Murder
To A
Slow Jazz Beat
Part One:
The Killing

Murder To A Slow Jazz Beat

Part One
The Killing

A Morgan Crew Murder Mystery

ART LEE

Murder To A Slow Jazz Beat
Part One: The Killing

A Morgan Crew Murder Mystery

By

Art Lee

ISBN: 978-0-9895073-9-4

THIS BOOK IS DEDICATED TO

Jackie, my wonderful wife

Who keeps me going when

I want to quit.

Thank you, Jackie

My love.

Other Books by the Author

The Morgan Crew Murder Mystery Series

A Storm In From the Sea
The Las Vegas Murders
A Deadly London Fog
The Four Seasons Murders
The Hawaiian Sunset Murders
The Spy Who Would Not Speak
The West Texas Murders
The Hawaiian Island Murders
The Top Secret Murders

Art Lee's Mystery and Adventure Series

Three Families
Wait Until the Dark of Night

Murder To A Slow Jazz Beat
Part One: The Killing

By

Art Lee

TABLE OF CONTENTS:

ONE - L'ange Bleu

It was ten minutes past four in the morning. The rains of spring would pass soon, and summer had its promise of warm, clear weather and blue skies to come. L'ange Bleu – The Blue Angel – is a jazz club in the cellar of an out of the way alley of the Latin Quarter of Paris. The club was sleepy that morning with moody and muted jazz flowing softly through a haze of grey smoke, both cigarette and marijuana, that hung from the cracked old wood ceiling. Soft, dreamy, and slow tones from a muted sax drifted through the club's small room and out into the mist to the deserted street.

Only a few patrons remained, several couples – men and women, men and men, and women and women – holding each other tightly as they swayed slowly and sexually to the music on the small dance floor. A few others sat at tables, eyes closed as they drifted through the sleepy dimness of marijuana and soul filled jazz.

The walls of the club are the old brick and crumbling mortar of a hundred years ago when the building was constructed. Dampness has eased its way through the bricks and mortar, bringing with it dark stains and a musty odor of age. That morning the tables each held the expected candle in an old wine bottle that was caked with the candle wax of many nights before.

Burning candles were strictly against Paris laws, but most things that occurred in L'ange Bleu were against French and Paris laws. Most of the candles that morning

1

however had already burnt out. Thin streams of smoke from what was left of the wicks drifted towards the ceiling from the remains of the candles. Three dull light bulbs with scratched and dented green painted tin, cone-shaped shades that were covered with dust of months gone by, hung from the ceiling on old wiring provided all the pale yellow light there was inside the club.

The Club's quintet was ready to call it a night even though a few customers were not. Adrien Garland, a cigarette hanging limply from his lips, slumped on the rickety stool at his small piano as his fingers flowed slowly across the ivory keyboard, finding the notes to Erroll Garner's 'Misty'.

Marc Baptiste was asleep, his arms folded on his drums, his bald head resting on the bass drum. Julien Marceau had propped his tall bass in a corner and sat in the wooden chair, leaning back against the bricks as he watched a particularly pretty young woman swaying her hips as she held her man tightly. Adrien's dreamy notes caught him; he stood and reached for his bass, setting a slow beat to the piano.

Patrice Laurent sat on the edge of the little stage, his foot tapping the music's beat on the dance floor, as he created wistful echoes of the music with his tenor sax.

LeRoy Manns was sitting at the edge of the stage in a scratched and bent, metal folding chair. His cornet sat lonely at his feet. The melodies from the piano and sax and bass wandered like a lazy slow stream to LeRoy. His eyes were heavy from cocaine. He reached for his muted cornet and followed along, ever so slowly and softly.

Adrien stopped his hands from seeking out the keys. He stood, crushed out his cigarette on the floor, and started for the door. He said in a coarse whisper, "Madelaine, elle attend pour moi."

LeRoy, the lone American in the group, understood, as did the others. Adrien's woman was waiting for him. She would be in their small bed in their fourth floor walk-up apartment. Her body would be warm, and she would fold her man into her arms whenever he came home. Adrien stepped away from the piano, lit another Gitanes cigarette, and walked from the little stage.

Julien wrapped his tall bass in its canvass case and leaned it carefully against the wall where it would wait for Julien to return the next night. Julien followed Adrien to the brick staircase that would take them from the basement club to the early morning street. They knew from use which bricks were loose and avoided them instinctively without looking for them. Tourists who had never been to the club before would stumble on the loose bricks but no one had hurt themselves recently.

Marc Baptiste and Patrice Laurent walked away, talking of where to get coffee and rolls before going home. LeRoy Manns, the last of the quartet to leave, cleaned the mouthpiece of his horn and stood. He closed his horn in its leather case and picked it up as he stood from the chair. He would not go home; he would go to see Germaine. He smiled at the thought of the woman. No matter how many days had passed since he went to her, she always welcomed him to her bed, no matter the time of day or night.

He started for the stairs, letting a few of the young people leave before him, but stopped when the door to the Club's offices opened and Alain DuSomme stepped through. He stood in the doorway, leaning against the door jam, looking at LeRoy who felt the fear rush up his back as it did every time he saw Alain. The thoughts of Germaine quickly left his mind.

Alain was a tall man, broad at his shoulders, with thick, muscular arms, who liked to dress very well. His clothes, shirts and suits and shoes, were all custom made and too expensive for the owner of a small jazz club. But the club was only a place for Alain to use as a front for his other business, which was murder. He watched the last of the club's patrons walk up the stairs to the street. LeRoy stepped closer to the stairs and stopped when Alain spoke.

"Monsieur LeRoy," Alain said and smiled a cruel smile. "Once again you and I seem to be alone." Alain spoke in English. His accent was heavy, but his English was good.

"I'm going home, Mr. DuSomme."

"Ahh, oui. You will go to the woman who welcomes you, yes? A warm bed on a cool early morning. What could be better, oui?"

LeRoy started for the brick stairs with the loose bricks but Alain moved quickly and stood in LeRoy's way.

"Please let me leave, Mr. DuSomme," LeRoy pleaded, his eyes lowered. He was frightened once again. He should have left with the others; he knew that. He had promised himself he would not again be alone with Alain DuSomme, yet his cocaine-clouded brain had slowed him this time.

"Tell me what you know, Monsieur LeRoy," Alain asked once again. For a month Alain had been suspicious of LeRoy. He felt certain that LeRoy had learned something, something that is dangerous for LeRoy to know. Alain knew that, but he had to have proof. Sooner or later, Alain knew, he would pull the truth out of LeRoy.

"I've told you before," LeRoy stammered. "I don't know what you're talking about."

"But I think you do, Monsieur LeRoy. I think you know

something that you should not know."

"Please Mr. DuSomme. I've told you . . . I don't know anything . . . Je ne connais rien."

"You are frightened, no, Monsieur LeRoy?"

"I am frightened, Mr. DuSomme," LeRoy said his voice a faint shiver. "I am frightened enough to just want to leave. Please. I'll leave the club and find someplace else to work. You'll never see me again."

"No, Monsieur LeRoy," Alain said as he took a step closer to the musician. "I cannot let you leave my employment. You will stay here, no? You see, I must keep my eye on you. Is that how you Americans say it?"

"I won't say anything, Mr. DuSomme," LeRoy pleaded. "Please."

"You won't say anything about what, Monsieur LeRoy? What did you hear that you won't speak of?"

"Nothing Mr. DuSomme," LeRoy pleaded. "I swear . . . Nothing."

"Go to your woman," Alain said, waiving towards the brick stairs. "Go to her bed and stay warm. You will be back here to play your good music tonight, yes? And you will speak of nothing, oui? What you know will remain with you, oui? Because you will not like what happens if you speak to someone, oui?"

LeRoy took hesitant steps to the side, afraid to turn his back on Alain. At the stairs he took them two at a time, ignoring the loose bricks, and ran out onto the damp morning alley. He ran as fast as he could down the empty streets, holding his prized cornet in its case to his chest, to Germaine's small apartment. He ran up the dark stairs to the third floor. Germaine never locked her door. Even in the dark streets of the Latin Quarter she felt safe as she had been born there so many years before and lived her whole life there. She knew everyone, and everyone knew her. LeRoy opened the apartment door quickly and closed it behind him. With his back leaning against the door he twisted the bolt to lock it.

Inside, LeRoy dropped his cornet onto the single chair in the small, one room apartment. Germaine was at the table, drinking coffee with the thick cream she loved so much, and smoking a cigarette. Germaine liked American cigarettes and bought them from American soldiers who sold them on the streets for either money or sex. Germaine paid in cash.

LeRoy ran to her and picked her up in his arms, holding her tight. She could feel the fright and tension LeRoy carried. He would not tell her what was wrong, but she knew something was wrong, something had happened recently. She would wait and comfort her lover as best she could until he felt it time to tell her.

Germaine could not be called a beautiful woman. Her hair was a dull brown, flaked with grey. Her pale white face was pockmarked and wrinkled, suggesting her age which was seven years older than LeRoy. She was neither short nor too tall. But her body was what filled LeRoy's dreams and thoughts. Her breasts were full and welcoming. Her skin was white and hadn't seen darkening from the sun in many years. Her hips were wide and strong, and held LeRoy as he lay on her when they made love. Her heavy legs wrapped him tightly to her, her arms pulled him down to her as they made love several times early each morning when LeRoy came to her.

"What is it?" she asked as he held her off the floor and kissed her hard. She pulled herself away and looked up into his eyes. "What is wrong, mon chéri?"

"Nothing," he said. "I just need some sleep."

"Then sleep, mon chéri. Sleep. I will not go to work today, oui?" Germaine was a waitress in a small café on a seldom travelled side street of The Latin Quarter. The same family had owned and run the café for three generations. Locals called there for glasses of cheap wine and good bread and excellent cheese. "I will stay at your side, yes?" She held her palm to LeRoy's sweaty forehead. He was warm, perhaps a fever, she thought. Perhaps he was sick. Something was not right; she could sense that.

Germaine stripped off LeRoy's clothes and he fell, naked, onto her bed. She pulled her dress, bra and panties off and lay beside him, pulling her thin blanket up, cradling him to her, and pressing her breasts against his back when he turned away from her. She felt his sobbing; her hand went to his face and found the tears.

"Sleep, mon chéri," she whispered. "Things will be better soon."

Germaine had no idea what was wrong with her lover. She could feel his dark skin was hot with sweat in the cool morning air. She loved LeRoy with a passion she had not felt in years. Oh, he was not her first lover. Many men . . . And several women . . . Both black and white had shared her bed in past years. But those were sexual lovers only. LeRoy was different.

LeRoy made her feel . . . Special was the only word she could think of. She felt like a woman, a desired and loved woman, wanted for more than sex. And the sex was more than Germaine had ever experienced before. The feelings of exotic pleasures had never been felt by Germaine before she felt the weight of LeRoy on top of her. She loved the man.

And his music . . . The soft and slow jazz that he

brought through his horn when they were alone in her apartment . . . It engulfed her and wrapped her in the music from dreams . . . It could only come from dreams, she often thought.

He would play the music of Coltrane and Miles, but he was able to turn that classic jazz into something soft as blue silk waving in a soft breeze. It mesmerized Germaine. She wished he could play only for her.

****

The sun had set when LeRoy awoke. He had slept through the day. He yawned, and his arm went to the pillow next to him to find Germaine. She was not there, but the sheets were warm. She was not long gone. She had gone to buy bread and wine he thought. He smelled the fresh coffee that she had brewed in the old metal pot. It was waiting for him across the room on the small, round, wooden table alongside two cracked cups and a small bowl of sugar. Germaine's thick cream sat in a soup bowl with the silver spoon that had been inherited from her mother. She would use the spoon to stir the cream into her coffee.

He lay in bed naked, having pushed the sheet and blanket away. The window was open at the side of the bed. The cool evening air floated in softly, gently. It felt good on his skin. His mind went to Alain DuSomme. What could he do? He knew DuSomme was a killer, and that knowledge frightened him.

He could run . . . But DuSomme was sure to find him. He had to protect Germaine somehow. And the only way to do that was to return to L'ange Blue night after night, deny everything, and do nothing to raise DuSomme's anger. He would do everything DuSomme demanded. Soon, he hoped, DuSomme would believe him and leave him alone to play his jazz.

LeRoy pulled himself upright and turned his legs off the side of the bed. He rubbed the sleep from his eyes as he sat on the edge of the bed. He knew he had to go back to the club that night, but the thought of not going back to L'ange Bleu ran though his mind. Once again he thought of running away . . . With Germaine . . . Somewhere. Maybe back to The States. He thought he might be safe there. It was the twenty-first Century, and if they settled up north, maybe Chicago, a black man and a white woman would be accepted. They might disappear in the big city.

But he was scared. He was scared for himself but more for Germaine. A man like Alain DuSomme could certainly find him anywhere. Why had he listened at the door to the phone conversation Alain had? He felt the anger and regret for listening instead of walking away burning inside of him . . . Anger against himself for his stupidity and regret for his curiosity. He should have turned away and walked away and his life would be music . . . And Germaine. Now his life . . . Would it end because of what he knew?

He dressed, considered a cigarette but no, that might hurt his throat and mouth and hinder the jazz that was inside of him from coming through the brass cornet. Coffee would be good, a quick cup as he shaved. But it was dark outside already, and the band would soon be waiting for him at the club.

He took his cornet and walked down the three flights of grey stairs to the street. He would miss kissing Germaine, but he would see her in the morning and make love to her over and over again, releasing the tension and fear inside of him.

A light, cool spring rain was falling from the cloud blackened sky. LeRoy pulled the collar of his tweed jacket up and shivered slightly. Over and over he had promised himself that he would buy an umbrella against the Paris spring.

He turned the corner onto the street where L'ange Bleu was hidden inside the dark alley, in the cellar of the old building. Lights suddenly lit the wet cobblestone road from behind him. He stopped and turned. It was a car, a dark Peugeot, not a new model, not moving, about fifty feet away. LeRoy turned away and started walking once again. He quickened his pace; the alley was close, and he could be safe there.

He heard the screeching of the tires. LeRoy froze and turned quickly, in time to see the car racing for him, the tires squealing on the wet cobblestones. It hit LeRoy as he stood, throwing him over the car. He twisted in the air and fell hard onto the street behind the car. His cornet in its case flew from his hand. The car stopped for only a second or two and then backed fast over LeRoy, crushing his chest and legs, and the brass horn. Then, again, the car raced forward across LeRoy's already dead body.

The narrow, old street of the Latin Quarter had been deserted in the cold rain that night. No one had seen or heard what had happened. The young jazz lovers would not arrive at the club for two or three hours. The few people who lived in the small apartments above the street were either asleep or busy with their lives.

Germaine found LeRoy lying in the wet street, covered in blood, as she walked home from her shopping. She had taken the shortcut home, through the street that was little more than a thin road. She found him dead on that cobbled street, lying in a pool of his own blood.

Her canvass bag of bread, wine and cheese fell from her hand. She wanted to scream but no sound would leave her. She ran to LeRoy, fell to her knees and with her hands, wiped the blood from his face. Finally a scream of never before felt heartbreak rose from her and filled the street.

TWO - San Marcos

It was late May but it was hot, foretelling the heat of a California summer that would arrive soon. I was trying to find some shade on the back deck of my home in the hills of San Marcos, California. I had thought out the design of our house in the hills after my mother and father passed away. I had been raised and lived in the old family mansion in San Marcos, California. I moved out soon after the funerals. I have a cousin living there now, who is president of one of the Crew Family banks and thinks living in the drafty hundred and twenty year old mansion makes him something special. He tells me every time we see each other, "Morgan, I sure am glad you gave me that place." I haven't told him I didn't *give* it to him; I just let him and his snotty wife and kids live there.

But for me, I like the simple life. I tried working in L.A. for a couple of years, at one of the family's corporations, sitting on the Board of Directors, but it wasn't for me. The Crew Family owns businesses and banks and ocean going shipping lines and real estate and construction companies and even a casino in Las Vegas and a lot of other things I try not to think about. That's all too much for me, even though I am considered the head of The Crew Family. All I do is spend a day or two in L.A. every year when accountants and lawyers tell the family about all the money it has.

Today I live in the four bedroom home I had built in the hills overlooking San Marcos harbor, on the Pacific coast, north of San Francisco. I play golf at the San Marcos Country Club. I go fishing as often as I can on some smelly old fishing barge. And I spend as much time as I can – which is a lot of time because I don't have to work – with my wife Sandy and our little girl, Caroline.

At our house there is a three level redwood deck out back, connected by stairs that run down the hillside. There are trees all over the place, all the way down the hillside and almost to the harbor below where all the commercial fishing boats tie up. There are Douglas Firs, pines, spruce, and redwoods all over the place, but at one in the afternoon with the sun directly overhead, not many of them were throwing shade onto the deck.

I slid the chaise with the thick pads I had been lying on, back to the railing of the upper deck to be under the branches of the tallest redwood in order to make use of one branch's small gift of shade. Pretty soon the sun would set, burning hot and red into the Pacific, setting the sky afire, and cool night air would flood in off the sea and up the hills. But right then it was too damn hot. I needed another cold beer, but that meant getting up and going to the kitchen . . . Too much like work for me right then.

Sandy had taken our daughter Caroline on a little vacation before our daughter started kindergarten in the fall. I took them down to San Francisco to the airport and kissed both of them goodbye. They took a Delta jet first to Phoenix to visit Sandy's sister and then on to Chicago to visit Sandy's mother. Now, I have nothing against either person. In fact Sandy's mother is a nice person. But . . . They are in-laws. 'Nuff said. So I decided to stay home.

It was too hot to play golf that day. I had played the day before and the day before that. I had eaten my meals at the Country Club, except for breakfasts which were mainly hot strong coffee and rolls slathered thickly with the rich butter Sandy would not let me eat if she were home. But that day was too damn hot to even leave home. I would search the fridge for something for lunch and then drive my old MGB with the top down to the Club later for dinner.

I was almost asleep on the chaise when Bob Sommers walked around the side of the house and opened the gate to the deck. Bob is the only detective on the nine cop San Marcos Police Department and generally assumed to be the boss there, surpassing the real head, an old man who has been on the City Council since I was a young man. Bob and I go back to our college years at Yale, when we wasted our time drinking beer, smoking a little dope, and chasing girls.

After college we enlisted in the Marines together, forgoing officer status for three years as enlisted mud-Marines. A couple of not too fun months in Viet Nam told us we weren't cut out for careers as Marines. I went home to San Marcos, and Bob signed up for the NYPD after we got out. He got married, and got divorced seven years later. With his divorce he took to the bottle too heavily, and three years later he was kicked off the force.

I took him in, dried him out, and because the Crew Family money controls most of San Marcos, I got him a job as a detective on the small, local police force. There hadn't been a detective on the San Marcos PD before. The cops took some time getting used to having Bob there as a detective, but they didn't complain openly. We are now, after all those years, close friends, almost the brothers neither of us has.

Bob today weighs in at close to 300 pounds, because he likes food . . . Any kind of food that is within arms' reach of him. Sandy tries to keep him healthy, but without speaking it, I know that she is waging a losing battle.

That day he carried a six-pack of beer and a paper bag that had grease stains on it, lunch that I really didn't need. But the beer sounded good.

"Hey, Morgan," he said, smiling broadly as he walked to me. He was wearing his normal grey slacks with grease stains across the lap and three day old white shirt with more grease stains. His blue tie was pulled loose around his neck, and the shirt collar was unbuttoned and stained with sweat. I guessed he had left his regular navy blue jacket in his car. "You awake? I got us some beer and a couple sandwiches."

"Hi, Bob," was all I could manage through my half sleep.

"Let's go inside," he said. "It's too damn hot out here."

I slid off the chaise and followed Bob into the house and to the kitchen. I had the A/C inside turned down to a cool 75 compared to the 90+ outside. He put four bottles of the beer in the fridge to cool off and opened two, handing one to me. I sat at the kitchen table and drank some of the warm beer. Bob sat across from me; he tore open the paper bag and slid one of the long hoagies towards me.

I drank some more of the beer and waited for Bob to say something. Rather than talking he bit into the sandwich of Italian meats and cheese and onions and oily dressing, letting oil and grease drip onto the table. I let my sandwich sit, still wrapped.

"OK, Bob," I said finally. "Tell me why you're here."

"Whataya' mean?" he slurred through a mouth overstuffed with food, letting bits of meat and cheese spill from his lips.

"Bob, I know you. When was the last time you brought beer and food here? Whenever you show up, it's to drink *my* booze and eat *my* food. Now, what the hell do you want?"

"Jeeze, Morgan!" he said. He laid his sandwich on the table ignoring the grease it would leave there. He wiped his mouth with the sleeve of his shirt, wiped his hands on his pants, and said, "Can't a guy sorta' repay a friend a little?"

"Sure you can, Bob. I would never complain about anything you do. You know that. You're my best friend. Now tell me what the hell you want?"

He drained his bottle of beer and went to the fridge to get two more bottles. When he sat at the table he twisted the top off his and drank some of the beer, laid the bottle next to the hoagie and slowly looked up at me.

"You remember a kid from college . . . Guy named LeRoy Manns?"

"Sure," I said. "He was that skinny little black kid who was majoring in English lit, but he really loved playing that horn of his. He just played what he had in his head, right? Great stuff."

And I certainly remembered LeRoy. Bob and I hit every college town party where girls and booze would be. And LeRoy was always there playing that bright brass cornet of his. The sounds that came out of that horn in no time at all had the room quiet as people became mesmerized by what LeRoy could do with a jazz piece.

Bob and I were never really close friends with LeRoy, but we were his friends. I slid money to him whenever he needed it, and Bob always managed to insure that the marijuana that was being passed around made it to LeRoy. In those days, a black kid wasn't yet fully accepted into the world of the wealthy whites of Yale. We made sure he was always welcome anywhere we were.

"Yeah, that's him," Bob said. His eyes left mine, and he looked down at the beer and sandwich. "He never did much with the English lit. But he played in the jazz clubs back east. I used to see him now and then when I was on the NYPD. He made the rounds of the nightclubs in Greenwich Village. His music was great but not too commercial, ya' know? He wound up over in Europe. I think he had a better chance over there . . . You know . . . Being black an' all. Never made it big, but he kept trying. I guess he never gave up on the jazz that was inside of him."

"You're talking about LeRoy in the past tense," I said. "Why?"

"He's dead, Morgan."

Now, I am a big fan of good jazz. That and the occasional classical CD is all I listen to at home and in the car. My musical range of likes is very limited. But I had not heard of LeRoy Manns since leaving school. He may have earned a living playing gigs, but if he had made it into the bigtime, I would have heard his music.

"That's too bad," I said. "LeRoy was a good kid. Lots of fun. I'll send some flowers to his family. Do you have an address?"

"No," Bob said, sadness in his voice. "I don't think he had any family . . . At least none who had cared about him. You know he never really got along with his folks."

I remembered more about LeRoy than his music. He had come from a prominent family in Philadelphia. His father had owned a chain of stores of some kind; I really never knew what. And according to LeRoy his father also owned a chain of slums that he kept the rents high on. LeRoy didn't like that. "I mean, it's his own people," he used to say. His father paid for LeRoy's college at Yale, bought him a nice car, paid the rent on a good apartment near Yale, and gave him a generous allowance that LeRoy would often just give away to kids who needed it more than he did.

But LeRoy and his father seldom saw each other, and when his father did visit it usually ended in harsh words being spoken between the two of them. LeRoy never made it big in college. His grades were just high enough to keep him from going on academic probation. I guess his father gave Yale enough money to ensure his son wouldn't be kicked out on academic expulsion.

LeRoy tried to be a good son. He promised he would work harder in class, but he would hide inside his music as soon as his father left. And the music was always a slow, sad jazz beat. His music was always sad in a way, but it always drew us in and folded us into its soft arms. I remember nights that drifted into mornings, listening to LeRoy's music. He would take cuts from Monk and Train and Dizzy and turn them into something special, his own music.

I finished the second beer and looked at the oil soaked sandwich. Before I met Sandy I would have devoured it. But after a few years of Sandy's love and care it didn't look good. I'd eat something else after Bob left.

"How did he die, Bob? He wasn't that old," I asked. "I hope it wasn't drugs."

"Auto accident," Bob answered. He drained the bottle of beer and then said, "Hit and run I'm told."

I waited and then I asked, "OK, Bob. You want something from me. So just tell me what you want."

Bob went to the fridge and took a third beer out, returned to the table, opened the bottle, and drank half of it before saying, "It's tough, Morgan. I hate to ask you to do stuff."

I knew it. I knew what was coming my way. My life, you see, is now and has been since I was a young man, putting myself at risk doing *for* other people what they cannot or will not do for themselves. Over the years I have been shot a couple of times – the scars remain to tell the stories – and tortured once, and I came close to death more times than I can count. But more terrible than that is that Sandy, the woman I love so deeply, suffered a gunshot wound and almost died in Las Vegas. Life without Sandy is unimaginable.

Well, I wasn't in the mood to go out putting myself at risk for other people right then. I wanted to spend the summer having fun with Sandy and Caroline. I wanted to take them to the beach and play in the surf. I wanted to take them to the mountains and hike in the cool air. I wanted to take Caroline to the pool at the club and watch her splash around. And I wanted to play golf, go fishing, and enjoy the wonderful food Chef Paulo prepares at The Club. Bob, like so many people I know, came to me in friendship to ask favors that all too often put me . . . And Sandy . . . At risk. I've helped him solve murders at home in San Marcos, and I helped him keep his job once when he was suspended by the City Council.

I could sense that something was wrong with LeRoy's death, and Bob wanted me to get involved.

"No, Bob," I said. "Don't even ask. I'm not going to do it."

"Do what?"

"Forget it, Bob. Whatever the hell you want me to do . . . Forget it."

"I don't want you to do anything, Morgan. Jesus, cut it out will you?"

"Then what do you want?" I asked.

"Me and LeRoy, we sort of kept in contact over the years. You know, Christmas cards and a phone call once or twice a year. I liked the guy, Morgan. LeRoy was playing out in Greenwich Village when I was having all that trouble back in New York. He was there for me, Morgan . . . Like you were. He even took me in when Dorothy kicked me out. Anyway, he's dead now . . . And I kinda' want to go to his funeral."

"So go," I said. "You don't need my permission to do that."

"I wanna' go . . . But . . ."

"Just tell me, Bob. Just tell me what the hell you want."

Bob shifted in his chair nervously. He could not look at me, and he was twirling the beer bottle around on the table, spilling drops of beer out of it. He finally said, "LeRoy, he's been living in Paris, Morgan. He had a good job there with a little jazz band at some little jazz club . . . You know. He had a girlfriend and everything. He was happy . . . Maybe for the first time in his life. He told me so a couple of times."

I waited but Bob still could not look at me. "Just tell me, Bob," I said again.

He looked up at me and said, "Hell, Morgan. I can't afford the plane fare. You know me; I can't keep five cents in the bank."

"Is that all you want! Bob, tell me when you want to go, and I'll book your flight and your hotel. My God, Bob!"

"Thanks, Morgan," he said. He finally looked up and tried to smile. "But there's one more thing. I want you to come with me."

"Sure," I said quickly. "I love Paris. As soon as Sandy and Caroline get home, we'll go. But don't ask anything else."

"Sure," Bob said, his head lowered, his eyes unable to look at me. He whispered, "But I want us to go now . . . To his grave . . . You know. The funeral was yesterday. I guess I missed it. I just heard he was dead. I want to go to his grave and maybe leave some flowers."

That seemed reasonable to me, and it didn't mean putting myself at any risk. So I reached out and touched Bob's arm. "OK, go home and pack. I'll get us tickets on the first flight out." He grinned like a kid who got the Christmas present he was hoping for. He slugged down the rest of the beer in the bottle, pushed his bulk to his feet, slapped me on the shoulder and left through the front door.

I tossed the sandwiches down the sink's garbage disposer, wiped the table clean, and phoned the travel agent I use.

THREE - In Paris

The Paris Ritz first opened its doors in 1898 and was the epitome of luxury for one hundred years. The Ritz was founded by the Swiss hotelier, Cesar Ritz in collaboration with the world renowned chef Auguste Escoffier whose cooking prowess fostered a generation of the best chefs around the world.

The hotel was constructed behind the façade of an eccentric 18th-century town house, overlooking one of Paris's central squares. It was reportedly the first hotel in Europe to provide a bathroom 'en suite', a telephone, and electricity for each room. It quickly established a reputation for luxury, with clients including royalty, politicians, writers, film stars and singers.

Through the 19th and early 20th Centuries the rich and powerful of the world could be found at The Paris Ritz. Politicians and Generals occupied the best suites at the hotel during The First World War, planning operations that resulted in the deaths of millions of their own people.

In between the European wars The Paris Ritz was popular with the 1920s wealthy, fun loving boozers of the world. When Nazi Germany occupied Paris the Ritz found itself the occupation home of Generals once again.

After the war The Paris Ritz went into a period of shame as the hotel deteriorated and began to show its age. In 2014 the hotel closed its doors for a major renovation and has recently reopened once again offering modern luxuries to those who can afford it, and once again standing tall as the model for what luxury should be.

Several of its suites are named in honor of famous guests of the hotel, including Coco Chanel and Ernest Hemingway, who lived at the hotel for years. One of the bars of the hotel, *Bar Hemingway*, is devoted to Earnest Hemingway, and the *L'Espadon* is a world-renowned restaurant, attracting aspiring chefs from all over the world who come to learn at the adjacent Ritz-Escoffier School.

The grandest suite of the hotel, called the Imperial, has been listed by the French government as a national monument in its own right. I booked a somewhat more modest two-bedroom suite for Bob and me.

We had seats in the first class section of the Air France jet from San Fran to New York and on to Paris. Bob took full advantage of everything offered for free in the first class cabin of the jets. The nine hour time difference caused us to arrive in Paris' Orly Airport in the evening when our internal clocks told us it was late morning. It took some struggled conversation between us and the Paris taxi driver, but soon he understood the words 'Paris Ritz' and he took us there on a thrilling high-speed drive. I remember wishing I had indulged in one or two more whiskeys on the jet just to calm my fears of getting killed on one of Paris' crowded streets.

We checked into the hotel with only a few small problems speaking English with French speaking desk clerks. The young lady at the front desk worked her computer and then looked at us. She said, using the best English she could manage, "You have the two bedroom suite, no? Monsieur Crew, this is the mistake, no? You and your partner desire one bedroom, oui?"

I laughed and stopped Bob from an angry response. "No, I guess you don't understand. We are friends only. Two bedrooms, please."

The young lady smiled kindly, shrugged her shoulders, and explained, "Monsieur, here in France we do not have the . . . How do you say? . . . The difficulties with you and your partner, oui?"

"He is my friend, not my partner," I said a little more forcefully. "Now, please let us have the suite I reserved. She shrugged her shoulders and began typing things into her computer. After a minute or two of standing there while other patrons and desk clerks grinned at us, misunderstanding our relationship, she handed us two plastic electronic key cards. She touched a brass bell next to her computer and a bellman ran to us, grabbed up our two suitcases, and walked away. The young lady behind the desk waived officiously, trying to tell us to go with our suitcases.

The suite at The Ritz was as grand as I had expected it to be. There were two bedrooms, a huge sitting room, and two full bathrooms. The sitting room opened out onto a balcony that was large enough for a wrought iron table and four wrought iron chairs, with a dozen potted flowering plants lining the wrought iron railings. The balcony was twelve by fifteen feet, with a red tile floor, and it overlooked a magnificent garden six stories below.

The entire suite was furnished in Louis XIV furniture, overdone as usual in gold leaf and red and gold upholstery. I've never found Louis XIV furniture to be very comfortable; my guess is that Louis XIV spent more time in bed with a lot of different women than he spent sitting on his furniture.

But there was one couch, ten feet long, soft and very comfortable, upholstered in beige silks with red and blue birds stitched into it, that I found I could sit on.

Both bedrooms were something out of a 17th Century bordello: red flocked wallpaper, lots of gold things everywhere, and huge beds. Inside the grand suite, Bob took the larger of the two bedrooms because it looked more expensive. "I'll take this one," he called out, telling me that the bigger of the two bedrooms was going to be his. It really didn't matter to me because both beds were as soft as pillows, and I sunk into mine easily.

The suite cost $2000.00 a night in American dollars. I guess they thought that might be cheap by French and European standards. But what the hell. Bob was impressed, and I didn't plan on being there very long anyway.

I unpacked my few things and headed to the suite's fully stocked bar. The bar was about six feet long and elaborately carved dark wood with lots of lion's heads and birds and fish carved into the wood. The bar top was black marble. On the wall behind the bar were three glass shelves that held a selection of glasses and crystal decanters of seven different kinds of booze. There was no bourbon, a problem I would soon correct. I have found that money can buy anything, even American bourbon in Europe. But there was Grey Goose vodka, so I poured a goodly amount of it over ice.

I was stretched out on the very comfortable and soft couch when Bob walked into the room and asked, "They got beer here?"

"I doubt it, Bob."

"Let's go get something t'eat, then. Maybe they got beer downstairs."

"There's a room service menu, Bob. Let's just eat

here and make it an early night. I'm really worn out."

Bob retrieved the menu, which was written in French only. He flipped the four pages and said, "What the hell is this, Morgan?"

"It's French, Bob."

He shrugged and went to the telephone. "Yeah," he said loudly thinking if he shouted someone would understand him. "How about a couple cheeseburgers and fries . . . Got that? . . . And maybe six bottles of beer, OK?" He waited but there was no reply.

"Hey, Morgan," he said, holding the phone out to me. "There ain't nobody there."

I got up and took the phone. I spoke softly, knowing a few words of French. "Bonjour . . . Deux . . . Hamburgers, s'il vous plaît. Et . . . Six . . . Bottles de bière." I guess someone understood because in short order our food was at the door. Bob ravished his hamburger and told me through a mouth full of food that, "This ain't as good as back home."

We did make an early night of it, and in the morning I had coffee and croissant sent to the room for me, and a very big cheddar cheese omelet with sausage for Bob. He retreated to the balcony and smoked several cigarettes while I showered and shaved. He came back into the suite and stood in front of me as I leaned back in a very uncomfortable chair and read the English printing of the European New York Times.

"I want to go to LeRoy's grave this morning, Morgan. And I want to speak with his girlfriend . . . Germaine."

"OK," I said. "Do you want me to go with you?"

"Of course," Bob said. "I'd get lost around here. None of these damn people speak English."

****

With only a small amount of trouble – the taxi driver spoke no English but eventually seemed to understand where we wanted to go – I was able to find the cemetery where LeRoy had been buried. His gravesite was in an out of the way and secluded corner of the Père Lachaise Cemetery. It was a grey morning that day in Paris with a light, cool rain falling . . . springtime in Paris. Bob swore quietly at having to walk in the rain – he never polished his scuffed leather shoes but griped about getting them wet and muddy – but I figured it was just the right backdrop for the solemn occasion of visiting a grave.

LeRoy had been a friend of both of us when we were in college, but Bob had been closer to him than I had been. I had not seen him nor talked to him in all the years since leaving Yale. I stood aside as Bob spent a few minutes at the graveside. He had bought a small bouquet of yellow flowers in the hotel lobby and laid them against the dark concrete headstone, marble being very expensive, and there probably wasn't anyone willing to pay for it. He seemed to be saying something, in a whisper, maybe a prayer I thought and then laughed at the idea. Bob and prayer were strangers to each other for as long as I have known him.

But I gave him what seemed like a fair amount of time at LeRoy's grave. I walked to him slowly and touched his shoulder.

"We need to find Germaine," I told him. "We should express our condolences and offer any help we can. And we need to get out of this rain."

"That's a good idea, Morgan. But how do we find her?"

I thought about that. Why had I suggested finding the woman? I had done what Bob had asked me to do. Why not just go home, I thought. Why try to find LeRoy's girlfriend? But the look on Bob's face, a broad smile and glow I had not seen in a very long time, told me my friend wanted to speak to Germaine.

So I suggested, "Let's go to the club where LeRoy played. Someone there will probably know where she lives."

That day in Paris I would have liked to do some tourist-type sightseeing, but it was cold and rainy all day which changed my mind. So Bob and I spent the day in the suite at The Ritz. I watched ESPN all day. The other channels on the TV were French. Bob slept on and off, raiding the bar and its bowls of chips and pretzels, and ordering food from room service in between his naps.

At nine that evening we left the hotel and took a taxi to the little alley that was home to L'ange Bleu. The driver seemed to know what we were talking about when I said the name of the club. The alley was not wide enough for the taxi to drive into so we got out on the street. The cobblestone walkway of the alley was wet and slick from the rain and probably years of not being cleaned. Trashcans and garbage lined the alley walls lending a not too nice odor to the damp air. I walked carefully and slowly, sliding a couple of times, but Bob caught me before I could land on my ass.

Paris jazz clubs are in a world all their own. 9:30 PM was early in their workday, which meant few people were in the basement bar when we walked down the brick staircase. And the people who were there were tourists who would have a glass of cheap wine and then head back to their hotel rooms for an early night.

But the small group of musicians that had once included LeRoy was there, playing something maybe a little close to New Orleans jazz to entertain the people there. The real jazz would begin sometime after midnight.

We sat at a table against a musty and damp brick wall. An old black and white photo of some park somewhere hung in a cracked brown wood frame. The photo was faded and looked as old as it probably was. The brick cellar walls of the basement club were barren except for a few such photos, all as old and faded as the one we sat next to. The three lights hanging from the ceiling did little to illuminate the place, but they did add a mood that seemed just right for such a jazz club.

Bob wanted to order some food, but I told him not to trust the food there. If the club's kitchen were as moldy and dirty as the room where customers sat, the food might be very dangerous. We settled for a couple of glasses of red wine served by a young, skinny girl with telltale needle marks on her arms from her heroin use.

Halfway through the glass of wine she brought us, the band took a break and started to walk off the stage. I stood and put my hand on Bob's shoulder, telling him to stay at the table. Bob is a good cop, but he is a cop and can be demanding and insulting at times. He started to stand anyway but I told him, "Stay here, Bob. Let me handle this." He sat and nodded. He picked up his glass of wine and drank it empty.

I followed the four band members through a door at the side of the small stage where they had played. A small round table and two mismatched chairs were at the side of the stage, blocking my way to the door. No one was sitting there so I just pushed the table aside.

Past the door, in a tight, dark hallway lit by a single dim bulb hanging on a frayed cord from the low ceiling, the four men stopped and turned to me. One of them spoke in

French . . . I smiled and shrugged my shoulders. One of the four took a single step forward and spoke in broken English, "American, correct?"

"Yes," I said. "And I'm afraid I don't speak French."

The same man frowned in deep thought trying to come up with the right English words. He said, "You not should . . . Be here, oui . . . Yes?"

"I'm sorry," I said. I took a couple of steps closer to them and held my hand out to the man who struggled with English. He took it hesitatingly and quickly drew his hand away. "I'm a friend of LeRoy Manns," I said. "I'm so sorry about his death. It must be tough on you."

"LeRoy? Oui . . . Yes. He . . . Good, yes? . . . With music, yes?"

"I'm sorry I didn't make the funeral. I visited his grave this morning. I'd like to speak with his girlfriend . . . Germaine. Can you tell me where she lives?"

"Germaine?" he asked. "Why?"

I tried smiling to ease whatever suspicion he had. None of the four were smiling, and all were obviously ill at ease. Maybe they were just not used to having American tourists invade their little sanctuary.

"I just want to tell her how sorry I am, that's all. I went to college with LeRoy. He was a friend."

The four musicians spoke together, in French. I understood very little of what they were saying, except I heard them mention 'Germaine' several times. Finally, the one man who spoke with me said, "Germaine . . . She will be here later. Come back later, yes? Or stay, oui?" he said, shrugging his shoulders to say he didn't care.

They turned and walked away leaving me alone in the

thin hallway. I called out loudly, my voice echoing against the brick walls, "When? What time should I come back?" They didn't answer.

Back at the table with Bob, who had finished his glass of wine and mine, I found he had ordered two more glasses of the cheap wine and was halfway done with his second. I sat and said, "There's something wrong here, Bob."

"Like what? They don't know Germaine?"

"They know her, and they told me to come back here later tonight. They said she would be here later. They wouldn't give me her address."

"So what's wrong with that? They don't know you. Maybe they're just protecting her from a rapist or strangler."

"It was their attitude," I said. I pushed the glass of wine away from me, and Bob grabbed it up. "They seemed frightened . . . Scared of something. I guess I just sensed that they were very uncomfortable . . . I think they might be hiding something."

"Like I said, maybe they just don't know you," Bob said as he started on the wine I had pushed toward him.

"I don't know," I said. "I just had a funny feeling they were hiding something. I think we should come back tonight after midnight."

"Hey, Morgan. Let's just stay here and wait for her. We can listen to the music."

"And drink the wine, too?" I laughed. "No. I think we need to keep our heads clear, Bob. Something just doesn't feel right here."

Bob looked deeply at me. He has known me for too many years not to trust my instincts. I had too many years behind me of sensing danger. "OK, Morgan. Let's go.

Damn I wish I had my gun."

"It may not be that serious, Bob. Maybe it's just something simple like one of them is having an affair with LeRoy's girlfriend. Let's just go and come back later."

I didn't mention it to Bob, but that little voice in the back of my head was telling me to "Run Away! Run Away!" That little voice speaks to me every time I am close to some kind of danger. I've heard it many times, and it's never been wrong. Every time I hear it, danger follows soon after.

And so we walked out, into the cold night rain. Taxis were far too few in that weather and that part of Paris at that time of night, so we ran until we found ourselves on the Boulevard Saint Michel. There we managed to waive down a taxi to take us back to The Ritz.

In the suite I showered while Bob raided the bags of pretzels and chips and other things. Later, as he ate a bag of something salty and apparently once fried to a crisp that only the French would recognize, I phoned Sandy. It was just past half past eleven in Paris and half past four in the afternoon in Chicago. I had to do the calculation on the time difference before phoning so I would be sure not to wake her.

After all the usual updates on how everyone was doing and how much fun our daughter Caroline was having being spoiled by her Aunt and Grandmother, I told Sandy about L'ange Bleu and Germaine.

"So you really think there's something wrong?" Sandy asked.

"I don't know for sure. But LeRoy's band people sure were acting strange. Maybe it's nothing . . . But they were acting very strange."

She hesitated for a short moment then said, "I think

you two should come home. LeRoy is dead . . . There's nothing you can do about that. Just come home, OK?"

"We'll leave tomorrow," I assured her. "But I think we should express our condolences to LeRoy's girlfriend. She might need help with his things. There was this really cheap concrete gravestone at the grave. Maybe she needs some money."

"OK, but you be sure to come home tomorrow. Caroline and I will be flying home tomorrow, too. Betsy will be finished with her semester in a couple of days."

Betsy, our daughter's nanny, was our 'Biker Chick' who we found when she was a rebel in trouble in Texas. Today she is in her second year of college and looking at medical school in her future. She is invaluable to Sandy and me; she takes our daughter away and protects her when we are away from home and putting our lives at risk. She hides with a biker gang down in San Francisco, a fact that I was very uncomfortable with until I found the gang to be trustworthy . . . At least in protecting Betsy and our daughter.

But Sandy is smart, the smartest person I know, with an instinct for what is dangerous that is unmatched by anyone I've ever met. I think she knew that I wasn't going to fly home the next day. I think she knew I would stay in France until I was sure there was no trouble with LeRoy's death.

After a moment or two of silence between us, Sandy said, "If you really think there is something bad going on there, I want to be there with you. Besides, a few days in Paris with you again would be nice . . . And maybe even romantic."

I knew that if there was anything remotely close to danger, Sandy would run towards it while I wanted to run from it. There was no way I would be able to keep Sandy at home when I was faced with any kind of danger. And I couldn't lie to her, I never have. So I said, "Let me phone you tomorrow. I'm probably just seeing stuff that isn't there."

❋❋❋❋❋❋❋❋❋❋❋❋❋❋❋

The rain had slowed to a cold mist under a black steel sky when Bob and I returned to L'ange Bleu. It was half past midnight when we walked down the stairs into the basement jazz club. The tourists with their cameras strung around their necks who had been there a few hours ago were gone, replaced with an eclectic group of young and old jazz lovers. There were hippies grown old and young people apparently in a haze of whatever drugs they were high on.

The crowded room was musty from damp age. A cloud of smoke, a mixture of cigarettes and marijuana, hung from the low ceiling, partially obscuring the three dim lights that, with a few tabletop candles, shed the only light in the basement club.

We found a small table in a back corner and sat. The quartet was in the middle of a slow, dream filled version of Billie Holiday's '*Willow weep for me*'. The sax man was blowing a tenor saxophone in some world far, far away from everyone around him. His eyes were closed, and he swayed in a dreamlike state.

The music caught me and pulled me into it. When the gig was done I realized that Bob had ordered two tall glasses of a bitter French beer. I looked up and saw the sax player looking directly at me. He nodded his head, directing me to the door and hallway where I had spoken with him earlier. It occurred to me for the first time that everyone in the little band was white, except for Leroy.

I whispered to Bob, "Wait here. If you hear any yelling . . . Come swing those big fists of yours and save my ass, OK?" Bob laughed and then drained one of the tall glasses of beer.

I stood and walked slowly, weaving my way through the tables, edging my way around the table to the side of the stage and in front of the door. Two twenty-something boys were sitting there; neither made any attempt to move for me. I eased myself around the table and went through the doorway. The sax man waited on the stage and then followed me. The remaining three musicians started another piece, it seemed without realizing that the sax man had left the stage.

Three doors lined the hallway; the one to my left was open, and light streamed into the tight hallway. The door to the right was closed. The third door, at the far end of the hallway was open, and it appeared to be a small kitchen; two men were working there at the time.

The sax man gently pushed me toward the open door on my left. I stepped inside. It was a small room, something of a dressing room I imagined. A metal clothes rack stood to the right and a small table to the left. A dirty mirror hung on the wall over the table, and a woman sat in one of the four chairs at the table.

She may have been seen as attractive by a few people, but she wasn't beautiful. Her hair was thick and mousy brown. Her skin was pale white. She was somewhere between thin and fat; her hips were wider than the seat of the chair. She wore a blue flowered dress that was wrinkled and faded. Her face was sad and without makeup. Her dark eyes drooped and were clouded with a grey sadness. She had been crying recently; her eyes were bloodshot, and the red surrounding her eyes told of the tears she was wiping away. She looked up at me, obviously frightened.

The sax man stood behind me and said, "This is Germaine. I will stay, yes?"

I turned and said, "That's fine. All I want to do is offer my condolences. Who are you, by the way?"

"I am Patrice Laurent. LeRoy, he was my . . . Ami . . . Friend is the word, oui? Germaine, she is my friend also. You will not hurt, oui?"

"Of course not," I said.

I pulled a chair from the table and sat. I said, "LeRoy was my friend from school. We went to college together. He and I had some good times. We went to a lot of parties together. His music talent was great back then; he must have been wonderful here. I'm so sorry to hear of his death."

Germaine's face revealed nothing to me. Then it occurred to me that she may not speak English. I asked, "I'm sorry. Do you speak English? I'm afraid I don't speak French."

A slight smile broke across her lips. She said in a soft voice, "Yes. LeRoy he has taught me some."

"Is there anything I can do? I went to his grave yesterday."

"Merci beaucoup. You can tell me who you are, please."

"Sorry. I'm Morgan Crew. My friend . . . LeRoy's other friend is out there. He'd like to see you, too. Would you speak with him?"

"LeRoy, he has mentioned you, Monsieur Crew. Is your friend who LeRoy says is Bob? He is the policeman?" she asked.

"Yes . . . Back home. Can he speak with you?"

Germaine looked past me at Patrice Laurent, a questioning look that had me worried. The sax man turned, looked outside the room first to the left and then to the right. He closed the door and nodded to Germaine.

She started, "LeRoy . . . it was not an accident. He was . . . What is the word . . . Assassine . . .?"

Laurent said, "Murder . . . I think, yes?"

That was not only a surprise; it hit me like a lightning bolt. "Murdered!" I said, maybe a little too loud. Both Germaine and Patrice jumped when I spoke too loud. Patrice went to the door once again, opened it and peered out. He closed it and nodded to Germaine.

"You're kidding," I said. "I'm sorry, I mean, are you certain? How do you know that?"

"How I know does not mean anything to you, Mr. Crew," Germaine said, her voice cracking as she tried to hold back the tears. She used a paper tissue to wipe her nose and then tossed it to the floor. Patrice handed her a cloth handkerchief that she used to dab at her eyes.

"Of course it does. He was my friend," I said, trying to sound compassionate. Patrice was scared, and Germaine was distraught. They wouldn't be unless they were right. LeRoy had been murdered. Once again that little voice in the back of my head started yelling at me, "Run away! Run away!"

"LeRoy, he has spoken of you many times," she said. "He has the admire . . . Is that the word, oui? He likes you, I think, yes? But you have not spoken with him in . . . How many years?"

"I know," I said. "I should have . . . But life gets in the way. I'm sorry. But what kind of trouble was he in? Or was he robbed and killed, maybe?"

She looked again at Laurent, still standing behind me. Out of the corner of my eye I saw him shrug. Germaine looked at me and said, "We will not talk here. Come to my . . . Apartment, yes? We can talk there, yes? Later . . . I will be there after three in the noon . . . I mean afternoon, yes?"

There was a lot more I wanted to know, but I wasn't going to learn anything then and there. I stood slowly, took Germaine's hand gently, and said, "I'm so sorry."

FOUR - The Lover

I didn't tell Bob what Germaine had told me that night. I managed to get him to leave L'ange Bleu after only one more beer. I had to remind him that back at our suite there was the bar with liquor and bags of stuff that he ate, all for free, that was being restocked on a regular basis. He was happy, happy to be on vacation, happy to be away from his work as San Marcos' only detective, and happy to be enjoying so much food and drink. Back at The Ritz, after Bob had too much to drink and too much stuff to eat out of strange looking bags, we slept until past ten that morning.

As I lay in bed that night, trying to fall asleep, that damn little voice that lives somewhere in the back of my head, started yelling at me once again. *'Run away! Run away!'* it kept telling me. I had heard that little voice so many times in the past that I knew what it was. I had the feeling I was about to be drawn into something very dangerous, something that I would be asked to do to protect someone else.

But that is my life. I do for others what they cannot or will not do for themselves. Not, of course, that I want to do those things, they are just expected of me.

I fell into a restless sleep. Blackness surrounded me and my breathing came very hard. I reached out, but I could not extend my arms fully. I reached up and the world ended not six inches above my head. Someone was speaking to me, softly, from far away, "Don't worry, Morgan. It won't hurt anymore. It won't hurt."

I realized then that I was in a coffin, that I was dead. Light suddenly shown all around me and I could see the pure white velvet of the coffin lining. But it was too soon. I had too much to do. I had Sandy. I had little Caroline. They needed me. I had to get out of the box. If I could just get out I would not be dead. I started clawing and pushing. I started shouting, pleading, "HELP! SOMEONE HELP! I HAVE TO LIVE! I HAVE TO LIVE."

I was shaking, thrashing around. I heard my name, "Morgan . . . Morgan . . . Wake up guy. Wake up."

It was Bob, and he was shaking me by my shoulders. "Hey, buddy," he said. "You were having one hell of a nightmare. You OK?"

"Huh? Yeah . . . I guess so . . . Yeah."

Bob pulled me to my feet and helped me into the bathroom where I splashed a lot of cold water on my face. My mouth was dry; I cupped my hands and drank from the faucet.

I thought the dream must have been a warning, telling me to get the hell away from whatever was happening with LeRoy's death. Bob was as worried as I was, but I told him to go back to bed. I assured him it was probably some bad food or strange wine working on my stomach. I told him I was going to go back to bed and he should do the same. I closed the door to my bedroom and lay on the bed, but fear had a strangle hold on me. I would not sleep the rest of that night.

But I would meet with Germaine as she asked. I had to; it was all part of my life, and I had to risk everything because that is what I am all about.

I would make some kind of excuse for Bob not to

accompany me. If there was something there, I didn't want him to become involved and possibly hurt. Whatever it was, I would take care of it myself.

Too much was running though my head for me to enjoy more than two cups of coffee for breakfast that morning. That's unusual for me because I really like strong coffee. It's not only the taste of it but the smell of it that wakes me up. And The Ritz has some really good coffee. It is delivered to the suite in a silver pot that is hooded in a fancy cloth to keep it hot. I would have liked a tall ceramic mug rather than the delicate little cups that came with the coffee, but what the heck.

The memory of the dream had my hands shaking. I spilled a little coffee from the china cups without Bob noticing. He was too busy eating.

So, after watching Bob stuff himself with a huge breakfast of eggs and ham and potatoes and rolls, I told him I had instructions from Sandy to buy her some things, ladies' things, which I knew he would interpret as panties and bras. "Yeah," he said. "You go do that. I'm gonna' go sightseeing. I've never been to Paris before. I brought my camera, too."

"Good," I said, satisfied that I could see Germaine without Bob knowing. "The weather looks better today than yesterday," I said, although the sky was grey.

Bob leaned back in his chair, and as he folded his thick arms across his ever expanding lap and sucked some food from between his teeth, he asked, "So I assume you saw Germaine last night?"

There was no sense lying again, so I answered, "Yes, in the back of the club."

"And I assume she wants you to do something for her?"

"I guess," I said simply. I held the coffee cup to my lips and drank a little to mask that fact that I wasn't telling Bob everything.

"OK, Morgan. I understand. I know you too well. Look, I've been away from home long enough. I'm going to fly out tomorrow. Is that OK with you?"

"Hey, Bob," I said. "You can stay as long as you want. After all, it's not costing you anything."

"No . . . I'd just be in the way. I'm a cop, Morgan. I can't be a cop here. I'd just be in your way, you know, holding you back like a cop would do. You do what you have to do and tell me about it when you come home."

✳✳✳✳✳✳✳✳✳✳✳✳✳✳

That day was much better weather-wise than the day before. It was cool, but it was dry, and the sky had cleared from steel grey to blue for a change. At the concierge desk I found a street map of Paris. It took me some time, but I found on the map the little side street where Germaine lived, in the Latin Quarter, not too far from L'ange Bleu.

It was too far to walk, even on a nice afternoon, so I took one of those Disney-thrill-ride speeding taxis. The driver seemed to believe that driving too fast and taking risks cutting in and out of traffic was the normal way to drive.

But I wasn't killed getting there anyway, and I guess I didn't tip the crazy driver what he expected from an American because he seemed to be swearing profusely at me when I paid him. Euros confuse me, and I guess the coins I gave him were too little. He drove away, into traffic, and flipped his 'fickle-finger-of-fate' at me out his window.

Germaine's apartment was on the fifth floor of a six story, dingy and old building. I was breathing hard by the time I reached her door. I knocked and stood aside trying to catch my breath, and then I knocked again. Maybe she had changed her mind about talking to me, or maybe she was just out shopping and would be late. I tried the knob and found the door unlocked.

That damn little voice suddenly started screaming at me, telling me not to open the door, but I pushed the door open anyway. Germaine was lying on her back, on the bare wood floor, her dead eyes staring at the ceiling. There were dark blue bruises around Germaine's neck. Her left cheek was red and swollen; her left eye was blackened. She had been beaten and strangled.

Stepping inside and carefully around Germaine, I knew I had to phone the police, but I wanted to look around first. I started walking around the apartment, and I realized that finding the dead woman had not affected me as it should have. I should have been shocked and maybe a little sick. But because she was not the first dead person I had seen and because she was not the first murder victim I had found, it didn't seem to bother me. I guess I was becoming cold to this violence, and that bothered me.

What would be abnormal to others had become normal to me, and I didn't like that fact. But I had been dragged into another situation where I was expected to do something for someone, in spite of my wanting to have nothing to do with it all.

Germaine and the sax-man Patrice Laurent were frightened about something. Germaine wanted to talk with me but only in private, not at L'ange Bleu. Now she was dead, and whatever it was she knew and wanted to talk to me about was dead with her.

Her apartment was small, and it was old. The furniture was not new, but everything was very clean. It was obvious to me that the three-room apartment had been searched very carefully; drawers were not fully closed, and pictures hanging on the walls were not quite straight. I had the sense that Germaine did not keep her small home out of order in any way; it was just too clean for an old place. That meant someone had been there searching the place for something after she was dead. Someone was looking for something that probably had something to do with LeRoy's death. Someone had killed Germaine for whatever they were looking for.

I went through the whole place again, perhaps not as neatly as whoever had been there before me. I used my handkerchief on everything I touched so as to not leave prints.

I had some idea of where people hide things: taped on the underside of drawers, inside the paper backing of framed pictures on walls, under loose boards in the floor, in canisters of sugar and salt. I looked in those places, and then using a coin I unscrewed the plates over wall sockets and emptied out the frost covered little freezer in the old refrigerator. I turned over a few chairs and pulled the sheets off the bed. I looked under the mattress and under the bed, and I pulled the caps off the brass headboard and footboard.

If there had been anything there, it was gone. Whatever it was that someone was looking for was a mystery. But the sax-man, Patrice Laurent, was still out there. And he was where I needed to go.

But first I had to report Germaine's murder. My hand reached for the telephone, but I stopped before picking it up.

Whomever I phoned would speak French, and I didn't. I was a foreigner, and therefore I would be a suspect. I could phone the American Embassy and ask for their help, but then I asked myself . . . Why? What would I gain? What would Germaine gain with me locked in a jail cell for a few days? It wouldn't bring her back to life. I would be subjected to a day or two of answering questions, and that would gain me nothing.

So I carefully went back and wiped everything I had touched once again, no sense taking chances. I took one more look around, looked down one final time at Germaine, and I left. I thought for a moment that maybe I should say a prayer for her. But after the life I've led, God would just have a good laugh listening to me say a prayer.

Someone else would have to phone the police. I might have been seen by someone, but in that neighborhood I imagined most people kept to themselves and away from the police.

I would go back to L'ange Bleu that night, but I had to decide what to do about Bob. He is my friend, as close as a brother, but he is a cop. He said he would go home, and if I told him about Germaine he might change his mind. If I was going to stay and find out who killed LeRoy and Germaine . . . And why . . . I didn't need a cop acting like a cop.

As I walked through streets I was totally unfamiliar with, I thought a lot about what to do. That little voice in the back of my head was screaming. As usual, I decided to ignore it.

After an hour's walk I did decide not to tell Bob of Germaine's murder. I would send him home. I would stay in Paris and do what I usually do, put myself at risk for someone else.

****

I treated Bob to a very expensive dinner at La Table de L'Espadon, the best restaurant The Ritz had to offer. As usual he ate and drank everything, not knowing what half the things were that he ate. The waiters were amazed and I am sure were making remarks about the crude Americans who ate too much and had terrible table manners. But Bob was happy, and I was happy just watching him. I did manage to order a lot of very rich food for myself, food that Sandy would not have let me enjoy had she been there. We stayed up late drinking over-priced French wine at The Ritz's Hemmingway Bar until Bob needed me to help him back to our suite and drop him onto his bed fully clothed.

It was probably all the wine that made me sleep so well that night. Or maybe it was the fact that I had stayed awake most of the night before. Either way, I woke up refreshed and feeling only a minor hangover – I'd had worse.

The next morning Bob was able to drink two cups of coffee, but he couldn't face any food, which was very unusual for him. I took him to the airport in a taxi and bought a first class ticket for him, knowing he would eat and drink too much of the free food and booze on the flight home. But what the heck; he is my close friend.

I waited until his plane took off and then returned to The Ritz and phoned Sandy. I had forgotten that there is a nine hour difference in time between France and San Marcos. I woke her at six in the morning her time.

"I'm sorry, babe. I forgot about the time."

"Yeah . . . I think I hear the baby, anyway. Are you coming home?"

"I sent Bob home this morning," I said. I wasn't going to tell her about Germaine yet. She would argue that I should come home right away. "I'm going to stay another day."

"I suppose you're going to surprise me with some expensive gift from Paris?"

"That's right . . . How did you guess?"

I knew my voice was going to tell her that I was lying. And it did.

"You better not be fooling around with some French babe."

She was joking but I was serious. I said, "You know me better than that."

"OK," she said, hearing my serious tone. I could hear her climbing out of the bed. She was holding the phone as she slipped into her slippers and pulled a bathrobe around her. I could hear all that as neither of us said anything for a minute or two.

She stood and demanded, "Tell me the truth."

There's no sense trying to fool Sandy. She is just too smart. So I told her, "There's something going on here . . . I don't know what yet. But I'd like to ask a few questions and talk to a few people."

"I'll be on the next plane out," she said quickly. I should have expected that.

"Is Betsy home yet?" I asked, knowing she would be home from college in a day or two. Betsy, our one time biker-chick-tattooed-runaway-teenager, was in college down in San Francisco doing pre-med. She is also our daughter's nanny when not in school.

I could hear Sandy sigh as she said, "Alright, but as

soon as Betsy is home I'm coming there if you aren't home yet."

That was good; that would give me at least a couple of days to try to find out what really happened to LeRoy and why he was dead. And why Germaine followed him into death.

We talked for ten minutes and then said our goodbyes, along with a few kisses over the phone. It was mid-afternoon in Paris, too early to find the people I needed to speak with. They are people of the night, jazz people who live in the night, and I had to wait for the night to find out what I needed to know.

I decided to have some lunch in the Bar Vendome restaurant in the Ritz's lobby. I was feeling good after a good night's sleep, so I dressed in the best Brooks Brothers sports jacket I had brought with me. It was dark grey so I wore light gray slacks with it. I had gone through the four ties I had packed back at home and decided to not wear a tie at all. I pulled a white silk shirt from the closet, and when I was ready to go to lunch I felt really good, and I told myself, as I looked in the room's mirror, that I looked pretty damn good, too.

Sandy would have ordered some fish or something else very healthy for me. Since she wasn't with me I ordered what I thought was a hamburger, wondering how the hell an American hamburger got on a French menu. As it turned out, my hamburger was beef but like nothing I had ever had before. The beef was almost raw and covered with raw onions and diced spicy pickles. The roll was a buttery, thick and chewy mound of sour bread. But the fried potatoes that came with it were delicious.

As I relished the undercooked meat a waiter, not the waiter for my table, brought a glass of red wine to my table.

"I'm sorry," I said, trying not to spit food at him. "That's not mine."

"Pardon, Monsieur," he said, smiling slyly as if hiding a secret. "The lady across the room, she sends this to Monsieur."

I looked where the young waiter was nodding; it would have been rude for him to point. A woman, perhaps mid-thirties and quite attractive was sitting at a small table. She held a glass of wine and smiled showing off gleaming white teeth.

Her hair was light blond, maybe out of a bottle but not cheap like some streetwalker might have. She wore a navy blue jacket over a light blue blouse; the top three buttons had been left undone. On the hand holding the glass of wine was a big diamond ring in a yellow gold band. It was on her left hand; I wondered if it might be a wedding ring.

"Please tell her thank you for me," I said. "But it's a bit too early in the day for me to enjoy wine." The waiter bowed slightly, took the glass of wine and walked to the lady.

In less than a minute the waiter was back at my table. He said, "Pardon again, Monsieur. The lady says she wishes you to join her at her table, oui?"

I said, "Again, please tell her thank you, but no. I am very married."

He walked away, maybe used to being the messenger between two people trying to pick each other up. Another minute passed and the waiter was again at my table. He was getting frustrated being a messenger boy I think.

"The lady," he said. "Please excuse . . . She said she does not wish to marry you or have sex with you. She wishes to speak with you." He was red faced and clearly embarrassed. I guess I was wrong in my uneducated opinion that all Frenchmen think about is food and sex.

"I'm very sorry," I said. I pulled a twenty dollar bill from my money clip and handed it to him. He seemed appreciative of that as I waived him away. Looking at the woman across the room, I pointed at the second chair at my table. She would have to come to me if she wanted to talk to me. If she were a hooker I would send her on her way quickly.

She stood, and I saw she was wearing very good quality grey wool slacks. Her shoes were low heeled and shiny black leather.

She walked slowly across the busy restaurant, her glass of wine in hand, obviously enjoying the stares she got from the people there as her eyes locked on mine. She was tall, slim, and as I said, attractive. Her hair hung softly to just above her shoulders. Her jacket was open and her silk blouse showed off her breasts very nicely. Her diamond flashed in the light of the restaurant. She had a small black purse hanging from a gold chain on her shoulder.

She stood at the empty chair at my table, her hand on its back, holding the glass of wine in front of her, and smiled down at me. "You are Monsieur Crew, I think, yes?"

"That depends on what you want," I said.

"May I sit, please?"

"For a moment," I said. She was waiting for me to get up and hold her chair for her. I was determined to make her wait forever for that nicety.

"Merci," she said. She finally pulled the chair away from the table as the young waiter ran to her and took hold of the chair for her. She dramatically lowered herself onto it, setting the wine glass very slowly on the white tablecloth.

She sat there smiling but saying nothing.

I broke the silence by saying, "OK, what do you want?"

"Perhaps wine, s'il vous plaît?" she said and drank the glass she was holding dry.

Without my asking, the young waiter brought the bottle of wine the woman had left at her table. He filled her glass and started for mine. I put my hand over it, telling him to forget it. He gently put the bottle on the table in front of her and all but ran from us.

"Now what do you want?" I asked. "I'm very married and not interested in any other women."

"Monsieur," she began, the smile dropping away from her. "I am the friend of Germaine."

I waited, saying nothing.

The woman leaned forward, her elbows on the table, and whispered, "She has been assassiné . . . Murdered, oui?"

"How do you know that?" I asked.

"I was on my way . . . To see Germaine yesterday. I saw you going there and leaving, oui? I waited and then went to her. Did you kill her, Monsieur Morgan Crew?" She had a frozen very slight grin on her red lips; her eyes bore into mine as she spoke.

"How do you know my name?" I asked her. I wasn't about to be questioned by someone I didn't know. This woman could be a cop out to arrest me for murder.

"I make the enquiries, oui?"

"That doesn't answer my question," I demanded. "Who the hell are you?"

"Pardon, Monsieur.   I am Lorraine Demeaux. Germaine, she was my lover, oui?" She said this without any restraint or attempt at hiding the fact. It seemed she was proud of having been Germaine's lover and wasn't about to hide that fact.

"Your lover?" I asked. I probably shouldn't have been shocked, but I was also skeptical. "Are you sure you're not some kind of cop?"

"Cop?" she asked. "You mean the police, oui? No, I am not the . . . Cop as you say."

"Then you wouldn't mind if I looked through your purse?"

She smiled and then handed her purse to me. Inside were the usual things a woman carries: lipstick, a small mirror, a few keys, an embroidered hanky . . . and a small chrome plated pearl handed pistol.

"Why the gun?" I asked.

"A woman alone . . . In the night . . . You understand, oui?"

I held her purse under the table and removed the pistol from it. I slipped it into my jacket pocket and said, "You can have that back when we've finished talking."

She nodded, and the tight grin went into a smile as I handed her purse back to her.

"You said you were Germaine's lover. I thought she and LeRoy Manns were lovers?"

"Oui, Germaine and LeRoy were the lovers. Germaine and I were the lovers, also. Germaine, she enjoyed the men . . . I don't. Germaine, she was free to do as she pleased, as I am."

"OK, I can buy that," I said. "So who killed her?"

"You did not?" Lorraine asked.

"No, I didn't. I want to find out what happened to LeRoy. He was my friend. I think LeRoy might have been murdered . . . Germaine told me that. If he was, then the same person who murdered him murdered Germaine."

"You and he . . . LeRoy," she said struggling to find the words. "You were the lovers, too?"

"No, of course not." I tried not to sound insulting but I knew I did anyway. "He was a friend of mine . . . From our college days, that's all."

"And you wish to know . . . I am sorry, I am trying to find the words . . . You wish to know the person who killed LeRoy?"

"How do you know he was killed? It was reported as an accident."

"It was I who went with Germaine to where LeRoy's body was kept. The Sûreté, they wished to have the body . . . I do not know the word, Monsieur."

"Identified," I said.

"Oui, that is the word. LeRoy, his body was greatly damaged, oui? Germaine and I were sure the accident was no. He was murdered, Monsieur, that is certain."

"You never told me how you know who I am."

"I followed you, Monsieur . . . To here . . . And I ask, oui? You will perhaps help me find the killer of Germaine?"

"Why me? Why not just go to the police?"

"The police, they do not like me, Monsieur."

"Why?" I asked.

Lorraine lowered her head and tried to smile. She

whispered, "Because I am the thief, Monsieur. I tell you because I need your help, oui? I cannot ask the questions. Perhaps you can?"

"You're a thief. That's quite an admission. What do you steal?"

She raised her head and again forced a smile to crease her red lips. "Whatever I can, no? The wallets from pockets . . . Things from the stores . . . Anything."

"So you're a petty thief," I said. "You dress well for a small time thief."

"Oui," she said, trying to defend herself. "I live well."

Maybe she was telling me the truth . . . Maybe she was making up a fantastic story. Maybe she was trying to hook me into something. I would be careful; I wouldn't let her con me . . . If I could that is. But if she was telling me the truth about her and Germaine, maybe she could be of a help to me. My French is abysmal. Her English wasn't much better than my French. But maybe she could be my translator and guide around Paris.

"OK," said. "I'm going back to L'ange Bleu tonight. Meet me there about ten, alright?"

"Oui, that is good," she said, now smiling a satisfied smile and relaxing back in her chair, knowing I would help her. "May I have the pistol, now, s'il vous plaît?"

"It's not dark outside. You don't need it in broad daylight. I think I'll keep it for a while. You can have it back . . . Maybe tonight . . . After dark . . . If I think I can trust you."

FIVE - Jean Paul Tavenier

A cool but sunny Paris springtime day had turned colder that evening, and a light rain was falling as I stepped from the taxi in front of the alley that held the jazz club, L'ange Bleu. Lorraine was waiting there for me, pulling a grey trench coat up around her neck. She wore a broad brimmed grey cloth rain hat that drooped from being wet. Her feet, wearing good quality black shoes with a two-inch heel, soaked from the rain, were doing a dance on the wet cobblestones against the cold. She smiled as she saw me, and she shivered a little from the cool night rain.

"Bonsoir, Monsieur Crew," she said as I approached her.

"Were you waiting long?" I asked. I was not late in my own mind. I had told her 'about ten' and it was nearly half past ten. To me that was 'about ten.' Lorraine was not a trusted ally . . . Yet . . . If ever she would be. Making her wait for me in the rain told her I was in charge, I was more important than she, and she would be taking a back seat to me if we were to ask questions together. I needed a translator, but I had to make her understand her place in our little arrangement.

"No," she said. "Not long in any case."

I started down the dark alley, Lorraine following a few steps behind me, our shoes clacking on the old cobblestones. I could hear the lilting tones of the jazz flowing from the basement club onto the alley. The band was playing a slightly upbeat version of Ella Fitzgerald's 'Summertime'. Although it was half past ten at night, it was still early in the day of the jazz world. The music would slow to dreamy wonder in the early morning hours.

We walked down the stone steps into the brick walled club, through a thin cloud of cigarette smoke that soon, later in the night, would share the air with smoke from marijuana. The club was only half full in the early hour. We found a small round table with two small, wrought iron chairs near the small stage where the four musicians played. Everything in the club had to be small because the basement room was small. The stage would have been a crowded stage if LeRoy Manns were still with them. It was unfinished wood, maybe two foot tall, and not very wide or deep. The musicians were crowded on the stage, but they didn't seem to mind.

The lack of LeRoy's horn was noticeable, but the four players were good, and the music was good, even if it wasn't the slow jazz I love so much.

We sat, and I ordered two glasses of red wine without asking Lorraine what she wanted, but she seemed to enjoy the cheap, strong wine anyway. The music glided into Herbie Hancock's 'Watermelon Man,' but without LeRoy's horn the music was lacking punch. Patrice Laurent on the sax tried to make up for that, but I could hear the difference.

Lorraine and I finished the glasses of wine as they finished a slower rendition of 'Here Comes The Sun.' When they had finished, the band laid their instruments aside and walked through the door at the side of the stage, without announcing they would be taking a break. No one seemed to complain.

I stood, and Lorraine followed me taking a step onto

the stage and down to avoid the table blocking our way to the door. We opened the door and walked into the hallway where the quartet had gone. The hallway was thin and dimly lit.

In the hallway the door to the left, where I had met Germaine, was open. I stepped into the little break room. There wasn't enough room for Lorraine so she stood in the doorway. The room was small, not more than twelve by twelve, and filled with five chairs and a miniscule round wooden table. The table was crowded with only a metal ashtray that was filled to overflowing with ash and cigarette butts. The walls were bare of any decoration. They had been painted a dull yellow years before, and nothing had been done to refresh them.

Patrice Laurent was the first to look up at us. He stopped us with a raised hand, standing from the rickety wooden chair he had been sitting in. "Monsieur Crew," he said, surprised to see me. "What are you doing here?"

"I need to speak with the four of you," I said.

Patrice looked at Lorraine and asked, "And who is this?"

So he didn't know Lorraine which meant he didn't know she and Germaine were lovers. Best to keep that secret for the time being, I thought.

"This is Lorraine Demeaux. She's helping me with my French, or lack thereof. I'm afraid my education lacked foreign languages."

Lorraine smiled a thin smile and nodded to Patrice. He and the other three musicians looked at her suspiciously, and I took note of that. Patrice sat back down, pushed the only empty chair away from the table with his foot and pointed to it, telling me to sit. I stood anyway. He crossed his legs and folded his hands in his lap, waiting for me to say something.

"Mr. Laurent," I asked. "Did you know that Germaine was killed yesterday?"

It was a direct question meant to elicit a response that would tell me if Laurent could be trusted or not. If he was surprised, shocked, or shaken, then he didn't know. It was a test question. For all I knew, he had killed Germaine.

His face went white, his eyes went wide, his legs fell apart, and he was jolted back in the chair as if he had been hit. "Germaine . . . She is dead?" He turned to his three friends and spoke in French, telling them. I looked at Lorraine, and she nodded ever so slightly, telling me he was telling them what I had told him.

The three musicians all began talking at once, none of them able to hide their surprise. I wanted to see if they honestly didn't know. Their reaction let me be assured they didn't know. Lorraine stopped them by saying something and answering their questions. She turned to me and said, "I tell them you wish to ask the questions, yes? They say they know nothing, but I think maybe they do."

"Ask them if they know why LeRoy was killed," I told her.

She conversed with the four for a moment or two, and then said to me, "They are surprised you think LeRoy was killed. But I think maybe that is not truth, you know, oui? I think there is something they do not say."

I looked at the four men as I asked Lorraine, "Tell them Germaine was murdered, and if she was murdered then LeRoy was murdered, too. Tell them I think they knew something that got both of them killed. If they know why, they need to tell me before the police hold them in jail for days for questioning."

She spoke with them once again, her tone argumentative and demanding. I wished I knew what they were saying. I could only hope that Lorraine was telling them what I told her to say.

She spoke to me, "They say nothing. But I think they are not speaking the truth, you understand? What is it you want to do?"

There was nothing I could do at that time, but I had an idea. I told her, "Let's go, but tell them I'm staying at The Ritz if they want to talk to me." She spoke to them again. I heard the word 'Ritz' so I assumed she had said what I told her to say. When she had finished, she followed me out of the small break room.

In the club I told her, "Go home. How do I get in touch with you?"

She reached inside her purse and pulled a scrap of paper and a small gold pen from it. She wrote her phone number down and handed the paper to me. I thanked her and asked if I could get a taxi for her. She shook her head and pulled on her raincoat and hat. She started up the stairs and out onto the street, walking very slowly. I wondered what she was thinking.

What I didn't know until this whole thing was over was that the four band members sat in the little break room arguing. The drummer, Marc Baptiste, was angry, more so than his fellow musicians.

Marc was a big man, not tall but fat. He was as pale white as a Caucasian could get. His hair was black and grey and oily and dusted with dandruff and uncombed most of the time. He liked his food and booze, and he spent his waking hours sitting behind his drums, resulting in a stomach of bragging proportions, legs that were too fat for most pants off the rack, and a series of fat folds under his chin. His eyebrows were thick and hung down almost to his eyelids. His lips were thick and puffy red. All in all, he was not a handsome man.

Marc was insisting that they do something . . . Anything . . . About their friend's death. At first he wanted to go to the police, but that drew astonished fear from his group. Then he wanted the whole band to go to The Ritz and tell me everything they knew. The others were against this, fear filling their silence.

After too much talk, rather than going back to work, Marc said, "You can do nothing. I will not. I'm going to Monsieur DuSomme right now. I will demand he tell me the truth."

"No! No!" they all shouted. But Marc was angry and he was not able to control that anger. Maybe he didn't want to.

"We all know what happened," he said. He struggled to get his bulk out of the little folding chair he was sitting on. The three tried to stop him, but he brushed them aside with one fat arm.

Marc stormed from the little break room and pounded loudly and heavily on the door across the hall. He waited then pounded again. From behind him his friends called to him to stop, but he ignored them. Rather than pound his fat fist on the door a third time he knocked. From inside he heard Alain DuSomme say, "Come in . . . Now that you do not break my door down."

Marc opened the door and took two steps into the room. Alain's office was bigger than the break room, and better kept. The walls were freshly painted a few months ago. The furniture consisted of a couple of nice chairs in front of Alain's desk, and a couple of file cabinets along the wall behind the desk. Framed pictures, good copies of good modern art, hung along the walls to the left and right.

Alain carefully laid the gold pen he had been writing with on the desk. He leaned back in his tall leather chair and asked, "So, Marc, what is it you want to see me about?"

The drummer looked at the two chairs wondering if he should sit. DuSomme saw this and said cruelly, "No, Marc. You are too damn fat. You will break the chair."

For the first time Marc Baptiste realized he may have made a mistake. He swallowed hard, took half a step closer to DuSomme, and convinced himself that he must follow through on what he wanted to say.

"Monsieur DuSomme," he began, speaking in the common French he had been raised in, his voice trembling, "LeRoy . . . I . . . We . . . I mean me . . . I think he knew something . . . Of you, I mean. If you did him harm I must go to the police. Please tell me if you . . . If you . . . ."

DuSomme put on a false smile and glared into Marc's wavering eyes. He asked, "Are you trying to accuse me of murder, Marc? I hope not. That is a terrible accusation. And one you will certainly regret."

"No Monsieur . . . No Monsieur . . . Certainly not . . . We . . . I . . . I only want to know why LeRoy is dead."

"Well now," Alain said. "That sounds very reasonable. But why ask me? Do you think I had something to do with his very untimely death?"

"No . . . Of course not . . ." Marc was shaking now. His face was red with fear and regret. He knew the reputation Alain DuSomme had. "But LeRoy . . . Did he know something?"

"Something? Like what, Marc?"

"I don't know . . . I hoped you would tell me . . ."

"And if LeRoy did know something he should not know, why in heaven's name would I know? And if I did know . . . Why would I tell you?"

Marc was shaking now. He felt the warmth of his bladder opening. He looked down; his pants were wet and a puddle surrounded his feet. "I am so sorry, Monsieur DuSomme. I am so sorry."

Alain looked down, laughed, picked up his gold pen and started to write. He said without looking up at Marc, "Go now . . . And be sure to clean up that mess."

❋❋❋❋❋❋❋❋❋❋❋❋❋❋

I watched Lorraine walk out of the club. Her hips swayed gently and seductively; I wondered if that was for me? Her legs were slim and eye-catching, and her hair swung softly under her rain soaked hat. She was attractive but certainly not beautiful as Sandy is. She kept herself attractive but she had no interest in men? That conundrum spun through my mind.

I walked back to the table we had sat at and waited. The quartet finally returned to the stage, late but not at all at ease and comfortable. Their music was restrained and almost forced. My conversation with them and the news about Germaine's death, obviously had affected them; at that time I did not know any other reason for their discomfort. I assumed by their faces, all white and ashen, that Germaine's death had affected all of them.

I had intended to stay until they quit for the night. I wanted to talk with Patrice Laurent alone, outside of the club. I felt he knew something, but he was afraid to tell me in front of his friends. I stayed through three hours, the music getting progressively deeper and slower and dreamier. My eyes started to burn from the cloud of smoke rapidly filling the club. I got up and decided to wait for Patrice outside, even if it was raining.

The thin alleyway that L'ange Bleu was in was dark and dirty. The rain had stopped, but the alley was wet and smelled like wet garbage and dirty dogs. Across the street from the alley was a small café, a coffee shop; three people sat inside, each alone, at separate tables. I decided that waiting there had to be better than waiting in the alley.

Sitting inside at the one window of the little shop, I was able to watch everyone going into the club and leaving. A long hour went by . . . Three espressos had me buzzing . . . When Patrice slunk out of the shadows. The three other band members were with him. Two walked away quickly; the fat drummer and Patrice stayed and were talking. I looked at my watch; it was a quarter to four.

They stopped in the alley at the sidewalk and talked, pressing themselves against the stone wall of a building at the alley entrance. As they talked they looked first right, then left, then right again, and stepped out of the alley. Even in the dark shadows of the night I could see they were frightened, almost shaking in fear.

Finally they decided to go home. Patrice said something and the drummer nodded in agreement. Patrice walked away quickly, and the fat drummer stayed to light a cigarette. He watched Patrice turn a corner and started to cross the street.

As his foot left the curb and touched the wet

cobblestones of the street Alain DuSomme walked from the shadows of the alley. He stopped the drummer and walked to him. He was speaking in angry terms although I couldn't hear what was being said. He was punching the fat musician with a finger as he spoke. The drummer raised his hands as if Alain's finger were a gun. Alain grabbed the drummer's suit lapels and twisted him around, pushing him against the wall of the alley.

I watched as DuSomme punched the drummer in his fat stomach, once and then again, and then a third time. The fat man fell to his knees on the wet cobblestones. DuSomme was yelling now, in threatening tones. He pulled a pistol from his belt and held it to the fat drummer's head. I could see the musician was pleading for his life.

I thought DuSomme was about to murder the man. But he didn't. He did stab the pistol barrel into the drummer's chest and then punched the fat man across his face. The drummer slumped to the ground. DuSomme slipped the pistol back under his jacket and walked away, back down the dark alley.

I at first froze where I was. I stood, stepped out of the coffee shop, and was about to cross the street to go to the poor fat man who was on the wet sidewalk, crying loudly. I realized I would be in danger if DuSomme saw me and I didn't even know the fat drummer's name. I quickly stepped backwards against a wall and then, keeping my back to the wall, I stepped sideways until I reached another side alley. I stepped into the shadows there and waited.

Time passed slowly, and I don't know how long it took for the drummer to get to his feet. He was leaning against the wall of the alley to keep from falling again.

My mind was racing with thoughts of what I should do. I could, of course, go to Marc . . . But why? What would it gain me? I had no idea who had killed Germaine. I had no idea who had killed LeRoy. What I did know was that DuSomme had threatened and attacked Marc who may have known something he should not have known.

People who knew something were being murdered. I guessed that Marc would have been murdered, but DuSomme needed him for his club. He was short one band member already; he could not lose another one. A threat would be enough.

Marc must have known what the others knew. How long would he remain alive? I had to find out what that something was that DuSomme had to hide.

The sky had not yet begun to brighten; night still enfolded Paris as I walked and found my way to The Ritz. It was a long walk, especially since I didn't know my way around Paris very well. I had been there for a week with Sandy on our honeymoon, but not since then. And on our honeymoon, tourist stuff was not high on my list.

I avoided taxis because I didn't want a record of me being anywhere near the attack. The doorman at the front of The Ritz, one I had not seen before and I hoped did not recognize me, opened the lobby door for me, and I made it to an elevator without drawing the attention of the few people in the lobby at that early hour.

I ran to the bar in my suite and drank down two large bourbons without ice or club soda. That steadied my shaking hands enough for me to phone Sandy.

"I'm sorry, babe," I said. "I forgot to check the time. Did I wake you?"

"No, of course not," she said. I think she could hear the nervousness in my voice. "It's only almost nine here. That makes it almost six in the morning where you are.

What's wrong? Are you in trouble?"

"I don't know," I said. I guess I just needed to talk to someone and get everything that had happened out of me. Sandy was the best person I knew to talk with, to talk about problems and get good advice. She is smart and calm . . . Most of the time, until she loses her temper . . . And she can reason through trouble. So I told her everything that had happened since arriving in Paris.

When I was done she was quiet for a moment or two, and then said, "I'll phone Betsy and ask her to come home tomorrow. I'm catching the first flight out. Please stay safe. We can't lose you."

We talked for more than an hour; I think Sandy was trying to calm me, to drain away the sick memories of the dead. She did that job very well. My hands stopped shaking, and I was able to breathe normally. And when we hung up our phones, sleep overtook me quickly. I was able to lie in bed, comforted and feeling light after getting everything off my chest. I slept a dreamless sleep, no nightmares once again.

Day light was streaming through the curtained windows of the bedroom when the pounding on the suite's door woke me suddenly. I kicked the soft down comforter away and struggled to get out of bed. I was still dressed in the pants and shirt I had worn the night before, less my shoes and socks that were wet from the night's rain.

My head spun as I stood too quickly and walked to the door. My fingers fumbled with the lock and chain on the door. Whoever was on the other side of the door was saying something. It was English . . . Sort of anyway . . . Heavily accented English . . . And the voice was demanding.

I was finally able to get the door open. A man, as tall as me but maybe ten years younger, stood there looking up and down at me as if I were some hobo he had found in a trashcan.

"Who are you?" the man asked. He was dressed like every cop I had ever seen; a cheap, off the rack, brown tweed jacket and mismatched brown slacks. His shoes were heavy soled black leather that needed some polish. His hair was dark. His eyes were dark. He was frowning with that cop-like threat they all use.

"Who the hell are you?"

"I am the Police, Monsieur . . . The Police Nationale. You are perhaps Monsieur Morgan Crew?" He pulled a brown leather I.D. case from his coat pocket and held it up in front of me. It could have been a Lone Ranger kid's badge from a box of Cheerios for all I knew.

I said, "I am . . . What do you want? You speak English well by the way."

"Merci . . . I should say . . . Thank you. I study . . . It is good that I can practice, no? May I come in?" His voice was an octave lower and he seemed a little less angry. I have learned over the years that an empty compliment does good most of the time, to swing conversations to my benefit and to lower the level of anger and threat facing me.

"Why? . . . What do you want?" I asked. I stood in the open doorway, my right hand on the door, my left on the doorframe, blocking his way in.

"I wish to speak with you on the attacking of Marc Baptiste last night, Monsieur."

"The word is attack, not attacking."

"I am sorry," he said. "You are right, of course. I will learn, oui? May I come in?"

I figured I could let this cop in and listen to him or

have him drag me off to some remote French jail to have someone beat the truth out of me. He wasn't about to ask the questions he wanted to ask while standing in the hallway.

I knew enough of French law to know that once a person was charged with a crime the accused was expected to prove their innocence; somewhat different from American law where the accused is innocent until proven guilty. So I stepped back and let him walk into the suite.

He was obviously impressed with the grand suite; his wide eyes took in everything appreciatively. I imagined this cop, living on a cop's salary, had not seen such luxury before, except maybe in museums if he could afford the entry fee. He stood a few feet inside the suite as he looked around the room slowly. I fully expected him to whistle, but he didn't.

I notice that kind of thing because it helps me determine the kind of person I am speaking with. This French cop obviously came from the middle class of French society. His appreciation of the grand suite told me I was right about him. He was not used to people who could afford the best.

I walked past the cop and sat in an armchair, crossing my legs and leaning back, trying to look at ease, but I knew my wrinkled pants and shirt, and my bed-hair, cast a different picture of me. I wasn't at ease realizing what I looked like, but I had to make him believe I was not nervous. I let the cop stand.

"Let's start with your name and some I.D.," I said.

"I am so sorry," he said as he took the brown leather case from his jacket pocket once again. He held it open, reaching his arm out towards me, for me to see. I had no idea what a French cop's I.D. looked like, but I had to make him believe I did.

He said as he held the case open, "I am Jean Paul Tavenier."

"OK," I said. The name on the ID card matched what he told me. "Do I call you 'Detective' or what?"

"Typically, I am called L'agent . . . But if we may be . . . Common is the word?"

"I think you probably mean informal."

"Oui . . . Yes, of course . . . Informal. Please, I am Jean Paul, yes?" His saying that told me he had done background on me and had learned what the name 'Crew' meant in the world. I carry a lot of privilege by having that name and the money and power that comes with it.

"That's nice, Jean Paul," I said. "And you may call me Mr. Crew. Now what do you want?" I had to let him think that I was better than him . . . Of course I didn't think I was better than anybody, but I wanted to get our positions straight before he started to ask questions. If I were his superior . . . In his eyes anyway . . . Then the questions would be polite and not too offensive.

"Last night a man was beaten badly. Marc Baptiste. He is now at hôpital . . . How you say this? You know this man, yes?"

"Is he the drummer at L'ange Bleu? I was there once or twice only; I think I saw him there. So he's in the hospital? Was he hurt badly?"

"You are not surprised that Monsieur Baptiste was attacked?" Jean Paul asked rather than answering my question. That was a mistake on my part. I should have been shocked and acted like it was a complete surprise. He saw quickly that I wasn't surprised by his news. Jean Paul was a good detective. He watched for signs in people's physical movements and words.

He was looking around the room at the several chairs and couches standing empty while he stood.

I asked, "Would you like to sit . . . Monsieur L'agent?" I said with a royal like wave of an arm. "And is Mr. Baptiste OK?"

He smiled and stepped quickly to the chair nearest me and sat with an appreciative smile on his pale pink face.

"Now," he said, relaxing back in the overstuffed upholstered chair, "You have not my question answered, Monsieur Crew."

"The proper English is 'You have not answered my question, Mr. Crew.' I'm here to help you as much as I can. And you haven't answered my question, either."

"And I am much thankful, Monsieur Crew. But please answer my question, yes?"

"I'm sorry," I said, delaying and being as obtuse as I could manage. "But what was the question?"

"Monsieur Crew," the cop said, frustration in his voice. He was getting impatient, and that was good for me, what I intended. When the opposition gets angry it puts me in control, and they often say and do things they would not normally say or do. "Why are you not surprised that Monsieur Baptiste was beaten?"

"What makes you think I'm not surprised?" I asked. Asking questions in response to questions being asked is an old trick I learned years ago when talking to the police. It's a trick the police use all the time when questioning witnesses and suspects – never answer a question, always ask a question. It only goes so far, and when the police reach the point of exasperation I start to cooperate . . . To some small extent anyway. Saying too much to the police . . . Or to an attorney for that matter . . . Is not very smart. Never volunteer anything.

"Because you do not . . ." he paused as he started to answer my question and smiled. "I know what it is you do, Monsieur Crew. Please answer my questions here, or I must take you to my poste . . . How you say? . . . Is it office, oui?"

I raised my hand palm up and said, "Wait a minute, OK?" I reached for the phone and dialed the International Phone Number for Harper, Harper, Jascro and Nettles, my family's attorneys. I had no idea what time it was in New York, but a woman answered the phone. Either it was midnight, and a lone telephone answerer was working, or it was daytime office hours. It made no real difference.

I told her who I was and that I needed an attorney very quickly. Since the Crew Family is the giant law firm's biggest client and biggest money maker, everyone there knows my name. I gave her my suite's number at The Ritz, and she said to stay there. The cop started to say something as I hung up. I raised my hand again asking Jean Paul to wait a moment.

The phone rang a minute or two later, and the man on the other end asked what I needed. He spoke very good English with a British accent.

"I have a detective from the Police Nationale here asking questions about an assault I was not involved in," I told him.

I handed the phone to Jean Paul and he listened, trying to get a word in edgewise but unable to do so. He tried unsuccessfully to interrupt what had to be the strong instructions and threats from my attorney. He looked deflated when he handed the phone back to me and I hung it up.

He said, looking down at the floor, unable to look at me as he spoke, "It is that your Embassy American will soon speak with Minister Feki, my boss. I have been asked to cooperate with you until Minister Feki is spoken to . . . I mean spoken with, oui? That I will cooperate with you is what Minister Feki will be told." He looked up at me with a not so friendly look on his face and asked, "Shall I?"

"Monsieur Tavenier," I said. "I intend to find out who killed those two people, LeRoy Manns and his girlfriend Germaine. I will work with you if you wish, but I will find out who killed my friend and his friend whether you and I cooperate or not."

Jean Paul nodded, perhaps accepting what he had to do whether he liked it or not. He asked, "So you think the deaths of Monsieur Manns and Madam LeFont are . . . What is the word? . . . Together?"

"I think you mean connected. Yes, I do believe that. I believe they knew something that got them killed. And I believe that the assault on the drummer last night is connected, also. I believe they all had some information that they should not have had."

"If that is so, why was not Monsieur Baptiste also murdered?"

"I don't know that right now," I answered. "I will find out. But it may be something as simple as DuSomme needs his band at the club. He's lost one, maybe he couldn't afford to lose another. Maybe a serious threat would work as well. I don't know right now. I can only guess that they all knew something they shouldn't know."

"And what would that be, Monsieur?" he asked and smiled. I believe he *knew* what I thought might be true. I believe he had some information that I wanted, but I wondered if he would share that information with me. Cops are often self-important people. Sure, they have a lot of legal power behind their badges, but it goes to their heads. They want to be in control of what they are investigating. Losing that control affects their self-importance often like being beat up by someone smaller than they are.

"Each of these people . . . ," I began and paused in mid-sentence. I stood and started to pace back and forth across the room thinking about what I would say to get the answers I needed. I had no idea if I was right or not, but my instincts have been fine-tuned over the years. I had this gut feeling that I was right.

I stopped pacing, turned to Jean Paul and said, "Each of these people had one thing in common . . . And that is L'ange Bleu, the club where LeRoy worked. Germaine and LeRoy were sleeping together. When people sleep together, and when they care about each other, they talk. I am fairly sure that LeRoy told Germaine something . . . Something that got her killed. The drummer . . . Marc is his name? . . . Must know something, too.

"I think it is very possible that whatever each of them knew is connected to L'ange Bleu. Marc Baptiste had to be close to LeRoy and Germaine. One or both of them probably told Marc whatever they knew," I said and started pacing again. I stopped after crossing the room once and turned to face Jean Paul. I said, "And I think you know what they knew about L'ange Bleu that got them killed."

He smiled again and nodded slightly. He said, "Oui, Monsieur. I do know something of L'ange Bleu."

"And what is that?" I asked after waiting for him to tell me.

"At this time . . . I think I cannot say to you. But perhaps in time I can. Perhaps after your Embassy American speaks with my superiors, oui? I must think of my position here, oui? Working without the instructions is a dangerous thing, oui? I assume you will continue with your own questions? Perhaps even if I say no to you?"

"And I assume your boss is hearing from the American Embassy as we speak. Yes, Monsieur L'agent, I am going to continue asking questions. But I have one question for you."

"Oui, and what is that?"

"Do you know a woman named Lorraine Demeaux?"

"I suppose I can say that this is one of many names the woman uses. She says she is a thief . . . But we suspect there is more to her than that. She is known, under many different names, all over Europe."

Now, that surprised me. I asked, "She told me she was Germaine's lover. Is there more than that?"

"Oui, I knew Lorraine had many of the lovers . . . Men and women . . . But that is not strange. In France . . . In Paris . . . Love is not strange, you know?"

He was not telling me everything; I could see that in his face and his eyes that would not look at my eyes. He was looking down one minute and glancing all around the room the next. He was nervous; I figured he was just frightened of telling me too much and getting in trouble back at his headquarters. I asked, "What else?"

"That I cannot say. Perhaps when I have the instructions to tell you I will. But not now. I can say that if you choose to continue, you will put yourself in the greatest danger. That I am able to say. And I cannot be the person responsible for you, oui?"

"One more thing," I said. "Can I see the autopsy reports for LeRoy Manns and Germaine LeFont?"

"Oui, I think that is possible.   Come to my office tomorrow . . . In the morning, yes?"

SIX - Threats

The policeman, L'agent Detective Jean Paul Tavenier, stood and turned. He nervously shifted back and forth, wondering if he should say 'goodbye' or just walk away. He looked at me, nodded without saying anything and quickly started for the door. He walked, almost running, out of the suite. I took that as he being very uncomfortable with the situation he had been thrown into. He knew things I wanted to know. He knew that, but to tell me police secrets was not within him.

He had said enough to make me certain L'ange Bleu was at the center of LeRoy's death. Without saying the words, he had told me that the French police knew something was going on at the club, something illegal if the police were interested, although he would not tell me what they suspected. And if I could find out why LeRoy was murdered, then I would know why another murder followed his, and I would know what was occurring at L'ange Bleu that the police were interested in.

But to know just who the hell Lorraine Demeaux was, was another question I may never get answers to. She was more than just a translator. But how much more? Lorraine Demeaux had said she would help me, but Jean Paul hinted that she had something to hide, something she hadn't told me.

I was lucky that the policeman who came to me could speak English. I realized I would have a hard time talking to people who could not speak English when I couldn't speak French. Sandy would be there with me in Paris as soon as she could, and Sandy can get along pretty well in French and Spanish, at least enough for her to be understood and to understand what others are saying. Rather than depend on Lorraine Demeaux I would wait for Sandy and then return to L'ange Bleu. That was the center of this whole mess, I was sure of that.

But on top of all that, all the things to consider and think about, there was that annoying little voice in the back of my head that was not yet screaming that morning but was speaking loud enough for me to hear. "Run away! Run away!" it kept repeating.

Over the years I have heard that little voice screaming at me, warning me every time I get close to danger. Although it is a sensible warning, I have never run away as it advises me. I laughed when I thought, 'Why does it keep yelling at me when I ignore it?'

I have been in many dangerous positions, and I have been frightened each of those times. I am not a hero like you see in the movies. I am scared of many, many things; truth be told I am afraid of everything. But I also know that I have to push past that fear and do what needs to be done. I have to push it behind me while remembering that fear also warns me to be careful.

I stripped off yesterday's clothes that I had slept in and stood in a hot shower for a long time. The stinging beads of steaming water did me a lot of good. The shower-head was adjustable to several forms of massage. I twisted it until I found one that was almost painful it was so strong. I let it hit my back and my neck for a long time, easing up the muscle strain from too much tension.

My sleep filled brain was awakened, and I could feel

some strength return to my body. The Ritz provided really big and really thick cotton towels. I used one to dry myself and another to wrap around me. I ordered a big pot of strong, black coffee and a plate of sweet rolls and croissants with thick, rich butter and sweet marmalade on the side – Sandy not being there to say "NO!"

After eating, I lay on the huge, soft bed all that day, listening to the voices in the back of my brain counsel me to go home. I flipped through the channels on TV, finding only programs in French, until I again found the one ESPN station in English. I guess even the French like American sports.

I did fall asleep out of boredom and woke in a dark room, the sun having set. The red numbers on the bedside table's clock told me it was twenty minutes to ten. I had slept the day away, and I was hungry. I ordered a steak and fries and a bottle of red wine from room service and showered and shaved while I waited for it.

Sandy would be with me the next day as she promised, so I took advantage of that to have a big steak, rare, and a pile of fries, something she would not have let me have were she there. I have no idea why, but with the stack of fries came a side of mayonnaise. Oh well, they were good even without ketchup.

Although I had decided earlier to wait for Sandy before returning to the club, I was bored. TV was all in French, except for the one ESPN channel, and although there was a selection of pay-per-view porn . . . Probably all in French anyway . . . I had to get out of the hotel awhile. At half past eleven I took a taxi to L'ange Bleu. I love good jazz, and a beer or two while enjoying the music there sounded like the perfect way to waste some time. I would be a typical tourist out for a night of jazz and cheap wine.

It was a pleasantly warm and dry evening in that

springtime Paris, known for its cool, rainy days and cold rainy nights at that time of year. By the time I got there the tourists had left to go back to their hotels to make an early night of it. The club was crowded with the 'Jazz Set' as the young Parisians are known who haunt the many hidden jazz bars.

I found a small table against the brick wall at the back and ordered a beer. The four remaining members of LeRoy's group had been joined by a woman playing a guitar and trying to sing. Her voice was raspy and as dull as she looked. She was middle aged, her rumpled hair was threaded with grey, she was slightly overweight, and her face was pockmarked. She wore an old flowery dress that a woman might wear at home while cleaning the house. But the people listening to her seemed to like what they heard. Or maybe it was the marijuana?

Marc Baptiste was behind his drums. His face was bruised, his right eye swollen and closed. I could see he struggled with keeping the beat of the music the band was playing. He was in pain from the beating DuSomme had given him. But he was there, doing the best he could. As with other great musicians, the music was the thing, the music was what made his world go round.

As I finished my second tall glass of pretty good French beer, Lorraine Demeaux walked down the brick stairs of the club, carefully avoiding the loose bricks, and approached my table. She stood there, looking down at me with a somewhat stern expression on her face.

"You did not say to me you were coming here," she said finally.

"Why should I?"

"That is the strange thing," she said, frowning. "It was understood to me that I would help you. Is that not the correct thing? Is that not what we had said?"

"And I thought I was to phone you when I needed you," I said flatly. "I had a conversation with a police detective. Jean Paul Tavenier. He told me things about you."

All Lorraine did in reply was to smile and shrug her shoulders.

The people sitting around us were staring at us, and one young woman, her pitch black hair combed down her too pale forehead into her black make-up circled eyes, said something in French and held a finger to her lips, telling us to be quiet. I guess we were talking too loudly and interfering with the music.

I pulled a chair away from the table and motioned for Lorraine to sit. She ordered a glass of wine from the only waitress there, who had glazed over, dreamy eyes from breathing too much of the pot smoke that filled the place and maybe enjoying some drugs herself. We listened to the soft and slow, dreamy jazz, trying to ignore the old lady who could just barely hold a tune. An hour passed along with another beer and two more glasses of wine for Lorraine. The music was good if the singing wasn't, and Lorraine said nothing.

The sleepy eyed waitress came back to our table. She took a deep breath, sighed, leaned toward me and whispered in my ear. "Go . . . to . . . office," she said very slowly, struggling to say each word separately, obviously having trouble with the English. She pointed to the door at the side of the low stage where the quartet and singer were performing.

Lorraine whispered close to my ear, "Do not go. It is not safe, oui?"

"Stay here," I said as I stood. The quartet stopped playing suddenly, in the middle of a tune, and they watched me walk to the door. The entire room was quiet as they turned to watch me walk slowly across the stone floored club, the heels of my shoes clicking loudly on the old stone.

The people at the table at the edge of the little stage that blocked my walk to the door stood and pulled the table and chairs aside. I opened the door and walked through. I probably shouldn't have, but I closed the door behind me.

The hallway was thin and dark with only the same one light on a cord from the ceiling casting a dim light, as it was the night I spoke with Patrice in the little break room. Further along the hallway were the two doors, one on the right and one on the left. And at the end of the hall was the little kitchen. Two men stood in the doorway wearing stained aprons and stained white T-shirts, looking at me, wondering what would happen to me.

The door on the left, the break room for the band, was closed. The door to the right was open; pale light cast from it. I walked to it.

I stood in the open doorway and looked inside. I saw a fairly good quality wood desk with a couple of nice chairs sitting at angles in front of it. The desk was crowded with a polished brass lamp and a pile of papers to the right of it. A couple of framed prints hung on the walls.

A man was bent over an old-fashioned ledger book, writing numbers in its columns with a gold ballpoint pen. He wasn't young; age was catching up with him. His hair was almost completely grey, but his thin mustache was still jet black.

But the man's physical appearance belied his age. Even as he was sitting, I could tell he was in good shape, strong and well-muscled. He wore wire rimmed glasses that hung low on his nose. I noticed a small gold and diamond ring on the pinky finger of his left hand. He wore a good quality French suit with dark blue pin stripes, a white silk shirt, and a red and blue diagonal striped tie. Nothing special there, but not what an average Parisian or the owner of a small jazz club would be able to afford.

He looked up as I stood there in the open doorway and dropped his pen onto the ledger. "Mr. Crew," he said. He smiled slightly but did not stand. "Please come in and sit."

I looked around, then pulled out one of the two chairs. I lowered myself slowly onto it, pulling the chair towards the desk as I sat. The man said nothing. He leaned back in his chair causing it to squeak loudly. I looked around the small office; it was much nicer than the breakroom. It was freshly painted, and I noticed that the framed prints on the walls were of good quality. Two gray metal filing cabinets stood against the wall, behind the man's desk and chair.

To break the silence I asked, "What did you want to see me about? And who are you?"

"Why are you talking to my employees, Mr. Crew?"

"Why shouldn't I?" I replied. "Who are you, anyway?"

"I am Alain DuSomme," he answered. He spoke very good English with only a trace of French accent. "I own this club, Mr. Crew and you are causing a disturbance."

"Well, I am very sorry if I disturbed anything. But I intend to find out why a friend of mine is now dead. Nothing personal, Mr. DuSomme."

"And who is this friend?" he asked. He took a pack of Gauloises from his jacket pocket, shook one out and lit it with a small gold lighter. He didn't offer me one, and I wouldn't have taken one anyway. I can't stand the smell of cigarette smoke.

"LeRoy Manns," I answered.

"Oh, yes." Alain said, shaking his head slightly. "A terrible shame. He was a very good musician. He is missed terribly here. The young people, they liked his music very much. I have been unable to replace him as yet. Perhaps you didn't know. He was hit by an auto. A hit and run I think you Americans call it."

"I understand that before the running part of the hit and run took place, the driver of the car backed over LeRoy a couple of times. Hardly an accident, don't you agree?"

"Accidents of all varieties happen all the time, Mr. Crew. You must be aware of that."

"The variety of the accident depends on the definition held by an individual. I call murder what it is . . . And murder is not an accident."

DuSomme leaned back in his chair once again, making it squeak as it did the last time. His left hand rubbed his chin, his right hand held the cigarette tightly between his index and middle fingers. I noticed that those fingers lacked the yellow stains of a heavy cigarette smoker. And he held the cigarette almost delicately. Almost royally, I thought. And I wondered just who the hell this guy was.

He glared directly into my eyes. I stared back without a flinch.

He leaned forward, straightened some papers on his desk almost too casually and moved his bent ballpoint pen an inch to the right. Finally he asked, "What is it you want, Mr. Crew?"

"You speak very good English, Mr. DuSomme," I answered, intentionally being evasive. Empty compliments again.

"Thank you," he said. "What do you want?"

"Did you study in school, perhaps?" I asked. I forced a smile and hoped it looked real.

"The military, Mr. Crew. I learned in the military. Now, please answer me, what do you want?"

"I want to know who killed LeRoy," I said.

"You want to know the name of the driver of the hit and run car?" he asked with obvious lack of understanding.

"I want to know who . . . And why, of course. Murder is not something that can be brushed aside easily, not by me anyway."

"The police," he said. "They have been here already and asked their questions. I suggest you go to them and ask your questions. Please do not bother my employees anymore. You are causing a disturbance. My customers come here for the jazz. The good jazz, you know? You are making my musicians uncomfortable, and then they do not play good jazz. I have lost one good musician . . . May God rest his soul. I cannot let my club suffer anymore. Now please . . . Go. And do not come back . . . You are not welcome."

"That sounds like a threat, Mr. DuSomme."

"Mr. Crew . . . I do not make threats. I only make promises. I promise that you will not like what happens if you come back here again. I know who you are, Mr. Crew. I know you are very powerful in the United States. But here you are just one more rich American who thinks money can buy anything . . . Including power. You are very wrong, Mr. Crew. Here your money can only buy . . . Peril."

"But I like the jazz," I said, smiling again. I leaned forward and folded my hands in front of me. Body language would tell him that backing away or folding my hands separately into fists meant that I was angry and frightened and threatening. I wanted him to think I was just asking questions without anger or threats.

I have been threatened dozens of times. Alain DuSomme's was just one more threat to be taken seriously but not run from. Threats like fear are to be pushed behind you. Once a threat is made then I know I am heading in the right direction. If this DuSomme guy weren't worried about my talking to people, he wouldn't make threats. LeRoy's death somehow involved Alain DuSomme. All I needed to do was find out that connection.

DuSomme crushed out his cigarette in a small tin ashtray. He blew a cloud of smoke directly at me, which I didn't appreciate at all because Gauloises cigarette smoke is particularly bitter and foul. He leaned forward, his elbows on the desktop, his fists curled separately, and smiled a particularly vicious and threatening smile. He said, "There are many jazz clubs in Paris. Go find a new one."

❋❋❋❋❋❋❋❋❋❋❋❋❋❋❋

I paused at the bottom of the steps leading out of L'ange Bleu. I looked back at Alain DuSomme who had left his office and was standing in the open doorway next to the stage, leaning against the door jam, watching me. His arms were folded in front of him, and an obviously mean look was frozen across his face. The club was frozen in a deadly silence. People were looking back and forth from me to DuSomme. The band stood ridged and silent.

Lorraine Demeaux was at the same table where I had

left her, but she had turned and had started talking with the young girl with the dark hair bangs across her forehead. Theirs was the only sound in the club as I stood at the bottom of the stairs. They stopped talking when they saw me at the stairs and DuSomme was glaring at me.

They had been passing a marijuana cigarette back and forth between them; both had been smiling and happy until the sudden silence crashed down around everyone.

I left the club and walked into the night-dark alley. My first thought was to wait for the band to leave and try to talk to them. But language was a problem. If none of them, except for Patrice, spoke English, I would only get them in trouble with DuSomme and learn nothing. Patrice was frightened; I would gain nothing new from him. I had no one to translate.

No, I would have to wait for Sandy to arrive. Tomorrow night I would speak with the remaining members of LeRoy's band. It was late, and I was feeling sleep wrap its soft arms around me once again. Beer does that to me. I walked a couple of blocks in the warm night air until I found a street with traffic on it. I flagged down a taxi and returned to the hotel.

SEVEN - And Now Panic

The telephone's red message light was flashing when I walked into the suite at the Ritz. It was from Sandy. She left her flight information and said she would take a taxi from the airport the next day rather than me meeting her. She said, "I need to buy some clothes . . . You know . . . Underwear and stuff. I had to pack quickly. I'll be at the hotel about noon, OK?"

So I slept deeply and late without leaving a wakeup call. It was half past ten that morning when I crawled out of bed. I showered and shaved and ordered champagne and strawberries from room service to celebrate when Sandy arrived. But I was hungry too, so I took advantage of my last chance for a big, unhealthy breakfast and ordered four eggs, a double order of crisp bacon, toast lathered in thick butter, and a big pot of strong coffee.

After I finished the breakfast I ordered a bottle of Dom Perignon with a bucket of ice to keep it cold. I had plans for some big time celebration as soon as Sandy walked in the door.

I sat staring at the champagne in the bucket with the melting ice, and watched the clock. One o'clock passed, then two, then three. I tried Sandy's cell phone a couple of times, but each time I got her voice mail. I was pacing around the suite when four o'clock came and went. The champagne was sitting in warm water.

I had her flight information so I called the airline and confirmed Sandy had been on the plane and the jet had arrived on time at 10:45 that morning. But where had she gone shopping? I had no idea.

Sandy is not one of those women who have to try on everything at every store before buying something . . . Or wind up just not buying anything. She is a quick shopper and buys what she wants without spending the whole day doing it. It was not like her, I knew, to spend five hours going from store to store, even if she was in Paris, the 'Shopping Capitol of the World'.

Another hour drifted by very slowly, and I began to worry. Was there an accident in the crazy Paris traffic? I fought the idea of renting a car and driving around looking for her. Paris is just too big for that. I would just get lost and probably wind up in a four car collision all by myself.

Desperation finally took me to the phone, and I called the Paris police, asking for Jean Paul Tavenier, the cop whom I had spoken with earlier.

"Monsieur Crew," he said, sounding surprised that I would phone for him. "And what can I do for you? I did expect you here to see the autopsy papers. Will you be late?"

"This may sound stupid, but I think my wife may be in some trouble," I started. I explained the situation and asked, "Can you check to see if she may have been in some kind of auto accident? I mean, maybe check the hospitals and that kind of thing? I can't do it myself because I don't speak any French."

"It is not the usual for Madam Crew to shop so late?" he asked.

"Very unusual," I said. "And she would have phoned

me to let me know she was going to be late."

"Oui, Monsieur Crew. I will do the check for you. You will be at your hotel, yes?"

"Yes, I'll wait here to hear from you. Quickly, please. I'm beginning to worry," I pleaded.

And so I waited. I paced and checked my watch against the room's clock every couple of minutes. I took the bottle of bourbon I had ordered specially and drank two glasses of it, over ice, and straight. They did little good. Maybe a third, I thought. But it didn't help either.

Sandy would not leave me to worry like that; she never had, and I knew she never would. Something had happened. In my mind I could see her lying dead in an auto accident, her taxi having crashed at 100 MPH. All I could think about was life without her. It was a nightmare. And how would I tell Caroline, our daughter?

The phone rang a few minutes before six. I jumped to it and picked it up before the first ring had ended.

"Yes! Hello! Sandy?" I said.

"No Monsieur Crew. This is the Detective Tavenier . . . Jean Paul, you know?"

"Yeah, OK. Have you found her?"

"No Monsieur. I have phoned all the hôpital . . . Hospital I think you say, yes? . . . And asked our . . . How you say it? Traffic . . . Is that correct? . . . The traffic police. Madam Crew has not been in the accident. Have you spoken with her?"

"No, I haven't," I said.

"Please stay at your hotel, Monsieur. I will be there shortly, oui?"

I paced around the suite some more, for twenty-five minutes – time that seemed like hours – until the detective knocked on the suite's door.

"Monsieur Crew," he asked as he walked into the room. It was late in the workday and he was dressed in clothes he had worn all day, looking like he had been out in the rain most of that time. His dark grey jacket and black pants were hanging wrinkled like a wet rag trying to dry out.

"You have not the word from the Madam?"

"No," I said. "Nothing. I want you to come with me to L'ange Bleu."

He stared at me; his forehead frowned, questioning what I was thinking. He asked, trying to make his voice sound as compassionate as possible, "Why, Monsieur? Can you mean the madam is there?"

"I've been there a couple of times. People who work there have been murdered. I spoke with Alain DuSomme, and he threatened me if I go back."

"You have been at Monsieur DuSomme's club? That surprises me, Monsieur Crew. That is not good. I did say it was danger to you, no?"

"I went, and he threatened me," I said. "I think he may have my wife . . . Trying to frighten me . . . Which he has done if he has her."

"He made the threats?" Tavenier asked.

"He doesn't want me talking to his people. I think he's hiding something. Damn it! I think he may have something to do with my wife's disappearance."

"You think Monsieur DuSomme has . . . What is the word? . . ."

"Are you thinking of kidnapping?"

"Oui, that is the word I think, Monsieur. That is the charge most serious, yes?"

"Will you come to his club with me?" I pleaded. I know it was a crazy charge to anyone hearing it, but I knew I was right. Sandy simply wouldn't leave me hanging without a phone call to let me know where she was and what she was doing. And if she weren't in an auto accident then she was in some kind of trouble. DuSomme was the only one who could be the cause of that trouble.

Tavenier took a minute to think. He glared at me, frowning, trying to digest the possibilities. He knew me and who I am and the influence I wielded at the American Embassy and in Washington, D.C. He finally relented. "I will go with you, Monsieur. But I must warn you against that which should not be."

"You mean I shouldn't beat the crap out of him?" I asked.

"That would be the bad thing, Monsieur."

He turned slowly, almost reluctantly, and I followed him out of the suite and down the elevator to his car waiting at the curb outside. Not a word was spoken between us as Jean Paul drove frustratingly slowly through the evening traffic to the Latin Quarter. He parked at the curb across the street from the alley where L'ange Bleu was.

Outside the club we stood on the curb at the entrance of the alley. I was trying to convince myself that going inside was a good idea. I had a hunch Tavenier was thinking the same thing, but he wouldn't admit it. The police knew something that I didn't yet know.

Would DuSomme be there? I didn't know, but I had to try. I had to do something to find Sandy, and I had a cop with me, so I felt safer than the last time I was there.

Tavenier followed me, reluctantly I think, as I started down the alley. The door to the club was closed but not locked. It was about a little after seven; the club would open about nine or a little later. Tourists would arrive as the club opened. The young regulars would not be there until after midnight.

I went first as we walked down the brick steps into the club. It was brightly lit inside; a row of lights across the ceiling were turned on, lights that were not visible in the hours the club was open for business. Dim lighting adds to the affects in a smoky barroom.

An old man was mopping the stone floor. Chairs had been turned upside down on the tables. A harsh smell of some strong cleaning solution permeated the air trapped in the basement club.

Tavenier spoke to the old man in French, just a few words from each that I didn't understand. The old man pointed to the door beside the small stage that led to DuSomme's office. The cop turned to me and said, "He says no one is here but he. He does not care if I go to the office of Monsieur DuSomme . . . So we go, oui?"

I nodded and followed him to the door and through to DuSomme's office. Tavenier, perhaps thinking of his own career, stood by the open office door as I started to search the room. The small desk was filled with the usual papers I assumed any small business might have. I asked Tavenier to translate a few of them, but I found nothing of any meaning among them.

A couple of gray, metal file cabinets stood behind the desk and chair DuSomme had been at when I spoke with him. Both were locked. I told Tavenier, "You might want to go outside for a minute." He smiled and stepped into the thin hallway, his back to me as I used a letter opener from the desk to force open the locks.

Inside were only a few files in the top drawer of the four drawers of one of the cabinets. The top drawer of the other cabinet was completely empty, but I could see small shreds of paper on the bottom of the drawer. There had been something there, but whatever it was had been taken away. I called Tavenier into the room and said, "They weren't locked after all."

"Yes, I see that," he said, smiling. He went through the few files I had found, translating for me, but finding nothing that would be out of the ordinary for a small business. Each of the next two drawers had the same kind of papers; the bottom drawer was empty. I showed the cop the empty drawers of the other filing cabinet and the remains of whatever had been there. He nodded but said nothing.

"So there is nothing," Tavenier said.

"Wait a minute," I said. I pulled the bottom drawer of the cabinet that was empty out and turned it over on top of the desk. An 8 X 10 piece of paper was taped there. Tavenier looked at it and said, "These are bank account numbers, Monsieur Crew. I find this very strange."

"I don't," I said. "I think DuSomme is a crook, and he's hiding money. I think this is where he's hiding it. And I think you think he's a crook, too, don't you?"

Tavenier thought for a moment about what he could and should tell me. Then he said, choosing his words carefully, "Oui, I have some thought that Monsieur DuSomme lives very well . . . Too well on the money he must make from this club. I will take this paper and do the investigate, oui?"

"I think we should leave it," I said. "Copy down what's on it, but if we take it he will know. It's better he doesn't know that we know."

"I see," he said, nodding. "You are right, certainement. He should not know."

I found some paper on the desk and we each copied down the bank account numbers. There were three phone numbers at the bottom of the page, and these we added to our notes.

"It is best that you return to the hotel, Monsieur Crew. It is much safer there, oui? I will do the questions of these, and I will come to you when I am done," Tavenier said.

"OK," I answered. "But I need to know what's being done to find my wife, too. Can you find out?"

"Oui, certainement. I will do that."

We left the office and walked into the club. The old man was leaning against his mop, looking disdainfully at us as we walked across his freshly mopped floor, leaving footprints for him to clean up.

****

Back in the suite at The Ritz I paced, unable to sit for any length of time, worrying about what was happening to Sandy. I tried her cell phone over and over but only got voice mail. I left frantic messages asking her to call back. I fought back the thought of having lost her. What could my life possibly be without her? How could I ever walk into the house that was our home? Thoughts ran through my mind: I would burn the house down; I would let it fall into an unkempt wreck for animals and the wandering homeless.

But without Sandy, I would never open the door to our house again.

A couple hours passed, and darkness had fallen outside. I flipped on a few lights and pushed aside the thought of going to the bar in the suite. I needed a clear mind, not a mind twisted with alcohol. I checked my watch every few minutes, but the time would not pass fast enough for me. Finally I had to know what was going on. I phoned the Paris Police Office.

"Morgan Crew calling for Detective Tavenier," I said.

The woman who answered the phone spoke in French, obviously asking a question.

"English, please," I asked. "Does anyone there speak English?"

Silence followed, and some clicking on the line could be heard. Then a woman's voice spoke, "I am Mary Huntington," she began. "I am with the American Embassy. Am I speaking with Mr. Morgan Crew?"

"Yes . . . American Embassy? . . . Why?"

"Mr. Crew," she said. "A complaint has been filed against you by a Mr. Alain DuSomme. The France Diplomatie . . . The Ministry of Foreign Affairs . . . has notified the Embassy."

I waited, but she said nothing else. I asked, "So what? I really don't care."

"The Ministry has agreed to let you leave the Country and return home, Mr. Crew. The complaint will be dropped if you do."

So now I was the next to get out of DuSomme's way. First murders and now get me out of the Country. I said, "Screw the complaint. I'll have a jet full of lawyers here in a few hours. I'm not leaving."

"Alright, Mr. Crew. Can we speak? Can I come to you?" she asked.

"On one condition, Ms. Huntington," I said and waited for her to speak.

"And what would that be?" she asked, finally.

"I want you to arrange full and total cooperation between me and the French police. And I want that complaint ignored by everyone in France who can ignore it."

She waited, thinking about that, and said, "I can try, Mr. Crew. That's all I can promise." I think she had become familiar with the Crew family name and the power attached to it. If she hadn't, I would make sure she became familiar in short order.

I hung up the phone and paced some more, waiting for her to arrive and talk with me about whatever could not be said over the phone. Not having the patience I should have, I went to the scrap of paper with the bank account numbers and phone numbers on it. It was a place to start.

I phoned Harper, Harper, Jascro and Nettles' offices in New York and asked for Peter Jascro. Peter was a close friend of my father and since my father's death has been an uncle to me, watching over me and doing whatever I need to have done.

"Hello, Morgan," he said cheerfully. "I hope we arranged some cooperation between you and the French authorities." I should have guessed that Peter and his international law firm had been working for me. He always does.

"Yeah," I said too abruptly. "Look, I need someone to run bank account numbers and phone numbers for me. They're probably all European."

I gave Peter the numbers, and he promised to get me what I wanted as quickly as he could. He said, "Morgan, I think you're in trouble again, right?"

"Sort of," I answered. It would only worry Peter if I told him all the truth. He's not young anymore, and he worries enough about me without knowing Sandy was missing. I hung up the phone before Peter could ask me anything else.

A knock on the door twenty minutes later told me Mary Huntington was there.

I opened the door and found a middle-aged woman who obviously spent too much time working and not enough time taking care of herself. She was . . . Well the best I can describe her is . . . *Dumpy.* She needed to lose a couple of pounds, and her hair could use a day at the beauty parlor; it was black with streaks of grey and rumpled as if she had forgotten to comb it for the last six or seven hours.

She was wearing a dark gray suit; its jacket and skirt were maybe a half size too small for her; the jacket being buttoned should have been left open. Her black shoes were low heeled and scuffed. Big, black rimmed glasses framed her tired pale green eyes.

Behind her were two men, big and mean looking like former Special Forces guys. Both had hair too close cropped. Both had too many muscles fighting to break out of their suits' sleeves. They both wore dark suits, white shirts and plain blue ties. Neither was smiling. And it was obvious from the lumps under their left arms that they were armed.

"Mr. Crew?" Huntington asked, holding her hand out. "I'm Mary Huntington."

I ignored her hand and asked, "And who are the two gorillas?"

She let out a single, short guffaw and answered, "They are Embassy security people."

"You must be very important to rank two bodyguards."

"Oh, they're not for me . . . They're for you, Mr. Crew."

"Me? Are you kidding? Why me? And what makes you think I want them hanging around?"

"Can we come in and sit, please, Mr. Crew?" she asked.

I waived her inside; one of the two guards closed and locked the door behind him. He stood with his back to the door as his partner went to each window and pulled the shades and curtains closed.

Huntington sat on the edge of the couch in the sitting room, and I sat on the other side of a glass topped coffee table in an uncomfortable, overstuffed chair copied from some dead French king's palace.

"So what's all this about?" I asked. I tried to look nonchalant and at ease, but I wasn't, and I think she and the two guards knew that.

"Alain DuSomme . . ." she began and waited for some reaction from me. She didn't get it. "He has been on our watch list for some time. State Department Intelligence has a thick file on him. So do the FBI, and I imagine the CIA probably does, also, but they don't talk to us. And the French authorities have him on their list to watch. Interpol has a file on him that they share with us when we ask."

She paused again; I had no idea what she was expecting from me. I waited a moment or two and then asked, "What kind of watch list?"

"That I can't discuss with you, Mr. Crew."

"Then get the hell out, Ms. Huntington. Why tell me

anything if you can't tell me everything?"

"Mr. Crew . . ."

"You either cooperate with me or get the hell out and leave me alone. Take your two gorillas with you."

"You have no idea . . ." she started, but I interrupted her again.

"Oh, I think I have an idea, Ms. Huntington," I said and smiled proudly. "In case you don't know, I've dealt with bad people before."

"We know all about you, Mr. Crew," she said.

"What's that line from Casablanca? *'We have a complete dossier on you.'* Then I say, *'Are my eyes really blue?'* Look lady, I really don't give a damn. My life's an open book thanks to the newspapers. I've been almost killed, and I've killed a couple of people. Don't try to scare me with all that top secret crap."

She paused once again, this time staring into my eyes with anger, as if she wished she could beat me over the head. Then she asked, "May I make a quick phone call, Mr. Crew?"

I nodded, and she got up, found the door to the bedroom and closed it behind her. The two burly guards stood looking down at me, arms folded in front of them, one at the door and one across the room at the windows. The one at the window looked at me and suddenly grinned and nodded once. He liked what I was doing, I guess.

Two or three minutes passed slowly and without words between me and the two gorillas before Huntington walked out of the bedroom. She retook her seat on the couch, took a deep breath and asked, "Are you absolutely certain you will not leave the Country?"

"Absolutely," I answered. "Not until I find my wife and I find out who killed LeRoy Manns."

"Alright . . . Then I have been given permission to discuss Alain DuSomme with you, but not the source of our information. Will that satisfy you?"

"Depends on what you tell me," I said. I was in charge; I knew it, and I would play it to the hilt, getting as much as I could from her. As long as my name was CREW and I carried the weight I did back in D.C., I would have to be physically tied up and flown out of Country to leave Paris without Sandy. And if they did that, which the two gorillas could easily do by looking at them, then of course, I'd get back on some private jet and be back in Paris the next day. I think she and others knew that.

She spoke for almost ten minutes, and I didn't interrupt. She told me that Alain DuSomme had been an Officer in the regular French Army and had transferred to the French Foreign Legion, spending ten years there before being recruited into the brigade des forces spéciales Terre, the BFST, which is the elite of French Army Special Forces, equivalent to our SEALS and Green Berets.

His record as a sniper in Afghanistan and Iraq was unmatched for his bravery and the number of kills he made. His war record ended with his discharge from the Army after killing seven people in Afghanistan, three men, three women and one thirteen year old girl, none of whom would tell him where a Taliban bomb maker was hiding.

Two years went by without Alain being heard about until the German BND, the German National Intelligence Service, reported finding the name Alain DuSomme on intercepted telephone conversations with a known member of one of the Russian Mafia Families working out of Bulgaria. He was questioned by the French authorities but denied having the conversation, insisting it must be some other person with his name or someone using his name. He was not charged, and after being released he opened L'ange Bleu.

American, French, German and Israeli Intel agencies had been following him since but had not been able to fix him with any criminal activity. Sources, which Huntington wouldn't name, had reported that Alain was now a very professional killer for hire for whoever would pay him. And his fee was reportedly very, very big.

I listened to everything she told me, but only a very little of it surprised me. I knew LeRoy Manns and Germaine didn't die for little reason. I had figured that DuSomme was into something bigger than selling pot to young jazz followers. LeRoy had learned something about DuSomme, he told Germaine, and each was sentenced to death for what they knew.

When she had finished her story I asked, "He lives a very simple life. His clothes aren't cheap but not extravagant. Does he have some palace somewhere where he lives?"

"Yes, of course" she said. "You're right about living a simple life. He has a small apartment in the 13th Arrondissement. That's not the best area of the City in case you didn't know. We have some information that his money is banked somewhere in the Caribbean and somewhere in Africa. Banking is very secret in both places."

I remembered the bank account numbers, but if Jean Paul hadn't told her, then I wasn't going to either. "One other thing, Mr. Crew," she said and took another deep breath. "He's very dangerous. We can only do so much to protect you."

"That's very nice Ms. Huntington. But I don't want to

draw unreasonable attention to myself. Having them with me will only draw unwanted attention. And I don't want to look like I want to start a gang war. So I will respectfully turn down your two guards. After all, he knows who I am already."

"That's not a good idea, Mr. Crew," she said; I think some honest sadness and concern filled her voice.

"Now, what about my wife?" I asked. "Where is she?"

"We don't know where she is," she said. I sensed some honest regret in her voice, sharing the words with her concern. That was nice but not helpful at all. "She was last seen getting into a taxi at the airport. Surveillance video recorded that, but the taxi number was false. No such number on record. I am sorry."

I thought for a moment and then asked, "Does DuSomme ever go out of town? Vacations? Maybe a girl friend? Anything like that?"

Huntington stood again and walked back into the bedroom, again closing the door behind her. She returned in short order, sat where she had been, sighed deeply and said, "I wish you wouldn't do what I think you're going to do, Mr. Crew."

She waited, looking at me, hoping for something from me which she didn't get. "OK, I have been told I can tell you that DuSomme has a small cottage in the Normandy region, in a little village called L'Copain. That's all I can tell you. For your own sake, please don't go there."

I stood to tell her our conversation was at an end, and she should leave. And I smiled of course, because I knew I was going to do exactly what Mary Huntington wished I wouldn't do. She stood and motioned for the two Embassy security men to follow her out of the suite. The man who had stood by the windows and signaled his approval to me whispered as he passed, "Good luck. Call me if you need me."

EIGHT - The Police

Sandy woke up lying on damp and musty straw inside what she thought must be a barn. No lights were on, and it was totally dark, but the smell of the cool air was filled with cows and goats and all sorts of barnyard animals. The outside air coursed through the building, which she assumed came through cracks in the siding and roof that revealed daylight to her. The smell of dampness and age almost overwhelmed the smell of animals. She sneezed against the dust of old straw.

She moved, wanting to stand, but her hands were tied behind her, and her legs were tied at her ankles. The slight movement caused streaking pain to shoot through her head. She didn't remember being hit, but she had a faint memory of two men jumping into her taxi from either side as the taxi turned a corner after leaving the airport. She looked at the one on her right and felt a sharp pin prick in the left of her neck. "Drugs," she said out loud. "Oh shit! Not again! What next?"

She lay back on the straw, closed her eyes and tried to relax her body, hoping the pain burning through her head would go away. After a few minutes it did begin to ease a little, although the discomfort of having her arms under her was there. She opened her eyes and slowly became used to the dark, and she could see a little of what was around her. Yes, it was a barn, and in a stall across the room from her there seemed to be an old, boney cow that was looking at her with a lot of interest. "What are you looking at?" she growled. The old cow answered with a deep *moo* and shook its head, sending dust floating all around the skinny beast.

Looking down without moving too much, she could see her ankles were tied with plastic zip-lock cords. They weren't as tight as whatever tied her hands behind her and were not as painful as whatever tied her wrists. She called out, "Hello! Hello! Anybody there? Hello!"

Sandy rolled around on the damp straw, but her wrists hurt, and her neck and shoulders hurt. The dark of the barn was suddenly broken when a door to her right opened, throwing bright daylight towards her. A woman walked in, taking her steps slowly and carefully, it seemed cautiously, and perhaps she was a little frightened, too.

She was a young woman, maybe twenty years old, maybe less, but she looked older from a life of hard work on the farm where she lived and where Sandy was being held. She was not slim by any means; her hips were broad, and her arms and shoulders muscular from years of the heavy work required on a farm.

Sandy lay still, looking up at her as she approached. The woman stopped and looked down at Sandy when Sandy spoke, "Where am I? Who are you?"

The woman put a finger to her lips and whispered, "S'il vous plaît, do not speak so loud."

She took a few steps closer to Sandy and forced a smile on her sun-reddened face and weather cracked lips. She wore a white peasant's blouse that was stretched across her large breasts and wide shoulders. Her blue jean pants were in need of a washing and were tucked into tall rubber boots that were covered in dark mud. Her hair, light brown, had been pulled tight behind her head. She wore no makeup, and even with professionally applied makeup she would not have been what one would call attractive.

Sandy tried to push herself up to a sitting position, ignoring the pain, and asked the woman, "Where am I?"

"On my farm," the young woman answered.

"Why?"

"That is not for me to know, oui?" she answered. Her English was fair and heavily accented, but Sandy spoke French fairly well. She asked in French and English, "Qui es-tu? Who are you?"

The woman shook her head and closed her eyes sadly. "I will bring food and water," she said. "When you need the . . . How do you say . . . Salle de bains?"

Sandy helped her. "Bathroom I think. Look I can speak French fairly well."

The young woman ignored her and said in English, "Oui, bathroom . . . I will be the help of you."

"Yeah, well I gotta' pee right now," Sandy said and waited. What she really wanted was to get onto her feet, have her hands and feet untied, and then fight her way out of the barn.

The woman turned away and spoke with her back to Sandy as she walked back to the open door, "I will bring something."

The door closed, and the barn went dark once again. Sandy twisted her feet trying to somehow loosen the zip ties, but all she managed to accomplish was to make her ankles raw and bloody.

Her low heeled shoes had been taken from her. She had worn comfortable slacks on the jet from the U.S. They were muddy now, and she felt dampness up to her waist. She had been, she thought, dragged through some mud at some point.

Within minutes the young farm woman returned carrying a rusted metal bucket. Sandy looked at it and the woman as she walked towards her. She laughed and said, "You expect me to pee in that thing? You've got to be kidding."

The woman stopped halfway into the barn, looked down at Sandy almost apologetically. "Pardon," she whispered. "Please do not speak so loud. They will hear."

"Who will hear?"

The young woman did not answer.

"Do you wish . . .?" she said softly after a moment, holding the bucket out towards Sandy.

"Do you really expect me to use that bucket?" Sandy said with a laugh. She was finding the young woman to be maybe a little sympathetic, and perhaps, Sandy thought, she could use that. "Look, how about you untie my legs and let me stand. Maybe I can use the bucket if I can stand."

Both women stared at each other until the young farm woman dropped the bucket and took three steps toward Sandy. She said, "I will do as you say. But outside there are men who will . . . They will be not happy, oui?"

"OK," Sandy said, smiling a friendly smile. "Thank you. I really need to pee."

The woman bent and drew a small pocketknife from the pocket of her jeans. She pulled the short blade open and cut the plastic zip tie at Sandy's ankles. She stood back and quickly turned toward the barn door to make sure no one was coming. She reached down and took Sandy's arm, helping her to stand. Sandy was taller than the farm woman when she was standing. She smiled gently and said, "I guess you'll need to undo my slacks."

As she said this, the barn door opened further than the woman had left it open. Two men walked in, each holding long shotguns. "Qu'est-ce que tu fais?" One was older than the other, with long, thick greying hair and a full beard. The other had close cropped hair, very dark, black, and the remnants of a black beard that may have been shaved two or three days ago. Both wore dirty blue jeans. The older of the two wore a blue plaid wool shirt. The younger's wool plaid shirt was red but very faded.

The young woman turned quickly and stepped back, away from Sandy. Sandy spoke up and said in English, "It's OK. Do you speak English? It's OK."

One of the two men, the younger, perhaps mid-twenties, answered, "I speak English, Mrs. Crew."

"Good," she said. She took a step forward, but both men quickly pointed their rifles at her. She stopped and said in as friendly a tone as she could manage, "I speak a little French but not very well."

"Why are you standing?" the man asked. His English was good and accented gently in an educated French tone. He had some good education somewhere; Sandy could hear that.

"I'm sorry," Sandy said. "I need a bathroom. This young lady was helping me, that's all."

The older of the two men spoke to the farm girl in rough, country French that Sandy understood most of. He said, "Why are you doing this, Michelle? Why have you freed her?"

"I'm sorry, Papa," she answered in French, bowing her head and folding her hands together at her hips. "She needed to use a toilet."

"Do you have any idea what will happen if he finds out

what you've done? Now, tie her up again. He will be here soon."

The younger of the two spoke, again in French, and Sandy was able to understand most of what he said. "Papa, let her use a toilet. It will take only a minute or two."

The older man, the father of the two, turned and walked away angrily. The young man spoke to his sister, again in rough, country French, "Take her inside . . . But hurry. Get her back here fast. He will be here soon. And use one of the plastic ties when you are done. He must not know."

Michelle, the young farm girl, took Sandy by her arm, and they walked outside. The sunlight was bright, but to the east dark clouds foretelling a storm were coursing towards them. Sandy looked around as they walked across rough, uncared-for grass towards a stone house roofed in dark wood shingles that were covered in green moss from years in the rain and winters.

Sandy spoke in French to the young girl, "This is your farm? It's very nice."

The girl looked quizzically at Sandy and said in English, "Your French is not so bad."

"And your English is very good," Sandy answered.

They reached the house and started up a flight of three worn wooden steps to the front door. As they did, a car, a Brown Peugeot, dusty from the long drive across country roads, turned onto the gravel drive to the farmhouse. The young farm girl saw it and immediately pushed Sandy down the steps onto the ground. She jumped down and knelt next to Sandy, holding her down by her shoulders. She whispered, "Please no sound. He will hurt me." Sandy nodded softly, understanding.

Alain DuSomme strode from the car to them. He spoke in French, his voice hard with anger, "What the hell is she doing out here?"

Michelle answered, "I'm sorry. She needed a toilet. She tried to escape and I pushed her to the ground. I will take her back and tie her legs."

"You better do just that," he growled. "And don't let her up again. Let her piss in her pants if she has to."

Michelle pulled Sandy to her feet and pushed her roughly towards the barn. When they were far enough away from DuSomme she whispered, "I am sorry, Madam. I did not have the choice."

"I understand," Sandy said. "Who is he?"

"He is the one who owns this farm. My Papa, he works for him here."

****

I returned to L'ange Bleu twice over the next two days, the first time in the early evening as the club was preparing to open. The quartet of what was left of the band was on the small stage, tuning their instruments. They stopped as I walked across the club's stone floor to a table very near them.

I pulled a chair off of a table and sat at the table, crossing my legs and folding my arms across my chest, waiting for someone to say something. The four musicians looked away and went on with their tuning, talking about something in French. They were probably talking about me. I waited over an hour, and I might as well have been invisible.

The old janitor who had watched Tavenier and me kept mopping. Two waitresses kept wiping tables and moving chairs. Everyone was carefully avoiding eye contact with me. I finally called out, almost yelling, to anyone who would listen, "Is DuSomme here? I want to talk to him."

No one stopped their work; they all ignored me. I got up and left. The next night I returned at midnight. The place was full of young people, drinking wine and smoking marijuana. I walked directly to the door at the side of the small stage. No one was sitting at the table blocking the door so I roughly pushed it and the two small chairs with it aside. I opened the door and walked through it. The tight hallway was dark, and no light shown from under either doorway. I went to DuSomme's office and tried the knob. The door was locked.

Back in the club the band was playing a samba, slow and hot. The woman who had joined the group was singing something in some language other than French, maybe Spanish or even Portuguese. I stood at the side of the stage and listened. The four musicians were good, and the vocalist was just OK. But the young people in the club seemed to like it. A few were dancing; most just sat, swaying to the music like reeds in the wind.

When they had finished and the kids in the audience had finished applauding, I called out for everyone to hear, "I want to talk with Alain DuSomme! Anybody know where he is?"

Everyone, including the musicians and singer, were looking at me, but no one said anything. Then, I guess ignoring me, the band started another piece, and the young people in the audience went back to their wine and pot and dancing.

I left, frustrated and angry, but with no idea what to do next. It was a sleepless night back at The Ritz. I had to find Sandy and know she was safe, and I had to find out why LeRoy Manns was dead. But how? I was in a strange land, without contacts and without the usual power my name and family fortune carried. I had only one hope and that was the policeman, Jean Paul Tavenier.

At six AM the next morning I ordered a big pot of coffee from room service and drank it as I waited for a decent hour to phone Tavenier's office. At five past eight I made the call and asked for someone who could speak English. A man came on the line and said, "Oui, Monsieur, I speak English."

"May I speak with Jean Paul Tavenier, please?"

The man said nothing, but I could hear his heavy breathing on the line. I said again, "Jean Paul Tavenier. He's a detective. I want to speak with him, please."

"And who are you, Monsieur?"

"I'm Morgan Crew. I was speaking with Jean Paul the other day. Is he in yet?"

"I think perhaps you should come into this office, oui? Right now, perhaps."

"Why?" I asked. "What's the problem? I just want to talk to Jean Paul, that's all."

"L'agent Tavenier, he is dead, Monsieur. Will you come here, or do I send some men to you?"

❊❊❊❊❊❊❊❊❊❊❊❊❊❊

I was ushered into a small room that was crowded with a four-foot long steel table, scratched and dented, telling me some bad things happened there on occasion. Three steel chairs were at the table, two on one side and the other across from them. The walls were covered with old white ceramic tiles, some cracked and broken. One wall held a long horizontal mirror, obviously a two-way mirror that hid people on the other side who would watch me being interrogated. I had seen police interrogation rooms before.

I sat alone in the room, trying to look as relaxed – and innocent of everything – as possible. I leaned forward, my elbows on the table, my hands folded, and looked around. I smiled at the mirror and even waived once to the people who were watching me on the other side; I tried to look bored as I waited for something to happen.

I was left alone for a long time while I did my best to control my temper. I think that is what they were trying to do, trying to get me uncomfortable and angry. I wasn't about to let them have their way. I leaned back in the uncomfortable chair and whistled a Disney tune . . . Just to piss them off.

Finally the door behind me opened, and two men and a woman walked in. One of the men made it very obvious that he was locking the door behind the three. The two men stood behind me, and the woman sat on a chair on the other side of the table, across from me.

She was dressed in a medium grey suit, jacket and pants, over a white shirt open at the collar. Her brown hair was cut short, almost masculine in style, and brushed back over her ears. She wore glasses, thick black plastic rims holding heavy lenses. I thought at the time that without all the dull accoutrements she might actually have been somewhat pretty.

She started by saying in English, "Mr. Crew, would you like an attorney . . . Or perhaps someone from your Embassy?" Her English was very good with only a slight, educated French accent.

"Why would I?" I asked. "Why am I here? I came here voluntarily, remember?"

"For the record then," she asked. "You do not wish an attorney or someone from your Embassy?" As she spoke I noticed that her teeth were in really bad shape. They hadn't ever seen the help of an orthodontist, leaving them misshapen and discolored.

"For the record?" I asked. "Can I assume there is a recording being made?"

"You may assume that, Mr. Crew," she answered. "Now, you have had contact with Jean Paul Tavenier?"

"Of course," I said. "You know that."

"And for what purpose?"

"My wife is missing . . . You know that, too . . . And a friend of mine has been murdered . . ." I began but she interrupted me.

"Mr. LeRoy Manns' death was an accident on our records."

"And you believe that?" I asked.

"You do not," she answered. It was not a question.

"No."

"And your wife . . ." she asked and waited for me to say something.

"Have you folks found her?" I asked. I hadn't moved since the three joined me, my elbows on the table and my hands folded. I think that fact was not missed by the three in the room and whoever was watching on the other side of the mirror.

"What do you know of L'agent Tavenier's death?" she asked, ignoring my question.

"Nothing," I said. "I first heard that when I called the police this morning. I am very sad about his death. He seemed like a good man, and he was willing to help me."

"How did he help you?"

"He listened to me, and I think he may have believed what I believe."

"And what do you believe, Mr. Crew?"

I waited a moment or two before answering her. What would happen to me if I revealed too much? What would happen if these cops weren't honest cops? What would happen if they had been bought? I have known a lot of police over the years. Most are good people who want to do a good job. A few are not so good and are easily converted to the dark side of society by money and sometimes drugs and sex. I decided to tell them a few things but not everything until I figured out what side they were on. And I would not mention too much about Alain DuSomme.

I began, "I believe my wife has been kidnapped in order to get me out of this Country. I believe my asking questions about LeRoy is scaring someone. And I believe whoever murdered LeRoy also murdered his girlfriend and now Jean Paul."

"That is what you believe, Mr. Crew? Nothing else?" she asked.

"Well, I believe one more thing," I said and leaned back on the hard steel chair. I smiled for the first time, a smart ass type of smile, and said, "I believe you need to tell me who the hell you are and why I am here. And I believe what you tell me better be the truth . . . If you know who I am, that is."

"Oh, we do know who you are, Mr. Crew."

"So who are you?" I demanded.

"I am Officer Marie St. John." She said. "And you may go now."

That surprised me. I had assumed I would be locked up and questioned over and over until the police got the answers they wanted. I sat back suddenly and asked, "What the hell do you mean, I can go now? Jean Paul is dead . . . A cop is dead . . . You call me in here, and that's all you can ask me?"

"Do you have something else to tell us, Mr. Crew?" she asked. There was something happening here, something I wasn't aware of. I felt like a lamb being fattened up for the slaughter. Were they setting some kind of trap for me? Did they think I had something to do with the murders? In a couple of movies I had seen they let the suspect go so they could follow him to . . . Whatever . . . The body or the gun or something.

But I wasn't going to fall for that. I wanted some information from the cops before I got up and left. I asked, "Tell me about Alain DuSomme. Tell me, and then I'll go."

Marie St. John turned her head and looked at the mirror to her left. A phone that was hanging on the wall behind her buzzed, just once. She turned without getting up and picked it up. She listened and said nothing. She hung the phone back on its cradle, turned back to me and said,

"You can go now."

"So you're not going to tell me anything about DuSomme?"

"You can go now," was all she would say.

"One last thing. Did Jean Paul have some papers . . . Maybe at his desk, or even in his pocket?"

"What papers?" she asked.

"That's not important," I said. I still had the bank account numbers and phone numbers. If the police didn't have Jean Paul's list that might be good for me, because if they did they might interfere in what I wanted to do.

"How was he killed?"

"A bullet. A single shot from a rifle."

I stood slowly; I guess I had nothing more to gain. They weren't going to tell me anything. I was halfway expecting one or both of the men standing behind me to hit me and beat the crap out of me. They didn't. One of them opened the door and motioned for me to walk out of the room.

I found my way out of the building and stood at the bottom of the steps outside, on the sidewalk. The clear morning had clouded over, and a very light rain was falling. I stood there in the rain, wondering what I should do, where I should go. Sandy was still out there somewhere.

If I did go home like people were telling me to do, would Sandy be hurt? Would I ever see her again? If I didn't go home how could I find her and protect her? Maybe DuSomme could be bought? I could go to him and offer him money, millions if I had to, if I could find him.

I looked to my right and to my left for a taxi. Then a car, a new black Mercedes pulled to the curb, and the rear door opened. Lorraine Demeaux was sitting inside. She said, "Please get in Monsieur Crew. You are getting wet.

NINE - Captivity

A chauffeur was behind the wheel. The inside of the Mercedes was elegant in tan leather and polished wood. Two crystal decanters and four crystal glasses were in a chrome rack. This was not the kind of auto a thief and lesbian lover would drive around the city in. Lorraine was looking at me, smiling, satisfied that she had surprised me, but saying nothing. I asked her, "Just who the hell are you, anyway? Jean Paul Tavenier told me you are not who you say you are."

"That is true, Monsieur Crew. I am Lorraine Demeaux . . . But I am not who I said to you. I am with Interpol, oui? You understand, oui?"

"Actually no, I don't understand." I was surprised and confused at what she said, but I couldn't let her know that. I had to keep myself, at least in her eyes, above what was all around me. If I showed confusion or any weakness, it would go against me, and I couldn't let that happen.

"Geneva . . . Interpol office, you know? . . . They have spoken with the Paris police and the Embassy américaine, oui? I have said it right? Interpol has been looking at Monsieur DuSomme for what is the long time. He is the bad man, you understand? He does murder, oui?"

"OK," I said. "I kind of figured that out for myself. So what? You're not telling me anything about DuSomme I haven't figured out for myself. Why are you talking to me?"

"We have thought that you might help, oui? Your wife she is held by DuSomme, and that may be in our favor. It would not be strange for you to go to her, no?"

"So Sandy and I would be your Judas Goats, right?"

"Judas Goats?" she questioned. "This I do not understand."

"You will sacrifice us to get DuSomme."

"Monsieur Crew," she began and sighed deeply. "We have the . . . What is the word? . . . History, is that it? The history of you."

"I think you mean you know all about me," I said. "Many of those stories you read about in the newspapers are overblown. I am not a hero, Ms. Demeaux. I run from trouble whenever I can."

"But you have killed, oui?"

"Why would I tell you that I have killed people? I have no idea who you are, and I want to know the people I speak with."

Lorraine laughed and opened her small black purse. She pulled a black leather card case from the purse and handed it to me. I took it and opened it. I had seen Interpol I.D. cards before, and what I looked at was in fact an Interpol I.D. card. It had her photo on it and all the right verbiage. So she wasn't lying . . . This time.

Of course, it could have been a counterfeit I.D. Any counterfeit I.D. and passport from anywhere in the world was obtainable for the right price. I had been told she was not who she pretended to be.

"So," she said as I handed the I.D. back to her. "Do you answer my questions now? You have killed . . . It is in the file of yours."

"When I had to," I said. "I don't go out of my way to take human life. Again, so what? What are you folks expecting me to do? If you say you want me to kill DuSomme for you, you are out of your flipping mind lady. I'm not a murderer."

Lorraine pushed a button on a row of buttons on the door next to her. A black screen rose separating us from the driver. When it was up she turned to me and said, "Monsieur Crew, we have the belief that Alain DuSomme has been hired by the Mafia. We have the belief that he will kill someone of the greatest importance. He must be stopped."

I forced a laugh to show my disbelief. Of course, I knew already that DuSomme was a killer. But the Mafia? That was crazy. "DuSomme runs a tacky little jazz club," I said. "Why would he be hired to kill anyone?"

"Monsieur DuSomme, he is the killer most dangerous," Lorraine said. "Many of us know that, but no one has been able to catch him. He is most intelligent."

"OK, so you expect me to . . . Catch him as you say . . . When cops from all over the world haven't been able to do that. That's crazy, lady. You know that don't you? And why the hell aren't you folks out finding my wife? I know DuSomme has her somewhere, and you should know that, too. Find her and you have DuSomme."

"We want you to find her, Monsieur Crew, and deal with DuSomme to do so, perhaps with the money, oui? In doing so, you may learn of who he will murder. He would not speak with authorities, no? He will speak with you perhaps."

It all made sense, of course . . . To them . . . But not to me. If some crazy Mafia guys wanted someone dead that was too bad. But it should be up to the police and military all over the world to stop that. It should not be up to me. Finding Sandy and protecting her was what I had to do. If Interpol, France and The United States could help me do that, I would make them work *for* me making them believe I was working *for* them. If doing so might help everyone find out who DuSomme was going to kill, I would do that but only as a second thought. My main objective would be to use them to find Sandy. I knew they wanted to use me to hang DuSomme, but that would happen only as an after effect of finding Sandy.

So I said, "I have some questions, lady. I believe DuSomme murdered LeRoy Manns, Germaine LeFont, and that cop Tavenier. I believe he did this because they knew something they shouldn't know. Why hasn't he killed me? He certainly has had the opportunity."

"You did not know the truth about him, Monsieur Crew."

"Now I do," I argued.

"True, and now you must be the man who is careful, oui? You have speaked with me only."

"Spoken . . . Not speaked," I corrected her.

"Pardon," she said. "You are right of course. But if you have learned of DuSomme from some other place, he would know. Only you and I know, oui?"

"Who knows you are with Interpol?" I asked.

"You," she answered. "And the driver here. The police, they do not know. Your Embassy they do not know. Only Geneva has spoken with them, and they do not reveal who I am."

"OK," I said. "DuSomme has a place in Normandy. Where is it?"

She took a map from a door pocket and was about to mark where the farm was. I stopped her and said, "No paper, please. Evidence. Just tell me. I'll find it."

❋❋❋❋❋❋❋❋❋❋❋❋❋❋

At the farm where Sandy was being held, DuSomme had watched as Michelle tied Sandy's ankles with a plastic zip tie as she lay on the straw. She waited until DuSomme had left the barn and whispered, "If you need the bucket, I can help," she told Sandy.

"Thank you, Michelle, but I think I'll wait awhile."

She whispered, "I did not make it too tight, Madam. But please, do nothing while he is here."

Sandy nodded and smiled her thanks. She lay back on the straw and watched as Michelle left the barn and closed the door. Sandy heard a lock being thrown. She would have to wait, wait for some chance to get away.

Her arms, tied behind her back, were aching. The plastic zip ties at her wrists were tight, and very little blood was flowing to her hands past her wrists. She rolled onto her side and tried to move her arms and hands to get some blood flowing, but all that did was cause a lot of pain.

Michelle's father and the younger man, who she suspected was Michelle's brother, had shotguns. They looked dangerous . . . But were they? They were more likely farmers who were being paid by the man Michelle warned her about. Sandy had to assume for the time being that they were dangerous.

She had made a friend of Michelle, the young girl. Perhaps she could make a friend of the young man who could speak English and might be educated, too. There had to be a way out. Or, she thought with a smile, she could just lie back and wait for me to come get her. She smiled at the thought. In her mind she pictured her Morgan Crew riding into town on a white horse and shooting the hell out of everybody. That made her laugh and forget the pain at her wrists.

Inside the farmhouse DuSomme sat at a small table in the kitchen. He spoke in French to the old man, Franc, the father of Michelle, "When I tell you to do something I expect it to be done."

"I am so sorry, Monsieur DuSomme. My daughter, she is young. Please forgive me. It will not happen again."

"It better not. I'm expecting some people here tonight. You and your son . . . Go into the village and spend the night there."

"What of Michelle?" Franc asked, frightened for his young daughter. He knew DuSomme was a dangerous man. What had he planned for Michelle?

"She will spend the night in the barn with the woman." He looked at Michelle and said, "If the woman makes one sound . . . I will kill both of them. Understand? Make sure your daughter understands."

✽✽✽✽✽✽✽✽✽✽✽✽✽✽

After speaking with Lorraine Demeaux I was refused

a ride to The Ritz and had to walk back to the hotel in the rain. I had hoped for a ride from her, but she was right when she told me we should not be seen together. I showered and put on dry clothes, waiting until L'ange Bleu would open its doors. I wanted one last try at talking with DuSomme. Maybe a large pile of American dollars would buy Sandy's freedom, and the two of us could go home. That, I thought, was better than me attacking wherever she was being held, all alone and armed only with Lorraine's small pistol.

Of course I was making an assumption DuSomme had Sandy. Why else would she have disappeared? For whatever reason, DuSomme hadn't killed me. He had killed three others but not me. I hoped that confronting him with an offer of cash would not cause him to kill me. Lorraine was probably right; I was supposed to know nothing of DuSomme's plans as the others he had killed must have.

I waited until midnight and flagged down a taxi to take me to the Latin Quarter and L'ange Bleu. The four remaining members of LeRoy's little group had been joined by new trumpet player. He was young and white and very thin. His clothes were old, un-ironed wool slacks and a wrinkled and faded pink shirt with sleeves that hung below his wrists. And he needed a haircut and shampoo badly.

His horn was muted, his eyes closed as he played. He was good, but I wondered if he was as good . . . Or better . . . Than LeRoy. The people in the club seemed to like what he played, but they had liked the fat woman who couldn't hold a tune when she sang. The soft jazz flowed up the brick staircase along with a cloud of cigarette and marijuana smoke as I descended down into the club.

Standing at the foot of the staircase, I waited for the set to end and then started for the door at the side of the stage. The new trumpet player turned to me. He was very pale skinned. He had dark eyes and sunken cheeks, and his lips were painfully thin. My first thought was that he had to be a heroin addict. He spoke in a high-pitched tone, almost feminine, in a thick French accent. "He is not here."

"Who isn't here?" I asked.

"The man you wish to see."

"And who is that?" I knew what he was saying, but I played with him anyway. Maybe he would get angry and say something he shouldn't.

"He is not here," he repeated. "Go away."

I looked past the horn player to look at Patrice. He was looking down, away from me, his shoulders slumped, his saxophone hanging from one hand.

The new trumpet player repeated, "Go away. He is not here."

I did a good acting job of laughing, pushed the table in front of the door away and opened the door. I left it open behind me and walked down the hallway. There was complete silence from behind me in the club.

DuSomme's office door was locked. The door across the hall was not locked. I opened it just out of curiosity and stepped inside. The windowless room was dark. I felt on the wall for a light switch, found it and turned it on.

It was a break room for the band but also a storage room. I hadn't noticed that the last time I was there. What one might expect in the back of a club was there: boxes piled on top of boxes, crates of wine, cleaning materials, a mop and bucket, and little more. The small table and the chairs were still in the middle of the room. The remnants of cigarette smoke from the band's last break were still in the air. From behind me the trumpeter spoke, "You should not be here."

"Why?" I asked, turning to look at him.

"You should not be here."

"Look, if all you can do is keep repeating yourself, you won't do yourself or me any good."

He closed the door leaving the two of us alone in the crowded room. Now, please understand, all my life I have considered myself a lover and not a fighter. The guy was shorter than I and thin in the arms and chest. But he had the look of a street fighter, with scars around his eyes. His nose was bent slightly from being broken at least once.

He came at me quickly, his hands raised ready to fight, but I was able to grab a box of empty wine bottles from a pile next to me and I threw it at him. As he brushed it aside I had time to take a bottle of unopened wine from an open case. I held it above my head like a club and said, "This is gonna' hurt you know. Now how about you just let me leave . . . Like you told me earlier?"

The man nodded and stepped aside. I kept the wine bottle raised as I edged past him, not turning my back to him. He looked out the open door which gave me the chance to swing the bottle and hit him above his ear, not hard enough to kill him but enough to make him fall to the side and to his knees. I dropped the bottle and ran.

When someone is hit on the head in the movies and on T.V. bottles shatter. In real life a wine bottle will not break but someone's skull will. I hoped, as I ran from the office, that I hadn't hit him too hard.

❋❋❋❋❋❋❋❋❋❋❋❋❋❋

Evening was falling as Sandy lay on the damp, odorous straw in the barn. Michelle sat on a rail of one of the stalls, the one where an old cow with a fat utter was contentedly chewing her cud. Michelle was obvious in not looking at Sandy, and she was nervous, frightened, and maybe even a little ashamed at what she was doing. Sandy saw this, and she would use this to her best advantage.

Michelle could be used if she thought Sandy was a friend and not a prisoner. She was not armed, at least Sandy didn't see any guns or knives hidden in the blue jeans or the too big shirt she wore.

Sandy spoke softly, "My hands are numb, Michelle. Any chance you could help me sit up for a while?"

Michelle climbed off the stall railing and walked slowly to Sandy. She looked down at my wife, thought for a minute, and then she bent and took Sandy's arm, pulling her up to a sitting position, pulling her back so she could rest against a stall's railing.

"Thank you, Michelle," Sandy said. She knew that calling the young girl by her name would personalize their relationship. "My name is Sandy," she said to the young farm girl.

Both Sandy and I had experience with being held captive. I had taught her to smile at her captives, use first names when known, speak to the captors like a friend if possible, and most importantly eat and drink everything given to her to keep her strength up.

Michelle returned to the railing of the stall and sat on the top rail without saying a word. But Sandy saw the frown on the girl's face and recognized that the girl could not look at Sandy. Michelle had second thoughts about what she was doing. Sandy would work on that.

Sandy struggled to stay sitting upright. She tried bending her legs back but the plastic zip-ties hurt. She started to slip down the stall rail. She asked, "Michelle, I hate to be a bother but do you suppose you can help me up? It helps if I can lean against the stall. My arms and back are killing me."

Once again the young girl slid from the stall's rail she was sitting on and walked to Sandy. Michelle took Sandy under an arm and pulled her back so she could lean upright against the stall.

"Thank you Michelle," she said. "That's a lot better. You're very kind. Let me ask you, Michelle," Sandy said. "Who is that man you're so frightened of?"

"I cannot speak of him," she said in a faint whisper.

"What harm can it do?" Sandy asked, sounding as kind and concerned as she could. "If he kills me then I can't tell anyone. If he doesn't, then maybe I can help you. My husband and I have a lot of influence. We can get you out of here. We can get you and your family away from him. We can even get you to America. I promise we can do that."

Michelle turned her head and looked at Sandy. "What is it you mean?" she asked.

"I mean I can get you away from him. Look, I know you're not happy here. I'm not blind. If that man doesn't kill me I can take you, your father, and your brother anywhere you want to go. You can have a life away from here."

The young girl turned away, climbed from the stall railing and walked away to the other side of the barn. Sandy watched and waited. The girl was thinking of her options, thinking of how she could really get away from the man who was holding her captive as Sandy was being held captive.

Minutes passed with Michelle walking aimlessly

around the barn, stopping now and then to pet a goat or a cow. Finally she stopped in front of Sandy. A single tear fell from her dark blue eye. She quickly wiped it away with the back of her hand. She looked up and said, her voice weak and broken, "I cannot stay in France, Madam. If I help you . . . Will you take me to America?"

"Of course," Sandy said happily knowing she had converted the young girl. "We can take you anywhere, and there will be money . . . Money enough to make you happy for the rest of your life." Michelle nodded, tried to smile a little, and walked away once again.

Night and darkness fell quickly. Sandy and Michelle fell asleep on the straw listening to rain on the barn's roof. Rain fell through the holes in the roof, soaking the straw on the barn's floor. Sandy pushed herself away from the pools of rain as best she could.

When she couldn't fight off sleep any longer, Sandy let herself slide down onto the barn's damp floor. Sleep for Sandy was not solid; she awoke several times, twisting and turning to try to ease the pain at her wrists and ankles. Michelle slept solidly, seemingly unaware of the rain falling through the barn's roof. She was dreaming of a life in The States where she could be anything she wanted to be, and not be afraid of Alain DuSomme.

The rising sun slipped beams of daylight through the cracks in the old barn's walls. The warmth of the rising sun caused clouds of evaporating water to rise inside the barn.

Michelle woke and found Sandy sitting up and looking at her. Sandy seemed happy and looked kindly at the young girl.

Michelle was smiling, feeling good about what she thought might be her future in The United States, when the barn door slammed open and DuSomme stood in the daylight. Two men, dark and bearded, stood behind him. They each carried an AK-47 rifle. DuSomme drew a pistol from under his jacket and fired twice. Michelle fell backwards onto the muck of the barn floor. Blood covered her blue plaid shirt.

DuSomme walked slowly to Sandy who sat on the straw, back straight, head held high. "I suppose you're going to kill me now?" she questioned.

"No, Madam Crew," DuSomme said. "I need you alive . . . For the time being anyway. These two men will stay with you for the time being." He walked out of the barn, leaving Sandy alone with the body of the young Michelle lying a few feet from her. The two gunmen stood at the open door.

Hours passed leaving Sandy sitting stoically, trying to avert her gaze from the dead girl. The two armed men did not move from the doorway and did not utter a word. The cow with the fat utter was mooing loudly, asking to be milked.

Sandy was terribly thirsty and hungry. Her head throbbed, her hands were numb and swollen; her back ached. But she did not ask the two men for anything. They were not a sweet young farm girl like Michelle had been. They were dark killers who would be more difficult to deal with.

She looked down at the young girl, lying in the blood soaked mud. Her life had been cut so very short. She could have been so happy had she not hesitated to let Sandy go. She could have had a life in America.

The sound of a car driving up to the barn drew the attention of Sandy and the two guards. Doors slammed and footfalls in the mud could be heard.

Michelle's father and brother pushed their way past the two Arabs still standing in the open doorway. They looked down at their daughter and sister and fell to their knees at her body. Franc screamed in French, "You bastard! You . . ."

The two Arabs at the doorway shot both Franc and his son, opening up their Kalashnikov rifles on full auto. The bullets tore the two men apart. They fell and lay dead next to Michelle. The two Arabs laughed and walked back to the open barn door.

TEN - The Bargain

I walked into my suite at The Ritz and saw the message light flashing away on the phone. It had to be Peter Jascro in New York . . . At least I hoped it was. I retrieved the message and immediately phoned him on his private line.

"Hello, Peter," I started anxiously. "I hope you have something for me."

"I do," he answered. "But not over the phone. That's why I didn't call you on your cell."

"So what is it?"

"There is a package waiting for you at the hotel's front desk. Get it immediately. Don't talk to anyone over a phone about this, and keep the information to yourself. And Morgan . . . Please be careful. I know it would be fruitless for me to tell you to just go home. But you're dealing with very dangerous people."

I assured Peter I would be careful . . . But I didn't say I would not stop at anything to get Sandy back. He didn't know Sandy was missing. What he didn't know wouldn't hurt anyone.

Running to the front desk, I asked for the package waiting for me. It was an attaché case, high quality grey leather. Besides the two combination hasp locks on it there was a small padlock that had been attached to a chain that had been screwed into the case in several places. Someone didn't want it to be easy to open the case. I had to sign for it, and once that was done, the clerk at the desk handed me a small sealed envelope which I found to contain the key to the padlock and the combinations to the two hasp locks.

Back in my suite I opened the case and found a thick file of papers. It took some time to read through them, but Peter's detectives and attorneys had found all there was to know about the bank account numbers I had found. They were numbered accounts in banks in Switzerland, Grand Cayman, Hong Kong, and South Africa.

I wondered just how they had managed it, but they had found the owner of each of these highly secret and protected, numbered bank accounts to be Alain DuSomme. The accounts were in different currencies, and one of them even had deposits of gold and silver. And the total of all the accounts when converted to dollars amounted to just over $52,000,000.00.

The owner of a small, out of the way, jazz club could not possibly have accumulated that much money. This told me that DuSomme really was a high-paid killer for hire.

The three phone numbers turned out to be cheap "burner phones," one time use cell phones that can be bought in any number of places. All of them had been used once. I assumed that once they had been used they would be destroyed and trashed.

So I had something to use against Alain DuSomme. I knew Peter and his people could drain DuSomme's accounts on a minute's notice, and if they couldn't, I knew that our nanny, Betsy Concanon could. She had done such things for me before. But I had to be careful not to let DuSomme know I knew about the accounts. Once he knew, he would move his fortune, and it would be nearly impossible to find it again. At the right time I would use this.

I closed the attaché and locked the locks. The hotel's safe would be a good place to keep it, and so I had it locked up there. I was satisfied that I was making some progress against the man I had to defeat. I felt good for a minute or two, until I remembered that Sandy was still being held captive.

****

I rented a Mercedes and managed to find a map in English in the hotel's gift shop that I could read. I had an address given to me by Lorraine Demeaux. I wasn't certain yet just who the hell she was, Interpol or a very strange thief and lesbian lover . . . Or maybe someone much more dangerous. But I had little choice except to go to the address she had given me. I had nothing else, and in fact, I had nothing to lose.

I packed a small bag, leaving most of my things in the suite at The Ritz. I figured I would be gone perhaps two or three days. As it turned out, I was wrong. But I felt assured that the hotel would continue to charge my Black AMEX card for the outrageous fee they charged for the suite so that it would be waiting for me when . . . And if . . . I got back from my trip.

Driving out of Paris is always a maddening affair. The traffic is crazy and always thick. The streets were planned a century ago, and the planners did not have heavy auto traffic in mind when doing the planning. Horse drawn buggies and marching soldiers did not take up as much room on the streets as a couple million cars. I got caught once on the merry-go-round of the streets circling the Arc de Triomphe, driving in circles until I just closed my eyes and turned the steering wheel to the right. Horns blared, but everyone avoided slamming into me, and I was back on crowded Paris streets quickly. I managed to leave the City and find the major roads to the northwest that were listed on the map.

Being on my own was something new to me. I am used to having a semblance of power, of being able to demand what I need, of at least being able to communicate with people I need to speak with. One example of my being out of my depth was when I stopped for lunch on the way to Normandy. I found a beautiful little inn with a thatched roof and flowering vines growing up the walls. It was a sunny and warm afternoon, unusual weather for France in the spring. I decided to stop for lunch, having had very little for breakfast.

I took a table outside, under a red and white striped umbrella, to take advantage of the warm sun. The woman who ran the place, a wonderfully fat and smiling woman whose red cheeked face reflected her love of life (and probably of good wine and good food) came to the table and stood smiling patiently as I pointed to a few things on the menu which was in French and unreadable by me. I hoped I was ordering something good and not something strange, like horse meat or something worse. The woman nodded approvingly as she listened to me, obviously not understanding a word of my English, even though I spoke very slowly and a little too loud. It seems I am not too much different from most Americans. When in a foreign Country we think that speaking English slowly and loudly will cause it to be understood by people who don't speak English.

I did know how to say "Vin rouge." She wrote everything down and disappeared. In the end she brought some food she thought I might like rather than what I must have ordered. A nice green salad followed by chicken in some kind of creamy sauce, with fresh vegetables on the side, and of course a really nice red wine was my lunch.

Of the six tables outside, two others were occupied, one by a family with two happy and noisy children and the other by a single man, reading a newspaper as he drank wine in the sun. The fat woman brought a bottle of wine to me, opened it all the while rattling off something in happy French tones that I understood not a word of. But she seemed to enjoy telling me whatever she was telling me. She laughed now and then in the middle of her story, her roly-poly body jiggling with each laugh.

She filled my glass, placed the bottle on the table and walked away. As I tasted the really good wine, the man reading the newspaper dropped it on his table, got up and walked to me.

"May I join you?" he said in good but French accented English. He was slightly past middle age, not too tall and not too short, not too heavy and not too thin. His hair, left slightly long over the top of his ears by his European barber, was brown, not too dark and not too light, and it had a slight wave to it. His face was that of a man who enjoyed life; the beginnings of jowls and pinkish flesh told me that drinking good wine in the sun was his favorite sport. His fingers were fleshy and his nails well manicured. He wore a very good suit, European cut in mid-blue wool. There was a white carnation prominent in the boutonnière of his suit jacket. And he wore perhaps too much cologne.

Yet, beyond what he looked like there was the unmistakable air of a man not to be trifled with. I doubted he was big enough to take me in a fair fight, but I knew out of experience that the people I was dealing with knew nothing about a fair fight.

My gut and that little voice I have in the back of my head told me I should say 'no' when he asked if he could join me at my table, that I should get up and run away, but I, as usual, ignored all that good advice. I said, "Sure, please sit."

He sat, pulled his chair close to the table, leaned his arms on the tabletop, and said in a soft voice, "Monsieur Crew. It is best that you return to Paris . . . Get on the first plane home . . . And go home."

"That's what's best?" I asked.

"Yes, to be sure."

"Why?" I insisted.

"Because your wife will follow you on the next flight after you leave."

I was pushing the right buttons; I knew that. Whoever had Sandy . . . And my money was on DuSomme . . . had her for one reason, to get me out of France for what they deemed was a very good reason. With what he told me I felt sure she would not be harmed as long as I was doing what they wanted. But what if I stopped doing what they wanted? What if I did not go home?

"OK," I said. "I'll leave . . . But I need to have my wife with me. Just bring her to the airport and watch us get on a jet together. Then all your worries are over."

The man was silent for a moment, and then he nodded. He said, "Do as I suggest, Monsieur Crew. Your wife will be on the next plane after you leave. There is no other way." He pushed away from the table, got up and walked away. He walked to the cars in the Inn's parking lot, got in a new brown Citroen SUV and drove away.

The smiling and happy fat woman brought my lunch to my table. I guessed I had ordered the right things because what she brought looked beautiful. But I had lost any appetite I thought I had. I picked at the food and thought about what I should do.

Trusting people who would kidnap Sandy was hard to do. If DuSomme was the person I thought he was and the person I had been told he was, then trusting him was out of the question. If I left France without Sandy next to me would I ever see her again?

I had his money at my fingertips. If all else failed I would leave him broke. Maybe I could trade his money for my wife? But if Sandy was hurt . . . I would leave him more than broke. I would leave him dead.

I finished my glass of wine, dropped some money on the table, and left.

❊❊❊❊❊❊❊❊❊❊❊❊❊

I had to stop and ask directions of a group of three children herding six white geese down the road. They didn't speak English, but they could read the address Lorraine had given me. They pointed down the road ahead, and one of them, the girl with her two boy herders who must have picked up a little English in school, said, "Three kilometers, Monsieur, three kilometers."

It was evening, and the sun was setting in a burning red sky to the west when I finally found the address Lorraine had given me. The little goose herding girl was right; it had been three kilometers ahead.

The area was pure farming country, very isolated but beautifully green and lush. Lines of grape vines filtered down the hillsides; fat cows grazed in the fields. A few cottages were scattered amongst the countryside hills. They were picture perfect with thatched roofs and flower filled vines creeping up the stone walls of the homes. The air was filled with pleasant florals, and now and then, as I passed certain fields where herds of cattle were fenced in, the smell of cow dung overtook the pleasant fragrances.

I turned onto the unpaved drive that led to the little farm house I had been looking for and parked the Mercedes near the house. I turned the engine off, rolled down the window and looked and listened. Nothing. Not a sound or anyone in sight.

I stepped out of the car onto the wet and muddy ground and started towards the farmhouse. The front door of the house was closed but not locked. I stepped inside the dark, cold house and looked around. The floors creaked as I walked around; the air was stale and musty. Total silence greeted me, telling me there was no one there; at least I hoped no one was there, waiting for me in some hidden shadow. I took a slow and careful look around the empty rooms and left the house.

The only other building in sight was an old barn about fifty yards away, the wood shingled roof and unpainted sides needing repair. I walked to it and opened a door. Inside I found an old cow in a stall; she was chewing her cud and mooed a sad call at me when she saw me. A couple of fat goats were in another stall, watching curiously what was happening amongst the strange humans.

Now, I'm not a farm boy, but I could see that both the cow and the goats needed milking; their udders were fat. No one had been there to take care of that chore.

The dirt floor was covered in damp straw and dung . . . And three bodies that had bled out, staining the straw with pools of dried blood. They lay next to each other having been lined up on their backs, their eyes gazing out into nothingness, a message to whoever found them, probably me. Bullet holes had riddled their bodies.

It took some work but using my cell phone I was finally able to get an operator to connect me with the Paris police and Officer Marie St. John. Two local cops from whatever little village was nearby arrived first; neither could speak English. I just waived them into the barn through the open door and waited outside in the cold night air.

It was near midnight when Marie St. John arrived with two cars full of police. They walked past me, without a word, as if I were invisible, into the barn. I waited patiently outside, and while waiting I saw Lorraine Demeaux's chauffeur driven car pull to the side of the road. The car, the engine running and headlights off, with I imagined Lorraine inside, waited on the street for a short time, and then it pulled away into the dark.

I was pacing around on the wet ground, pulling my light sports coat around me trying to stay warm when Marie St. John and another cop, neither in uniform, walked out of the barn.

The man with Marie was tall and broad shouldered. He was not young, a fact betrayed by his short cropped grey hair. He had a military bearing about him. He asked me something in French, and Marie translated. "Why are you here?"

"I'm looking for my wife," I said. "You know that."

Marie went on translating back and forth, "But why here?"

"I had a lead," I answered simply.

"A lead?" she asked before translating to the tall cop.

"What is the lead?"

"I had information that my wife might be here."

She translated and then asked, "What information? Who told you this information?"

I wasn't sure who Lorraine Demeaux was. She had told me she was either the lesbian lover of Germaine LeFont, a petty thief, or an Interpol Agent working undercover. It was maybe a good bet that she was lying about everything she said. Until I was sure I decided to keep her to myself. I answered, "A little bird told me."

Marie frowned and translated to the tall cop. He and she spoke a few words with wondering looks on their faces. And then she asked me, "I do not understand. Who is this . . . Petit oiseau . . . Little bird?"

I had to laugh at that, and she didn't seem amused. I said, "I have a source I cannot tell you about I'm afraid."

She translated to the tall cop, and when she had finished he pulled a set of shiny, chrome plated handcuffs from under his jacket and told Marie to tell me, "You are under arrest, Monsieur Crew."

"For what?"

"For our suspicion of you of the murder of three people." Marie translated what the cop had said, but she hesitated before telling me. She was obviously unsure, but she did tell me what her boss had said.

"I suggest you phone the American Embassy first," I demanded. "Speak with a Mary Huntington. I think you'll change your mind about arresting me." Marie translated.

Marie and the tall cop had a short conversation before he put his handcuffs away. He told Marie to tell me, "The Government of France and the Government of the United

States have the agreement that you do what you wish to do. This is not the thing that we want. But it is what we must do. I assure you that murdering people is not included in the agreement between our two Countries. If we find you have committed the murder on these three people you will be arrested and charged."

They turned away and walked back into the barn. Marie was following the tall cop, a few steps behind him. Before she could walk into the barn I called to her. I went to her and asked, "Who are the dead people?"

"They are the family who work this farm," she answered. "You know why they are dead, Monsieur Crew?"

"I have a suspicion that my wife was being held here," I said. "Why these people were killed . . . I don't know."

"And your wife?" she asked.

"I have reason to believe she is still alive."

"And you will not tell me why you have this reason?"

"No . . . Not now," I said. "But I do have a question. You said the three dead people 'worked this farm.' Does that mean they don't own the farm?"

"We are investigating that, Monsieur Crew."

That wasn't so strange to me. Lorraine had told me that DuSomme owned this place. I told Marie, "I suggest you look at Alain DuSomme as the owner of this place."

"And why do you say this?"

"That little bird told me," I said and laughed.

Marie nodded with a questioning look behind the nod, I assume trying to understand. She walked into the barn, and I decided to go to my car to get out of the cold night air.

I sat inside watching the ambulances arrive and the

three bodies, in black body bags, carried from the barn to them. It was past two in the morning when the last of the police drove away. I saw Marie sitting in the back of the last car looking out the window at me as she passed by.

She had a worried look on her face; maybe she was worried for my safety or maybe she was worried that she would have to eventually throw my ass in jail. Whatever, I waived at her, nodded and smiled as she rode past. Mixing politics with criminal investigations all too often gets no one anywhere and all too often slaps the cops across the face. I really didn't want to have Marie St. John mad at me; I needed a cop who could speak English. And she seemed honest enough.

I started the engine . . . But where was I to go? I sat in the car, listening to the deep, soft engine and trying to think. I switched on the radio and dialed through the channels. I stopped on one that was playing fairly good jazz. I didn't recognize what was playing, something in the 'New Age' group of musicians whose talents fell short, in my humble opinion, with the jazz musicians of the fifties and sixties.

Should I go back to Paris? Or perhaps just get on a jet as the man at the Inn told me? I had very few choices at that time. But I had to know that Sandy was safe. There was no way I would trust a man I felt sure was a killer and kidnapper to keep his word and send Sandy home.

The idea occurred to me that I could drain DuSomme's bank accounts. That would surely bring him out of wherever he was hiding. But would doing that also get Sandy killed?

Before I could do anything an auto's headlights reflected in the rear view mirror. A car, a new Citroen, a brown SUV, pulled up behind me and stopped. A man got out and walked to the side of my car. It was the man from the country Inn where I had lunch who had sat at my table. I rolled down the window halfway.

"Monsieur Crew," he said. "I see you have not taken the good advice I have given you."

"It didn't sound like advice," I said. "Sounded more like a threat."

"No, no, you don't understand. All we want is to be left alone."

"OK, turn my wife over to me, and I'll leave you alone."

He shook his head and laughed a little. Then he said, "There is another offer. Please follow me. It is but a short ride."

He walked back to his car and backed away. He turned left out of the farm's drive. I followed at what I hoped was a safe distance. If he made a sudden stop and started shooting at me, I had room to turn around quickly and get the hell out of there.

We drove slowly along an unlit, thin and winding lane. It was roughly paved and very bouncy with a lot of potholes that needed filling. Turning a tree shrouded corner I found myself in the middle of a small village of grey stone buildings, some with thatched roofs, some with more modern clay tile roofs. All of the buildings were dark except for one; the Citroen pulled to a stop in front of it, and I pulled in behind. There were a few very old streetlights that cast faint light down on the cobblestone street. I looked up at one and saw an owl sitting on top of the light, looking down on us. He was probably thinking I was pretty stupid for doing what I was doing.

The man got out of the car and looked back at me,

still in my car. He smiled and waved, telling me to follow him inside, which I did, still unsure if it was some kind of trap. But once again, I had little choice. I would either get my wife or get killed.

The building was a small tavern with a door of old wood that had an old stained glass window in it. Inside the tavern was old but nice and in good condition, with lots of polished wood on the walls and stone, smoothed by many years of age, on the floor. The air inside was perfumed with a hundred years of wine, liquor, and tobacco smoke.

Three round tables filled the room in front of a short bar with a polished stone top. Behind the bar was a single shelf holding about a dozen bottles of booze; none of the labels were of something I was familiar with. A good sized barrel protruded from the wall under the shelf. My guess was it contained the local red wine for the local farmers to enjoy.

At the center table of the three sat Alain DuSomme, facing the door. No one else was in the tavern. He had a bottle of red wine on the table and two glasses, one of them empty and waiting for me.

"Please do sit, Mr. Crew," He said.

I sat and asked, "Where is my wife?"

"That is what we shall talk about, now isn't it?" he said. Again I was surprised at his skill with English. He had spent years in the military but that was no place to become highly fluent in a foreign language. He was smart, and that allowed him to speak so well.

"What is there to talk about? Just give me my wife, and we'll be on our way home and out of your hair."

"But I have work to do," DuSomme laughed as he said this. He filled the empty glass with wine and slid it across the table to me.

"I don't really care what work you have. I just want to get my wife and get on a plane home."

"The job I have to do, Mr. Crew . . . Has suddenly involved you. So . . . Your wife will remain safe, and you will help me do this job."

"You're kidding right?" I said. "Let's get serious. You want money? How much? I'll even get you a suitcase full of cash if that's what you want. Just let us get out of your hair and leave you to do whatever the hell it is you want to do."

"No, no, Mr. Crew. Having you in my . . . Shall we say, in my employ? Having you working for me will make my job much easier."

I had no idea what this guy wanted me to do, but knowing who he was, I knew it wasn't legal. I had been told he was a criminal, a hired killer. But if he thought I was going to help him kill someone . . . Or worse yet if he thought I was going to kill someone for him, he was crazier than I thought he was.

I took the glass of wine and drank half of it. I'm not a wine expert, but that stuff was pretty damn good. I drained the glass, laid it on the table and DuSomme refilled it. I picked up the glass and held it as I asked, "Do I have a choice? Is there something I can offer you?" It was too soon to threaten DuSomme with his fortune. If I told him I knew of his bank accounts and could easily take them from him, he would probably kill me, kill Sandy and move his money, all very quickly. No, I would wait.

"Oh, Mr. Crew," DuSomme said feigning a sad look. "I am afraid you have no choice."

"My wife," I said. "If I'm going to do something for you I want to see her. I want to know she's OK. And I promise you that if you've hurt her in any way . . . I will see you dead, Monsieur DuSomme."

DuSomme laughed at that, but he stopped when he recognized the look on my face. I glared into his eyes, unblinking and deadly. I saw right away that he might have felt just a little bit of fear. Then he called to the man who had taken me to him.

"Take Mr. Crew upstairs," he said. "Let him talk to his wife." Then he spoke in French so that I could not understand what he said. He told the man, "If he tries something stupid take him and the woman back to the farm and kill them quickly." The man I had followed there nodded and started for the staircase.

I stood and followed him across the room. There were sconces on the walls of the staircase, but they were turned off. It was dark, but at the top of the stairs I saw a thin bead of light from under a closed door. We went to that door and stopped.

The man had his hand on the doorknob as he turned to me and said, "You may speak with your wife. Tell her nothing. If you do anything, you and she will be killed. Understand?"

He opened the door, and light flooded out into the dark hall. I stepped inside, the man shutting the door behind me. He waited outside in the hallway.

Sandy was in a hard wooden chair on the far side of the room. Her hair was a mess; there were bits of straw in it left from the barn where Michelle and her father and brother had been murdered. Her slacks and blouse were rumpled and dirty. Other than that she looked in good shape.

Her face lit up when she saw me in the doorway. She smiled broadly and said a little too loudly, "Hey, Morgan!

What the hell took you so long?"

I turned to my left and right. Two men were standing against opposite walls. They were dark men with dark beards and hair. They each held an AK-47 and looked as mean as two guys could look. I looked from one to the other and said, "How you doin' fellas? Can I borrow a light?"

Neither answered, and both looked at me like they didn't understand what I said. To be sure, I added, "Hey, you two guys are each other's girlfriend, right?"

I went to Sandy as she pushed herself from the chair. I took her in my arms and kissed her, holding her tight. Her hands were still tied behind her back but her ankles were free. She whispered in my ear, "What's going on? What do they want?"

"Not now," I said. "I think these guys may not understand English, but I can't be sure. Are you OK? Have they hurt you?"

She backed away and spoke without a whisper, "No, these bastards haven't hurt me. But I'm hungry, thirsty and tired."

I looked behind, opened the closed door and spoke to the man who had brought me to Sandy, "I want food and water here . . . NOW! And I want her hands untied!"

He nodded, and I slammed the door in his face. I sat Sandy back in her chair and looked at her hands. They were red, and her fingers were swollen. One of the armed men raced to me and pushed me aside with the butt of his rifle. I pushed back, pushing him away from me. "I'm going to get my wife's hands untied. You two sons'a bitches have rifles. Are we gonna' hurt you?"

He stepped back against the wall, and I went back to Sandy's hands. There was a small desk in the room. On it was a brass cup that held two pencils, a pen, and a small pair of scissors. I grabbed the scissors and worked at cutting the plastic zip tie.

When she was free she shook her hands to get the blood flowing again. She said softly, but loud enough for the two guards to hear, "I don't know if these guys speak English or not. Be careful what you say. They killed three people back at some farm not too long ago."

"I know," I said. "I was there. I called the cops, but they don't know what's going on. Do you have any idea what the hell DuSomme wants?"

"No . . . But I know he's a stone cold killer. He killed the girl . . . Michelle. Just shot her without even thinking about it. These two killed her father and brother."

I pulled a hard backed wooden chair from the other side of the room and sat in front of Sandy. She smiled and asked, "We're in it again, right? What do they want?"

"I'm not sure yet," I said. "Look, I think I'm going to have to leave you with them for a couple of days. At least until I find out what they want."

She wrapped her arms around me and kissed me hard. As I held her she put her head against mine and whispered, "What now?"

"Stay here," I said for her ear only. "These guys have guns and we don't. Let me try to work something out."

I sat her in the chair she had been tied in. As I turned, DuSomme's man walked into the room with a small tray that held a plate of meat and cheese. Next to it was a small glass of red wine. "You eat," I told Sandy. "I'm going to talk with DuSomme."

Downstairs, inside the deserted tavern, DuSomme sat at the same table. I pulled the chair I had been in to the table quickly and sat. "I want my wife released immediately."

"I'm afraid I can't do that. As I said, I need you to do something for me," he said.

"You talk pretty tough," I said, grinning, although I was just talking a big bluff. "As long as you have guys with guns. How about just you and me step out back?"

DuSomme laughed and leaned back in his chair. "Oh, Morgan . . . May I call you Morgan? You may call me Alain. You have no idea what you're saying. Anyway, your good and beautiful wife stays with me until you finish the little job I have for you. I assure you she will be well treated. She will have food and water and some good French wine. But she *will* stay with me until you finish the job I have for you."

"And suppose I agree to whatever you want and come back with a couple dozen armed men and kill you and your buddies?"

"If you can find me," he laughed. "And if you do, then your wife will be the first to die," he said.

I was trapped; I knew that. If I had some freedom I might figure a way out and a way to save Sandy. And the only way I could have any freedom was to accept DuSomme's 'offer'. If what he wanted me to do I could do alone, on my own, without his people watching me, then I might be able to do something.

So I feigned thought, frowning my forehead to make DuSomme believe I was considering what he had said. I leaned forward and said in a defeated voice, "I suppose I have no choice, as long as those two bearded thugs are upstairs. But that's something that has to change. Depending on what you want, I may do it. But Sandy has to remain safe. I want those two guys out of her room. Let them guard the door out in the hallway, but I want a woman in the room with her. And if she is harmed in any way . . . I promise you I will bring the darkness of hell itself down upon you."

He laughed again, but his laughter went away when he saw that I meant what I said. I think he had done some background research on me. I think he may have known what I was capable of. The Crew Family had power all over the world. And I controlled the many billions of dollars the Crew Family was worth. I think that knowledge maybe frightened him just a little.

"Alright, Morgan. I will do as you say. Your wife will be completely safe. I will have a woman with her at all times. She will not be bound unless I move her to some other place. As I said, she will eat and drink well. Now will you do what I tell you to do? Or will that safety end quite quickly?"

ELEVEN - The Chateau

What DuSomme wanted me to do seemed easy enough. I was to go to a 400 year old chateau in the French Alps, the home of an international banker by the name of François DeLocke. I was to spend a few days with him, draw a map of the chateau's layout and surrounding area, make notes of any security at the chateau, and find out DeLocke's travel schedule for the next month. If he was expecting guests, I was to find that out, also.

It was spring and the snow season would have ended. The mountains would have green grass and flowers emerging from the left over snow. It would be, if nothing else, a nice time of year to be in the mountains. But all that alpine beauty would be lost on me. My mind was filled with what was happening to Sandy and how I could get her out of the claws of that man.

I had met François several times over the years. His bank had financial interests in some businesses my family had over the years. He was a fat and obnoxious man who liked to hunt, taking a particular liking to killing small animals and watching them die. But he also killed deer and small bears and other assorted larger animals if they came within range of one of his rifles. Rather than walk through a forest seeking game he would sit comfortably behind a hunter's blind and wait for animals, baited with food and scent, to come his way.

He liked his food and ate too much of it, and drank too

153

much, too. And he liked young girls. Even his wife of twenty-eight years knew that. I had met her a couple of times. She was fat and homely. She seemed to be itchy constantly as she was always scratching herself, often in unseemly places. And she smelled bad on top of all that.

I didn't like the man, but he and I had never argued, mainly to keep him on the good business side of my family's businesses.

Dropping in on François without notice might be a problem. So I had to figure out a good reason for knocking on his door and asking to stay in his castle for a week or two. Back in Paris, at the suite in The Ritz, I phoned New York and spoke with Peter Jascro, the man I could always rely on to do what I needed to have done. Peter has been like an uncle to me since my father passed away years ago and he has never refused me anything, no matter what I asked.

I explained the problem to him, getting into the chateau, without telling him about DuSomme and Sandy's captivity. Peter, as usual, agreed to help although I could hear the suspicion and trepidation in his voice. I think he knew I was doing something dangerous, that I was in trouble once again, but he would do as I asked anyway. And as he had asked, no mention of DuSomme's bank accounts was made over the phone.

****

François DeLocke was at home in what he called his 'castle'. His castle was in reality a two hundred fifty year old chateau overlooking a green valley within the French Alpine region. François had bought the chateau, and befitting his enormous opinion of himself, he immediately started referring to it as his 'castle'. It didn't take long for friends, mainly business associates and contacts, as François had very few other friends, to start calling his home a castle. But when they did, they did it with a mocking laugh when François was not within earshot.

The chateau was today a rambling structure of thirty-three rooms, having grown from the original twenty-four room home of a man with a royal title who owned the farmland in the valley below. François had added nine more rooms and a ten foot tall wall of stone to surround the building, along with two towers reminiscent of towers from the Middle Ages.

An iron gate at a winding hillside road was the only entrance and was just wide enough for cars but not trucks to drive through. Deliveries were made outside the gate and brought in to DeLocke's castle on small electric carts or by hand.

He was sitting at his desk in his office, gazing at the big computer screen on his desk, paging through his bank's financial records. The Bank de Lyon had branches throughout Western Europe, Asia, South America, and North Africa. François had attempted to infiltrate the United States' banking system but found the banking regulations and Government oversight too stringent for his type of banking, which included financing several semi-legal (and a few totally illegal) business operations, as well as laundering illegal money if his profit was worth the risk. The bank also financed several dictators in Africa and South America and offered secret and secure depository for people who couldn't have their money become public.

The Crew businesses had, once or twice, gone to François's bank for financing when starting a business or buying a business in those parts of the world where purely honest banking was not available. As titular head of the Crew family I had the disagreeable duty of meeting with François several times over the years. I never could understand why, with all the money the family had, why we went to a bank for financing. The accountants and lawyers all assured me it was wise business practice to use 'other people's money.' But did 'other people's money' have to be Francois DeLocke's money?

That morning François looked up from his computer to the walls of his office. He smiled at the memory of having killed all the animals whose heads and ivory filled the walls. The killing was good, he thought. He liked to see the blood rush from an animal he had shot, particularly if the animal had been shot with a powerful gun that tore the animal apart. He was always careful not to damage an animal's head however. He needed them for display. If the animal had to die a slow death, bleeding to death, that was acceptable if the head were preserved for mounting.

And one day he would be able to hunt and kill a person, he dreamed. That would be the pièce de résistance – the most substantial dish in a meal – for his hunting career. He was working on that, but it would take time to arrange such a thing without repercussion from the law. One of the dictators he financed would soon arrange that, he was sure of that. His people were working on it.

One of the five phones on his desk rang. He picked it up slowly, wishing it had not interrupted his memories of the killings and blood.

He spoke in French, using his usual common dialect, not an educated French, "Yes, hello, who is it?"

"Monsieur DeLocke?" a man asked.

"Yes," François said letting his voice sound angry. "Who is this? What do you want?"

"I am Henri Trousatte," the man said. His voice was educated and he spoke slowly with perhaps a 'better than thou' tone to the words. "I am an attorney in Paris."

"Yes," François said again, even more impatiently. "What do you want?"

"I am phoning for Crew Minerals International. You are familiar with the Crew industries?"

"Of course I am," François said, sighing audibly to let his impatience be known. The attorney was obviously trying to sound better than DeLocke. It was important to DeLocke to sound bored with the man.

"Crew Minerals International wishes to begin mining a new discovery of tin in Indonesia," the attorney said and paused.

François waited for him to say something else. When he didn't, François shot out, "Get to the point man! Do you think I have all day!"

"Crew Minerals wishes funding to start the mining operation. Indonesia has insisted in being awarded an interest in the mining operation in order to approve local bank funding."

Again François said nothing, waiting for the attorney to say something. Finally he said, "So what? How does this concern me?"

Trousatte answered, "Crew Minerals International wishes to obtain financing through The Bank of Lyon thereby bypassing the demands of the Indonesian Government."

François said, "So have them go to the bank and fill out the papers. Why are you phoning me and wasting my valuable time? Do you have any idea who you are talking to!"

"Your branch in Indonesia must report all transactions to the Government. Crew Minerals International wishes not to have that happen."

François immediately brightened. Something not quite legal was being proposed, and that meant money in his pocket. If a transaction sought to work around some laws, then he would be able to demand a higher price for his bank's services.

"Alright," he said in a softer voice and a little more pleasant tone. "What do you propose?"

"This cannot be done publicly as you might assume. Mr. Morgan Crew would like to come to your home to discuss the particulars. May I report that you will meet with Mr. Crew?"

"Of course," François said. He pulled up his calendar on his computer. "The second and third weeks of next month are impossible," he said. "When may I expect him?"

"I believe Mr. Crew is in Paris on other business," Trousatte said. "May I have him phone you directly?"

"Of course," François said and hung up before Trousatte could say anything else.

****

Two hours later, as François was pacing in circles around his office in his castle, one of his phones rang again. He ran to it and answered, speaking again in French.

I was on the line and said, "I'm sorry, I don't speak

French. This is Morgan Crew."

In accented English, François said in a particularly polite and overly gushy tone, "Yes . . . Please . . . Monsieur Crew. I was expecting the call. How may I be of help?"

"May I come to your home?" I asked. "I don't want to talk over the phone."

"Certainement . . . Excuse me . . . Certainly. When would you like to come here?"

"I can be there tomorrow," I said. "In the afternoon if that's OK with you?"

"That would be fine," François said, almost licking his lips at the thought of the profit he would not have to pay taxes on. He would demand an extravagant amount of cash to be paid for the Crew business to get its financing. He could almost taste the cash. "I will have the dinner prepared, oui?"

"Terrific," I said. I was trying to sound relaxed and businesslike, but thoughts of Sandy being held captive filled my mind. I had to work quickly, but I also knew I couldn't be part of a murder. I had come to the conclusion that DuSomme was going to kill François DeLocke . . . For whatever reason someone would want him dead. Someone had hired DuSomme to do the job. But I would think about that later. First I had to free Sandy.

I took a small private jet from Paris and landed at a private airport in San Germaine, about fifteen miles from François' home. The only rental available was a five year old Citroen that belched smoke as it struggled through the foothills and valleys. But I made it as I had promised.

François' twenty-two year old maid, at least that is what François called the girl who shared his bed occasionally when his wife was not there . . . And sometimes when she was, opened the tall double doors of the castle and stepped aside as I walked into the dark house.

Inside the entry was all dark wood and stone with mounted animal heads lining the walls everywhere. The girl was saying something in French which I couldn't understand as she led me through the long room.

An elevator, so small that it was a tight fit for the two of us, which seemed to please the young girl more than it pleased me as she faced me and pressed herself to me, took us on a slow ride up to the fourth floor of the castle. Again I followed the girl as she continued to speak in French. I assume she was greeting me and telling me all about the castle because she kept pointing at things as she spoke. Finally she stopped at a bronze door, opened it and stood aside for me to enter François' office.

"Ah, Monsieur Crew!" François said effusively as he walked quickly to me. He held out his hand which I took in mine. I found his hand to be cold, soft, and damp and his handshake weak. I felt I was shaking the hand of a dead man. I think he wanted to hug me and maybe lay one of those European kisses on me. I leaned back out of his reach.

"Please do come in and sit," he said, waving at a chair sitting at a round table of polished mahogany. It was about four foot in diameter, big enough for two people to sit at. The chair he waived me to was upholstered in silk with red and gold stitched deer. One other chair was there, taller than the one he wanted me to sit at, which François sat in after I was seated.

"And so," he said, smiling broadly. "I am told we have the business of money to speak about, N'est-ce pas?"

"You get right down to business I see," I said as jovially as I could manage. "I thought you would have a meal waiting. Isn't that what you said on the phone?"

François laughed nervously and spoke to the young girl still standing in the open doorway. He spoke quickly and in French. I thought I heard a French four-letter word I had heard somewhere. She nodded and walked away.

"Some wine, I think, no? And perhaps some cheese? The village here makes so good cheese, oui? Perhaps some meat? I have a boar that has been smoked, yes?"

"Before dinner?" I said. I had to delay as much as I could. I needed time to do what DuSomme wanted. "A small snack, of course. And wine sounds good after my trip here. Then perhaps you can tell me all about this beautiful castle of yours? What little I've seen is fascinating. There must be interesting history here. And you must tell me all about the . . . Animal trophies," I said, waving a hand around the trophy covered walls.

"Certainement," he said, perhaps some disappointment in his voice. "But you must spend the night, oui, Monsieur Crew?"

"I had hoped you would ask. I have a suitcase down in the car."

I managed to delay talk of business for three days. I controlled the conversation and kept it about the chateau and the grounds, asking question after question. Day after day I kept it up, except to convince François now and then when he showed signs of frustration that my family was prepared to give him a lot of money to secretly finance what he thought was a mining operation.

He gave me an almost foot by foot guided tour of his home . . . all of it . . . while I memorized the floor plan and doors and windows, and reduced it all to paper before sleep each night. I insisted that he show me everything, playing on his ego and pride, while tossing in suggestions of the business he was expecting. I asked about everything I saw, all the furniture and especially all the dead animals which he seemed to relish telling me about.

When I had seen all of the castle, including a massive wine cellar that held hundreds of bottles of wine, and François' own private blood splattered taxidermy operating room – which I found really disgusting – I asked for a tour of the surrounding grounds.

After four days of this I could see that François was getting anxious and nervous about my visit. I had to calm him, so I suggested we spend an afternoon discussing how he would hide the money my company supposedly would give him. He smiled and relaxed and spoke for two hours on how he had surreptitiously moved money around in the past. He took great pride in how well informed he was in illegal money transfers. He was almost as proud of that knowledge as he was of all the animals he had murdered.

After dinner that night I asked again for a tour of the land surrounding his home. He promised that would happen the next day, but only if business could be finalized. It was time to give in and start talking business, as best as I could. I would make most of it up as we went along, and I hoped he wouldn't figure out all I said were lies.

We spent a few hours talking about money and what his money would cost. I made a show of the 'mining' operation in Indonesia and what huge profits could be expected. Labor, I emphasized, was cheap. He seemed to appreciate that and commented once or twice on the difference between the classes of people around the world. He seemed proud of the knowledge he said he held of the difference between the dark skinned poor and his own class.

Several times I reminded him of the secret nature of

the financing. He smiled at that, licking his lips at the unspoken thought of what that secret financing would cost the Crew Family.

"That's terrific," I said feigning happiness when we shook hands on the agreement we had reached. "Now, my people can be here within three or four weeks to sign the papers. Is that convenient for you?"

"The second and third weeks of the month next are not good, oui? I have . . . Business plans for that time. But other times are good."

"Fine," I said. "Now, dinner and then bed. I am tired. But your home is absolutely beautiful, Mr. DeLocke. And we must go hunting sometime. I'd love to get an elephant. Never killed one of them."

"Oui, that will be fine," he said. "After the business, oui?"

The next morning the young girl who greeted me at the door when I arrived drove me around the estate in a new Rolls Royce while I sat in the passenger seat. I took photographs of everything, including the exterior of François' castle. DuSomme would probably appreciate that, I thought, and might speed him into releasing Sandy to me. Then I could go to the police and warn them of DuSomme's pending attempt on François' life.

It seemed so easy at the time.

TWELVE - Off To The Rescue

After leaving François's castle I spent the time on the small dual prop airplane – the local airport was little more than a landing strip with one steel building and no private jets to rent – handwriting out some more details of what I learned at his home. DuSomme had, in my opinion, only one reason for wanting to know these details. He was going to murder François DeLocke and wanted a way into and out of the chateau.

DuSomme was a hired killer, so I had been told and what I believed. Someone wanted François dead, probably because of one of his business dealings gone wrong. I imagined that François had cheated someone and he would pay the price with his life. What other reason could someone like Alain DuSomme want such details of François DeLocke's home and schedule? He had to know when DeLocke would be home alone. And he needed to know how to get in and get out of the chateau.

After a long and very bouncy ride in the years old four seater plane, I stepped out onto an airport a lot like the one I had left from, a concrete runway with weeds sprouting through the cracks.

I drove a rented four year old Mercedes that smelled of cigarettes to the little tavern where I had spoken with DuSomme and visited with Sandy. It was bright inside the tavern when I arrived there in the late afternoon. I could hear voices inside and an accordion playing something I didn't recognize. The tavern had been deserted the last time I was there, but that was late at night, and the local farmers would have been in bed. I looked around to make sure I was at the right place. I was.

Inside was crowded with farm type men and a few women. All the talk ended, and someone playing a small squeeze accordion stopped in mid-song. Everyone looked at me, a stranger in a small town. I walked across the room to the bar and asked if Alain was there.

The man behind the bar, an old man with grey hair and beard that needed a comb, stared at me not knowing what I had asked. I turned and asked, "Does anyone here speak English?"

No one answered. The stairs I had taken to see Sandy were to my left. I went to them and took them without anyone stopping me. There were four rooms on the second floor. All were empty. Sandy and DuSomme were gone. But to where?

I was lost. I didn't know what to do. Did DuSomme just want me out of his way while he murdered someone else? Was my trip to the chateau just a waste of time, a red herring as they say? And where was Sandy? Was she still alive?

Not knowing what else to do I took the long drive back to Paris in the odorous Mercedes and went directly to The Ritz and my waiting suite. I handed over the keys to the car and told the doorman, who I think spoke some English, to have it returned to where I rented it. I'll never know if the car was returned or sold to someone.

I needed a hot shower to try to feel clean after so many days with François DeLocke, a man I felt was rancid in appearance and nature. I can't believe my family has done business with that man and I made a mental note, if Sandy and I ever got out of our current danger alive, to instruct the lawyers and accountants and all the business managers to never again speak with François DeLocke or have any business with his bank. If we had money on deposit in his bank it would be withdrawn totally and quickly, and all ties cut.

I tossed my small suitcase through the door into the bedroom and went to the bar. The bar in the suite had a small bottle of brandy. I poured a glass of it and downed it quickly. It did little good. And I was scared, frightened because I did not know where Sandy was or if she was safe. I had to get to her and free her from Alain DuSomme. But how?

There was a small beige envelope waiting for me, propped up against the telephone in the sitting room. Opening it I found a single sheet of paper with *'TONIGHT AT MY CLUB'* handwritten in big printed letters in pencil. It was not signed, but I knew it was from DuSomme. He wanted my report on DeLocke, or maybe he would laugh at sending me off on a wild goose chase while he committed some crime. I had to go, I had to do what he told me to do; I wanted Sandy. I would go there as soon as the club opened.

****

It was early in the evening when I walked down the brick stairs into L'ange Bleu. The band, now only four musicians without the female singer and the skinny trumpet player who was with them the last time I was there, was playing some hot New Orleans jazz piece. The tourists there seemed to like it, but I could tell the band didn't have their hearts in it.

I didn't wait long enough to listen to what they were playing. I stormed to the door at the side of the stage, pushing the empty table and chairs aside. I opened the door slamming it against the wall. I left it open behind me and walked as fast as I could into DuSomme's office.

He was at his desk, writing something that had no interest to me. I pulled a chair to his desk and sat. "OK, I'm here," I said. I wasn't happy, and I wanted him to know that. Whether I was not happy with having to do his work for him or that he still had Sandy I would keep to myself. Actually I wasn't happy about either thing.

"So you are," he said, smiling. "And you have what I asked you to get?"

"Let's get this straight," I said. "You didn't *ask* me to get anything. You coerced me, you threatened my wife's life, and you gave me no choice. But you didn't *ask* me to do anything for you."

"And so it is. But let's not argue over semantics. Give me what you have, please."

"Give me my wife," I replied firmly.

"Your good wife is safe and unharmed. She is eating well and enjoying very good wines. She has received her luggage from the airplane, and I have had some new clothes bought for her. She will be released soon. But first I have to know that you obtained what I need."

"Why do you need this?" I asked. I pulled a sheaf of papers, folded in half lengthwise, from my jacket pocket. I held the papers on which I had written everything but did not hand them to him.

"That is not for you to know, Mr. Crew. Please," he said, holding out his hand to take the papers.

"If you intend to kill François DeLocke . . . I will be implicated. I don't want that."

"If it makes you feel better . . . I do not intend to kill Monsieur DeLocke. Now, I will have what you are holding."

"If I give this to you . . . I fully expect to have my wife with me no later than tonight . . . And very soon tonight."

DuSomme only smiled and held his hand out for the papers. If he had lied, if I gave him the papers and he killed me, if Sandy was already dead . . . What could I do at that moment? I had to take the chance that he wasn't lying to me.

I had little choice. I handed the few sheets of paper to DuSomme. It was at that point that I made up my mind to stop him. Whatever he had been hired to do, whoever he had been hired to murder, I would stop him. I would free Sandy somehow, and if I had to kill DuSomme to do those things, I would kill him myself.

"When will my wife be freed?" I asked. "Where can I go to get her?"

"Soon, Mr. Crew . . . Soon. When I have finished what I have been hired to do."

"What!" I stood and pushed the chair away. "That wasn't the deal! I want my wife now!"

"Soon . . . Soon. I assure you she is safe and watched by a woman as you asked. But first I must be assured that you will not go to the police. So as long as you do not do that, your wife will be safe and unharmed. As I assured you, she has excellent food and very good wine, also. She is happy, do not be fearful."

"Then send me to her. I'll wait there . . . Until you're done with whatever you're going to do."

DuSomme leaned back in his chair, folded his hands in front of him, smiled a little and said, "That would be unwise. You see, you would be missed. You are a famous person throughout the world, Mr. Crew. Your good wife is not as famous. Few people even know she is in France. If you were missing, inquiries would be made. The police would certainly look into your disappearance. Your American Embassy would insist, I'm afraid. No, you must remain free and in public. And you must remain quiet, of course. If you speak of this to anyone . . . Well, your wife would then be killed."

There was no sense arguing with the man. He held the winning hand in the game we were playing. I had little to work with. All I could do was wait for my chance to kill the man.

Arguing and even pleading would do no good. All I had left was to stop him from murder and free Sandy . . . All on my own.

****

The American Embassy is on the Avenue Gabriel in the 8th Arrondissement in the heart of Paris. Tall walls surround the building, and heavy traffic fills the roads in front of the Embassy. Armed Marine guards in full dress uniforms stand duty at the iron gates where pedestrians enter. And still more armed Marine guards in combat fatigues are stationed at the gate at the rear of the Embassy which controls truck and auto traffic into the Embassy grounds.

I climbed out of the taxi that took me to the Embassy and walked to the closed iron gates; the two Marine guards stood on the other side looking suspiciously at me through the iron bars.

"Hi," I said hoping to sound friendly enough. "I'd like to see Mary Huntington, please."

"Do you have an appointment, sir?" one of the guards asked. He had a lot of stripes on his sleeve and a tough look on his face.

"No, I'm afraid not. But she knows who I am, and if you call her, she'll want to see me."

The two Marines looked at each other for a short moment before the one with all the stripes backed away to a telephone hanging in a box on the wall near the gate. He punched in some numbers and turned his back to me as he spoke. He returned moments later and opened the gate. As it happens, it wasn't locked. Only a sliding bar kept it closed.

"Inside," he said simply, not looking at me and with a not-too-happy glare on his tough, military face.

Following the Marine at a discrete distance, I walked up the four steps at the front of the Embassy and stopped at the big double doors. The Marine turned and walked away, leaving me standing at the doors not knowing what to do. If I just opened the doors would I be shot? I looked for a button to push, but the doors opened without me doing anything and I stepped inside. Two more Marines were inside, standing next to a metal detector, looking very serious. These two were dressed in tan shirt and slacks. Both had a lot of stripes on their arms and rows of medals pinned over the left pocket of their shirts. They also had really big pistols in shiny holsters on their hips. I decided not to mouth off at them or challenge their authority. As worried as I was about Sandy's wellbeing I'm not stupid.

"Please empty your pockets," one of them said. I did and was waived through the metal detector. No alarms sounded so I guessed I wasn't going to be tackled or arrested or maybe both.

I was in a long hallway with glass doors lining each wall. As I retrieved what I had taken from my pockets, an elevator slid open and Mary Huntington stepped out.

"Good morning, Mr. Crew," she said without a smile in greeting. I wasn't sure, but I think she was wearing the same drab suit I had seen her in last time. "What can I do for you?"

"Well, I'd like to talk with you if you don't mind."

"About what?"

"Can we go somewhere less public?" I asked. I was trying to look friendly and not dangerous. I forced a smile, but I am sure I looked more frightened than anything else.

Mary Huntington was shorter than I, not more than 5'6" tall. And she looked even more disheveled than the last time I had seen her. She looked like she may have slept at her desk the night before and hadn't bothered to even comb her hair that morning. She turned and started back to the elevator as she said, "Follow me, please."

I stood against the back wall of the elevator with Huntington in front of me as we rode up five floors. Standing behind her, all I could focus on was the dandruff flakes all over the collar and back of her jacket.

I followed her out of the elevator to an office, which

turned out to be little more than a broom closet. A small, pale, wood desk with a small secretary's chair behind it and a hard wood chair in front of it filled most of the little room.

"Please excuse the mess," she said as she squeezed herself sideways behind the desk and sat in her chair, which squeaked loudly as she sat. Without being invited to do so, I sat in the only other chair in the room. I reached behind me and made sure the office door was still open, not only to have some room to breathe a little fresh air, but also to be sure I had a means of escape if I needed it.

There wasn't much in Mary's office. The four walls, painted a kind of sickly pale green, held only one cheaply framed photo of our President.

"Just what is your job here, Ms. Huntington?" I asked.

"Is that what you wanted to see me about?"

"No . . . I was just wondering . . . I mean . . . This is your office?" I stammered.

"My office?" she asked. "Yes, it's all I have. I translate for others," she said apologetically. "I studied French language and history. I have a Master's Degree in both. I had hoped for something better, but this is what I have. So I translate for others who are more socially adept than I am. Now, what do you want to talk to me about?"

At first I laughed at what she had said. Then the laugh went away when I saw she was glaring at me. I said, "That's not possible. You came to me with two big guards and you knew things. You phoned people, and you told me things a mere translator wouldn't know. Who the hell are you, anyway?"

She said nothing. Her glare was slowly shifting to a sour scowl. I was not making her happy, and that would get me nowhere. She was hiding her true worth at the embassy.

I had the idea that the little room we were in was not her office. But I had to drop my suspicions and get her to help me.

So I decided to get right to the point, although I had an idea that Huntington wouldn't help me. "What do you know about François DeLocke?" I asked.

"Mr. DeLocke is a well-known banker and financier," she answered and looked up at me wonderingly. The scowl had suddenly disappeared. I had surprised her with the question.

"Is that it? That's all you know about him?"

"What else would you like to know?" she asked.

I took a chance and said, "I'd like to know who might want to kill him?"

"Kill him? Do you know something that should be reported?" she asked, honestly surprised. She reached down into the one drawer of her small desk and took out a pack of Marlboros. Taking one from the soft pack, she held it out to me. I shook my head, and she lit her cigarette with a cheap, plastic lighter.

She blew a cloud of smoke up and away from me. I watched the smoke curl up towards the water stained ceiling. I asked, "Do you know you've got a water leak up there?"

She ignored what I said and asked again, "Do you know something that the police should know?" I had to remind myself that pushing it, no matter how badly I wanted to challenge her authority, would get me nowhere.

"I'm afraid I can't go to the police right now," I said. "Maybe later but not now."

"Why?"

"I'm afraid I can't tell you that either. Look, who do I

talk to if I want to find out something about DeLocke? I thought you were more than a clerk. Who should I talk to?"

Mary reached down to an imitation leather attaché on the floor and pulled a laptop computer from it. Pushing aside a pile of papers, a few of them falling to the floor unnoticed, or maybe uncared, she opened the laptop and started typing at the keys.

After a minute of this she leaned back, looked at me and said, "François DeLocke is highly politically connected. His bank loans money to Governments. He has political friends in very, very high places around the world."

"And doing that he might well have made some enemies, too," I said, almost speaking to myself. I asked her, "What political dealings has he had recently?"

She typed in more stuff and then said, "There are some things that have been classified."

"Classified?" I asked. "That means I'm not supposed to know about that stuff, right?"

"I'm afraid so . . . And I'm not privy to these things either by the way, so don't ask. I'm just a clerk you know."

I chose to ignore her lie and asked, "Classified by who?"

"You mean by *whom*?" she asked.

"Yeah . . . Sure . . . Whatever," I said. I should have known that but college to me meant chasing girls and playing sports. Mary Huntington obviously had a better education than I had.

"I'm afraid I can't tell you that either," she answered.

"I guess if you have something about DeLocke on your little computer, then it was some U.S. Intelligence guys somewhere who classified it."

"That could be," she said and smiled knowingly. "But we cooperate with many other Countries, and they cooperate with us. Don't assume that what we have is from U.S. sources."

"That's all you can tell me?" I asked.

"Yes," she said simply.

I decided to take a chance on her. I don't know why, but maybe I felt she was dissatisfied with presenting herself as a translator-clerk. All people have an ego. Some people have a huge ego, others control their ego, but everyone wants to feel important, even an intel agent like I was sure Mary Huntington was. So I decided to play that card thinking she wanted to feel important.

So I told her, "Look, I'm in trouble. You said you folks and the French decided to let me find my wife and take care of DuSomme. I need help doing both those things and I can't explain why."

"I sort of guessed that, Mr. Crew. But you want information on François DeLocke. But what else can I do for you? That seems to be out of the limits our two Countries have agreed on."

"And if DuSomme is somehow connected to DeLocke?" I asked.

Mary leaned back in her chair causing it to squeak again. She folded her hands casually in her lap and grinned as if she knew something I didn't know and would not know from her.

I figured I had learned all I was going to learn from her. So I moved on and asked, "Those two guys who came with you the other day. Who were they?"

"U.S. Embassies hire independent contractors to provide the real security at Embassies and Consulates, Mr.

Crew. Marines handle the gates, but contractors do the real security and protection. They are contractors."

"I want to hire them . . . Sub-contract so to speak. How do I do that?"

She had this really strange look come onto her face as she looked up at me. She scratched her head and rubbed her chin, and then she said, "Let me get this straight. You want to hire Embassy contractors? To do what? I don't get it."

"It's simple enough, Ms. Huntington. I want guys with guns who can help me out here."

"Please step outside for a minute," she said.

I did and stood in the open doorway with my back to her. I wanted to listen to what she was saying on the phone. Of course she could be calling a bunch of 6'6" 300 pound Marines in to beat the crap out of me. I didn't know what she was doing, but I had little choice but do what she said.

"Please close the door," she asked. "I want to make a phone call."

I closed the door and waited. There were no benches in the hallway, so I began pacing nervously. Maybe, I thought, I had said the wrong thing and gotten myself in hot water with the Ambassador. Maybe a couple of men would turn the corner and arrest me . . . Or show me to the door.

As it turned out, Huntington called my name from inside her tiny office. I opened the door and stepped inside the broom closet sized office.

"Mr. Crew," she said as she held out a small scrap of paper for me. "Go to this office, please. It's on the fourth floor. The elevators are to your left. And please don't involve me in anything again. Thank you. Please go now."

I took the paper and looked at what she had scribbled on it. Simply an office number; no names or anything else. I walked out without thanking her, leaving her office door open assuming that she would leave that small space and return to her real office, in spite of the fact that she yelled, "Please close the door!"

The elevator she had directed me to was an old one, doored in brass that needed some polishing. The main elevator from the front lobby was new, clean and shiny. The elevator doors opened, and I stepped inside and rode alone to the fourth floor.

Arriving there, as the doors slid open I was greeted by a very tall Marine in combat fatigues that just barely covered all the muscles on the guy. He asked me who I wanted to see. I handed him the piece of paper Huntington had given me and told him, "I was sent here by Mary Huntington."

He nodded and told me to follow him, which I did humbly and silently. We turned right and left and right again through hallways that progressed to be thinner and thinner as we walked through them, and they were poorly lit. At the dead end of the last hallway the Marine pounded loudly three times with a closed fist on a wooden door that needed a coat of paint. Without waiting for a reply to his pounding on the door the Marine opened the door and stepped inside, holding the door open for me.

Inside was a waiting room of sorts. The room was small, probably not more than twelve by twelve. There were four grey metal framed chairs with black cloth seats along the wall to my left and a desk to my right. At the desk sat a young man typing away at an old desktop computer. With all the income taxes my family pays I wondered why the hell they couldn't afford a newer computer.

I stood a few steps past the Marine and looked at the

young man. He stopped typing long enough to say, "Take a seat." He went back to his typing.

I started to say, "I was sent here by . . ." but he interrupted me and repeated, "Take a seat."

So I sat, and the Marine left, closing the door behind him. I kept checking the passage of time on my Rolex. Ten minutes crept by, and I asked the young man, still typing away with flying fingers, "Excuse me, why am I here?"

"Please wait," was all he said, without stopping his typing or even looking up at me.

More minutes passed as I fidgeted in the very uncomfortable and very hard metal chair. And then the office door opened once again, and Officer Marie St. John walked in. She was dressed in expensive looking grey slacks and a good quality navy blue jacket over a pale blue blouse. A thin gold necklace hung around her pale neck. For the first time I realized that she might actually be pretty . . . Just a little pretty.

I stood, and the young man at the computer stood. St. John nodded to him, and he walked to a door behind his desk. He opened it, and I followed St. John into a much larger office.

Inside, sitting at a very nice, polished, dark mahogany desk about five feet wide, better than the one in the waiting room, was a woman dressed in a very impressive Class A Army uniform.

Across her chest were four rows of ribbons, including one with a silver star on it which told me she was some kind of hero somewhere. There was a silver parachute insignia above the ribbons. I saw the silver eagles on her shoulders so knew I would be speaking with a full colonel with a lot of combat experience. I decided to be on my best behavior. I didn't want a woman to beat the crap out of me.

Her black hair was cut short and combed back revealing minute streaks of grey. She didn't wear a lot of makeup, just some lipstick and the faintest touch of eyeliner. Small diamond studs sparkled on her earlobes, her only sign of femininity. She filled the uniform out nicely, and I tried to keep my eyes off of her uniform's breast area.

Behind her, hanging on the wall above her head, was a really great looking sword, curved like a cavalry saber in a red and gold sheath, with a gold tassel hanging from the hilt. At her right side, again on the wall, was a glassed case with two matched, chrome plated Colt .45s. And on the wall to her left was a triangular folded American flag in a glass case.

She sat there not looking up at me, almost like royal prerogative. She was surrounded by trophies and military stuff of all kinds, indicating she was very athletic and a combat veteran.

After what seemed forever, she put the gold pen she had been writing with down on her desk, leaned back in her tall black leather chair, and folded her hands across her lap. She looked at me without a trace of expression on her face.

Marie walked to a chair in front of the colonel's desk and sat. Not knowing what to do and without being told to, I sat in the chair next to Marie and waited. The colonel was glaring at me with just a crack of a nasty grin on her face. I thought she might be deciding which of my arms to break first. Suddenly she spoke after I had settled down into the chair, "Please close the door, Mr. Crew."

I forced a chuckle at that, hoping she wouldn't notice how worried I was about what was about to happen, but I did get up and close the door. Yet another thought went through my head as I went to the door, that I was about to be arrested by both the French police and the military. Would they fight over who would throw my ass in jail? If they did, I hoped it would degenerate into a cat fight. I would sit back and enjoy watching two women roll around on the floor, fighting over me.

Sitting down again I asked, "So what? Why am I here?"

"Excuse me?" the colonel asked without moving. I caught the military command in her voice, which was deep from years of giving orders that were immediately obeyed. "I thought you had asked Mary Huntington if you could hire some of our civilian security contractors. Was I wrong about that?" I would hate to be a buck private standing in front of this tough woman.

I have never been one to be easily intimidated by people who think they are very important. Once people know what my family name is, they tend to lose some of that self-importance. I changed my mind about being nice.

So I sat forward, smiled like I hope some tough guy would smile, and said, "Cut the crap, lady. I don't give a damn if you're a colonel, a general or a God damn private skinning potatoes in the mess hall. Who the hell are you, and why am I talking with you? And why the hell is this Paris cop here?"

She broke out in laughter and shook her head at that. She spoke softly, unlike the military voice I had just heard. "Ordinarily . . . In other like circumstances . . . I would throw your tiny ass out a window and watch you bounce off the parking lot. But we've been told . . . By people pretty damn high up in D.C. . . . That we are supposed to cooperate with you and give you whatever you want. So . . . I will put my temptation to break some of your bones aside for now. Tell me who the hell you are. Why does a guy with a gut hanging over his belt draw such power out of Washington?"

I had to laugh at that, and unconsciously I sucked in my stomach a little. Sandy would have agreed with her. My gut is too big. I know that, and Sandy has been working for years to reduce it.

I said, "I am Morgan Crew. My family supports a couple dozen people in Congress. I have relatives who play golf with the President on a regular basis. I played in a tournament once with him. As long as our money flows freely into D.C. then there will be people back there who want me to have everything I want."

"And what is it you want, Mr. Morgan Crew?"

"I told you . . . I want two of your civilian security contractors. I don't want to have to explain that again. The two who came to see me with Mary Huntington will do, but if they're not available I will take any two contractors like them. And I want them armed. And I want others available to me if I need them. I want what we call SWAT teams back in the States. Heavily armed commando types ready when and if I call. Get on the phone and have those two contractors come here . . . Armed."

Marie St. John sat forward and spoke for the first time. She was grinning as she spoke. "Here in France, Monsieur Crew . . . It is not like your wild west. We do not have the guns and the cowboy and Indians shoot outs . . . As they say on the television, oui? Having people carrying the rifles in the streets . . . That cannot be, oui?"

"Officer St. John," I said, calming my voice because although I could probably intimidate most people from the United States, I doubted I could pull that off with a French cop. "It is my understanding that your Country and mine agreed to let me have a free hand dealing with Alain DuSomme. Was I wrong? Did something change on your side? If you think you can gather evidence on what he has killed three people here in Paris all on your own . . . Just say so, and I will step aside and watch."

"Monsieur DuSomme has done not the crimes in Paris. We do not have the evidence. We do not do the arrest of people only because a person has said Monsieur DuSomme has committed the crimes."

"So DuSomme, as far as you are concerned, is a good, law abiding citizen. But I know for a fact that he has my wife, and I want her back. How I know that, I can't say . . . Right now anyway. If I did tell you how I know DuSomme would kill my wife. So you can't do anything . . . But I can. Now do I get what I want or not? Believe me, I can start a really big international brouhaha over this if I have to."

Marie St. John smiled and lowered her eyes shyly. She admitted, "Nothing has changed, Monsieur Crew. But you should know that I have strongly made the objection. That will go on the file record we have of you. If you kill someone, my objection will be noted by the courts, and you will be prosecuted."

So as not to piss her off too much, I said, "I appreciate that. You have a duty, and I know that. But I have a responsibility, too. I have something that needs to be done. Murders have occurred, and more murders will occur soon. I have to stop that and protect my wife. I hope you can appreciate my side of this thing."

She nodded and looked at me, that same grin on her face. She didn't ask me about 'murders that will occur.' That was not lost on me. She knew something I didn't know. She said, "It has been decided that I will accompany you, Monsieur Crew. It has been decided by people with much high positions that I will be the . . . 'Cop' as you say . . . And you will work for me. Is that something you can do?"

I smiled and laughed a little, shaking my head in

disbelief. But I also knew there was no sense arguing with her. I was in a foreign land with foreign rules that I could not control even though our two Governments came to an agreement about me.

I was in a land where my money meant very little, outside of the demands of the U.S. on the French government. Only the influence of my own Government, influenced by the Crew Family money, on the French Government got me as far as I had. So I agreed. Inside of me, unspoken by me, I would allow her to accompany me as long as she didn't get in my way or interfere in keeping Sandy from any more danger than she was already in.

Trying to keep things as light as possible I wanted to say something like, "Wow! Do I get a deputy's badge and a six shooter?" But I didn't. Why piss people off when I needed them to work with me?

"Welcome aboard," I said cheerfully, instead of what I really wanted to say. "I hope you carry a very large gun."

"I have the . . . How do you say? . . . Authorize is the word? . . . I will have a weapon. You will not, oui?"

The Colonel shouted, "OK, come in!" I jumped when she shouted. Marie St. John didn't.

The door to her office opened, and the two civilian contractors, Manning and Phelps, walked in, leaving the door open behind them. They had been waiting outside as the Colonel had told them. They were dressed in dark grey suits and white shirts and red ties. I guessed they spoke to each other every morning about what they would wear.

I stood and held my hand out to them. Each shook hands with me but neither smiled or seemed happy to see me. Their grip on my hand was light and quick. They weren't happy to see me, I guess. They seemed to recognize the silver eagles on the colonel's shoulders. They stood at rigid attention with their hands at their sides; my guess was both had military experience, or maybe they were current military, killers for the Government.

"Stand at ease," the colonel said. The two men spread their feet apart and locked their arms behind them. 'Yep,' I thought. Military types. I'd seen men like them before, leg breakers and widow makers. Just the kind of men I needed.

I was standing between them and the colonel. I said to them, with my back to the Colonel, "You'll be working for me for a few days. How much do you want?"

Rather than answer me, they both looked at the Colonel. She answered for them, "I have been instructed to assign these two to you for no more than seven days. No cost to you, Mr. Crew." She paused for a short moment and went on, "But if any sort of violence occurs within those seven days . . . You will be held responsible. Mr. Manning and Mr. Phelps will not be held responsible for anything that happens. They will protect you only. If they use their firearms for any other reason . . . It will be recorded that you have used the firearms, not them. If they harm anyone . . . Other than to protect you . . . It will be recorded that you have harmed those people. You will be surrendered to the French authorities if those things occur. Is that clear?"

"Crystal," I said. To the others in the room I said, "OK, team. Let's go."

THIRTEEN - Who Do I Trust?

We had plans to make, and I had no idea what those plans might be. We sat around the comfortable sitting room of my suite at The Ritz, drinking coffee and gazing at a plate of delicious looking pastries on the table. Everyone was waiting for someone else to grab the first one, as I explained the situation. I told them about my wife and Alain DuSomme. I told them DuSomme had told me that if I would leave France, Sandy would be on the next flight out.

Marie St. John asked, "And why have you not done this, Monsieur Crew? It seems the best way to free your wife without trouble."

"Simply because I don't trust Alain DuSomme. I have reason to believe he is a hired killer. I don't think it wise to trust anyone who kills for money."

I didn't mention François DeLocke. I had questions to ask before doing that. I simply added that I had something else to do that I could not discuss at that time. She wasn't happy about that; she leaned back in her chair and a disapproving look, to say the least, crossed her face.

Officer St. John sat quietly, listening but not saying anything more. I knew she had her doubts about what I was doing, but she did have her instructions. I also knew that she would let me go only so far before she stopped me.

My intention was to send the two contractors after DuSomme and do whatever was necessary to find out where

Sandy was being held. I said to them, "I have a suspicion you two know how to get people to talk."

When I suggested this, St. John spoke up very quickly, stopping me from doing what I wanted to do. "That, I am to fear, cannot happen, Monsieur Crew. I cannot allow a violent crime, oui?"

"And what do you suggest?" I asked her.

"This I do not know, Monsieur. It is not for me to do the plan. I only look on, oui? We have not the evidence to accuse Monsieur DuSomme of anything more than perhaps selling marijuana. That we will not waste the time doing."

"That's not absolutely true, Marie." I called her by her first name for the first time. "You apparently do one more thing very well."

"And what is that?"

"You are very good at being a pain in my ass," I said; she laughed but I didn't.

Manning and Phelps were grinning but didn't say anything.

Phelps finally did ask a question that I was afraid would be asked. "Why does DuSomme have your wife, Mr. Crew?"

"Right now I'm afraid I can't tell you that. The reason is something I have to look into independently. I only have suspicions. My only concern is getting my wife back. Everything else I will take care of myself. I am open to any and all suggestions on how to free my wife. The one limitation is that we will have only one chance to be successful."

"What does that mean?" Phelps asked.

"It means she will be murdered if our attempt fails."

"This sounds pretty strange," Manning said. "It would be helpful if we knew all the facts."

"In time . . . In time . . . Maybe," I said.

"Monsieur Crew," St. John said softly. "I will talk with Monsieur DuSomme. Even in the world today, the police, we still have the influence, oui? I will speak with him and perhaps this can be . . . Résoudre . . . How do you say? Is it *resolve*, oui?"

I said nothing because arguing with the police, particularly when the police don't know you or care about you, is a waste of time. St. John stood and walked out of the suite, leaving me alone with Manning and Phelps.

When the door was shut behind her I said to the two, "OK, now that she's gone, how do we go about getting our hands on DuSomme?"

****

Officer Marie St. John waited at the locked door of L'ange Bleu. Spring weather had finally found Paris bringing with it a warm afternoon and the promise of a dry evening, so different from the rainy days and nights since I had been there.

Two women arrived, cleaning ladies who would make L'ange Bleu as presentable as possible for the evening's jazz fans. A few minutes after them the old janitor who I had seen there previously arrived. The three spoke for a minute or two and then went to work.

Cleaning the rough brick walls and stone floors was

the job of the old janitor. The one very old bathroom that male and female patrons shared, and the kitchen was a job for the two women. St. John showed them her I.D. card, and they let her into the club without argument. She sat at a table near the stairs that led up to the street. She was waiting for DuSomme to arrive at the club, not realizing that the club would not open until well into the night.

An hour and a half later the janitor and the two cleaning women had finished their jobs and walked up the stairs, leaving St. John alone in the dimly lit club. The small tables had their chairs turned upside down on top of them. The stone floor was still wet in spots from mopping, and the smell of strong cleaners permeated the club.

She wished she had not quit cigarettes three months ago. Pacing around the empty club, she walked behind the bar thinking there might be cigarettes there. But she found none.

She was scared, although she would not admit that to anyone. She knew, as every police officer in Paris knew, that Alain DuSomme was a dangerous criminal. For years the Paris police had been building a file on him, but to that date they had never been able to gather evidence of any crime committed by him.

Three bottles of red wine that had been opened the night before were sitting corked on a shelf below the bar. Perhaps one glass of wine wouldn't hurt, she tried to tell herself. After all, Inspector Renard, her immediate boss, drank openly at his desk whenever he wanted to. His bottle of American whiskey was famously always sitting on his desk. So she took a bottle, found a clean glass and filled it with the dark red wine.

The 'nose', she told herself as she sniffed at the wine, was not terribly good, but the alcohol of the wine was unmistakable. She sipped at it, found it acceptable, nodded her pleasure, and then drained the glass. "One more won't hurt," she told herself. She filled the glass to its rim and quickly drained it. The wine seemed to calm her nerves a little. Maybe a third glass would work even better?

Footsteps on the brick staircase made her flinch before she could fill the glass again. She quickly hid the open bottle and glass under the bar and walked fast around to the dance floor. Alain DuSomme stepped off the stairs and stood looking questioningly at St. John.

He spoke in French, "Et qui pourriez-vous être?" (And who might you be?)

She pulled her I.D. card from her purse and speaking in French she said, "I am with the police. I want to speak with you, Monsieur DuSomme."

They continued, speaking in French.

He walked past her to the bar, sat on a stool at the front of the bar there and asked, "About what?"

"Madam Morgan Crew."

"And who is that?"

"I think you know, Monsieur DuSomme. I have spoken with Monsieur Crew. He believes you have kidnapped his wife and you are holding her somewhere."

"And why would I do that?" he asked, smiling.

"Monsieur Crew would not tell me that. Please answer the question, do you have Madam Crew hidden somewhere?"

"That's foolish," he said standing. "I have work to do. Please come to my office and we can talk. But if you plan on arresting me . . . Please leave now. I will have my attorneys phone you."

"I have no intention of arresting you, Monsieur DuSomme. I merely want to ask you some questions. We can go to your office if you wish."

DuSomme sniffed in the air, as a very special person with special privileges would do when faced with authority from below, and he smiled. He nodded, walked behind the bar and found the open wine bottle and glass. Pulling both off the shelf, he carried them as he walked through the door at the side of the small stage. St. John followed.

She stood in the doorway watching DuSomme sit in his chair behind his desk and pour wine into the glass St. John had used. He took a second glass from his desk drawer and filled it.

"Please sit, officer," he said, holding out her glass to her.

She hesitated but finally sat and took the wine.

DuSomme raised his glass and said, "Here's to law and order, Madam Policeman . . . I am so sorry. I mean Policewoman. I do apologize."

He drank some of the wine and St. John followed, drinking from her glass.

"So," DuSomme began, "This Monsieur Crew thinks I have kidnapped his wife."

"I never said 'kidnapped,' Monsieur DuSomme. Maybe she is just off having a good time with someone? You perhaps?"

"Me? That would be funny! Why would I be having an affair with another man's wife?"

"Then, if you have her somewhere . . . If she is not with you voluntarily, then you in fact have kidnapped her," St. John said and drained her glass. The wine wasn't a good one, but it was warming and it felt good going down. It had its effect on her; her head began to spin. She laid her glass on the desk and asked, "Do you have a cigarette?"

"Of course," DuSomme said, pulling a pack of American Lucky Strikes from his desk drawer. He knew that Europeans were impressed with American cigarettes. He left his own Gauloises cigarettes in his jacket pocket.

As St. John was lighting the cigarette DuSomme filled her glass once again. She drew deeply on the cigarette, coughed, and took the glass filled to its rim to her lips. She could feel the wine working on her head and eyes and stomach. But it felt good. It had been more than a month since she had been drunk.

As she smoked the cigarette, DuSomme filled her glass twice more and she drank each quickly.

She laughed as she looked for an ashtray, finally dropping the cigarette on to the yellow vinyl floor and missing as she tried to crush it under her shoe. She laughed again.

DuSomme suggested, "Perhaps I should come to your office tomorrow morning? We could talk more then?"

"Oh, yes," she said, her voice garbled from the wine. "What a good idea! Tomorrow . . . Yes. May I have just one more glass of wine before I leave?" It seemed like a good way for her to escape her fear of interviewing Alain DuSomme.

The last of the wine from the bottle barely filled her glass half way. She shrugged and drank the glass dry. She stumbled as she stood and held onto the wall and chair. She almost fell as she walked from DuSomme's office.

The stairs were a problem for her; she almost fell backwards half way up because of the loose bricks. But she found the door to the alley and stepped outside.

Evening and the unlit street were surrounding her. It was mid-week, and no customers had arrived at the club yet. She leaned against the alley wall and breathed the cool evening air deeply. Her head was spinning, her throat was burning, and her stomach was twisting. She held back the feeling that she would vomit.

She walked down the alley to the street. She stumbled as she stepped from the curb to cross the street, and where LeRoy Manns had been murdered a car raced to her. She was hit to the ground and the car ran over her legs. She tried to scream but all she could do was open her mouth; no scream left her. The car stopped and backed over her chest. She was dead and an autopsy would reveal the alcohol in her system. It may have been a hit and run, but she was drunk and still on duty. Only the very basic investigation would be done.

****

The day crept into night. I spent the day talking with my two civilian contractors . . . Although I felt sure they were active military. We had dinner sent to the suite, steaks covered in grilled onions and fries on the side, and we finished a bottle of good wine. But between the three of us, we had no idea what to do about freeing Sandy. We just had to wait for Officer Marie St. John to get back to us and work with her within the laws of France. Manning and Phelps demanded that.

At half past ten that night Manning and Phelps left to

go to their homes. I showered and went to bed. Dreams of Sandy in terrible jeopardy filled my sleep. When I ran to her, the earth opened and I fell into a black, bottomless pit. I could hear Sandy screaming, yelling for me to come to her, to save her, but all I could do was spin endlessly into nothingness.

I jumped out of bed before I could die in the pit. I rubbed the sleep from my eyes and stumbled to the bar in the sitting room. I poured a strong brandy but thought better of it. I left the filled glass sitting on the bar. A clear head seemed to be more important than the cooling buzz of booze.

Sitting in a tall chair near the big window of the suite, I turned the chair around and pulled the curtains to the side. I stared out on the lights of Paris. It is, without a doubt, a beautiful city, but a city that could bring death to me . . . And worse to Sandy.

And it seemed like an endless city. There had to be thousands of places where Sandy could be kept. And then there was the entire Nation of France. She could be anywhere, and where do I start?

Sleep found me as I sat in the chair. The sun and the phone woke me.

My eyes were still foggy as I found the phone. "Hello . . . Yes . . . What?" I said.

"Monsieur Crew?" a man's voice asked. He spoke slowly and the words were in a very deep tone.

"Yeah . . . What? . . . Who is this?"

"Monsieur . . . Please excuse my poor English. I am Inspector Renard . . . Police Paris, oui?"

"Yeah . . . OK . . . What do you want? I just woke up."

"I am . . . So sorry, Monsieur," Renard said, his English hesitatingly slow. "Officer Marie St. John. You know her, oui?"

"Of course," I said. I needed coffee but I would have to hang up on the cop to order it.

"She is dead, Monsieur," Renard said. The words did the job of waking me fully. "When, s'il vous plaît, did you see her last?"

"Dead? Marie is dead? I don't . . ."

"S'il vous plaît, Monsieur. When did you see her last?" the Inspector demanded.

"Last night . . . I think," I answered; sleep was still clouding and slowing my brain. "Early. We met at the American Embassy. She was working with me to find my wife. Two American Embassy people were with us. She insisted on speaking with Alain DuSomme. That's the last time I . . . The last time I saw her, I guess. I can't believe it. Did DuSomme have anything to do with it?"

"This thing we do not know, Monsieur. I will speak with Monsieur DuSomme this day. Please do not leave the City for now," the Inspector said with more than a little authority in his voice. He looked on me as a suspect. I accepted that; it seemed reasonable, to him anyway.

The two Embassy contractors had left phone numbers for me. They were housed on the Embassy grounds, but they had private quarters and private phone lines in their apartments. I phoned Phelps first. There was no answer and no voicemail to leave a message. I phoned Manning's number. Again, no answer and no voicemail.

I had no idea what to do next. I was in a land not familiar to me with a language I couldn't speak, and I was all alone. Marie St. John was my last hope for help. Now she had joined the group of dead people. Each of them had one thing in common, Alain DuSomme.

Life was easier back in San Marcos. But I wasn't there, and I had to do whatever I could do, no matter how impossible.

I ordered coffee, but food just didn't sound good right then. My stomach was knotted up, and I was too worried and nervous to eat anything. A cold shower while I waited for the coffee woke me up.

I sat on the couch in the suite's sitting room, drinking the coffee that had been left there while I showered. I was naked, the cold air conditioning doing its best to chill me into thinking. But I had nothing. I had nowhere to go. I was lost in a City I knew nothing about, with no one to turn to.

I knew DuSomme had murdered Marie. It would be a very broad coincidence that all the people now dead were the results of accidents outside DuSomme's jazz club. I knew that but how do I prove it? The police would talk with him, but I knew he wouldn't be arrested. After years of murdering people he still walked free. There would be no evidence that he murdered Marie, as there was no evidence he had murdered LeRoy Manns and the others. And now he was planning another murder, the banker François DeLocke. DuSomme had to die. I had to kill the man. There was no other way to stop him. I made that decision as I sat there with the coffee cup in my hand.

I couldn't go back to the Embassy to find out where Manning and Phelps were. I couldn't ask anyone at the embassy or the police about François DeLocke. If I did I knew DuSomme would kill Sandy, as he said he would.

Three cups of the hot, strong coffee did nothing to help me. A soft knocking on the door made me jump.

"Who is it!" I yelled.

"Lorraine Demeaux," she answered. Lorraine . . . Was she Germaine LeFont's lesbian girlfriend? . . . Was she an Interpol Agent? . . . Was she some kind of thief or maybe a con artist? Was she a partner of DuSomme? But then, what the hell difference did it make? Letting her into the suite and talking with her would not make my position any worse. Maybe I could find out something from her.

"Wait a minute," I called out. I went to the bedroom and threw on a bathrobe. Returning to the door, I opened it and found Lorraine smiling up at me.

After a moment or two of standing silently staring at each other, she asked, "May I come in?" I checked the robe to make sure I had tied it tightly and nothing was showing that shouldn't be showing.

She was dressed in better and much more expensive clothes than I had seen her in before. Her grey slacks were light weight wool and obviously custom cut with a sharp crease running down both legs. Nothing off the rack could fit so well. Her shoes, low healed and what looked like good leather, were expensive looking as well, probably Italian.

Her silk blouse was a pale green and similarly custom made. She wore a simple gold chain around her neck, falling to her cleavage that was exposed by her blouse open three buttons down the front, and the chain had not been bought at Kmart. It was real gold, no mistake on that one. On her right hand was a wide diamond ring, gold again with a diamond that had to be four or five carats surrounded by a lot of smaller diamonds.

A small black leather purse hung on a gold chain over her left shoulder. This was not someone's lesbian lover, not a petty thief. Could Interpol pay its people enough for them to afford the clothes Lorraine was wearing?

"Of course," I said when she asked to come into the suite. I stepped aside, holding the door open for her.

As she walked past me I asked, "Why are you here?"

"I could ask the same, Monsieur Crew. Why are you here still?"

"This is where I'm staying while in Paris," I answered.

Without my invitation she sat in an armchair at the side of the coffee table, laying her purse on the floor at her feet. She looked longingly at the silver pot of coffee. Two cups had been delivered with the coffee as usual, even though I was registered as one guest. Maybe in France they just expect overnight guests? I sat on the couch and said, "Please help yourself."

"Merci, Monsieur Crew. I have not had the coffee this morning."

She filled a china cup and brought it to her lips. She smiled in appreciation of the very good coffee. As she did I asked again, "Why are you here?"

She held the delicate cup on its saucer and said, "You have been speaking with the police, oui? And some persons at your Embassy, oui?"

"Yes," I said. "So what?"

"And, Monsieur . . . What help have they been?"

That was the truth. She had gotten to the truth very quickly. I'd spent two days trying to find help, and I was nowhere closer to finding Sandy than I was at the beginning. And the only Paris cop who had been willing to help me in any way was dead . . . Murdered, I was sure . . . After having spoken with Alain DuSomme.

Lorraine said, "They have not been of the help, then. And what will you do now?"

"Honestly," I said. "I don't know. I want to grab DuSomme and beat the crap out of him. But that wouldn't help, would it?"

"No, it would not be of the help . . . And Alain, you could not beat in the fight," she laughed. "He is very good at the combat of all types, you know?"

"So . . . You have a suggestion?" I asked.

"Oui, Monsieur, I do."

I waited but all she did was stare at me without any expression on her face.

"Ok," I said, maybe a little too loudly and impatiently. "So tell me what the hell that suggestion might be."

She stood, delicately and carefully placing the cup and saucer on the table. She walked into the center of the room, her hands held behind her back. She was thinking, deciding what she could tell me, to what extent she could trust me. And I was wondering the same thing. I had no idea who she was. Would she be truthful . . . Or would she tell me lies to trap me?

She stopped, turned to me and said, "We have the wish to bring an end to Alain DuSomme . . . As you do . . . But for different reasons. I think perhaps that end could be done if we help you in the finding of your wife and free her."

"And who is 'we'?" I asked.

Lorraine laughed and began pacing back and forth again. She was thinking, trying to decide what was best for me to know, what she could tell me and what she couldn't.

She stopped suddenly and quickly spun around to face me. "I believe I have told you that I am with Interpol? Did I not say this?"

"Yeah, you did," I said. "But I'm having a hard time

believing you. First you're a lesbian lover, then a thief, now Interpol. Lady . . . I'm having a hard time believing anything you say. And did you use your Interpol expense account to buy those clothes? Why not tell me the truth for once."

She laughed again and shook her head in disbelief. "Monsieur Crew," she said. "Who else do you have the trust for but me? Will you go back to your Embassy? Do not trust people there. Monsieur DuSomme, he has the friends there. And he will be told you have gone there. When he has been told this . . . What will he do with your wife? And the police, he has informants there, too. He is not afraid to kill a police now is he? No, you have no one to trust in but me, oui?"

"I have two civilian contractors, security people, well-armed men, who I can trust."

"Monsieur DuSomme has the plan to kill these men, too. We know this."

"And just how the hell do you know that?" I asked, astonished but unsure if I should believe her.

Rather than answer, Lorraine said, "If you wish them to be not murdered, you should not contact them again. You and I, we will find your wife together . . . And I will bring the end to Alain DuSomme."

"And just how will you do that?" I asked. "I mean, if you don't know where he's holding my wife, how do you intend to find her? And how exactly do you intend to 'bring an end' to DuSomme?"

"How I will bring the end to Alain, that is my business," Lorraine said. "How we will find your wife . . . You and I will do that."

"And just how the hell do you suggest we do that?"

FOURTEEN - The Safe House

It was half past two in the morning on a Thursday and the spring rain of Paris was with us again. Lorraine and I were in a black Mercedes GLS SUV. The windows were blackened so no one could see inside, and we had a hard time seeing out because of the rain. The engine was turned off, the windows closed. After a few hours of waiting, the air inside the car was stale, hot, and musty. We had to keep wiping the fog off the front window.

We were parked at the curb a block away from the entrance to the alley where the L'ange Bleu jazz club was. We hadn't spoken a word in over an hour, spending that time staring at the alley, waiting for Alain DuSomme to leave. People, alone and in pairs, were leaving, some walking some running, through the rain.

Lorraine suddenly spoke, "The wipers cannot be used." I don't know why she said that. Maybe she was talking to herself, answering her own unspoken question.

"Yeah, I know that," I said. "I've done this sort of thing before." Using the wipers would tell someone that we were sitting in the car. It had to look like a parked car and nothing more. When Alain finally left the club he could not know we were sitting there waiting for him.

Lorraine nodded and went on gazing out the rain soaked window. Blurred figures of people occasionally moved outside, people leaving the club. I wondered how we would recognize DuSomme. Lorraine seemed not to worry about this. It was her idea to wait for DuSomme and follow him, so I had to trust she would be able to recognize him.

Time slipped by. I asked, for no more reason than to break the interminable silence, "Is this your car?"

"No," she answered. "It is stolen."

"Stolen!"

"Yes . . . Do not worry," she said softly and calmly. "No one will know, oui?"

"What the hell!" I had slumped down in the front seat of the car. I pushed myself up straight. All I needed was for a Paris cop to tap on the window and arrest both of us for Grand Theft Auto or whatever they call it in France. "Someone is going to report this thing stolen! The cops will be looking for it!" I said.

"Do not worry mon chéri." She laughed. She patted my knee as she would a frightened child and said, "I have changed the . . . What do you call them? . . . The numbers, no?"

"The license plates?" I asked.

"Oui, the license plates."

"And where did you get them?" I asked, almost afraid to find out.

"I stole them, of course," she said as if it were a stupid question. I shook my head trying to believe and understand this woman.

Time dragged by, and the rain continued. Lorraine surprised me by once again breaking the silence saying, "Under your seat, there is the pistol, oui? Please take it and be careful not to shoot me. This would not be good." She was laughing but never took her eyes from the street and alley where sooner or later Alain DuSomme would appear.

I didn't know if she was joking or not about shooting her. In any other situation with any other person sitting next to her, it might have been good advice. If Lorraine had done any study of my background, she would have known that this was not the first time I held a pistol in my hands.

But the pistol was there, a 9MM Beretta M9A1. A really big gun but one I had used before. I checked the clip and found it full. I eased the slide back and found a round in the chamber. I nodded my thanks to Lorraine, flipped on the safety, and slid the gun under my belt at the small of my back. Whether or not I would need it, I now had a way to put a bullet into DuSomme's head when I had the opportunity.

We waited at the same curb for three nights running. Each night, in the early morning hours, before the sky lightened, we watched DuSomme leave the club and drive his Jaguar to his apartment home.

At half past one in the morning of the third night, a Saturday, a night of dry weather and a clear, starlit sky, we sat in the same stolen car, waiting. Just for something to say, I asked Lorraine, "I wonder if the police have looked at his car? I mean, I *know* he plowed down a couple of people. There has to be damage to his car."

"Morgan," she said. And it was the first time she had used my first name. "Alain, he has the use of many cars. He may steal a car as easily as I have. The killing, they look as accidents, no? He does things so. He is not the stupid man. He would not use his own car to kill. And if he had, the car it would have been repaired quite quickly. He can do that. He has ways."

I could accept that, and in truth I had thought that myself. I just had to say something to break the maddening silence in the car.

On the fourth night of our waiting, he drove his Jaguar again but this time not to his home. Lorraine did a masterful job of following Alain without being spotted by him. She managed to stay four car lengths behind and whenever possible let a vehicle come between us.

She drove in silence, keeping her concentration on following DuSomme, and kept her speed steady. Most of the time she drove with the car's headlights turned off, driving in the dark, waiting for the sun to rise across the horizon to the east, when lights were no longer necessary.

We drove for a couple of hours, out of the city, to the northeast. The city and suburban roads turned into country roads and then country lanes. We kept driving, speeding up when DuSomme did and slowing down when he slowed. More hours passed, and I began thinking that maybe he knew we were behind him, and he was leading us on a wild goose chase. Lorraine seemed to read my mind. She said without my asking, "Do not worry. I have done this before."

The sun was rising high in the sky, and Lorraine pulled even further back so as not to be spotted by Alain. She stayed now at least six to eight car lengths behind him. I thought we had lost him several times as the narrow roads twisted and turned, but Lorraine seemed to know what she was doing. Every time we came to a corner or turn in the road and we had lost sight of DuSomme, when Lorraine made the turn, there he was ahead of us.

She suddenly braked, bringing the car to a skidding stop, and turned off the engine. I was about to ask what she was doing when she stopped me. "Ssshh, mon chéri," she said. She reached up to the interior roof of the car and switched off the interior lights so they would not come on when the doors were opened. She opened the door of the car and slowly stepped out. I did the same, being as quiet as she was.

I followed Lorraine into a field of grape vines lined up as straight as soldiers on parade. We were near the top of the gentle hillside the grape vines grew on. We followed the line of vines for a hundred yards. The pebbled ground was soft from days of rain, but leaves and twigs were everywhere. I tried as best as I could to step softly so as not to make any noise.

Lorraine was bent low so she would not stand above the tops of the vines. I did the same, following her lead. She stopped and I stopped, waiting.

Lorraine put her finger to her lips, telling me to be very quiet. She pushed the thick vines apart and pointed through the opening. The grey, early morning light, shrouded with a thin, misty fog hanging low to the ground, was enough for me to see a small stone cottage about twenty yards away.

A man, tall, dark and bearded, stood outside at the lone door of the cottage. He held a Kalashnikov rifle casually by its barrel, letting the stock touch the ground. He was stamping his feet on the ground against the cold morning air while smoking a cigarette. He was dressed in faded blue jeans and a faded, light blue work shirt. He wore a dark blue sleeveless quilted jacket that hung open enough for me to see the grip of a pistol tucked into his belted jeans.

I couldn't be sure from that distance, but he looked like he was one of the men who had been at the Inn where Sandy had been held. If not one of them, then another Arab man. There was no mistaking that. If it was one of those two, I wondered where the other was.

Instinctively I looked behind me and all around. No one was behind us. But I knew Sandy was inside that cottage. My hand went to my back. I touched the Berretta just to make sure it was still there.

DuSomme's Jaguar was parked at the side of the

stone cottage, under a tall tree with umbrella branches. He wasn't in sight, but dim lights from inside the cottage shown through the windows. He . . . And Sandy . . . had to be inside. My first thought was to rush the guy standing outside, shoot him and bust through the door. But that would just get Sandy killed. I took a deep breath, and I waited.

Lorraine bent low and pulled at my arm. I bent and listened to her whisper, "This place I do not know. It is perhaps where Madame Crew is. DuSomme he is here. The man outside I have seen before. There can be no other reason for him to be here, oui?"

"OK, so what do I do?"

"You do nothing, Monsieur Crew. These are the most dangerous people. I will have dangerous men come here. They will do what is necessary."

"I don't understand," I said. "If my wife is in there and shooting starts . . . I don't want that."

"My people they will do what is right. They know how. It is best. Madame Crew, she will be safe . . . We will do our best, oui? DuSomme, he will die . . . That is most important."

Lorraine pulled a cell phone from the pocket of her jacket and started to dial a number. She pushed the send button on the phone and stopped when we both heard footsteps crunching on the wet gravel coming from our left. Whoever it was, they weren't making any attempt to be quiet. Their footsteps crushed twigs and leaves noisily, and they were standing straight rather than bending to hide behind the vines as Lorraine and I did. If these were her people, they weren't as good as I would have hoped.

Through the morning mist I saw Manning and Phelps,

the Embassy security contractors, walking casually towards us. They made no attempt to hide themselves. I waved at them to get down but they just kept walking towards us.

Lorraine stood, dropped the cell phone to the ground, and her hand went to her waist, under her jacket. Phelps pulled a big pistol from his belt and said, "Forget it. Just stand . . . Both of you . . . And drop the gun lady."

Lorraine stood and raised her hands above her head. I followed her lead. At first I wanted to stand behind her, using her as a shield, and pull the Berretta from my belt and start shooting. But getting myself and Lorraine killed would not have helped Sandy.

Manning pulled a gun equally as big as Phelps' and eased his way past us, carefully, not getting between his partner and us. He stood behind me and patted me down, searching for a weapon. He found the Beretta and pulled it from my belt. He did the same to Lorraine and found a six inch long stiletto in a scabbard strapped to her left arm.

"What the hell's going on here?" I demanded. "You know who I am. They have my wife in there," I said pointing at the stone cottage. I looked that way and saw a man had joined the guard we had seen. The man was as dark as the first, and bearded. He was probably the second man I had seen at the Inn.   Both of them were laughing; Alain DuSomme walked out of the stone cottage, stood next to them, and started laughing with them.

Manning ordered, "OK, let's go."

Lorraine and I walked along the row of grape vines to the road and along it to the little stone cottage. As we walked, with the two contractors behind us holding their pistols at our backs, Lorraine said, "I told you to not have the trust with your Embassy." Phelps laughed at that.

As we walked to the cottage DuSomme opened the door for us and stood aside. Inside was dimly lit but light enough for me to see Sandy sitting in a chair, legs crossed, drinking a tin cup of coffee. She was not tied up as she had been in the barn and at the Inn, but she was wearing the same clothes she had on at the Inn.

She saw me and said, "Well, it's about damn time. What the hell took you so long this time?"

"You said that last time," I said.

Lorraine followed me into the cottage, the two contractors behind her. It was a small cottage of stone walls with a stone fireplace against one wall. A warm fire of cut wood was ablaze and filled the little cottage with welcome heat in the early morning cold.

DuSomme spoke to the two bearded men in French. They seemed to complain, but they did go outside as DuSomme had apparently told them. They closed the door.

Other than a threadbare, stained, upholstered chair that Sandy sat in, there was no other furniture, yet it was crowded with the six of us. Manning and Phelps stood with their backs to the wall on either side of the door. DuSomme stood in the middle of the room, and Lorraine had moved close to the fireplace.

I went to Sandy and took her in my arms. "Are you OK?" I asked.

She dropped the tin cup of coffee to the floor. "Yeah," she whispered. "I just wish I knew what they wanted."

The air inside was warm but musty with age. Morning light was let in by two small windows of dirty glass. DuSomme stepped across the room, his feet kicking up dust from the bare wood floor. He handed a thick brown envelope to Manning and said, "Thank you. I will phone when I need you again."

Before the two could turn and leave the cottage I asked, "Why? I thought you worked for the Embassy?"

Phelps answered, "We work for whoever pays us." Manning looked at me and with a thin smile he winked. I had no idea what that meant.

The two walked away. It didn't surprise me that they had taken money from DuSomme. I've dealt with mercenaries before. Many are people who use their military skills to do what people cannot do for themselves. They fight wars that no one else would fight, to free people. But I have also met a few who fight only for money, willing to kill anyone for a price, willing to change sides in the middle of a battle for money.

When they were gone, DuSomme spoke to me, "You will stay here, Monsieur Crew, with your lovely wife. I am afraid this is the best accommodation I can supply for now. It will be for only a few days. You will have food and water . . . . But I'm afraid you will have to sleep on the floor. I apologize. I will have blankets brought to you."

He turned to Lorraine who had edged her way against the wall next to the door. He smiled and said, "You did very well following me, Mademoiselle. I almost didn't see you a couple of times there. You are very good."

Lorraine said nothing. The look on her face was completely blank, revealing nothing of what she was thinking.

"Please do not try to leave, Mademoiselle. The two men outside have no respect for women. They will kill you without a thought. And by the way, who are you . . . I mean really . . . Who are you?"

"I am only a friend of Germaine LeFont and LeRoy

Manns."

She didn't seem frightened of DuSomme. She was either crazy or maybe I could trust her . . . Maybe both. After all, the two Embassy contractors were not the ones I should have turned to. Who did I have left?

DuSomme grinned and shook his head at her answer. He said, "For now that will do. I do not have the time to find the truth. Soon I will have the time . . . And I will find out who you are. You will stay here, and I will decide what to do with you later."

He opened the door and said as he was leaving, "If you need something, ask the two men outside. They speak some French but no English I'm afraid." He closed the door, and I could hear a lock being snapped shut.

As the sun rose, it filled the little cottage with light, streaming through the two windows. Thin clouds of dust floated aimlessly in the sunbeams of light. The three of us wondered what we could do.

Lorraine seemed to be deep in thought. She walked back to the fireplace and leaned against the stone wall next to it. She lowered herself to the floor, pulling her knees up to her chin. She sat quietly as Sandy and I spoke of what had happened, what brought us to that place. I didn't mention what I had done for DuSomme, going to François DeLocke's home. Maybe, just maybe, Lorraine shouldn't know that.

I asked Lorraine, "You said DuSomme had plans to kill Manning and Phelps. What happened?"

"Money happened, Monsieur Crew. It is much easier to buy someone than to kill someone. One must dispose of bodies. It only takes money for the other. Those people, like others who kill for pay, can easily be bought by someone with the money to do so. Later they may yet be killed."

"And do you kill for pay?" I asked her. I was upset with Lorraine, and I still wondered if she could be trusted. She had led me into a trap.

"Monsieur Crew . . . Like you, I have been the killer when I had to kill. But like you . . . I hope . . . It is not to be enjoyed, oui? Other people . . . They hire themselves out to kill. And often they have the liking to do it."

My stomach was telling me I hadn't eaten anything in twenty-four hours. Sandy told me that the two guards standing outside would bring food if we asked. She spoke enough French to be able to get what she wanted. But that could wait.

I asked, "What happened to the woman DuSomme promised? He said a woman would guard you."

"Yeah, and you believed that? The man's a real bastard. I think he may be insane."

I was about to go to the door and call to the guards when Lorraine stopped me.

"Wait," she said, holding up her hand like a cop on the corner.

"Why?" I asked. "Aren't you hungry?"

"Wait," she repeated. "Stand away from the door, please."

Sandy stood from her chair, and she and I stepped to the corner furthest from the thick wooden door, holding onto each other. Something was going to happen. Thoughts ran through my mind as we waited. Sandy looked up at me, fear in her eyes. I hadn't before seen her frightened . . . At least as frightened as she was that day.

Time was frozen. Lorraine simply sat and smiled, her arms holding her knees to her chin. Then Sandy and I jumped at the sounds of four very quick gunshots, so fast they seemed to be fired all at once.

The door swung open, and a man walked in holding two very big semi-auto pistols, one in each hand. He wore a white shirt, the sleeves rolled up to his elbows. His blue jeans were old and worn at the cuffs and knees. His black hair was cropped close and a mustache crowned his upper lip.

I went to the open door and saw the two bearded guards lying dead on the ground. Their eyes were now merely holes; blood and brains streamed from the holes.

Lorraine stood and shook the man's hand. They spoke in what sounded like German. I asked Sandy if she understood what was being said.

"Not really," she said. "A word or two. But it sounds something like maybe Hebrew."

I interrupted their talk, "How the hell did he get here? How did he know where we were?"

"Monsieur Crew," Lorraine said, answering what to her was a stupid question. "Do not you remember that I dropped my cell phone outside? It is quite the easy thing to trace its location very quickly."

I asked Lorraine, "OK, just who the hell are you? And what just happened?"

"Mr. Crew," she said, ignoring what I had asked. "I have to leave you now. You and your wife may, of course, come with me and return to Paris if you wish. Or you may make your own way to wherever you wish." Her English was suddenly better. Very little accent covered her words. All I could think of was 'What the hell is going on here?'

"Wait a damn minute," I demanded. "Interpol doesn't go around killing people like . . . Like what just happened.

And I think you two were speaking Hebrew. And what the hell happened to your thick French accent? Who the hell are you, anyway?"

"It would be better if you don't know," Lorraine said. "If you want, I can take you back to Paris. What do you want to do, Mr. Crew?"

"I want to know the truth," I said. "So far everybody's been lying to me. You . . . DuSomme . . . The police . . . Even my own Embassy. All of a sudden you don't have any accent. People are being killed and I'm being used as a pawn. I want to know just what all the secrets are."

"And you have the secrets, too, Monsieur," Lorraine said, smiling, suddenly the French accent was back. "You know of things. Tell me."

Sandy pulled at my arm, backing away from Lorraine. She whispered to me, "Look, this woman seems to have saved us. I don't know who she is . . . And maybe that isn't important right now. If you know something, maybe you should just tell her. Maybe if it's really important she and whoever she's working for can handle it and we can go home."

That made a lot of sense to me. After all, who am I? If DuSomme, supposedly a professional hired killer, wants to kill some rich banker how could I stop him? Lorraine, as mysterious a woman as she was, seemed to be associated with someone . . . Some group or organization . . . Maybe even Israel . . . I might never know. Maybe Sandy was right. Let the professionals take care of the professionals.

Whomever she was with, they didn't seem to mind killing people. If that was the case, I thought, perhaps it would be best to tell her about DeLocke's chateau and what I thought was DuSomme's plan to murder him. It might be best to let her go off and kill DuSomme and save DeLocke.

Let her do whatever was needed. If she could kill DuSomme, well that's what I was in France for anyway.

Of course, I wanted to kill him myself. He had kidnapped Sandy and used her to make me case the chateau. He had really pissed me off. I wanted revenge for that and for LeRoy and the others. He had used me. But maybe that was not possible. DuSomme was a professional with what seemed to be an organization. I was alone. 'Let Lorraine do it' seemed like a good idea. She had some kind of organization, too.

Lorraine was standing in the open doorway. She was watching her killer-helper drag the bodies of the two guards behind the cottage. They would not be buried but left in the tall weeds for the birds and animals that would find them. I really didn't care.

Sandy and I went to her. I said, "Lorraine, I want to talk to you."

"Oui, it is best," she said, her French accent as strong as ever. I wondered what nationality she really was. She was a woman with a lot of secrets and apparently a lot of personalities.

I told her about DuSomme ordering me to go to François DeLocke's chateau and what he wanted me to find out. I left out nothing, and I added my opinion that DuSomme was going to murder DeLocke.

"And you did this, Monsieur? Why?" she asked, her tone telling me she did not believe I would do his work.

"He had Sandy and threatened her life," I explained. "I had no choice. The question is, why did he *want* me to do that? If he wanted to kill DeLocke, I'm sure he could do it without my help."

"Oui, that is true," she said. "But perhaps it is not this

Monsieur François he wishes to kill? Perhaps it is someone else?"

"Like who?" I asked. It made sense, of course. A man like Alain DuSomme could easily kill someone like François DeLocke. I had the feeling Lorraine already knew who DuSomme was targeting and it wasn't DeLocke. I added, "I wish you'd keep to one language lady. You're really confusing me." She laughed.

She began, "François DeLocke is the banker all over the world. There is one place he wishes to have his bank that he does not."

She smiled, waiting for me to ask. So I did, "OK, where?"

"That place is Iran. And Iran has not allowed his banks."

I looked at Sandy, and as usual she and I were in sync. She asked, "So DuSomme's pissed off at the Iranians? He's been hired to kill some Iranians? Who would hire him to do that?"

"No, Madame Crew. DuSomme has been hired to kill business people of Israel and Lebanon. For this Monsieur DeLocke will have his bank in Iran. Those two men outside now who are dead, they are Iranians, oui? They are Iran Revolutionary Guard Corps. They are bad men for the world."

Now I was really confused. I asked, "So you're saying Iran hired DuSomme to kill some . . . Some guys Iran hates? Why doesn't Iran do that itself? They must have soldiers and spies who can do that."

"Once again, I must say no," Lorraine said. "There is a group of very bad men. They have the name L'armée d'Allah . . . The Army of Allah. A silly name to be certain, but they are the most terrible of people. They have the approval of Iran and use money from Iran. They are French originally from Algeria, and they are Muslim. It is these people who have hired Alain."

Sandy and I looked at each other, both of our brains spinning around the grey fog that envelopes the world of spies and killers. For people who are not part of that world, it is not possible to break through that muddled curtain to understand the reason these people do something. So I said, "I don't get it. Is this all about Iran having plausible denial . . . Putting a buffer between Iran and the killings?"

"Oui, Monsieur," Lorraine answered. "This is correct, oui. The buffer as you say."

Sandy added, "All that may be true, but I'm still confused. Can these business people be all that important?"

Lorraine smiled and nodded. She said, "Oui, it is natural. What happens in the world often is very . . . étrange . . . What is the word?"

Sandy offered, "Strange. You mean what is going on is strange. And I think you knew that. English isn't that tough for you."

"Oui, it is strange. Now, do we take you to Paris?"

Sandy and I looked at each other, neither one of us knowing what to do. But in my mind I knew what had to be done. I was once again in the swamp, with my ass surrounded by alligators. There was no way out for me. I had to accept that. This very, very strange woman might be my only source, my only way of getting to DuSomme. I had no idea who she was, and I couldn't bring myself to trust her.

I asked Sandy, "What do you think?"

"I think we need to get on the first plane home. This is a morass that we should have no part in."

"I think you're right," I said. I turned to Lorraine and said, "Take Sandy to the airport and put her on the first flight out. Make sure she gets on the plane safely. Drop me at The Ritz. I have no place else to go. And I need a gun. Can you arrange that?"

"Wait a damn minute, Morgan," Sandy said with anger in her voice. I'd heard that anger before. Every time I decide to face some kind of danger, she wants me to run away. And that little voice in the back of my head had joined in her chorus, yelling, "RUN AWAY! RUN AWAY!"

"Sandy, I need to stay here awhile longer. It's what I came here for."

She pushed me away and said, "No you didn't! You and Bob came here to go to a funeral, nothing more! All that's over with! Now let's go home!"

"You know I can't," I said. "You know what I have to do."

"You mean you want to kill that DuSomme guy? That's what you mean?"

"I have to at least stay here long enough to know that he can't kill anyone else, Sandy," I pleaded. "After all he's done . . . I have to."

"No you don't have to!" she demanded. "Let the professionals do what they need to do. Let this crazy woman . . . Whoever the hell she is . . . Do it. You're coming home with me before you get yourself killed!"

It took some arguing with Lorraine standing aside, enjoying every minute of it. Sandy threatened to not be home whenever I got home . . . If I ever got home she added pointedly . . . If I stayed and tried to kill DuSomme. I knew it was only a threat . . . A threat to be honest I'd never heard before. She had never threatened to leave me before. She was frightened, more frightened than I had ever seen her.

It took a lot of tears and hard words, but Sandy did fly home leaving me in Paris. The reasons I used to convince her were simple enough. We had our daughter, Caroline, at home, and Alain DuSomme had really pissed me off.

****

I stood and watched the jet take off, carrying Sandy away from me. It was my fault for having her come to France in the first place. Had I not done that, looking foolishly for a translator who I could have hired somewhere, she would never have fallen into the hands of Alain DuSomme. She had been his captive for weeks while I did what I thought I had to do to free her. As bad a man as Alain DuSomme seemed to be, he had kept his word, and Sandy was not harmed during her time as his prisoner.

As I watched the plane rise into the clouds I said a silent prayer of thanks to God for allowing no harm to come to her. I cannot imagine life without Sandy. And as I prayed the thought raced through my mind that if I didn't kill DuSomme, if he killed me, would Sandy be able to imagine life without me.

Lorraine and her gunman were waiting for me in the parking lot at Charles De Gaulle Airport. It was mid-afternoon, and a light rain was falling as usual – springtime in Paris – when I left the terminal and walked to their waiting car. I slid into the back seat of the black Mercedes. Lorraine and her gunman were in the front seat, the engine of the Mercedes running to keep the chill of Paris springtime away.

And lying on the seat as I got in the car was a pistol, a Glock 9MM.

"Where do you wish to go?" Lorraine asked from the front seat without turning to look at me. Her gunman-partner was behind the wheel, the engine purring lightly.

"I need a driver," I said. "Someone who speaks English and knows Paris and all the rest of France."

"That can be arranged," she answered.

"Thank you for the gun. I'll need extra clips and ammo."

"That can be arranged."

"And I need a place to sleep. I can't go back to The Ritz. DuSomme will be looking for me there."

"That also can be arranged," she said.

"And I need one more thing."

"What is that, Monsieur?"

"I need to know who you are. Interpol? Mossad? Or what? I know you're not some petty thief and gay partner of Germaine LeFont. And I know that French accent of yours is a phony. So who are you?"

Lorraine turned and looked at me for a moment without saying anything. She turned away and said, "That, Monsieur, is something you cannot know for now, oui? Perhaps at some day to come . . . But not for now." I guess she was going to hold onto the accent for a while. Maybe she enjoyed it.

"OK," I said, accepting that for the time being. "So are you going to kill DuSomme?"

Without answering my question she asked, "I think perhaps you wish to do the killing of Monsieur DuSomme?

Is that not true?"

She wasn't going to tell me what she was going to do. Was she going to stop DuSomme from killing DeLocke, if that was his plan? That was the obvious thing, but in the dark world of killers and spies, the obvious was not always what would happen.

Would she be sure the 'business' at DeLocke's chateau would succeed or fail? It was easy enough to speculate that Lorraine would be the one to kill DeLocke and the others. As easy as it was to speculate that she would save them. I had no idea, and she wasn't going to tell me.

Once again I had no choice but to accept secrets. Once again I was embroiled in a world I knew little about. But I was learning. Even though I was looked upon as a child playing a man's game, I would use what I had. I would use these people every way I could. I would take from them what I could, and in doing so I would do what I had to do.

Alain DuSomme, I had learned, was a professional killer. If I were to stop . . . Somehow . . . His planned murder of François DeLocke and whoever he was hosting at the chateau, for whatever business reason they might have, and allow DuSomme to live, he would be a danger to my family and me. If he lived, and I was able to stop his planned murders, he would hunt Sandy and me any place in the world we might go.

And then there were the murders of all those people starting with LeRoy Manns and the kidnapping of my wife. It had to be done if for no other reason than vengeance.

I had one ace up my sleeve. DuSomme's bank accounts. I could drain them and leave him broke. But would that stop him from coming after me?

No, Alain DuSomme had to die. That was the only

way to protect my family. Whether Lorraine did that or I did that really made no difference. He had to die.

After these few moments of thinking, as the Mercedes pulled from the parking lot and drove from the airport, I asked, "So you have a place I can stay?"

"So you will not answer my question? You will try to kill him then? I will leave you to that. Oui, Monsieur Crew," Lorraine answered with an overly dramatic sigh. "There is a place. It is not what perhaps you are used to, but it will be safe, oui?"

"And the extra ammunition?" I asked.

"In the place you may sleep . . . There is a box. It has in it what you need, Monsieur. Do you need to know how to load the clips?"

"I am familiar with how to do it."

"Très bien. It is in a drawer beside the bed, oui?"

"And from now on I'm on my own?" I asked.

"It is true," Lorraine answered, with a slight grin. I hope she was telling the truth. "We will take you there, to the house where you may stay, and say au revoir."

"I won't see you again?" I asked.

"You will not," she said. "I will go to say the prayer at your funeral."

"My funeral?"

"Oui, Monsieur DuSomme will put the bullet in your head I think."

❋❋❋❋❋❋❋❋❋❋❋❋❋❋

The 'safe-house' Lorraine took me to was a long, deserted, auto mechanic's garage with broken windows on a deserted side road in a part of Paris I had never been in, and I would bet few other people would ever venture into. As I got out of the car I asked where I was. Lorraine and her driver laughed as they sped away without telling me anything.

A tall sliding door seemed to be the only entrance to my new, temporary home. I struggled to open it on its rusting steel wheels. Inside it was dark and smelled like overripe garbage, oil, and dirt. I left the door open to get some fresh air inside.

I found a single light bulb hanging from the ceiling. I couldn't find a wall switch, but I found that the bulb was loose in its socket. Twisting it caused the bulb to come to life, and the garage was lit a little.

At the back of the garage was a green door of cracked wood hanging open. Inside was a toilet that needed cleaning badly. It was hidden in a small closet that passed for a W/C. A room only slightly larger, without a door, was next to it. That appeared to be my bedroom. A bare mattress, stained and dirty, lay on the floor. On a table next to the mattress was a single burner hot plate without a pot or pan to be used on it. On a small table next to it was a lamp without a shade. I lit the lamp's dim bulb to light the room. And there was the drawer in the table holding the lamp Lorraine had said would hold the ammunition I felt I needed. It was the only drawer next to the 'bed', so it had to be it.

I opened the drawer, and inside I found two oil stained

boxes of French bullets. I couldn't read the writing on the boxes, but I did see the 9mm printed on each. The boxes themselves were old. I hoped the bullets inside weren't too old. There were two extra clips for the Glock.

So this was where Lorraine thought I could live while doing what I had to do? It might have been called a 'safe-house' by some people, but it wasn't what I expected. Staying there for however long it took to kill DuSomme might kill me.

I took the two clips and the two boxes of bullets with me, deciding that was not the place for me to stay. As I turned to leave that place a rat as big as a cat ran across the oil and dirt covered floor. It stopped me before I could leave, standing in my path, up on its haunches, waving its fists at me, challenging me to a fight maybe. I considered shooting the damn thing, but that would only draw someone's attention. I stamped my feet a couple of times and yelled at it. It ran away and so did I.

FIFTEEN - Mickey

The light spring rain had let up, but the sky, black with the threat of more rain, darkened the afternoon streets. I had no idea where I was so I just walked. To feel a little safe I kept my hand on the Glock inside my jacket pocket. I was wearing the same grey checked sport coat and black pants I had worn for two days. My clothes smelled and were wet from the rain. But that was the last thing on my mind.

Where could I go? Except for the clothes on my back, everything I had was at the suite at The Ritz. DuSomme would certainly be watching there, waiting for me. I could risk it, I suppose, maybe going there late at night or early in the morning. That would be a last resort.

I had cash and my credit cards so I could buy what I needed, but where would I sleep? I turned a few corners, hoping to find a major street with some kind of hotel. The area of Paris I was in was old and mainly decrepit, made up of factories and buildings that had been deserted years ago. No people were on the streets, no cops anywhere. The rare car or truck passed by as if I were invisible.

Turning yet another corner, I came to a sudden stop at a Paris taxi parked at the curb a half block away. A Black man, a really fat Black man with a thick, full beard and thick, black rimmed glasses, leaned against the taxi's front door. The rear door hung open over the sidewalk.

"Hey man!" the Black man said, calling to me as I

stood trying to decide if I should run or pull the Glock to warn him. He was smiling broadly showing off big yellow teeth. "You gonna' git you'self soaked any time now, man. Gonna' rain like shit pretty soon. Looks like you needs this here taxi."

He was dressed in blue jean bib-overalls and a white flannel shirt that was hanging untucked on his right side. His shoes were white Nikes and looked brand new.

I walked to the man and the taxi, ready to draw the pistol if I needed it. "Were you waiting here for something?" I asked.

"Yes, sir," he said brightly. "Us Yanks gots t'stick t'gether. I been waiting here f'you."

"You were waiting for me?"

"Ain't you Morgan Crew? Lorraine, she done tol' me t' take care a'you. Come on an' get in. I gots this place you can stay. Better than that ol' trash place she dropped you at. She was just jokin' wit' you 'bout that. She a real funny lady, that one."

I got in the taxi, and what I hoped was my new friend sped away. He drove fast, too fast to make me feel comfortable, taking corners on screeching tires, tossing me around in the back seat. He turned his head slightly to say to me, "I bet you hungry, ain't you?"

"Who are you?" I asked.

"Name's Mickey," he answered.

"You're American," I said, more of a statement than a question.

"Yeah, you bet," he said. "Love 'Merica! You bet! Best place in the whole damn world!"

"Why are you here? I mean, in France."

"Can't go back," he said. "Done kind'a dropped outta' the Army one day. They's wan' me t'go to that damn Eye-rack. I ain't gonna' git my ass shot off fo' nobody. Got here . . . Changed my name . . . Got me a good woman."

"And Lorraine sent you?" I asked as he sped through the City.

"She says she tol' you 'bout a driver can speaks French. Well that be me, Morgan. S'alright I calls you Morgan?"

"And you can speak French?" I asked, just a little misbelief hiding behind the words.

"Peoples says I speaks French better'n English. Guess they right," he laughed. "I gots me this here S'othen ways of talkin' English. I done learn French the proper way."

"So, Mickey, you work with Lorraine?" I asked although I assumed he did.

"Yeah, man. 'Course I do. Now's an' then I suppose. Hey, you got that gun?"

Not being sure who this man was I chose not to answer. I felt the weight of the gun tucked in the pocket of my wet jacket.

"What do you do for Lorraine?" I asked instead of answering him.

"Drive, man. What you think?"

I had to know more about this man before I trusted him. He could be anyone . . . He could be working for DuSomme . . . He could be one of the duplicitous contractors from the Embassy.

"Are you armed, Mickey?"

He laughed. Instead of answering me he said, "Got

me a woman, but me and her, we ain't ready fo' no damn weddin' yet. We got two kids, though. Nice kids. I suspects they would like t'see a weddin'."

I asked, "So who is this Lorraine Demeaux?"

"She a woman, man. She gots money t'hand out. What's mo' ya' gotta' knows?"

I was quiet for a moment or two and then decided to push. I needed to know who I was dealing with.

"Is she Interpol? . . . Mossad? . . . What?" I asked.

Mickey laughed but didn't answer. I asked, "She puts on a French accent, doesn't she? Do you know why?"

"Man," Mickey said. He shook his head and almost laughed, but he didn't. "You gotta' watch you'self, man. You inta' stuff you ain't gonna' like too much. Better you stay not knowin', man."

"Do you know Alain DuSomme?" I asked.

"Sure . . . 'Course . . . Me an' the ol'lady goes to his club now an' then. Fine place that."

"Tell me about him."

"Nah, man. You best stay 'way from that man. He a real bad ass motha'."

OK, so I was to be kept in the dark. I knew little of the people I was dealing with. And because of that I could trust no one. I wasn't about to trust Mickey. He was too convenient, too evasive, and too coincidental. And I have learned the hard way to never believe in coincidences. They don't exist in the real world. I was on my own once again.

Mickey drove on in silence, slowing down as we got into more populated areas. We said nothing for almost ten minutes until he stopped the taxi, pulling to the curb in a fairly nice section of the city.

Small shops lined the street on both sides. Two boulangeries on opposite sides of the street seemed to be in competition. A wine shop had a window full of bottles of red wine. A women's clothing store had two mannequins in its window, one fully dressed in a nice, summery blue dress, the other naked. The neighborhood looked like a nice, middle class place.

"This here is my place . . . Upstairs I means," he said, pointing above the dress shop. "Ya'll can stay here f'while if you'se wants. We got's some room."

A nice looking restaurant and a coffee shop were on the street just steps from Mickey's little third floor apartment. Three big windows up at his home faced the street. They had lace curtains across them and lights were on inside. The streets were clean, and they were filled with happy people shopping.

When we got out of the taxi I could immediately smell the bread baking in the boulangeries. Mickey led me up the brightly lit blue carpeted stairs and to his apartment door which was painted a bright red. He stepped aside to let me walk in.

It was a small place but nicely decorated and clean. A woman was in the kitchen as we walked in. She was white, tall and thin. She wore a flowery house dress, and she was barefooted. Her brown hair was thick and curly and pulled up on top of her head. She wasn't pretty, but she was attractive in her own way, and she smiled happily to see Mickey.

"Bonjour, mon cher," she said, not stopping stirring the pot of wonderfully aromatic cassoulet of some kind on the stove. It would cook there the rest of the day until supper that evening, filling the home with wonderful aromas.

"Hey, babe," Mickey said. "I got us a house guest here."

****

Mickey showed me to a bedroom where his two children sat in the lower of the bunkbeds along one wall. "This here is Billy," he said pointing to the boy of the two children. "He the oldest so's I give him a 'Merican name. An' my sweet little girl there is Monet. Named her after that painter guy who did all them's pictures and shit."

A thin daybed was against the opposite wall. "Ya'll can sleep there," Mickey said. "It ain't much, but a sight better than that ol' shitty garage."

Following Mickey back to the tiny kitchen, I sat at their small table and enjoyed a cup of very good coffee. "You wants a sandwich or sump'tin?" Mickey asked. Because of exhaustion, food didn't sound good. I finished the coffee and went to the day bed where I slept the afternoon away. Sleep was peaceful without nightmares, and I awoke refreshed and feeling a lot better than I had in days.

Dinner was the cassoulet of wonderfully seasoned pork and vegetables that had been simmering on the little stove when I arrived there. True, in France a cassoulet was for centuries 'poor folks' food, but it had matured over the years into a dish relished by everyone, especially foreign visitors who wished to brag back home about the 'gourmet' food they enjoyed on their week in Paris.

Mickey and his woman, who he introduced as Lilly,

treated me to a second bottle of really good red wine, not a labeled vintage wine, but a really good wine of the people. They each lit a cigarette, offering one to me which I politely declined.

Conversation over dinner and coffee was about Paris, sites to be seen and little known museums and restaurants to be enjoyed. Mickey translated some of what I said; Lilly understood some English. After an hour or so the pleasantries slowed to an end and I said, "I'm going to step outside and make a phone call."

"You be careful out there, man," Mickey said in a dreamy voice filtered by a lot of wine.

I nodded, touched the gun tucked in at my waist under my jacket, and rose from the chair at the table. It was dark outside as I looked for a quiet place to phone Sandy using my cell phone. The street was busy with locals shopping and enjoying the neighborhood's food and wine.

The streets were lined with three and four story buildings, the upper floors being the homes to locals. Each home seemed to have a small terrace from one or more windows, wrought iron railing lining them. And from almost every railing a planter box had been hung, each containing colorful flowers hanging from them. They made the streets look like gardens. I remember wishing I had had a camera with me.

I phoned our home line and Sandy picked up the phone on the second ring. She had made it home safely and told me Caroline, our daughter, was demanding that I come home, too.

"Tell her I'll be there as soon as I can. She's old enough to understand the things I need to do."

She had no answer for that. Sandy knew what my life

is all about. And she knew that sooner or later Caroline would have to know, also.

We talked for a few minutes, the weather in California being better than in Paris, although the evening I phoned from a street corner was clear and dry, the sky dotted with thousands of stars, the moon almost full and very bright.

We spoke for a few minutes about how quiet San Marcos is compared to the bustle of Paris. Our home, in the hills above the harbor of San Marcos, California, is a quiet little town . . . Until murders occur or until criminals invade. But I love it there and would never move away. In the back of my mind I hoped silently that I would see it and my family again.

It was almost 9 PM, but I trusted that the Paris Police worked late. After speaking with Sandy for a full ten minutes, I phoned the Police Headquarters, and with some language difficulty I was transferred to Inspector Renard.

"Inspector," I said, my voice revealing how unsure I was doing what I was doing. "This is Morgan Crew."

"Oui, Monsieur Crew," he said, sounding surprised. "I was told you went home."

"My wife did," I said. "I stayed."

"For why?"

"As I told you, I need to find out who killed LeRoy Manns and why he was killed."

"That is a job of the police, Monsieur. It is not for you to do."

"Look, Inspector, I don't want to argue with you. My Government and yours have approved my doing what I want to do. So putting that aside, what have you learned about the murder of Officer Marie St. John?"

"And this you know it is murder?" Renard asked suspiciously. "How do you know this?"

"I'm just asking, Inspector . . . Speculating I guess. She was killed the same way and in the same place as LeRoy Manns. I don't believe in coincidences, Inspector. Do you?"

"Coincidence? . . . What is coincidence, s'il vous plaît?"

"Two similar things happening by chance . . . Not related."

"I see . . . What I know you cannot know. Perhaps some time but not now."

That answer told me that he knew her death was murder, even if he didn't mean to tell me. He refused to answer my question, telling me he actually, without saying so, thought the two murders were connected. If he knew they weren't he would have told me. His silence was his answer.

I touched the 'end call' button on the cell phone without a goodbye to the cop.

The meal at Mickey's was good and filled the empty space in my stomach. I needed to add a drink to it. There was a bar on the opposite side of the street at the far corner, so I went there.

It seems the French knew the word whiskey. The bartender, a bald headed man with a pock marked face and a protruding gut that he seemed to be proud of, smiled and poured what I recognized as an off brand of scotch into a short glass. He held up a glass pitcher of water as if asking me if I wanted to ruin the already not-too-good scotch. I said 'no', a word I guess the French understood.

As I was on my second scotch I heard sirens outside.

They were easy to recognize as Paris police sirens, strange wailings up and down, and ear piercing. I turned from the bar and looked out the window at the street. The police cars, three of them, stopped across the street and at the far corner, near Mickey's apartment.

Throwing down the last of the bitter whiskey, I got up and walked outside. Police were surrounding Mickey's building, some running inside, some staying outside to keep the growing crowd away.

I walked toward the crowd, slowly so as not to attract attention. My cell phone rang so I stopped and answered the call while no one was watching me, their attention on the fleet of cop cars and cops rushing around looking very efficient.

The voice on the phone was muffled and whispered. It could have been a man's voice but maybe not. It could have been a woman using a cloth over the phone to mask her voice. The voice said, "Mickey is dead. You are next. Go home." The line went dead.

I stood there, a half block away, until the crowds started to walk away, bored with the show of routine police work. Two black plastic wrapped bodies were taken from the building and slid into a white ambulance. Then the crowd came running back to see what was happening. All but one of the police cars drove away with the ambulance, quietly, without sirens blaring.

Left standing on the sidewalk in front of Mickey's apartment building were two uniformed cops and two plane clothes detectives. They stood together talking, three smoking. A car pulled to the curb at my side as I watched the four cops. I turned to look at it as the driver's side window rolled down. It was Inspector Renard.

"Monsieur Crew," he greeted me with a not-too-friendly look on his face. "Why are you here?"

"Just rubber necking, Inspector," I said. I bent down so I could look directly at the Inspector.

"Rubber necking?" he asked.

"Yeah," I said. "Just watching. Like everybody else."

"Oui, I understand. But why are you here? Why are you at this street?"

"I was at that bar," I said, pointing at the bar behind me where I had the mediocre scotch.

Renard looked at me, suspicion masking his face. "Monsieur," he started. "Paris has many . . . How you say? . . . Les tavernes . . . Why do you choose this one?"

"I don't know. I was just walking around. You know, touristy stuff."

He didn't say anything, so I asked, "What happened?"

"Two people were killed."

"Oh really? Who?" I forced myself to sound disassociated and curious.

"A black American and a woman," he said.

My stomach turned and I almost spit up the whiskey. Mickey and Lilly. How about the two children? I had to ask. I swallowed hard and asked, "That's weird. Anybody else?"

Renard looked at me suspiciously again. I felt my face losing color, and I felt cold wipe over me. I think he saw this. He asked, "And why is it I think you know?"

"Hey, just asking. You know . . . Just curious." I forced a smile and put my hands in my pants pockets to keep them from shaking. I felt the sweat beading on my forehead. I wanted to wipe it away but I didn't. It would have told the Inspector too much.

He said, "There were two children. They were not hurt. A neighbor has taken them."

"Oh really?" I said trying to sound as innocent as I could.

He asked, "I think perhaps you know of these killings, no?"

"The short answer is *no* Inspector. As I said, I was just having a drink across the street, that's all."

Renard quietly stared at me without blinking. It was a frightening glare. He knew, but he could not prove it, and he could not pull me into police headquarters for three or four days of questioning. Our two Governments had said he could not do that.

I had run into cops like Renard all over the world. Tough and dangerous, smart and hard working. They had instincts that the average person didn't have. He knew I wasn't telling him everything I knew, and I knew I wasn't going to tell him everything I knew. I was alone, on my own; I had no one I could trust.

Finally Renard said, "Monsieur Crew. I advise you to be the most careful person. You are in the greatest danger, oui? You do not know the people around you, oui?"

"Thank you for the advice, Inspector. I will be very careful. By the way, have you taken DuSomme in for questioning yet?"

Without answering me he pulled away from the curb. He made a quick U-turn, stopped at the police standing on the street at Mickey's home, spoke with them, and then drove away quickly.

I stayed on the corner watching the crime scene like

any good, curious, uninvolved person would do. There were still the four cops across the street watching me, obviously having taken instructions from Renard, and I didn't want them coming after me. I didn't want to look suspicious.

After what I thought was a safe time, I turned and walked away slowly. I turned twice to look behind me, to see if the four cops across the street were following me. They weren't, and I felt good about that.

I knew nothing of French police operations and French law. It could be they had no reason to come after me . . . And it could have been the deal the U.S. made with France. Whatever it was, I was being left to work on my own.

Mickey was dead. He and his woman were dead because of me. Guilt was rushing through me. They would be alive had it not been for me.

It hit me as I walked slowly through the unfamiliar streets that Lorraine had arranged for Mickey to meet me. Or had she? I had only Mickey's word for that. He could have taken me to his home on orders from DuSomme as well as Lorraine . . . Or anybody else. I didn't know and I had no way of learning the truth. Once again the fog of the un-reality of the world these people live in confused me terribly.

I was alone again. And I had no idea where I was. Walking a few blocks away, I found a small hotel that had a book store next to it. It was still open at nearly ten that evening. In the book store I found a street map of Paris which I bought. The old man in the bookstore looked wonderingly at me and helped me count out the Euro coins for the purchase. He rattled things off in French that I nodded to and smiled at, not having any idea what he was saying. And with only a little bit of trouble I was able to get a room in the hotel next door for the night.

I had planned to open the map in the room to find out where I was, but exhaustion, probably mental exhaustion rather than physical exhaustion, and the nagging guilt I felt at Mickey and Lilly's deaths, caught up with me. I found my hands shaking, and I was sweating. I needed to lie down. Bourbon would be good, but there wasn't any, of course.

The bed in the room was small and lumpy, but I fell asleep fast on it, without stripping off my clothes or shoes. My dreams were filled with Sandy and San Marcos. They were pleasant dreams but were suddenly interrupted by the red curtain of blood and murders all around me and the people who lived double and triple lives that were filled with lies.

A bright and warm sun, filtering in through the room's only window, covered by a yellowed lace curtain, woke me. My wristwatch said it was a quarter past eight. My head was clear, and my thinking was whiskey free. I realized upon waking that whoever had killed Mickey and Lilly . . . And my money was on DuSomme . . . Had been after me. But how did he know where I was? Someone had told him. But who? Did DuSomme have such a wide organization that he knew everything . . . Everywhere?

My stomach twisted as the thought came to me that maybe Mickey worked for DuSomme. When DuSomme came to his apartment to kill me, maybe he was just angry at Mickey letting me walk away when I was supposed to be there to be killed? Could DuSomme be that insane?

I sat on the bed thinking, rubbing the sleep from my eyes.

A bathroom was located down the hall past three other rooms. In there I splashed cold water on my face and decided that I had to take a chance and return to The Ritz. It was time for me to stop playing it safe. I had to be aggressive or I would be waiting around for someone to put a bullet in my head. Who else would have to die because of me? I had to bring it to an end.

My hand went to the small of my back, feeling the Glock resting under my belt. There were fifteen rounds of 9MM in the pistol, and I had the two boxes of bullets and two empty clips. I was glad I had the spare clips because taking time to reload a clip was death waiting for me. In any kind of battle I would need the extra clips.

But then, if I killed DuSomme I would be arrested and either spend the rest of my life in a French prison . . . Or do they still use the guillotine? The hard way would be to prove DuSomme killed my friend, Leroy Manns . . . And maybe stop him from killing the people at François DeLocke's chateau. Would a French court and jury convict him on what evidence I could collect? Probably not. To put an end to DuSomme, I had to kill him and somehow get away with it.

I mean, why not? I looked at myself in the cracked mirror of the tiny bathroom in the cheap hotel and asked, "Why not?"

Outside, I walked a couple of blocks and finally found a taxi. I was further away from The Ritz than I had imagined. The Taxi pulled under the portico and the doorman opened the door for me. I looked around before getting out, just maybe seeing someone waiting for me. The doorman recognized me but obviously wondered about the dirty and wrinkled clothes I had been wearing and sleeping in for several days. My hand went to my chin, and I felt the stubble that had been unshaven for too long. I figured I looked like some hobo off the streets.

I got out and walked quickly into the hotel, almost running to the elevators, and up to the eighth floor where my suite waited for me. When the elevator doors slid open I peered out, into the hallway, my hand on the Glock in my jacket pocket. The hallway was deserted as far as I could tell.

Making sure the door to the suite was still locked, I opened it and walked in carefully, the Glock in my hand, ready to shoot. The suite looked the same; it had been kept clean waiting for my return. The little red light on the telephone wasn't blinking – no one had left a message for me. I locked the door behind me and put the little chain in place, even though it would not stop anyone who really wanted to get into the suite.

I went from room to room and looked in every closet, behind the drapes, even going so far as looking under the beds in each bedroom. It was crazy, I know, but I knew I was alone, and I felt somewhat safe for the first time in days.

I went to the big bedroom, stripped off the clothes I had worn for too long, stepped into the big shower and stood under the steaming hot water for a long time. The water stung magnificently. After shaving the two days of stubble off my face I ordered breakfast from room service and called to have my clothes taken for dry cleaning. And since Sandy wasn't there I ordered everything that she wouldn't let me eat, bacon and sausage and croissants and eggs and thick butter. And of course a big pot of strong coffee. It was great.

After breakfast I sat in the biggest, softest chair the suite had to offer. The thick cotton robe the hotel provided was warming and comforting. My mind raced around all the things I *wanted* to do, but I couldn't grasp onto *how* I would do those things. My eyes went to the suite's bar. It was too early for bourbon, and I needed a clear mind, not one softened by booze. I needed information but had no one to go to for that information . . . Well almost no one.

There was Mary Huntington at the American Embassy. She had come to my suite with armed civilian contractors. She was nothing but a low level translator . . . So she said . . . But she might be able to give me what I needed. I had to worry about the two contractors, Manning and Phelps. If they were working for DuSomme, was Mary Huntington working for him, too?

I picked up the phone and dialed the Embassy. Going through the usual bureaucracy, I was finally connected with her.

"Good morning, Ms. Huntington," I said as cheerfully as I could. "This is Morgan Crew."

She said nothing.

"I said good morning," I repeated. "Can you hear me?"

"Where are you?" she asked very seriously.

"In my suite at The Ritz. But you'll know that by tracing the call if you don't have caller ID. I have a hunch your real office is bigger and better than the one I was in with you. And it probably has all kinds of electronics like caller I.D. And if you're planning on sending those two goons out to get me, I am armed and I will kill people if I need to."

She said nothing once again.

"Are you angry with me, Ms. Huntington?" I asked somewhat jokingly.

Again, she said nothing.

"Look," I said. "If you're calling the police go ahead. I won't be here when they get here."

"I'm not phoning the police, Mr. Crew. You have too much pull all the way back to D.C. Why are you calling me?"

"I have two questions, and you are the only person I know who can answer those questions."

"And what are those questions?"

"Those two contract security people . . . Manning and Phelps. Do they work for you?"

She was silent once again.

"Am I wasting my time?" I asked. "Do I need to make an overseas call to some people in Washington?"

"Mr. Manning and Mr. Phelps are . . . On temporary assignment. And I am merely a translator."

"That's bullshit, Ms. Huntington. You're more than that. You and I both know that."

"I am a translator, Mr. Crew. Anything else I do is none of your business."

"What the hell does that mean? Who are they working for?"

"I can't answer that, Mr. Crew. If you are on a first name basis with the President of the United States, perhaps he can order me to tell you. Other than that . . . I can't tell you."

"OK," I had to accept what she said. I was alone and I had to work with what I had, which was nothing so far. I asked, "François DeLocke is hosting some people at his home soon. I need to know who these people are and when they will be at DeLocke's."

"Why?" she asked.

"I can't tell you."

I added with as much mockery in my voice as possible, "Unless, that is, you are on a first name basis with the President of the United States. You can phone him and he can order me to tell you." I just love being nasty to people who have too much authority in their own minds.

She said nothing again. I was getting tired of holding the phone to my ear while she refused to speak. I felt the anger rising in me. If Sandy were there she would have taken the phone from me and by being nice and polite, she would have found out what I needed to know. But Sandy wasn't there.

I took a deep breath and tried to sound conciliatory. "Look, I'm sorry I have to bother you with this, but you're the only one who can help me. You must know that there are important people meeting at DeLocke's. And you must know that there is going to be trouble there. I have an idea when, but I don't know who. Please . . . Please help me."

"Why do you want to know this?" she asked. "Do you think you can do what other people can't? Are you some kind of Superman?"

It was my turn to try silence. I waited as patiently as I could manage. Finally, Huntington said, exasperation in her voice, "Representatives of the Government of Israel and the Government of Lebanon are meeting to discuss a trade deal between the two Countries. That's all I can tell you."

That cleared up a lot of confusion in my mind. If Israel could be friends with yet another Arab Country, it would be a big step toward peace in the Middle East. It also cleared up the 'why' about DuSomme being so interested in DeLocke's home. He needed to know how to get in and how to get out, and when the meeting would take place. I had, unfortunately, gotten all that for him without knowing the depth of the danger. Now I had to stop him.

And of course, if Mary Huntington was telling the truth, François DeLocke had a personal interest in the success of such a meeting and trade deal. I assumed his bank would be financing much of the deal between Israel and Lebanon. So he offered his chateau as a place to meet and discuss the deal in return for . . . For what?

Lorraine had said he wanted to have his bank operate inside Iran. And the deal would assure that. What the hell? How could a business deal between Israel and Lebanon get DeLocke's bank into Iran? I couldn't tell who was lying and who was telling the truth. The world of spooks and spies and killers had nothing to do with truth. Maybe both people were lying? All I could do was try to stop DuSomme from killing whoever he was going to kill.

"OK. And when will this meeting take place?" I asked.

I could hear her sigh deeply before saying, "They are there now." So I was wrong. DeLocke had lied to me. She paused again and then asked, "What are you going to do?"

I answered, "Like you, Ms. Huntington, I can't tell you that."

"You know you're going to get yourself killed, don't you? You're being very stupid, Mr. Crew. There are things in motion, and when you interfere you will be hurt."

"Who is going to hurt me, Ms. Huntington? When we hang up are you going to report to Alain DuSomme? Are you working for him? Are you going to send Manning and Phelps after me again?"

The phone line went dead. She had hung up on me. She would be reporting the phone call to someone . . . But to whom?

SIXTEEN - Rescue

Working with the hotel's concierge desk I was able to rent a Mercedes with a built-in GPS. I would need that if I were to be my own chauffeur. The last time I had seen DeLocke, I had taken a jet to his 'castle', as he referred to his home. This time I would drive, so I would have some freedom of movement . . . And perhaps surprise anyone I would meet there.

I tossed a small overnight bag into the rear seat of the rental and slid the Glock, the two spare clips that I had loaded and the two boxes of ammo into the glove box. Using the GPS, programmed to speak to me in English, I made it out of the heavy Paris traffic without too much trouble and onto the less crowded highways leading to the French Alps and DeLocke's chateau.

At the hotel's gift shop I had purchased a small book of English / French translations. I used my Black Amex card to get a cash advance of 5000 Euros, cash enough to last the few days I would need to bring Alain DuSomme to one end or the other, either death or jail.

With all that at hand I drove toward the mountains that held François' chateau. The weather to the east was sunny and dry, better than it was in Paris. It was a long drive. I was tired by the time I reached a little village about twenty miles from François' chateau. I found a small Inn, grey brick and covered in vines flowering in bright red. I stopped there to enjoy good, local wines and meats and cheese. I had to keep my strength up, yet I hoped I wouldn't get there too late.

Using the translation book, I managed to get a room at the Inn overlooking the one road into and out of the village, perfect for seeing someone come after me before they could see me. I needed time to rest and think . . . And gather my courage. That damn little voice in the back of my head was screaming at me to "GET AWAY! GET AWAY!"

I sat on the bed, which was quite soft and comfortable, and smiled, trying to push the fear behind me. But that smile disappeared quickly when my mind went to work. I was twenty miles from François DeLocke and the people meeting at his chateau. I was twenty miles from where DuSomme would kill. Just what the hell would I do? The question ran through my mind alongside that damn little voice in the back recesses of my mind, shouting *"Run away! Run away!"*

Was he there already and had he killed the people there? I went downstairs to the Inn's front desk, and using the little book of translations I was able to phone DeLocke's chateau. A woman answered the phone, the young woman who had greeted me at the door when I was last there. She didn't sound panicked, so I assumed DuSomme had not arrived there yet. I hung up without saying anything.

I knew I had to put a stop to DuSomme, but I had no idea how to do that. My hand went to the Glock pistol resting at the small of my back. If it was simply murder, I debated whether or not I could do that. LeRoy Manns was a friend but not a close friend, whom I hadn't seen in decades. Others had died at DuSomme's hands. DuSomme had kidnapped my wife and held her. These things needed to be answered for.

Revenge . . . I tried to remember the old saying from

somewhere . . . Revenge is a dish best served cold. Or something like that. So, if I had no choice, I would murder DuSomme and worry about what that act brought on later. I had an army of lawyers to work for me. Maybe I could stay out of jail. I had killed and walked free before. Maybe I could do it again.

I paced around the bedroom, thinking, trying to make a plan. How could I stop him? I could wait in the road, wait for him to turn a corner and then start blasting away. Stupid.

I could get into the Chateau and warn the people there. Would they believe me? Probably not.

I could wait for DuSomme inside the Chateau. If I started shooting inside the confines of some room inside the chateau, he would shoot back. But what use was that? I knew I was not a cop or a trained military type as was DuSomme. It was useless. He had more chance of killing me than I had of killing him.

I am not a murderer nor am I a criminal. I cannot think like they do. Finally, I realized I had only one chance to bring justice to Alain DuSomme.

He would come to François DeLocke's castle to do what he was hired to do. I would go there and wait for him. I would probably be killed, but I had to take that risk. At least I would try and not run away like a coward.

❋❋❋❋❋❋❋❋❋❋❋❋❋❋

I knocked on the tall oak doors of the chateau. François' twenty-two year old maid opened the door. She was surprised to see me. This time she was wearing a modest black dress that hung just below her knees. Her shapely legs were covered in dark stockings. She wore simple, low heeled black shoes. An equally simple string of white pearls hung low from her neck. Her hair was pulled back and twisted tightly behind her head. Her twenty-something pretty face had light and simple make-up on it.

"Pardon, Monsieur," she said. "Le Baron, he is expecting you, please?"

"No," I said and stepped past the little girl into the dark house. She stepped aside for me. I was bigger than she was, and she had no choice.

"I was in the neighborhood and thought I would just drop in to say hello."

"Pardon," she said quizzically. "I do not understand." The English words were forced by her and hard for her to speak properly.

"That's fine," I said. "Just close the door, and go tell Mr. DeLocke I'm here."

She paused, her hand on the brass knob of the open door, not knowing exactly what to say or do.

I smiled to reassure her and said, "Go ahead. It's OK."

She closed the door and almost ran for the elevator. I waited in the hallway, walking around, my footsteps echoing across the highly polished, dark wood floor. I was looking at the mounted animal heads, the paintings, the ancient weapons of war, and the armor and shields covering all the dark wood walls. It took only a few minutes for the girl to step from the elevator into the hallway once again. She stood in front of the open elevator doors and waived to me, telling me to go to her and to the elevator for the ride up.

She wasn't smiling.

The small, tight little elevator took us on another slow ride up to the fourth floor. The sweet but nice cologne she wore filled the elevator around us. Once out of it I followed her again to the big bronze door of DeLocke's office. She opened the heavy door and stood aside for me to enter. DeLocke was not there; no one was in the room. As I looked around, the girl slammed the door closed, and I heard a keyed lock being thrown.

After trying the door, I went to the windows. I was four stories up, so climbing out seemed a little silly, but I had to check anyway. The office was in a corner of the chateau, with two windows on each of the two outside walls. All four had been caged with heavy steel bars on the outside, the windows themselves built into their frames and not meant to be opened.

DeLocke's desk had phones on it. I went to them and found each to be dead; there was no dial tone on any of them. I would only have hurt myself if I tried to break down the big bronze door, so I sat in DeLocke's tall chair and waited . . . Waited for something to happen.

Sitting back in the leather chair I could feel the Glock tucked under my belt at my back. I pulled it out and held it in my shaking hand. It gave me a semblance of comfort, knowing I could at least put up a little bit of defense and resistance if I had to.

Time dragged by. I kept checking my wristwatch, but the time on it seemed to have stopped. The sudden sound of the door's lock being opened startled me. I jumped to my feet and my hand gripped my pistol tighter. The door swung open. The young girl stood aside, and François DeLocke walked into the room, the door closing behind him.

"Monsieur Crew," DeLocke said, surprised to see me.

He looked at the pistol in my hand. I quickly put it under the belt at my waist. He asked, "I assumed our business had been completed, oui? Was I wrong?"

He was dressed in an expensive and very impressive double breasted business suit, blue pinstriped. It fit him well, even over his big stomach. His shirt was white and crisp; his blue and red striped tie was probably evocative of some 'old school' background of his. And he had a white carnation pinned to his lapel. He was ready for high level business.

I ignored the question and asked, "Do you have people here? People from Israel and Lebanon?"

DeLocke was stunned and was unable to hide it. He took a step backwards, his face flooded with red. "Monsieur Crew," he stammered. "This is not for you to know."

"I do know," I said. "And I also know that people are coming here to kill you and the people you are hosting."

DeLocke seemed ready to faint. A sheet of pale white covered his fat face. His eyes widened and his jaw dropped open. His weight and his profligate lifestyle – too much food, too much liquor and wine, too many women – put him in condition for a heart attack or stroke. I went to him before he could collapse, took him by his arm, and led him to a chair in front of his desk. He sat and seemed bewildered. He was sweating; the collar of his white shirt was ringed with sweat. His hands were shaking.

I stepped back, and the sudden realization of what was happening hit me like a punch in my gut. I said, "No! I'm wrong! You aren't a target! The people here from Israel and Lebanon are! You arranged this whole damn thing! You want banking access in Iran! You're working with Iran! You're waiting for DuSomme to get here and kill them!"

His head rose, and he looked up at me with dazed

eyes. "Quelle? . . . What? . . . Je ne comprends pas." He was stuttering, and spittle was dripping from his fat lips. His face was white, and his eyes were bulging from their sockets.

"I'm sorry," I said. I really didn't care if the man dropped over dead at my feet. But I had to know. I asked, "I don't speak French. Do you or do you not have people here meeting secretly?"

"Oui," he said, his thin voice shaking and weak as he stared up at me. "But . . ."

"Please listen to me, Mr. DeLocke. I don't know when, but I know the person you hired will be here soon to kill them. If they are killed you will be held responsible. You will go to jail. The only way for you to stay out of jail is to stop this. You need to do something to stop this. You made a big mistake, François. Too many people know what's going on. Too many people know Alain DuSomme is on his way here. And I know you arranged this whole damn thing."

DeLocke pushed himself from the chair. I hadn't noticed but the young girl who had greeted me was in the room, standing with her back to the bronze door. She said softly and calmly, "There is security here, Monsieur Crew. You cannot leave here, and no one can get in."

I turned to her. "Security? Where? I came to the door here without seeing anyone. You let me in easy enough."

She walked towards us and spoke in French to DeLocke. I had no idea what she said, but it caused DeLocke to panic even more. His jaw hung open; his eyes were inflamed and bulged as if they would explode from their sockets. I wanted her to be angry with her boss. Maybe she was. He did not react as if she were trying to calm him.

The man, I guessed, had no idea what he was getting into when he arranged the murders of the Israelis and Lebanese. He understood now, and panic had overtaken him.

The girl reached for one of the phones on DeLocke's desk. Then she pulled another from its cradle. I knew she would find no working phone. She said something to her boss in French.

DeLocke nodded, and the girl pulled up her dress. She was carrying a small chromed pistol in a holster strapped to her thigh. She pulled the pistol out and pointed it at me. She said, "You will stay here. Do nothing."

She ran for the door. As she opened it she turned to me and said once again, "Stay here. Do you understand?" Her English was near perfect, not the stage play accent she had used on me up to then. Lorraine did the same trick; switching accents on a regular basis.

She closed the door, and I heard the lock being thrown once again. DeLocke was slouched in the chair and he was crying. Tears ran freely across his fat, red face. He was mumbling something in French. I thought he might be saying a prayer. If he was, he just might need some help from above.

I went to the two windows that looked south onto the chateau's property. It was a bright clear day; a few wispy clouds were drifting across the snowcapped mountains. The chateau was in a low valley of sorts, in the mountain range but surrounded by high, snowcapped peaks on all sides. The grounds below the window were green grass and well maintained. Decorative plants and trees had been well placed. A wide stone path ran from the house, winding casually across the lawn.

The two windows on the east side revealed gardens

much like I had looked at from the other windows, except that in the middle of the green lawn, the snows of winter having melted away. I saw a man and a dog, both lying prone in uncomfortable looking positions on the grass. I had seen the dead before, too many times, so I knew right away that the man and his dog were both dead.

DeLocke said something, almost mumbling through his tears. "Please . . . Please . . . Please . . ." I didn't understand anything else he tried to say. I think he must have known that his plan had not been well thought out. I think he must have known he would be prosecuted for the crime that was happening in his home as we stood by helplessly . . . If he survived, that is.

The ancient lock on the big bronze door was loud enough for me to hear it being opened. I drew the Glock from under my belt and held it out in front of me. It occurred to me that I needed to put a round in the chamber if I were going to shoot somebody. So I pulled the slide back quickly and let it fall forward as the door opened. The gun's hammer locked back; my finger seemed frozen on the trigger.

The girl walked in. I lowered the pistol quickly as her face showed the surprise she felt on seeing the Glock.

"You are armed?" she asked needlessly.

"So are you," I said.

"Are you here to kill?"

"I'm here to try to stop the killing," I said as I walked towards her. She held her pistol, smaller than mine but lethal anyway, pointed at me. "You know your outside security is dead, right?"

"Yes," she answered, closing the door behind her.

"What of the people from Israel and Lebanon?"

"I have put them in a safe room. It is like a safe in a bank. They are alright . . . For the time being. Will you help me?" Her French accent had disappeared completely. Her English was as good as any well-educated European could manage; only a tinge of accent could be heard.

"That's what I'm here for. Is there help you can call in?"

"Yes, but the phones . . ."

I handed her my cell phone. She looked wonderingly at it and said, "The mountains . . . There is no cell service here."

"Are any of your security people still alive?" I asked.

"No . . . There were only two . . . With dogs . . . They are dead."

"Inside the house," I asked. "Anybody who can help?"

"There is a cook and two maids. They are hiding in the wine cellar."

"Outside? Gardeners or anybody like that?"

"They come in only three times a week. They don't live here."

So that was it; we were alone to fight off the professional hired killer Alain DuSomme and whoever he brought with him.

"So who are you?" I asked. "You speak very good English. Do you know a Lorraine Demeaux?"

"Yes," the young girl answered.

That explained the accent changes. This young girl worked with Lorraine. But that didn't answer the question of who the hell they worked for.

"OK," I said. "Where is this safe room?"

"On this floor," she answered. She was a professional; she was obviously not frightened at all. "It is a small room . . . Concrete . . . A steel door. As I said, like a bank vault."

I looked at DeLocke, still sitting in the chair, his hands covering his face as he cried. He was shaking; his feet were stomping on the floor and his pants were dark from having pissed through fear without knowing it. He would be of no use to me.

"Can you stay here with François? I'm going to check the doors and windows on the ground floor. I assume DuSomme is inside already. If he is, I want him to have a difficult time getting out. I'm going to try to find him. Lock the door after me and don't open it for anyone but me."

She nodded, but I saw her hand, holding her pistol, start shaking. She may . . . Somehow . . . Be working with Lorraine, but she was young.

I put my hand on her shoulder and smiled, trying to calm her a little. "What's your name?" I asked. "What do I call you?"

"Nancy," she said. She tried to smile, but it was difficult for her. I think she had just begun to realize how dangerous the situation she and I were in. I held back the urge to ask her how she was associated with Lorraine. That could wait until all this was over.

"OK, Nancy. We'll be OK. There are people who know we're here. The police know, and they will be here soon. We'll be OK." I was lying, of course. I tried to believe the police would be there, but it was only a hope, nothing more.

I left François' office and heard Nancy close and lock

the office door behind me. Standing in the hallway I listened . . . For anything. The hallway was eerily silent. I would have thought that whoever killed the guards and dogs outside were now in the chateau searching for the people they wanted to kill. But there was nothing.

François' office was at the south end of the hall. I walked slowly, hugging the wall, my pistol raised and ready to shoot. At the far end of the hall a door stood open an inch or two. Other doors I passed had been closed. I eased the door open and peered in. I saw a glass doored bookcase had been pulled away from the wall to the right. Behind it was the steel door Nancy had described. It was solid and . . . I hoped . . . solidly locked from the inside.

A wide staircase was to my right. My thought was that the elevator would be too confining, and I wouldn't know who would be waiting for me when the doors opened. I took the stairs down . . . Very slowly, step by step, holding onto the thick mahogany handrail with my left hand while holding the Glock up, ready to shoot.

Reaching the third floor, I walked that hallway and listened. I checked each door and room. Still nothing. The second floor was the same. The chateau was huge, with many rooms and hallways extending off of hallways. It was a maze that I would not be able to search completely. I stayed in the main halls, carefully moving forward; assuming a group of killers . . . Or just DuSomme . . . Would not be in hiding but would be openly searching for their targets.

On the ground floor I found two doors in the main hall: the entrance I had come through and a twin door at the far end of the hall. The big doors at the formal entry were closed. I found heavy locking-bolts at the top and bottom of the doors. Both were lying open. I threw each tightly closing them and locking the big doors.

I walked towards the other door holding my back to the wall. If there were intruders in the chateau they would be there. I held the Glock out in both hands, ready to shoot. As I got halfway along the hall, a door opened. I stopped, crouched, my finger went on the trigger.

Lorraine Demeaux stepped into the hall. She was dressed in blue jeans and a tan shirt that was tucked into her jeans. Her breasts tugged at the buttons of the shirt. Her hair was pulled back into a tight bun on back of her head. That was unusual as every time I had seen her prior to that, she wore a dress or expensive slacks and looked very feminine. This time she held a very large pistol in her left hand.

"Monsieur Crew," she said. "I had hoped you would not be here."

"I am . . . And you are, too. Is DuSomme here?"

"We are looking," she said.

"The guards outside . . ." I began.

"Oui, we have found them. It is bad. And Monsieur DeLocke?" she asked.

"He's safe . . . Upstairs."

"And Nancy . . .?"

"She's OK. She's with DeLocke."

"Très bien. The people who are the guests, they are with him, oui . . . And safe?"

"They are safe," I said. "There's a very secure safe room. They are there."

"And where is this place?" she asked. As she did, four men walked out of the same room she had been in. They were armed with nasty looking submachine guns. I did not try to hide my surprise. Lorraine saw this and said, "Do not be afraid, Monsieur Crew. These men are to protect."

I nodded and lowered my pistol to my side. Lorraine repeated, "This safe place, where is it, S'il vous plaît?"

"Upstairs," I answered. "But they're OK for now. Shouldn't we be looking for DuSomme? I mean he's here . . . Somewhere. He killed the guards outside, right?"

"Oui, this is right. But first I must be certain the people are safe. S'il vous plaît . . . Please . . . We will go to the people, oui?"

"OK," I said. "Leave your men here. We have to stop DuSomme from going upstairs . . . And from leaving this place."

"This is correct," she said. She turned to the four men and spoke in what Sandy thought might be Hebrew. The men nodded. She said to me, "Oui, these will stay here and keep Monsieur DuSomme out of the chateau . . . Or in if he is here. We shall see to the people now?"

Lorraine walked at my side to the elevator. As we walked she said, "It is good you wish to do the help, oui? But it is very . . . How you say . . . dangereux . . .?"

"Dangerous," I suggested. "I suppose so, but I have a personal reason for being here."

"Oui, I understand. It is your . . . Ami . . . Your friend, Monsieur Manns."

As we walked the hallway I asked her, "Why the phony accent, lady? Nancy does the same vaudeville show. Why not just English?"

She smiled but would not answer.

We rode up the three floors and stepped out of the elevator. The hallway was silent; our footsteps were loud on the white marble floor. When we reached the door to François' office I knocked. Nancy's voice was weak as she said, "Who is it?"

"Morgan," I said. "I have help with me. We're OK. Let us in."

Nancy opened the door and stood aside as Lorraine and I walked into the office.

Lorraine took Nancy into her arms and hugged her. She whispered something. François was still in the chair, shaking and crying. Nancy started to say something when Lorraine raised her pistol and shot Nancy, once in the middle of her forehead.

"What the hell!" I screamed as I pulled my own pistol from my belt and stepped in front of François.

"Step aside, Monsieur Crew. It is not you I wish to kill."

Without thinking about it too much I pulled the trigger of the Glock. Nothing. I pulled the trigger three times more. Still nothing.

Lorraine laughed a small laugh and said, "Did you think I would give you the gun that works?"

I dropped the Glock and feinted a look to the left. Lorraine reacted, looking quickly to her right. I jumped on her, grabbing her gun hand and pushing her back. She slipped on the slick polished floor and fell backwards. I fell with her, on top of her, and heard her head hit the hard oak floor with a terrible cracking sound. She lay still, her eyes wide in surprise, dark blood seeping from the back of her head.

It was hard pushing myself to my feet. Lorraine was dead, there was no mistaking that. I had seen black blood flow from the open skull of people before. She was lying near Nancy. And Nancy was supposed to be working with Lorraine. What the hell was going on, I asked myself. Lorraine was supposed to be the good guy. Maybe Interpol . . . Maybe Mossad. François was leaning back in the chair, his jaw hanging open and loose in a silent scream.

I walked in circles, my head in a dizzying spin. The room was twirling around in front of me; my stomach twisted. The morass of all that was around me was too much for me. Suddenly, the room stopped spinning and I stood looking down at DeLocke.

I wanted to go to him but the office door slammed open. One of the men Lorraine had with her on the first floor stood in the open doorway, looking down at Lorraine lying in an expanding pool of blood and brains. He looked at Nancy and then up at me. His confusion allowed me time to grab Lorraine's pistol from the floor. I fell prone onto the floor and fired. I killed the man with two shots to the chest.

Dragging the dead man into the office, I closed the door and locked it. I slid a heavy chair against the door. The room was as secure as was possible, which I knew would not stop three men who wanted in to kill me. François was on the floor, in the furthest corner, on his back, kicking with his legs, making insane sounds through lips wet with foamy drool.

I struggled to pull the fat man up. I was difficult but I managed to drag him across the floor, his heals leaving a trail of skid marks on the waxed wood. I sat him back in the chair. His wide eyes had a crazy gleam to them. He mumbled something, just sounds. If they were words they were nothing like I had ever heard before.

I grabbed him by his shoulders and shook him. "François! François! Listen to me!" It took a hard slap and then another across his face to break him out of his frozen horror.

He slowly raised his arm and wiped his wet mouth with his sleeve. The tears had stopped. His face was red, and his breathing was short but steady.

"François . . . I need to take you to the safe room . . . François . . . Do you hear me?"

François looked down at the bodies on the floor. "Nancy?" he said softly. "Nancy?"

"François," I said shaking him by his shoulders again to get his attention. "I have to take you to the safe room. Come with me. I can't carry you. You must walk. There are people here who will kill you."

He nodded slightly, mumbling something I could not understand; I did not care what he said. He pushed himself from the chair. I picked up the gun Lorraine's man had brought with him.

It was a Tavor Bullpup submachine gun, an Israeli weapon used by that Country's Special Forces and Mossad. I had seen these before but never before had I laid hands on one. I hoped it would fire when I pulled the trigger.

The dead man had a military vest on which held two spare clips for the gun. I took these and put one in each of my jacket's side pockets. There was a small radio in a pocket of the vest. I took it; knowing what the other two men had in mind might keep me alive.

François stood beside me as I carefully moved the chair away and unlocked the office door. I held the Tavor out with my finger on the trigger. If the hallway was not empty I hoped the weapon would work for me.

Opening the big door slowly, I peered out and then opened the door wide. No one was there. I stepped into the hallway and pulled François behind me.

"OK," I whispered. "We're going to the safe room. Walk fast."

He nodded and pointed to the left. We walked, side by side, down the hallway, very slowly. There were stairs and the elevator behind me. As we walked I turned every two or three steps to look there.

François stopped at a door on the right. "À l'intérieur," he said. "Inside." I opened the door and pushed François ahead of me. I closed and locked the door behind me. I gave François another shove. He stumbled to the bookcase across the room and slid it to the right easily with one hand, as I had. The steel door, like a bank vault door, was still closed.

"Open it," I demanded to François.

A key pad on the wall to the left of the steel door was lit in cold blue. François touched a series of six numbers slowly with shaking fingers. I watched and almost laughed at the stupidity of the man. He used numbers 1 through 6 as a code to unlock and open the door.

It took all my weight, but I managed to pull the six inch thick door open. Inside were four men, huddled together, in fear of impending death. The room was a box, four walls, floor and ceiling, of grey steel without any furniture. One light caged in wire housing on the ceiling lit the room. It was meant as a place to hide for a time and nothing more.

I said nothing but pushed François roughly into the room. The four men inside all began talking at once, indistinguishable babble as far as I was concerned.

"Stay here," I said. "Stay here."

I closed the door, and using the key pad I touched the six numbers and heard the bars of the door slide, locking the men inside. As I slid the bookcase back finding it very easy to move, I thought, "And if I get killed . . . They'll die in there."

For the first time I looked around the room. It was a bedroom, elaborately furnished in expensive 16th Century furnishings. A bit overdone for my taste; I laughed at the thought. Then I realized I had to leave that room and see if Lorraine's three killers were in the chateau, and decide what I would do if they were.

I sat in a very uncomfortable armchair with an upholstered, very hard seat and a back too hard and straight. I tried to figure out just what the hell I would do. Then chatter started on the small radio I had taken from the dead man. It was, to me, just gibberish in a foreign language I could not understand. But it did tell me that Lorraine's men were still somewhere nearby.

The talk on the radio sounded panicked. My guess was the three men were nearby and probably had found Lorraine, Nancy, and their partner in François' office. If that were true then they were very near me.

Looking around the room, I figured I had two options. One was to barricade some furniture around and shoot it out with the men when and if they came into the room. The other option was to lock myself inside the safe room. I have no idea why at the time I chose option one. Thinking back on it, I guess I would rather get shot than suffocate inside the safe room.

I started moving furniture around the room; flipping the big bed onto its side and piling chairs in front of it. I figured I had a 50 /50 chance of winning a gun battle there. I knelt behind my little barricade, ready to shoot, and wondered.

Lorraine had surprised me. I had thought that she was going to help me stop DuSomme. As it turned out, I had to stop her. In past years I had made mistakes in trying to judge people as good or bad. Lorraine had conned me into believing she was one of the good guys, when in fact it was she who had been hired . . . For some reason I had to find out . . . To kill the Israeli and Lebanese people at the chateau.

Then I heard the loud explosions of rapid gunfire in the hallway. It was a short gun battle but a violent one, and then it ended. Less than a minute of rapid shots had filled the air. I laid the Tavor on the raised edge of the bed and prepared to fire. Someone was knocking on the door, and that seemed out of place. I had expected the door to be blown open.

I said nothing and listened to the heavier knocking on the door. "Mr. Crew," a familiar voice called out. "Mr. Crew . . . Are you in there?"

"Who are you?" I shouted, trying not to sound as frightened as I was.

"Doug Phelps," he answered. "Ryan Manning and I have some people here to protect you."

Manning and Phelps, I thought. The two traitors who had sold their services to Alain DuSomme. I said, "Help me? . . . Or turn me over to DuSomme again? I am armed . . . So just go away and nobody else will get hurt."

"We're not here to hurt you, Mr. Crew," Phelps said. "We found Lorraine Demeaux. Are you all right?"

I said nothing and crouched down behind my barricade, ready for them to break down the door. Instead, Ryan Manning must have joined Doug Phelps and said through the door, "We know there's a safe room in there, Mr. Crew. Are DeLocke and his people in there?"

I did not answer. Instead I called out loudly, "Tell you what! The two of you and all the people with you, go outside under the window in his room. Lay all your weapons on the ground. Then back away about a hundred feet. Once you've done that, you Manning, and Doug Phelps take off your jackets and leave them outside. The two of you come on back up here. I'll unlock the door and let you in. But know that I have two pistols and a loaded and ready to shoot Tavor I took from a dead guy. If you come back here, and there's anyone else with you, I will shoot to kill."

I heard them talking softly, and then I heard them walk away. There was quiet outside the locked door.

Moving to the window overlooking a small garden of roses that had yet to bloom in the early spring, I watched as six men walked out of the house. Manning and Phelps were the last of the six. They were dressed in combat camos, each with a Kevlar vest on.

They laid big long guns on the ground, and each took a pistol from a holster at his side, laying it with the other guns.

Four of the men walked away, leaving Manning and Phelps by the pile of guns. Manning and Phelps slipped out of their brown, military-like jackets and laid them over the pile of guns. They spoke to each other, and then they slipped off their Kevlar vests and dropped them to the ground.

I pushed the heavy brocade drape aside and raised the window and called out to them, "Turn around . . . Slowly . . . With your hands in the air!" They did that, and I called again, "Now pull up your pants' leg . . . I need to know you don't have guns strapped to your ankles!" They did that while shaking their heads in disbelief.

"OK," I called out once again. "Now the two of you can come back up here. Remember . . . Come alone or I start shooting!"

I closed the window and for some reason I threw the lock on it. I waited. It took only a moment or two for the two men to walk up the three flights of stairs to the fourth floor. Doug Phelps spoke from outside the locked door. "OK, Mr. Crew. We're here, now open the damn door."

I checked what I thought might be the safety on the Tavor and held it ready to fire as I unlocked the door. Opening it only an inch or so, I peered out, and all I could find were the two men. But I knew these men were professional, and I had to be ready for tricks. I stuck the gun out in front of me as I slowly opened the door.

Manning looked down at the Tavor and said, "That's a damn dangerous weapon you've got there, Mr. Crew. How about pointing it someplace besides my nuts and take your finger off the trigger? That thing can cause really bad accidents."

I realized I had had the gun only inches from Manning's crotch as I looked down the hallway for people other than these two.

Pulling the gun away, I backed away so the two could walk into the room. I backed up, holding the Tavor pointed at them. When they were in the room I ordered, "Close the door and lock it."

Phelps did that quickly without arguing.

"Pull a couple of chairs from my barricade and put them against the door and sit," I ordered again.

They looked at each other quickly, but they did as I told them to do. When seated, Manning crossed his legs casually and asked, "How about the safe room? Are we in it?"

"First a few questions," I said. I leaned against the wall as far from the two of them as I could get. I asked,

"Why Lorraine Demeaux?"

They looked at each other like they didn't understand the question. Ryan Manning looked at me, a frown on his forehead, and asked, "I don't understand. What do you mean?"

I sighed deeply, faking the bored sigh like an actor on stage. I explained, "Lorraine came here to kill François and his guests. Why her? I thought DuSomme was going to do that."

"So you had it all wrong," Phelps said. "Seems like everyone knew you would. I think you were told to go home . . . Weren't you? You got yourself in the middle of something way over your head."

OK, I'd been conned a couple of times before. Lorraine had done a good job fooling me, but she was dead and I was alive. So, I thought about that and felt good thinking it. Who was the smart one?

I asked, "I want to know who you're working for; The Embassy or DuSomme?"

They looked at each other, seemingly communicating silently. Phelps looked at me and said, "Sometimes it's a dark world out there, Mr. Crew. Sometimes secrets hide the truth. You aren't written in to anything happening here. You don't get to know the truth."

"Let's remember one thing here gentlemen," I said, I smiled broadly as I said it. "I have the guns here. If you want to walk out of this room . . . Alive that is . . . You're going to . . . How did you say it? . . . Write me in to what's happening here."

Manning laughed and said, "You're going to kill us. I mean, you actually think you're capable of murder?" He laughed again.

"Who said anything about murder?" I asked. "Oh, yeah, I did kill Lorraine and her man in the other room. That's true. And I guess I have killed other people over the years. But with you two . . . I won't kill you . . . I'll just put a bullet in each of your knees. That'll sort of end your working careers, won't it? Now, please let me know what the hell is going on around here."

Ryan Manning laughed again, but Doug Phelps took me a little more seriously, especially when I took a step towards him and lowered the Tavor, pointing it at his right knee.

"Now wait a minute! Wait a minute!" he said, pushing himself back, sliding the chair back against the big door.

"Shut up, Doug!" Manning said.

"Fuck that shit," Phelps said. "I'm not gonna' let him cripple me for this stupid shit."

"He's not going to do anything," Manning said laughing again while looking me in the eyes, challenging me.

I slowly lowered the Tavor pointing it down, away from Doug Phelps, holding it in my left hand. Manning smiled a bragging smile, assuming he was right and I would give up, surrendering to him. But I drew the pistol I had taken from Lorraine from my belt and fired one shot at the floor. The bullet tore into the wood floor an inch from Manning's toes. He jumped up, kicking the chair out from under him. "You son of a . . ."

I interrupted him, "Sit down," I said. "I might just take a few of your toes out before I shoot your knee caps all to hell."

He reached behind him and pulled the chair upright. He sat, glaring at me, red faced with anger.

"Now," I said, calmly as I felt I was really in charge.

"Let's start at the beginning. Who are you working for . . . And forget the crap about secrets."

Manning's eyes did not unlock from mine. Phelps looked at him, shook his head, and turned back to me. "What I'm going to tell you cannot reach the press, understand?"

"Sure," I said. "Just between you and me." I, of course, didn't mean it. I had to bring some right to everything that had happened. I had to right the death of LeRoy Manns. And I had to learn what DuSomme was responsible for. If it meant making things public that shouldn't be public, I would do that, too.

Manning shot back, "Shut your damn mouth Doug!"

"No, Ryan. I'm sick of this. It's time it all ended." Phelps turned to me and began, "We knew about the meeting here. The American Government, I mean. The French knew, the Germans knew, everybody knew, except the Israelis and the Lebanese. The people meeting here intended to make money for themselves and sacrifice their own Countries to do it. They intended to break their own laws. And DeLocke was the man who arranged the whole thing. He wanted access to Iran, and he thought this would do it.

He cleared his throat, looked for a second at Manning, and then went on, "Iran and Lebanon traded some promises . . . I don't think they ever intended to keep those promises . . ."

Phelps was stopped in the middle of the sentence. Pounding on the door and shouting from the hallway made Manning smile, Phelps worried, and me ready to shoot it out with whoever was outside.

Phelps raised his hand to me and called out to the

people outside the room, "We're OK!" he said.   "Stay outside!"

"Tell them to go back to the yard and stay there," I ordered.

"It was the gunshot," Phelps said. "They heard it and came running."

"I said to tell them to leave the chateau. Tell them to wait outside."

They must have heard me. Listening, I could hear the men walk away, all talking amongst themselves. I looked at Phelps and said, "Go on. Tell me what this is all about."

Manning spoke before his partner could. "Are they nearby? Are the people who were here nearby? Are they still alive?"

"Yes they are still alive," I said. "As soon as I know what's going on . . . And as soon as I feel you're not here to kill them, I'll bring them to you."

Doug Phelps nodded as a defeated man would nod and went on telling me the whole story. "Anyway, Iran made some promises about slowing their nuclear programs if we allowed these people to make their deal.   I guess Washington thought getting Iran to do what they said they would do was more important than an illegal business deal. But somebody out there . . . We still don't know who . . . Somebody wanted all the people who wanted to make the deal . . . Dead. They didn't just want the deal stopped . . . They wanted the people from Israel and Lebanon dead."

I asked, "And you still don't know who wanted them killed?"

"No," Doug answered. "At least at our pay grade. Could be people in higher places know, but we haven't been joined in that."

I could easily accept that as the truth, except I knew DeLocke had arranged the killings . . . For somebody . . . So he could open banks in Iran. But why Iran? The dark clouds of International spies were impossible for me to see through.

If all else he had said were true, a couple of contractor security people wouldn't be brought into the depths of secrets.

"So why were you guys working for DuSomme? Back there at that stone cottage?"

Manning looked at Phelps, nodded, and Phelps explained, "It may have looked like we were working for DuSomme, but we were protecting you and your wife. All we and others wanted was for the two of you to get the hell out of France and go home. Lorraine had ideas to kill both of you. She had to know we were nearby. Us being there, knowing you were there with her, stopped her from killing you and your wife."

"What about Lorraine Demeaux?" I asked. "Frankly, she surprised me when she showed up here with guys to kill everyone."

"Yeah, we knew that," Phelps said. "We've been following her. But our orders were to do nothing . . . To let her kill everyone."

"And you didn't question that?" I asked. "You were just going to sit by and watch her commit murders?"

Ryan Manning spoke for the first time. He said, rather sarcastically, "We know all about you, Crew," he said, dropping the Mister and making that very intentional. "You've been involved in operations like this before, when . . . People, so to speak . . . When people are hired to kill. Don't be so naive. Governments have their reasons."

"The point being," I said. "I have never accepted the

right when it comes to murder. Sometimes it is necessary but never right."

Manning snickered at that. I figured he would be trouble for me before this whole thing was over. Phelps had given up, and it wouldn't have surprised me if I never saw him again. I think he had a conscience, something that Manning might be missing. Maybe he was just plain scared.

I paced around the room, thinking. All that Phelps had told me made some sense . . . If you added into the calculation the twisted thinking of people in the weird world of spies. But there was one thing that hadn't been answered for me yet, and I needed an answer. I turned to the two men and asked, "How does DuSomme figure into all this?"

Manning laughed, this time an honest laugh at the humor of what I had asked. Phelps merely shook his head and, looking down at the floor, he said, "Nothing."

"What the hell do you mean 'nothing'?" I asked, bewildered now more than a half minute before.

"I mean Alain DuSomme wasn't involved in this in any way. You thought he was, and we let you think that. I mean, the order was given that if you weren't going to leave France, then let you go on thinking DuSomme was involved. It would keep you out of the way."

"Then why did he kidnap my wife and send me out here to find out what the inside of this place was like? And why the hell did he kidnap Sandy? And you said you were working for DuSomme."

Doug Phelps looked sideways at Manning, questioning if he should say anything more. Manning just shrugged his shoulders. Phelps turned to me and said, "We were following you and the Demeaux woman. DuSomme's people would have killed you and your wife. I . . . We . . .

Didn't want that to happen. I don't know why he sent you here. You'll have to ask him that. All the intel we had pointed to Lorraine and not to DuSomme. We have no idea what DuSomme was up to."

Now the spinning in my brain turned into a dark, deep whirlpool. It was all too confusing for me. But I had to be certain of one thing before letting Manning and Phelps go. I asked, "And you're certain that Alain DuSomme had nothing to do with attacking this place?"

"Based on what we know," Phelps said. "He had nothing to do with this operation. But we aren't told everything, you understand. People tell us what to do, and we do it. Up the ladder, someone might know something we don't know."

I started pacing in circles again, trying to make some sense out of everything. If DuSomme wasn't intending to attack the chateau, did he really kill LeRoy? And if he did kill LeRoy and the others, why?

I tired of pacing and pulled another chair away from the little barricade I had built. I set it in front of the two contractors and sat, sighed deeply, and said, "OK, if I show you where François DeLocke and the others are hiding, what will you do?"

Doug looked sideways at Manning again, questioning without words what should be said. Manning turned to me with a deadly glare, spat on the floor, and said, "We were supposed to verify that everyone was dead. If they aren't . . . Then I guess we will report that. I don't kill outside of work. We'll just go back to Paris and tell Ms. Huntington what happened here. The rest is on your shoulders. But I will tell you this. The plans made at the meeting that was to take place here had to be stopped. It will be stopped. There's no way the U.S. will allow what these people want to do, in spite of what Iran wants. And you're in the way, Mr. Crew. What that means is . . . You will die if necessary. Somebody out there will kill you if you keep sticking your damn nose into what is none of your business."

I looked at Doug Phelps, hoping for some kind of verification of what Ryan had said. He closed his eyes and nodded. That's all I needed.

I stood and walked around my little furniture fort. The bookcase slid easily away from the steel vault-door. I tapped in the silly combination François had used, and the door sprung open. I pulled it aside and saw François and the four other men huddled against the back wall, all frightened enough to be sweating and peeing in their pants as they held onto each other.

For the first time I looked at the two Israelis and two Lebanese. They were businessmen, all dressed in dark suits of good quality and all with white shirts, opened at the sweat-stained collars.

They weren't looking at me but at the Tavor submachine gun I was still holding.

"You can come out now," I said to them. "No one is going to hurt you."

They didn't move. I propped the gun against a wall and took a step away from it. "It's OK . . . Really . . . You're safe," I tried to assure them.

One by one they walked out of the safe room, DeLocke the last in line. They took in the little barricade wall I had built from the room's furniture and the two men, still seated in front of the door to the hallway. All five of them were out, nervously waiting to be told what to do.

Ryan Manning reached inside his camo shirt and pulled a small semi-auto pistol out. As I put my hand on the pistol I still had tucked under my belt, Doug Phelps jumped on his partner.

Both fell to the floor, rolling on top of each other. One muffled gunshot rang out and both men lay still. Manning took a second or two to push his bleeding partner off of him. He started to raise the pistol as he lay prone on the floor, but before he could bring it up and point it at anyone I shot him once, the bullet piercing his right eye and exploding out the back of his skull.

Doug Phelps lay on the floor, his hands covering the bullet wound on his left side, under his shoulder. He looked up at me and saw I had my pistol pointed at him. He said, "No . . . This was not planned . . . At least I didn't know about it."

By that time the men who had been waiting downstairs were at the door; they smashed it open. They quickly looked around the room and at their dead comrade. Then their focus shifted to me, and they raised their weapons.

Phelps called out, "No! It's not what you think! It's not Mr. Crew!" I dropped the pistol onto the floor quickly and raised my arms high over my head.

❋❋❋❋❋❋❋❋❋❋❋❋❋❋

The rest of that day was taken up waiting for an ambulance, waiting for the French police, waiting for American Embassy people and finally for French Government people who took François DeLocke and his four business conspirators into custody. The people from my own Government talked the French Government people into letting me go with them.

A helicopter was waiting in one of the gardens, having crushed rose bushes and a couple of tall, thin, green trees when landing. I was roughly pushed into it. Sitting back, between two really big Marines, I relaxed for the first time in a couple of days. I knew nothing was going to happen to me. The Crew family name carries a lot of weight in D.C. I might be held and questioned, but in the end I knew I would be released.

Once that happened, I had to find out why LeRoy Manns was murdered and who murdered him.

SEVENTEEN - My Rescue!

The helicopter landed on the rooftop helipad at the Embassy. I was shuffled off, not too gently, by the two Marines who had squeezed against me in the helicopter, to a basement cell and locked away without words being spoken. Inside the eight by ten foot cell was a steel bed hanging from the concrete wall by two chains. It was solid steel and without a mattress. A dirty metal sink with a dirty toilet under it was hanging on the opposite wall. There was nothing else in the eight foot by ten foot cell.

It was a little prison not advertised nor known to the public. But I didn't complain. I was alive. I let the system take its own time, knowing I would be in that cell for only a short time.

I stretched out on the metal bed, my arm crossed under my head, and waited. There not being a window in the cell, time would have stood still if it were not for the fact that I was left with my Rolex wristwatch. In fact nothing had been taken from me except my weapons. I was not 'patted down' or searched in anyway. Oh well.

Trying not to check my watch every couple of minutes, I had waited there for close to four hours before Mary Huntington opened the cell's solid steel door.

"Mr. Crew," she said. "Please come with me."

I could have been mistaken, but it looked like she was dressed in the same clothes I had seen her in the last time we spoke. Maybe I was wrong. Maybe she just had a couple dozen outfits that all looked alike.

I made a show of swinging my legs off the bed and then struggling to stand. I moaned dramatically and said, "You might think about a better bed in here."

I followed her up three flights of narrow stairs and through a door onto the main floor of the Embassy. She and I walked down a hallway to an elevator and stepped inside. It stopped at the top floor, and again I followed Huntington silently to the left and to the end of the hallway.

She stopped at an oak door with a keypad lock and touched a few numbers, carefully blocking my view of the code with her left hand as she touched numbers with her right. The door swung open automatically, and we walked into a nicely furnished room. Comfortably upholstered chairs were arranged decoratively in well planned places. A tan and red carpet, almost an inch thick, covered the floor. A marble fireplace was across the room, cold that day, but the room was warm anyway. It would have been a midrange motel room except for the bars on the windows.

"You'll stay here for a while," Mary said. "You can order food . . . Use the phone over there," she pointed to a beige colored phone on a small table in the far corner. "There is a bedroom and bathroom to your left."

I interrupted Mary by saying, "I want to phone my wife."

"For now," she said, a little hesitant, "that will not be possible. No outside calls of any kind, please. The phone will only connect with the kitchen."

The 'please' surprised me. I expected an order; I got sort of an irreversible request.

"But . . ." I started. She turned quickly, leaving the

room and locking the door behind her.

For the next three days I relaxed in the room, reading the New York Times European Edition that was brought to me with breakfast every day and watching TV shows in French, not understanding anything that was being said. I managed to find the ESPN network and watched a lot of sports that were only a little bit interesting to me. I had too much on my mind . . . Like what was going to happen to me.

Someone had gone to The Ritz and packed most of my clothes in one suitcase. It was dropped on the floor in my apartment/cell without words. I was comfortable but bored.

The fact that I knew phone calls were being made between DC and the Embassy kind of eased my mind. People in Washington depended on my family's money. After all, a person in Congress making $150,000 a year or thereabouts, had no hope of becoming a millionaire without the money my family filtered to them, legally or otherwise. I just had to wait until enough of them sounded off and used their political power to tell the people at the Embassy to let me go.

The only break in my boredom was when two or three times a day someone, sometimes a man, sometimes a woman, would come to the room and 'interrogate' me. To make them feel "welcome" in my room, I ordered coffee and rolls in the morning and booze if they showed up late enough in the afternoon or the evening. I asked politely if they wanted lunch or an early dinner. They seemed a little insulted at this, but they drank the coffee and ate the rolls and had a drink or two anyway.

Once one guy, younger than the others, said a ham sandwich would be nice. Before I could order that for him, the phone in the corner rang. I answered it, but it was for the young interrogator. He listened and then hung up the phone.

"I guess I won't have that sandwich after all," he said, a little disappointed. That told me the room was wired and probably had cameras hidden somewhere, too. That evening I showered and made a show of drying off in the sitting room, making sure whoever was watching enjoyed seeing me naked.

The interrogators would each ask basically the same questions: What relationship did I have with all the dead people? Why was I at the chateau in the first place? Where did I get my information from? Who was cooperating with me? I answered each question the same way, withholding a few truths from them, bending and twisting a few other truths, but never really lying to them. It was all over, so why lie? But I had to protect myself, and I had a job to do once they let me go. If they knew I wasn't simply going to go home, they might keep me there forever. I knew that probably wouldn't happen, but they would at least escort me home and take my passport away.

I found the whole thing amusing, partly because they knew more than I knew about François DeLocke and his business friends, and partly because I knew more than they did about what was going on in Washington, DC and Paris.

I answered each question as vaguely as I could, not lying but not revealing any details either. I stayed calm and watched each of my questioners lose patience with me and get up and leave. It was fun, but also boring after a while. Sort of like watching the same dumb TV show over and over again.

I wanted to get out of there, and I wanted to do that without a fight, a fight I would most certainly lose. If I were patient enough, I would soon be set free. Eventually they would learn that they had nothing to gain by keeping me there.

Congressmen and Senators were being inundated with lawyers defending me and working to get me released from the very comfortable prison. Plus, money was being passed around to "re-election campaigns."

And everybody working to get me free did their work very well. On the morning of the fifth day the door opened. I expected the breakfast I had ordered – pancakes and bacon and coffee – but two Marines in combat camo, carrying very large pistols at their sides, walked into the room.

I stand a little over six foot one inch tall. These two guys towered over me, and their camos were stretched under their muscles. They each took one of my arms and pulled me from the chair I had been sitting on.

"Hey! . . . What the hell! . . ." I demanded. They said nothing but roughly pulled me between them, out the door, down the hall, to the elevator. They held on to me tightly as the elevator went down. I imagined being thrown into that secret little steel and concrete cell in the basement. As we went down in the elevator I said, "Where are we going? What the hell's going on?"

They ignored me. The elevator door slid open; they pulled me out. We were on the main floor of the Embassy. To my left I saw the lobby of the Embassy. My Marines pulled me to the right, to some double glass doors which opened onto a parking lot. They opened the doors, and I was pulled down five steps onto the concrete and then pulled across the lot to big iron gates. Another Marine stepped from a small gate shack and opened the gate. The two Marines holding tightly to my arms pushed me toward the open gate and out onto the street. They let go of me and stepped back, and the gate was closed, leaving me on the outside and them on the inside.

I was free, but I had no idea what I would do being free. I was standing in a wide alleyway, behind the Embassy, used only to bring cars and trucks into the guarded parking lot. It was morning, cool, and a light drizzle was falling from a cloudy sky. I thought, 'Would Paris spring ever end?' I started walking, not knowing where I would go.

Turning at two corners, I found myself on the Avenue Gabriel. It was morning, ten minutes past seven according to my watch, and the traffic on this main road was beginning to thicken. I needed a taxi to take me back to The Ritz.

Taxis passed, but they were all taken. I waited, and I waived at a few, but none stopped. A black Renault pulled to the curb in front of me and stopped. The passenger window rolled down. Paris Police Inspector Renard bent low inside.

"Bonjour, Monsieur Crew," he said happily, smiling like he was a friend. "I heard the rumor you were . . . Shall we say 'free'?"

Renard was wearing a crisp white shirt with a too bright red tie. His Navy blue suit coat was draped over the passenger seat. From the open window a thick sweet flow of aftershave flooded out.

I ignored the cop, turned and started walking away. The black Renault crept along the curb, keeping up with me. Renard called out again, "I think perhaps you need the ride, oui? May I offer you the ride to your hotel?"

I didn't stop walking, but I walked very slowly. Half way through the block two cops in uniforms stepped from a doorway and stood, blocking the sidewalk. I stopped and turned to look at Renard.

"Monsieur," Renard said, this time in a more official

voice. "I no longer offer the ride. You will get in the car . . . Now."

To my right the two uniformed cops were walking slowly towards me. Renard had a hard glare on his face. I figured I could turn and run but I had a better chance if I just did what the cop said and trusted that my influence in Washington would continue.

As I took my first step to get into Renard's car, a blare of horns from a dozen cars on the street started. A white Mercedes, driving crazily was cutting in and out of traffic, darting in front of the dozens of cars, speeding along Avenue Gabriel. Drivers were yelling profanities as the Mercedes came too close to them, almost causing a few accidents. But the driver finally made it to the curb and slammed on brakes, stopping an inch or two from slamming into the rear of Renard's Renault.

The passenger side door opened, and Sandy, bless her heart, shouted, "Get in!"

I took four fast steps to the open door and slid in as Sandy threw the car into reverse to back away from Renard, and then threw the gear shift into forward and slammed her foot on the gas pedal pulling into the heavy traffic. Thankfully other drivers, smart enough to avoid crashing into us, got out of her way.

Holding on tight to the seat, I tried strapping the seat belt around me. Sandy didn't slow down as she weaved between cars. I asked, "What the hell are you doing here? I thought you had gone home."

"Yeah, I did. But I spoke with a bunch of people in Washington and found out what was going on here. Betsy convinced me that I needed to be taking care of you. She said she could take care of the baby and I shouldn't worry about that."

Betsy Concanon, as I mentioned before, is our daughter's 'nanny'. Once a tattooed, green haired, biker chick, she was hired by Sandy to help care for our daughter, Caroline. Betsy had an immediate connection with our daughter and has taken care of her over the past few years when Sandy and I were in trouble. Today, Betsy is in college, pre-med, and her hair is no longer green; she has let it revert to a natural brown. She remains our invaluable friend, as close to a daughter as she could be.

I knew better than to argue with Sandy about returning to Paris. We've been married and together long enough for me to have learned that I can never win an argument with her. So I just shut up and held on tight as Sandy sped through Paris. Finally we ended up at the front of The Paris Ritz. I sat in the car trying to catch my breath as Sandy stepped from the car and gave the keys to the valet. She stopped at the front doors of the hotel, turned and waived to me to follow her in. I hadn't gotten out of the car yet.

The Ritz had held our suite for us as I had told them to, charging my Black Amex card a little more than $2000 a day for the privilege. Inside, I collapsed on the couch in the sitting room, spreading my legs out and slouching. Sandy was at the window, looking out onto Place Vendôme traffic below.

She said, "I think we're OK. Doesn't look like the police are coming after us."

"Oh, that's just great," I said as sarcastically as I could manage. "So the cops are after you for something? Did you get into the Country illegally?" I wouldn't put that past her; she's done stranger things to get us out of trouble.

She giggled at that but said nothing. I got to my feet, went to her and turned her around, bringing her to me. I kissed her and hugged her as tight as I could. I had missed her, although I was glad she hadn't been with me at the chateau. Too many bullets were flying around. I whispered, "I'm glad you're here . . . But why?"

"Oh, Morgan . . . I wasn't able to sleep knowing you're here all alone." She pulled away from me, looked up at me, and that beautiful smile of hers radiated the entire room. She said with a laugh, "I mean, all those French women chasing after you! I had to protect you!"

It was still early in the morning, not quite 8 AM. I was hungry, and the thought of wonderful French croissants, cream filled pastries, fatty ham, rich cheese, and dark, strong coffee filled my head. But the few days of enjoying the best food France had to offer were over now that Sandy was there.

She went to the phone and ordered yogurt, fresh fruit, wheat toast, orange juice and coffee. Well, at least the coffee would be good.

We sat next to each other on the couch . . . Very close to each other . . . And Sandy asked, "So, tell me what you've been doing."

There was no sense withholding any truth from her. She would, as usual, find out everything sooner or later, so I told her the whole story, from the moment she left for home on the jet. Breakfast . . . Such as it was . . . Was delivered as I finished the story.

"Morgan," Sandy started. "You killed those people . . . And you're walking free. How?"

Now that was a good question. Maybe that's what Inspector Renard wanted me in his car for? But that was something I was trying to figure out. I tried to explain what I was thinking. "Whatever was going on . . . Between

DuSomme, DeLocke, and Lorraine . . . Is something that someone thinks I can figure out better than they can."

"Does that make sense, Morgan?"

"Sandy," I said, a slight bit of humor behind what I was saying. "How many times have the cops let us go our own way to do what they can't do . . . Legally?"

"Yes, of course," she said. She put her hand on my knee, a motherly gesture I was used to when she would try to talk me out of doing something dangerous. "But we're not at home. We're all alone in a foreign Country. We have no resources . . . No one to help us."

Putting my hand on top of Sandy's I said, hoping to explain how I felt deep inside of me, "I came here to find out why LeRoy was killed. I can't just walk away from that. Yes, I was used by everyone in that . . . Whatever it was . . . That thing at DeLocke's chateau. I have no idea why they let me do what I did. But that's over. I need to find out what happened to LeRoy and why it happened."

"And that means confronting Alain DuSomme again," Sandy said.

"Right. Got any ideas, sweetums?"

She laughed, uncomfortably, and said, honestly but not wanting to say it, "We have to go back to L'ange Bleu."

✱✱✱✱✱✱✱✱✱✱✱✱✱✱

Paris in the spring brought more of its rain that night. We bundled up as best we could and bought a big, golf size umbrella in the hotel's little shop. I figured besides keeping us dry, it might just make a good weapon.

The cobblestone alleyway that was the home of DuSomme's L'ange Bleu was puddled and slippery. We heard the slow, soft jazz filter through the green door of the basement club as we approached. The club's door had not been shut completely by the last person to enter – or maybe leave – the club. I pushed it open to let Sandy step inside, out of the rain, while I shook the wet from the umbrella.

The stairs down into the club were wet and a little slippery. I held onto Sandy, and she held onto a rusty metal handrail hanging on the brick wall to our left. We both carefully avoided the loose bricks on the stairs.

It was only a quarter to ten in the night, early for jazz clubs and those who frequent such places. But a few tourists were there.

L'ange Bleu boasted fourteen small tables, all mismatched, six of which were not occupied that night. We took the one nearest the stairs, just in case we had to make a fast exit.

A young man, eyes clouded with some kind of drug stumbled to our table. "Qu'auras-tu?"

"What?" I said. Sandy smiled, touched my arm lightly, and said to the waiter, "Vin rouge, s'il vous plaît. Deux."

He turned, sort of unsteady, almost tripping over his own feet, as if in a dream, and walked away. I wondered if he had heard Sandy. But it made no difference. The door at the side of the little stage opened, and Alain DuSomme walked through it. He stopped at the side of the stage; the quartet was deep into their own rendition of Trane's 'Slow Blues.'

He nodded knowingly and the smile that crossed his

lips was halfway between 'Glad to see you' and 'Now you're dead.' He walked very slowly across the stone floor, never taking his eyes off of us. A few of the young people who had started to come to the club for the jazz, the wine, and the marijuana watched him, curious at what was going to happen. All the tourists turned to watch, a few of them, sensing some kind of danger, got up and quickly left. The band, one by one, stopped playing in mid-song.

DuSomme stopped at our table; he stared down at us, his glare moving from me to Sandy and back to me. After a moment or two, I thought his glaring threats might go on forever so I said, to break the trance, "Pull up a chair and sit."

He nodded very slowly and pulled a chair from a nearby table. He sat across from us, leaning his arms on the small table. It took another minute, a very long minute, for him to say, "What the hell are you two doing here?"

His accent, I remembered was very slight. There was only a tinge of French in the words. I answered, waiting for Sandy to tell me not to, which she didn't, "I want to know why you murdered LeRoy Manns."

"What makes you think I murdered LeRoy?"

"Because he was afraid of you . . . The reason he was frightened of you I will find out sooner or later."

People were looking at us. The quartet had stopped playing. The room was eerily quiet. Everyone was staring at us. DuSomme was aware of this, as were Sandy and I. He said, "I won't discuss this with you here."

"Then where?" Sandy asked.

He obviously had to think about that. If he thought we would just go away because he denied killing LeRoy, he was wrong. I think he knew that.

"You will not leave me alone, will you?" he asked.

Sandy answered; her eyes locked on DuSomme's, "No."

"Very well," he said. "I will send a car for you in the morning. It will take you to my apartment. We can talk there."

I let out a quick guffaw and said, "I don' think so. I don't trust you. Back in the States being 'taken for a ride' usually means a one way ticket. You come to our suite at The Ritz. Come for breakfast. Nine o'clock. We can talk there."

The strange smile on DuSomme's lips faded quickly. But after a second or two, he nodded, stood, and walked away.

The drugged out young man, obviously oblivious of what had just occurred, brought our two glasses of red wine. The glasses had not been washed after the last customer's use; bright red lipstick was on one of them.

I dropped a few Euros on the table, and Sandy and I walked to the stairs and out into the cold and wet evening.

❋❋❋❋❋❋❋❋❋❋❋❋❋❋

We had a breakfast of a few fresh fruits, croissants, a few pastries, and a very large pot of coffee delivered to the room at a quarter to nine that morning. I had told room service to send three cups and three plates with the food. I frankly didn't expect DuSomme to show up, but I wanted to be ready just in case.

I wished I could order a very large pistol from room service. I anticipated staying in Paris trying to find out the reason for LeRoy's murder and being shot at a few times while trying to do that. But guns were not on the room service menu.

At exactly Nine AM the buzzer doorbell at the suite's door rang. Sandy started to get up to go to the door. I stopped her and pointed to our bedroom. I whispered, "Go. Say in there. We don't know if that's DuSomme or some killer he hired. They didn't call from the desk to let us know he's here."

Sandy went to the bedroom without the argument I had expected. She left the door open an inch or so, to see and hear. The front door of the suite had one of those peepholes in it. Looking through it, all I could see was an empty hallway. The door buzzer rang again. I knew I had to eventually open the door. So I did.

I had absolutely nothing to use as a defense. So, I would just fight as best I could . . . And I hoped Sandy would run to join in the fight. She's pretty good when she can swing a lamp or chair at somebody.

I swung the door inward very slowly. And when I could, I looked out. Alain DuSomme was standing there. His hands were folded in front of him, and he was grinning like a kid playing with a doorbell and then hiding.

"Are you alone?" I asked.

"Certainement . . . Excuse me, I mean certainly, Mr. Crew."

He took a step and stopped when I didn't move aside. "Will we talk in the hallway, Mr. Crew?"

I did take a couple of steps backward, and DuSomme

laughed and shook his head as he walked past me into the suite. He was dressed casually in tan slacks and brown loafers, highly polished. He wore a pale blue Polo shirt, unbuttoned at the neck. His clothes were dry even though it was raining lightly outside. I noticed that immediately and thought it very strange. He wasn't announced by the front desk, and he wasn't wet from the rain outside.

I had not noticed him wearing any jewelry when I spoke with him several times at his club, but on his right hand little finger he wore a gold ring with a single diamond on it. And on his left wrist he wore a diamond encrusted Rolex, bigger than my own.

He looked around the room approvingly, nodding and smiling, and finally took a seat in a soft chair near the couch. He crossed his legs, leaned back, and looked to his side at the table set for breakfast for three. He asked, "Will not your wife be joining us?"

The door to the bedroom opened, and Sandy walked into the room. She was carrying an eighteen inch tall statue of a woman that had been carved in stone, holding it at shoulder height, a club ready to be used. DuSomme took great amusement at that, laughed broadly and said, "Oh, Mrs. Crew! There will be no need for weapons! I am here to talk and nothing more."

She put the statue on a small table near the bedroom door, and both she and I walked to the couch and sat.

"We had some breakfast brought up," she said. "Can I get you some coffee?"

"Mrs. Crew . . . I am here to find out why the hell you two are so bothersome to me . . . Not to eat. Why are you . . . Une puce sur mon cul . . . A flea on my ass, as they say?"

"I think," I began. "No, I know . . . You killed a friend

of mine. LeRoy Manns. And I want to know why."

The smile never left DuSomme's face. It was a forced smile, a smile that was meant to hide his feelings, but I could see there was the threat of danger behind it. His eyes shifted from Sandy's eyes to mine and back to Sandy's. Behind his stare I could see the dangerous man he really was. I had seen that look before. DuSomme, I had been assured, was a hired killer. I had no reason to disbelieve that.

"I am the very curious one, Mr. Crew," DuSomme began. "Why is it you believe I am the person who killed your friend? I respected LeRoy's talent and the people who come to my club came to hear him above the other band members. Why would I kill him?"

"Because he heard something from your office at the club," I said.

"Is that so?" DuSomme was beginning to get nervous, but he was hiding it well. "And what was this thing that LeRoy heard?"

"I don't know that . . . Yet," I said. "When I do, I will know why he died. And when I do know, I will know why Germaine died and why Marie St. John died, and why Jean Paul Tavenier died, and why Mickey and Lilly died. I will have the evidence to see you prosecuted for murder."

DuSomme said nothing but continued to shift his gaze from Sandy to me. To break the silence, Sandy asked, "Look, I need to know why you kidnapped me. I think that may have something to do with LeRoy's murder."

"Not in the least," DuSomme said, and I believed him. I knew Sandy was trying to break through a different door to get at the truth. He had held her and had me go to DeLocke's chateau. If not for the meeting there, then what?

DuSomme went on, "I had a job to do. The two of you were in my way. I have no wish to harm either of you. I had to get you away for me to do what I was hired to do. I knew Lorraine was hired to kill those people. So I put you into that. To keep you out of my way, do you understand?"

Sandy said, "No. I don't understand. You had people rough me up at the damn airport. I was tied up in a shack and threats were made. Those three people at the farm . . . I saw you kill one of them."

"And you had me off on some kind of wild goose chase," I added. "You didn't want anything to do with the damn chateau but you had me . . . Case the joint, like the crooks in the movies say . . . I had to report to you about the layout of the chateau. Yet you say you had nothing to do with the people there. I think that's a damn lie."

That caused the easy smile on DuSomme's face to fall away really fast. I doubted he would kill us right in the middle of The Ritz. How would he get two bodies out of the hotel? Then the realization hit me that the desk hadn't phoned ahead of him coming to see us. Maybe no one saw him enter the hotel? Maybe he *could* get two dead bodies out without anyone seeing?

He glared at me, his quick hot anger obvious. But that quick anger also told me that, he being the professional I was told he was, the anger would disappear just as fast. He leaned back in the chair, and the forced little smile crept back across his lips.

He said, finally, "That is . . . OK as you Americans like to say. I understand the insult; I understand what you are doing."

"And just what am I doing?"

"You are trying to get me to say something I should

not say . . . Am I correct?"

"And what is it you're not supposed to say?"

DuSomme laughed a short, sudden laugh. He threw his head back and slapped his knee. He stood, straightened out the crease in his expensive slacks, snickered and shook his head in disbelief. He said, "I'm leaving now. I have a particular job to do. Do not stand in my way, please. You will not like what happens if you do. I have avoided killing you, but I may not be able to avoid that much longer."

He started for the door, but I stopped him. I asked, "Tell me if LeRoy was killed because he knew something he shouldn't have known. Not something about you . . . Just something he shouldn't have known."

He stood still for a moment, shook his head in his disbelief that I would push ahead in spite of his threats. He said in a dark whisper, "Believe whatever you want to believe."

DuSomme closed the suite's door softly, leaving Sandy and me alone.

EIGHTEEN - The Old Man

It was cold and wet at three in the morning as Sandy and I sat in the rented Toyota. I kept the windshield wipers on a slow interim wipe to clear the rain that had been falling since early evening the day before, even though I knew that was a bad idea; people would know someone was inside the car. We were parked a block away from the alley that was home to L'ange Bleu, where Lorraine had parked her car when she and I had waited for DuSomme.

"I'm cold," Sandy complained.

"Me too," I said. I wasn't about to keep the engine running; the wipers were enough to draw attention to us without having the engine running too. We were waiting for the club to close. It was mid-week, and we guessed that the club would be closing before the sun rose.

And we were right. At half past three people started to leave, huddled under umbrellas or just walking in the rain, ignoring it because of too much marijuana and too much bad wine. We would wait until we saw the band members leave. It was Patrice Laurent we were waiting for.

Well past three we saw Patrice walk out of the alley. The other members of the band were with him. They stood in the rain at the entrance to the alley, talking in the rain, under umbrellas. They pulled the collars of their coats up around their necks as some little protection. The umbrellas did little to keep the heavy rain away.

After a minute of talking they split up and started walking away, towards their homes I imagined. Patrice crossed the cobblestone street and turned left at the corner. He was walking fast, without an umbrella, and he was hunched over, pulling his long trench coat tightly around him.

When he was at the next corner I started the engine and pulled away from the curb to follow him. I left the headlights off and drove slowly. We watched him turn left at the corner. As I turned the corner we saw him use a key to open a bright blue door on the right side of the street. I stopped the car immediately and we waited for him to go inside the building.

I spoke to Sandy, "Wait here. I'm going to try to talk to him."

"Like hell," she said as she opened the passenger side door and stepped out into the cold rain.

The door that Patrice went through was the entrance to a six unit apartment building. The door, etched glass panels revealing a dark hallway inside, was locked.

On the wall at the side of the door were six tarnished brass buttons without names on any of them. I shrugged my shoulders and pushed each button, one at a time. A moment later a buzzing sound threw the lock, and the door opened a half inch. I pushed it open, and Sandy followed me into the unlit hallway.

A staircase was to the right of a dark hallway. A dim, single bulb suddenly flashed on. The light couldn't reach the foot of the stairs but at the top we saw Patrice Laurent standing there. His right hand was on the stair's railing, his left hand held a revolver, held at waist height.

"What is it you want?" he said.

"We want to speak with you," I said. I put a foot on

the bottom step of the staircase.

"Do not walk up the stairs, Monsieur Crew!" he ordered. He raised his pistol and pointed it down at Sandy and me.

"All I want is to talk with you Mr. Laurent. Nothing more."

"You talk with some people . . . And they die, no? Why is it I should so suddenly talk with you?"

"Because I think you were friends with LeRoy and Germaine. And I think you know why they were killed. I want to find out why they were killed . . . And who killed them. Help me."

Patrice was thinking. He knew what I had said was the truth, and I knew he knew that. He had cared about his trumpet player friend, and he had cared about Germaine. I felt that inside; he was a good man surrounded by very bad things. The weight of the revolver brought his hand down to his thigh. That told me he wanted to do something about LeRoy's death as much as I did. He was just scared.

"Bien," he said reluctantly. "Come up . . . But you must leave soon."

Sandy followed me, racing up the stairs that creaked loudly under foot. Patrice turned and walked into his apartment. We followed.

Patrice stood at the door, holding it open for Sandy and me to walk inside. It was a small, dark, one room place. A round table sat under the lone window that was curtained in a tattered yellow cloth, thin with age. One old wood chair was at the table. A bed with white painted metal head and foot, a lot of the paint having been chipped away, filled most of the room. A red flowered quilt, frayed at its edges and torn in a corner at the foot, was rumpled around a woman who lay on the bed.

She sat up in bed as we walked in, leaning back on her arms. The quilt was at her waist, her bare breasts exposed, her hair rumpled from sleep. She was not a young woman, her age revealed by her hick grey and black hair. She was a light skin black woman with dark, piercing eyes that shot back and forth between Sandy and me. Her breasts hung low, her skin was wrinkled, her arms thin.

She spoke to Patrice in French, her voice foggy from sleep, "Qui sont-ils?" 'Who are they?' she asked.

Patrice looked at us and said in French, "They want to talk to me, mon chérie. Cover yourself."

The woman pulled the quilt up slowly as she glared at us. She lay back on the bed, and pulled the quilt up over her head.

I asked Patrice, "Is there someplace we can talk? In private I mean."

"Here . . . Pourquoi pas? . . . There is no other place, oui? And she does not know the English, oui?"

Sandy was glaring down at the woman in the bed. She asked Patrice without looking at him, "You live here?"

"Non . . . No . . . You followed me . . . I know that. It is not for you to know where I live. I come here so you do not know."

I looked around the room; the lone chair was the only place to sit. Patrice guessed what I was looking for and said, "S'il vous plaît, you will not be here long enough to sit, oui? What do you want?"

"I want to know what you know about LeRoy Manns," I said.

Sandy was still glaring at the woman under the quilt. I

elbowed her gently to get her attention. She nodded and relaxed a little.

Patrice said, "LeRoy, he was the good . . . What is the word . . ."

"Musician?" Sandy asked.

"Non bien sûr que non," Patrice started. "LeRoy, he was more than as you say the good musician. He was the man who would do good . . . Do the good for others, oui? You understand?"

"So, what did he know that got him murdered?" Sandy asked.

Patrice lowered his gaze from us. He was scared, frightened of what truth he must have known. His voice was cracking and soft as he said, "I know nothing . . . Nothing."

I said, "Patrice . . . Somehow I don't believe that. What you tell me will remain between you and me. No one will know that you spoke with me."

Patrice shook his head and nodded towards the woman in the bed. I understood, he could not talk freely in front of the woman even if she did not understand English. I imagine he had the idea that Sandy and I would simply leave, but we didn't.

I said, "Come with us. We can talk at our hotel."

"No," he said. "I cannot be seen with you . . . No."

"Where then?" Sandy asked. I could see she was losing her patience with all this. She kept looking sideways, down at the quilt covered woman in the bed who had started snoring loudly. Sandy was either uncomfortable or offended at the woman who had little care about being naked in front of strangers.

Patrice thought for a moment or two and then said,

"Go to the hotel. I will speak with you soon."

****

"Damn it! I want to go back to the club and confront DuSomme," Sandy demanded.

We had not left the suite at The Ritz for two days. We ordered meals from room service, we slept little, and we paced around the rooms and looked out the windows at the springtime showers Paris is famous for. But Patrice had not contacted us yet.

"What good would that do?" I asked her. "Are we gonna' beat the truth out of him? I think not. We just have to be patient."

"And while we wait here patiently our daughter is back home."

"Betsy is taking care of her," I said.

"I'm going to phone and say hello to her," Sandy said, "Before she forgets who I am."

She stepped quickly toward the small polished Louis XIV style work desk and the phone there. Her hand was reaching for the phone when it rang. She picked it up quickly.

"Hello, yes, what?" she managed with short anger in her voice.

She listened and turned to me. She spoke into the phone, "OK, send them up."

"It's Patrice," she said. "He has someone with him."

I stood, and we both walked to the door, waiting there. 'Someone' could be DuSomme or one of his killers. Maybe we had gone too far, and DuSomme had had enough of us. I looked around the room for some kind of weapon. Maybe a lamp . . . Maybe one of the small statues . . . Or that statute Sandy had found in the bedroom the last time DuSomme had visited us.

The door buzzer sounded; I stopped Sandy from opening the door. I put my eye to the eyehole in the door. Patrice was there, and with him was an old man, a foot shorter than Patrice, with grey hair balding on the top of his head while hanging over his ears. Three or four days of grey beard hung under a full and thick, grey mustache, yellowed by tobacco smoke. He was bent over from age and perhaps life. But I doubted he was a killer, so I opened the door.

"Bonjour," Patrice said. He wasn't smiling, and he looked left and right up and down the hallway. "Please, we must not stand here."

I stepped aside, and both men walked in quickly. "Close the door," he said. He was sweating and visibly nervous. "Please lock the door, Monsieur Crew."

It was mid-morning, and Sandy had ordered coffee for her and me. It lay untouched on the elaborately inlaid coffee table. She offered it to Patrice and the man he brought to us. Patrice declined, but the little man smiled a grandfatherly smile and said he would like a cup.

"Yes, pretty lady," he said. "I would like a cup, please." He walked to the couch and sat as Sandy poured a coffee for him. He nodded towards the silver cream and sugar service. Sandy sweetened the coffee for him while he smiled appreciatively. He took it, sipped at it and smiled up at Sandy once again. "It is so good," he said. "Is there perhaps more sugar . . . And perhaps just a little more cream?"

His accent was heavy but not French, possibly Germanic. Sandy and I drink our coffee black, but she had ordered cream and sugar in case anyone wanted it. She tipped the creamer and filled the old man's cup to its brim. He took the spoon from the sugar bowl and poured three full spoons into his cup, coming close to spilling coffee from the delicate china cup.

Sandy looked at Patrice and said, "Won't you introduce us to your friend?"

"No, pretty lady," the old man said. He laid the cup and saucer gently onto the coffee table. "I am here to give you . . . Is the word Inform? Not to be social."

"Information?" Sandy suggested.

"Yes, of course," he said. "But who I am must remain with me. Now, Herr Laurent says you wish to know of your friend Herr Manns. What can I tell you?"

Sandy sat on the couch next to him, and I went to an armchair at his side. Patrice remained standing and remained visibly uneasy. I thought he might turn and run from the suite at any minute.

I asked the old man, "Who killed LeRoy?"

"That I know who killed your friend is something I would wish for."

"Then why are you here?" I demanded.

"The *who* is often not the same as the *why*. I can help you understand the *why,* and when you understand the *why* you may know the *who*," he said and smiled again. He sounded like a kindly grandfather teaching something of value to a child. "The young want to rush to the end while with age comes patience. One thing at a time, Herr Crew."

"OK, why?" I said.

"Patience is something you may not have not yet learned," he said, shaking his head sorrowfully. "I will tell you, but you must be calm, yes?"

We said nothing; Sandy and I were both almost glaring at the old man, our 'patience' close to an end. If he knew something, I just wanted him to say what he knew. But the old man had a story to tell and he would tell it, knowing well Sandy and I were impatient to learn what he knew. I think he enjoyed knowing he was frustrating us.

He began, "I do not know when I was born. But the Nazis were conquering Europe, and I have been told I was sent, as a baby, to Palestine. I am told the people who may have been my mother and father were sent to the gas chamber. You see, I am Jewish. I was raised by a good family on a Kibbutz where we grew oranges and lemons and vegetables. It was a good life for a boy. Even if I often wondered who my parents were.

"There was sunshine and good food and friends. But war came, and I joined the Haganah and I fought for my homeland. I was just a boy; I was told I was not yet a teen, but in truth I didn't know my real age. I carried a rifle, and I killed when I had the chance. I killed Arabs who would kill me and my friends at the Kibbutz. For more than sixty years I have been fighting for my Country and homeland. For more than sixty years I have been killing Arabs."

The old man stopped talking for a moment. He took a deep and sad breath, his eyes clouded with tears at the thoughts of his childhood years. Sandy put her hand gently on the old man's shoulder. She whispered, "It's OK. We understand." He took the cup from the table and drank some coffee.

Laying the cup on the table carefully and slowly, he smiled thankfully and went on. "For all my life, for more than sixty years, there have been people who want to destroy Israel. Bombs, terrorists, war . . . All have been used in attempts to kill us and drive us from our homeland. But more recently there has been a group of people who would destroy Israel by destroying Israel's economy."

He paused once again and looked at me with a wondering smile on his ancient face. I asked, "Do you mean the meeting at François DeLocke's chateau?"

"Ah!" he said. "You are very cognitive, Herr Crew. Not many people would make the connection."

I explained, "Mr. . . . Whoever you are. I've been in this for a long time. I don't believe in coincidence. I know DuSomme is somehow involved in that. I need to know why and how that is connected to LeRoy Manns' death."

Patrice had stopped his pacing. He stood four or five feet away, staring at us. He was sweating profusely; his hands were at his side, shaking uncontrollably. In a quaking voice he said, "Non, I cannot be a part of this. I leave now." He turned quickly and ran from the suite.

"Do not be angry with him, Herr Crew. Fear, it is a terrible thing."

I nodded and said, "Go on with your story."

"Story? Story you say? It is not a story, Herr Crew. It is a sad fact that so much of the world hates Jews, and the rest of the world, who don't hate Jews, turn a blind eye to this hate for oil and money. What I tell you is not a story. It is very sad fact. We fight for our lives, Herr Crew."

"I'm sorry," I said. I didn't know what else to say. Yes, I've seen on the TV news all the killings and hatred. I've read in all the papers about the Arab Nations whose sole goal in life is to destroy Israel. And what have I done about it? Nothing but change the channels and turn the pages of the newspapers.

The old man went on, "Your friend was murdered because he knew certain things. Others would have shrugged their shoulders so to speak and gone on with their own small lives." I felt almost ashamed. Was he speaking to me? "But your friend would not do this. You should admire him as well as think of him as a friend."

The old man said this with a lot of recognizable anger. I answered, "Over the years I have come to admire anyone who faces evil rather than run from it. But if I'm going to do something about who killed LeRoy Manns, I need to know more from you."

"Yes, of course," he said. "The meeting of the people at that place was not a business meeting. Criminals . . . Some would call these men Arab fanatics . . . Others would call them Arab terrorists . . . Criminals from Lebanon who were working with Iran, paid by Iran, were there to buy secrets. Israeli secrets. But the people who would sell the secrets were to be killed by people hired by Iran rather than paid for the secrets."

He paused again, reached for the cup of coffee and drank. He smiled at me, holding the cup and saucer in both hands, waiting for me to say something. To give him what he wanted I offered, "Military secrets."

The old man shook his head, satisfied that I was wrong. He said, "No, these secrets are economic. Government and corporate money accounts, passwords, computer programs. Things in today's world that are money," he said with a derogatory wave of his hand in the air. "These things, if known to the criminals, would destroy Israel's economy . . . Or at the least weaken Israel's economy long enough for it to be unable to protect itself against attacks."

"And François DeLocke knew this?" I asked.

"The man is a greedy bastard," the old man spit out. He would have been paid a great sum of American dollars. What he didn't know was that those American dollars were counterfeit, printed in America. Oh, they were very good copies. Even a man such as François DeLocke would not know they were mere copies, forgeries."

I thought but did not say that getting a lot of counterfeit dollars would have been a good thing for the man. I asked, "How about Alain DuSomme?"

"Ahhh," the old man said as he laid the cup and saucer again on the table. He nodded and seemed happy at the thought of DuSomme. "There is a group of people who would do what they can to protect Israel. We . . . Excuse me, I mean they . . . Often work outside the normal channels of Governments and the law. This organization had planned to kill the people at DeLocke's home. But you, Herr Crew, did the job of stopping what those people had planned. Unfortunately, you left them alive."

He paused for a moment in sad thought and continued, "It would have been better that they had been killed. But that cannot be helped. This organization I speak of will kill these people because we . . . I should say they . . . Know they will try once more.

"Alain DuSomme," he went on, "now has a new contract with some very disreputable people. He has been retained to kill someone."

A few slow moments slipped by with me looking at the old man and him looking at me, with a catlike grin on his grey face.

I asked, "And that someone is you?"

"Very good, Herr Crew. But I have seen many years . . . As you might assume as you look at me . . . And there have been many people who have tried to kill me. And as you can see . . . I am still here, and many of those people who have tried to kill me are dead, damn their souls to hell."

Sandy's face was pale; her jaw was open; disbelief or perhaps a driving need to not believe as some sort of protection filled her mind.

"Morgan," she said, her voice weak and filled with trepidation, "Let's get out of here. This is more than we can handle."

She was right, of course. But all the old man told us had, as yet, nothing to do with LeRoy Manns' murder.

I asked the old man, "How does all this relate to my friend's death?"

"Herr Crew," he said, his voice revealing his sadness at what life has to offer. "The death of your friend . . . Although unfortunate . . . Has little to do with a war that has continued for over two thousand years."

"Mr. . . . Whatever the hell your name is . . . I fully understand the history of the Jewish people. Don't patronize me. I may have stepped into some horse shit at the chateau, but I did that not knowing you folks had your plans. All I've done since arriving in Paris is try to find out who killed my friend. I wish you well on what you do, but if you know why LeRoy was murdered and who killed him tell me now . . . And I mean that as a threat . . . If you want to leave this room. I'm not much of a killer but someone as old as you wouldn't stand a chance against me."

The old man looked up at me and said, "Your friend heard something he should not have heard. He had left the little stage at L'ange Bleu to use a rest room.   Herr DuSomme's office door was open.   He was on the telephone." He laughed and said, "We have been listening to his phone calls for some time.   The discussion was with an Arab man . . . His name is not important now . . . An Arab man who wanted to be certain the meeting at DeLocke's was successful.   We . . . I mean the men who would stop the meeting had to be eliminated by DuSomme.   Your friend overheard and he was murdered."

"By DuSomme or someone who works for him?" I asked.

"This I do not know.   But be assured he was responsible." I could almost feel his eyes gazing into mine. He asked, "And what will you do, Herr Crew?"

"I will have him charged with murder . . . Or kill him."

Sandy gasped; her hands went to cover her lips. "Morgan! Can you hear yourself?"

"LeRoy Manns, Germaine LeFont, Jean Paul Tavenier, and Marie St. John were all murdered by DuSomme.   It seems the police can do nothing to bring DuSomme to justice. I have pressed that Inspector Renard. All he can say is that there is no evidence. I was let go by the police and the American Embassy because I might be able to do what the police and two Governments cannot do because of the restraint of law. I think I'm expected to end DuSomme's murders."

Sandy was almost in tears. She said, "Oh, Morgan!"

The old man stood, the groans of old age accompanying his efforts. He said as he stood, "I will leave you now, Herr Crew. I wish you the best. But I cannot be of help to you. Do you understand?"

"I understand," I said. I knew, as usual, I was alone.

My life is to do what others cannot or will not do for themselves. My family has too much money to count, and I could live a life of ease and decadence if I wanted to. But I have found that I have other things to do with my life, like bringing Alain DuSomme, a professional killer, to justice . . . Or to death.

I watched as the old man walked slowly out of the suite. I went to the bar and poured a tall bourbon with just a splash of club soda. Sandy was at my side as she poured an equally tall vodka over ice and drizzled in a little tonic. The hotel had a hard time finding Wild Turkey 101 for me but it had a supply of Absolute vodka. I drank something the Europeans called 'bourbon,' but it wasn't. Oh well. I am in the habit of making the best of everything that confronts me, even imitation bourbon.

We stood next to each other, drinks in hand but not drinking them. After a long silence Sandy asked, "What now?"

NINETEEN - Burglaries

We found ourselves in our rented Toyota once again, waiting in the street again at half past three in the morning. We didn't have much to go on to bring Alain DuSomme down. I had told Sandy that, as nasty as it sounded, I really wasn't interested in what the Arabs, the Iranians, the Iraqis, and all the rest of the bunch were up to. "Let the old man and his organization take care of that. I just want to get DuSomme for LeRoy's murder and go home."

It had been an unusually dry day for springtime in Paris, and the dark sky that night was cloudless and filled with stars. We had spent the afternoon walking, finding our way to The Avenue des Champs-Élysées where we stopped for coffee at a nice little sidewalk café. We watched the young people walk by; the shoppers and wealthy women with little poodles on rhinestone leashes. Sandy ducked into a few very outrageously expensive women's clothing shops and bought nothing.

After wandering a few more streets, not knowing where we were, we found the Eiffel Tower. Taking the elevator up, we ate an outrageously expensive lunch – I mentioned to Sandy as we ate that maybe everything in Paris was outrageously expensive. After finishing lunch, we peered over the railing of the tower and took in the glorious view of all of Paris, laid out before our eyes. It was a beautiful, clear day, and the city looked magnificent. We wished we were on a fun-filled, relaxing vacation so that we could take the time to see more of the beautiful buildings and sites that Paris had to offer.

As the sun was beginning to set we took a taxi back to The Ritz and tried to eat some food in our suite. But our appetites just weren't there. Worry about what we had to do filled our minds and the few words we spoke.

Well after midnight we went downstairs to the rented car we had waiting and drove away. Near four in the morning the young patrons of L'ange Bleu had wandered away; the four band members had gone their separate ways after standing in the street, talking for a few minutes. We waited for Alain DuSomme to leave. We had spent the night waiting in the car talking about what we would do. Actually, we didn't have the faintest idea what we *could* do.

Sandy had used her cell phone to phone home twice during the afternoon, just to speak with our daughter. I knew she was scared; we were away from home and away from familiar territory, with no friends and little power. Hell, I was scared, too.

As we sat in the car talking and waiting, she said three times that she wanted us to go home, but I think she knew I wasn't going anywhere until I saw Alain DuSomme in jail . . . Or dead. This whole thing had become very personal with me. He had done too much to me . . . And to Sandy.

We had been silent for over an hour as we watched and waited. Sandy was about to say something when DuSomme walked from the dark alley onto the street. He stopped at the curb, looked left and right, and then turned left and started walking away from us.

"Do we take the car or follow on foot?" Sandy asked.

I didn't answer because I didn't know. We watched DuSomme walk a block away and stop. He looked behind him and in the street ahead of him. At that hour of the morning, in that arrondissement, few people and cars were on the street. DuSomme crossed the narrow street, stopped again, looked left and right again, and then pulled open a garage door. He stepped inside and we waited.

A dark blue Jaguar F-Type backed out of the garage and turned left on the street.

"Now we follow," I said.

I pulled away from the curb but left the car's headlights off. It was dangerous driving without headlights, but it was necessary. At that time of the morning if DuSomme saw headlights he would know he was being followed.

We followed DuSomme at a distance. Not having any other cars on the street meant we could follow him without getting close enough to be seen. He drove slowly, lower than the speed limit. It was maddening not knowing what he was doing, but we went on because it was all we had.

We followed for over half an hour. DuSomme was obviously being very careful. He made turns left and right and doubled back on himself several times. Finally he pulled his car to a stop in front of a grand 19th Century building in the grand Saint Germain-des-Prés neighborhood of the 6th Arrondissement. Lorraine and I had followed DuSomme several times but never to that place. The thought occurred to me that DuSomme had known he was being followed back then and led us on a wild goose chase.

A man ran down the front steps as DuSomme got out of his car. He handed the keys to the man who bowed slightly and drove the car away. DuSomme took the eight steps up to the front door of the building two at a time. He stopped at the door with a single key on a gold chain in his hand. He once again looked left and right, and then unlocked and opened the tall, etched glass door and went inside.

"Now we know where he lives," I said.

Sandy nodded and asked, "So what do we do now?"

"We go back to L'ange Bleu."

Sandy looked sideways at me and asked, "Why?"

"Chances are DuSomme has something . . . Some evidence of what he does . . . And chances are he has that either at L'ange Bleu or inside his home. Of course he may have someplace else he does business at. But L'ange Bleu is a place to start. Tomorrow, while he is at the club, we'll get into his home. Right now we'll get into L'ange Bleu."

"I thought you told me you searched his office once . . . With that Cop Tavenier?"

"I did, and I found his bank account numbers. But there has to be something about what he has planned.

"You know you're crazy, don't you, Morgan?" Sandy said, smiling. "But I love it. You're an exciting person, and you get me excited, too."

✳✳✳✳✳✳✳✳✳✳✳✳✳✳

We walked down the thin, damp and dirty, unnamed alley where L'ange Bleu was located. I had bought a flashlight at the hotel's gift shop. It wasn't much, just a plastic flashlight that gave off a dim light, but it was better than not having anything.

It was a thin alleyway, lined with garbage cans and musty odors. A black cat jumped from an uncovered trash can and ran across our path. I shined the light on it as it ran.

Sandy said, "A premonition of bad things?"

"Yeah," I said sardonically. "We both know that ain't unusual."

We approached the door to the club with slow, short steps. I think we were both expecting someone to jump from the shadows and fall on us. But we were alone in the alley when we reached the paint flaking wooden door. It was locked of course.

"What now, Mr. Cat Burglar?" Sandy asked.

"There was a cleaning lady here the last time I was here. But that was in the afternoon. I guess we missed her."

I started walking further into the dark alley. There were no lights so my little flashlight had to do. The three little windows down at our feet I knew were there. But we were too close to the street to break any of them and try to climb in.

At the end of the alley we found what at first sight was a dead end and an eight foot tall battered wooden fence that was lined with trash that had been lying there . . . Forever judging from the smell of it. I shone the light at the fence and along it. The fence ran behind the building, about three feet from the back wall of the old building. So it wasn't a dead end after all.

Sandy followed me as I walked along the back of the building. The place stunk of rotted garbage, rotted fish, and old urine. But I kept going anyway.

I kicked some of the filth away from the brick wall of the building and found a small window down near the cobblestone alley. It was perhaps a foot and a half tall, or maybe a little more, and perhaps twenty-four inches wide. It was bigger than the three windows along the alley, big enough for us to slip through if we could get the window open.

I bent and knelt on a pile of old, wet newspapers. I tried pushing on the dirty glass. It was either locked or frozen with age and grime. So I stood and kicked the glass. On the third kick the glass broke. It sounded like a bullet going off, but I knew it really wasn't that loud, and we were in a back alley in a time of night that no one would be awake to hear it.

"Oh, that's just perfect, Morgan, dear," Sandy said sarcastically. "Now I can tear my clothes and cut myself up a dozen times climbing through."

But I knew what I was doing. I knelt again and carefully reached in through the broken window, avoiding the broken shards of glass. My hand felt the lock, and I forced it open. I pushed the window up. It squeaked loudly, but it stayed open. I brushed the broken glass away from the window frame and, feet first, I climbed through, dropping to the floor inside.

Sandy followed; I caught her as she slid through and gently lowered her to the floor.

"That's a tight fit, Morgan," she said. "I'm amazed you made it through. You just have to lose those twenty pounds I've been telling you about. As soon as we get home I'm putting you and me on a diet." I didn't tell her about all the good and very rich French food I'd been eating while she was in California. I'm not stupid you know.

After the years I've spent with the love of my life I've learned not to argue with her, especially about my weight. So, I knew I'd be eating light as soon as all this was over and we were back home.

It was pitch black inside whatever room we were in. Since giving up cigarettes so many years ago I haven't carried a lighter or matches. Sandy took her ring of keys from the small purse she carried. On the ring was a small flashlight meant to illuminate a lock she would use her keys on. It didn't throw off much light, but along with the small flashlight I had we could at least not walk into walls or trip over anything in the dark.

The room was a storage room filled with boxes of wines and liquor. Too much for such a small club, I thought. DuSomme must have some criminal use for all that, I assumed. The young people who frequented his jazz club drank cheap wine and smoked marijuana. Only a few of the early-night tourists enjoyed half way decent liquor and better wines. And there was too much there for the few tourists to drink.

In a corner near the only door out of the cellar was a plastic bucket holding a mop, a broom and a few bottles of cleaning stuff. The door was closed; I hoped it wasn't locked because breaking it down would be difficult . . . For me anyway.

Sandy started for the door, walking too quickly. She didn't have the experience I had with breaking and entering. I called out in a whisper, "Sandy! Don't touch the door! Don't touch anything! If DuSomme calls in the police, they'll look for finger prints."

She stopped and nodded. She understood that we could not leave any evidence of having been there. DuSomme would see the broken window of course. He would know someone had broken in. Since none of the wine and booze would be missing, he would probably guess it was me, but he wouldn't know for sure.

In my mind I felt sure DuSomme was not going to

report the entry to the police; he had too much to hide. All that good wine and liquor, and I felt certain he had a stash of marijuana . . . And probably more dangerous drugs . . . In the cellar could not be revealed to the police. But he might be able to trace us via fingerprints we might leave. Alain DuSomme was not a petty thief. He would have resources all over the world, and one of those many resources would be a means to retrieve and trace fingerprints.

I used my handkerchief to open the door from the storage room to the club. It wasn't locked as I had hoped it would not be. A wooden staircase led up to the club, only a few steps but they were old and noisy. We took them slowly, one at a time, to another door that had to lead to the back of the club, to the hallway in which DuSomme's office and the band's break room were.

I was right as we stepped into the kitchen at the end of the dark hallway. Sandy followed me down the short hall to the door that led to the club itself. It was dark inside the basement club but not as dark as the storage room. The three little windows along the alley did very little to let any moonlight in. But two dim lights hanging on opposite walls were lit and cast enough light to walk through the club without walking into tables and chairs.

After making sure no one was in the club I turned back to the hallway. "Where are we going?" Sandy asked.

"To DuSomme's office."

"You think there's something there that will incriminate him in the murders?"

"I don't know, dear," I said. "I'm just kind of playing this by ear. I found where he keeps his bank information. Something else might be there. I'm just playing this by ear."

The door to DuSomme's office was closed and

locked. "Now what?" Sandy asked.

'What the hell' I thought. I broke the window, why not the door, too. DuSomme would know someone had broken in by the broken window.

I hit the door with my shoulder. The thin door frame splintered as the door flew open on its hinges. There was a loud crash that echoed throughout the hallway. But the club and the hallway were in a basement, below ground. If anybody had been out on the street, it would have been unlikely they would have heard.

"Oh, that's just real nice," Sandy said. "Now no one will know anyone's been here." I reminded her that there was a broken window down in the storage room.

Inside the office I found a light switch on the wall. Two florescent tubes flickered to life. The two gray colored metal filing cabinets that I had rifled through with Tavenier were still there and were still standing against the wall behind DuSomme's desk. Both were locked, a button lock at the top of each had been pushed, locking the drawers.

Sandy stood at the open door, watching and every now and again shaking her head in disbelief at what I was doing. I found the metal letter opener on the desk and used it to force open both locks, both basic and not meant for real security.

I went through each of the eight drawers and found nothing but the same routine business papers for the club that had been there the last time I was there. One of the manila folders contained payroll records. It seems DuSomme wasn't paying his band members very much more than a basic living wage. Yet they seemed to stay in his employ for a long time.

I filed that away in the back of my brain. They were

good for club musicians and could have moved on to better pay, yet for some reason they stayed with DuSomme and low wages. Fear is a great argument for them to stay.

Turning away from the cabinets, I said, "There's nothing here." But Sandy wasn't there. A dim light from a room across the hall had been lit. It was the breakroom the band used. Sandy was in there, searching through everything.

I looked for the bank account papers but they were gone. I had told Peter Jascro to keep an eye on the accounts, to keep a record of monies in and out. He would have told me of major transfers. I had an idea how to use those bank accounts, and I needed to keep track of them. Peter would do that for me.

The band's break room hadn't changed much; a small round table circled by five folding metal chairs filled the small room. A scratched and worn wooden cabinet from someone's old kitchen lined a third of the back wall of the room. The top was old green vinyl, tattered and torn.

Standing at the open door I watched Sandy as she opened the four doors of the cabinet and looked inside each. Inside the fourth she found the thin back wall of the cabinet hanging loose just a half inch or so. She pulled it aside and found a small round wall safe, the kind with a dial and handle to open it. It was sunk into the wall between the breakroom and the club on the other side.

"OK, big guy," she said to me. "How are you at opening safes?"

"Other than what I've seen on TV, I have no idea." I said, "I haven't had to do that yet."

It was on one of those old TV shows that I remembered seeing something about wall safes. The front of safes, and often the sides and top, are usually built very strong. But the back of wall safes, because they are to be built into walls, are often not as strong.

I left the breakroom and went to the stage where the quartet played. The wall was thin wallboard. I tapped on it until I heard a solid sound. Kicking at it with the heel of my shoe I managed to crack the wallboard. Tearing out the broken pieces of wallboard, I was able to expose the back of the little safe. Sandy was watching, and I felt a little masculine pride. I hoped she was impressed.

"OK . . . Now what?" Sandy asked.

I went back to the wooden stairs to the storage room and found a light switch on the wall we hadn't seen. The room lit up. In a corner, on the floor, next to a stack of boxes, I found an open cardboard box with a few tools in it. I pulled a hammer and a long neck screw driver from the box.

The back of the safe had been spot welded to the walls of the safe. It took some time and some work, but using the hammer and screw driver, I managed to chip away the welds. When that was done the back of the safe fell off easily enough.

Inside I found a small ledger book. It was two thirds full of names, dates, money amounts, places, and notations, all in French. The safe had nothing else in it.

"That has to be important, Morgan," Sandy said.

"We'll take it with us. I hope you can translate enough of it. Let's get out of here. We've been here too long already. That cleaning lady is bound to show up any time now."

Sandy looked around the mess we had made, laughed and said, "Yeah, no one's gonna' know we were here."

I wiped my finger prints off of the hammer and screw driver. Sandy wiped the back of the safe I had ripped off. We went back to the band's little break room and wiped everything very carefully. We did the same in DuSomme's office.

We took one last look around to be sure we hadn't left any evidence of our thievery and went out the small window in the storage room we had come in through. It was much harder getting out than getting in, and I managed to tear my slacks at the knee.

That we had gotten away with such a small crime, one that would never be reported to the police, made both of us giddy. We wanted to run and laugh like a couple of kids who just stole a candy bar from the shop up the street. But we walked slowly back to the car so as not to draw attention. We drove away like normal people who weren't burglars.

✳✳✳✳✳✳✳✳✳✳✳✳✳✳✳

Alain DuSomme was asleep in the arms of a young woman he had met at his club that night. It was a few minutes past six in the morning when his phone started ringing. He wanted to rip the damn cord from the wall but he picked up the receiver instead. It was his cleaning lady at the club. She was yelling something in her guttural French that DuSomme had to tell her to repeat a couple of times to understand what she was saying.

The club had been broken into during the night, at least that is what he thought she was saying. He slammed the phone down and got out of bed.

"Reviens au lit," the teenage girl said. "Come back to bed."

DuSomme ignored her. He dressed quickly in the clothes he had worn that night and had dropped on the floor as the girl undressed. He told her to go home as he left his apartment. He drove his jaguar breaking the speed limits to get to L'ange Bleu. If someone had stolen some wine or liquor, or even a bag of marijuana, he didn't care. It was all bought cheaply from thieves anyway. But he had a book there, and that is what he was worried about.

"I should never have left it there," he said out loud, talking to himself as he sped through the deserted streets. He hit the steering wheel of the Jaguar in his anger at being so stupid. But it was in the safe, he thought. And hidden. No, someone just stole some wine.

He slowed down before the police could stop him. The police couldn't know of a break-in. Even the wine could not be reported because no tax would be paid on it. He had bought it and everything else on the black market. No, the police could not know. He would handle the theft himself. He knew people, he thought. People who would know who the thieves were. He would find the thieves and extract revenge as full payment.

He pulled to the curb on the cobblestoned street in front of the alley, the Jaguar skidding on the wet street. He got out of the car and locked the doors. The sun was just rising up above the horizon, and a few people were already on the street, passing by in cars, on their way to work.

He waited on the curb, smoking a cigarette until the street was empty of people who could see him walk into the alley. The door to the club was hanging open, light pouring from it into the alley. His cleaning lady was standing in the open doorway, shaking with fear.

DuSomme gave her twenty Euros and told her to go home. He added another ten Euros and told her to not tell anyone of the break-in. She nodded, not sure why her boss wanted the burglary to be kept a secret, but she would do what he told her to do. No one . . . But maybe her old husband at home . . . Would know.

Inside, DuSomme's eye immediately went to the hole in the wall behind the little stage where the quartet played. He swore and tossed a chair across the room. Someone had ripped open the safe from the rear, and it was now empty. His ledger was gone. Anger filled his head, but he quickly calmed himself. He knew he had to remain calm and think clearly. Evidence of his murders and all the money he had received, all the people who had hired him, all the bribes he had paid, everything was in the hands of someone. He punched the wall swearing at how stupid he had been to trust the little safe at the club.

Then the name 'Morgan Crew' flashed before him. "Of course," he spoke out loud again. "That bastard," he said. He threw another chair across the room; it crashed against the brick wall and shattered into pieces.

At the end of the hallway, past his office, was where waiters and waitresses poured drinks and made espresso for customers. DuSomme went there, poured himself a tall brandy and drank it down. It didn't help. His anger hadn't subsided. "I'm going to kill him," he said to himself, speaking out loud once again.

✤✤✤✤✤✤✤✤✤✤✤✤✤✤

We sat in the rental car a block away from DuSomme's home. We watched him leave, taking the six stairs from the front door to the street in two steps. He ran around the corner, and less than a minute later he sped away in is Jaguar. The cleaning lady had come to the club and found what we had done as I suspected she would. She had phoned him, and he raced away in a panic.

While DuSomme was storming through his office, Sandy and I were at the front door of his home, wondering just how the hell we were going to get in. It was easy enough breaking into the club, but his home had doors with glass panels that would make a lot of noise if we broke them. And all the windows were barred.

"I guess that's it, Morgan," Sandy said. She touched my arm knowing I would be disappointed at not being able to search DuSomme's home.

"Let's go around back," I said. I started down the stone stairs before Sandy could object.

We had to climb a seven foot tall wrought iron fence, topped with sharpened spear-like points, and drop to the lawn below. It was dark, so we edged our way along the side of the building using our hands to find our way.

Finally we came to the rear and found a thin alleyway. "Must be for trash collection," I guessed speaking in a whisper. There was no gate on the alley, it was open to the street; it would have been easier using the alley instead of climbing over the iron fence. Oh well, we aren't professional burglars.

There were street lights to our right where the alley met the street. We stepped to the left and found a door at the bottom of two steps. I went to it and found it locked with a heavy padlock.

"I need something to break this," I said to Sandy. She turned and looked around. The only things nearby were two plastic trash cans. But the walls of the steps were brick. She pulled on a couple of them and with some effort one came loose.

"Will a brick do?" she asked.

"Maybe."

She handed it down to me. I started hitting the padlock, chipping away at the brick without harming the lock. The sun was coming up, and people would be out. I was making a lot of noise, but would anyone be interested enough to stop and see what was going on as they went to their jobs?

I lost my famous temper with it and hit the lock with a full arm swing. The lock remained undamaged, the brick crumbled in my hands, but the hinge screwed to the door and holding the lock was on torn away from the door.

I pulled the wooden door open on loud, rusted hinges. My guess was that this door wasn't used very often. There must have been some other way to get the garbage from the house to the trash cans.

I walked into whatever the door and padlock had protected. It was dark as pitch in the low ceilinged basement.

"Got a match?" Sandy asked.

"If I did you'd accuse me of smoking. Get that little flashlight out, will ya'?" I said as I turned on the flashlight I had bought. Once again, together they threw enough light ahead of us.

Between the small keychain flashlight and my small flashlight, they did little to light our way but did manage to keep us from walking into something. A staircase across the basement led upstairs. The bare wood treads were old and squeaky; we took them slowly, hoping no one was home to hear us. I had no idea if DuSomme had live-in domestic help. The door at the top of the stairs was not locked.

"Listen to me, dear," I whispered to my wife. "If there's anyone in the house, I want you to run. Get out the way we came in. Get as far away as you can and find the cops."

"And you, my dear, will fight off all the bad guys all by yourself? Like they do in the movies? No, dear, I'm staying with you."

"Sandy, one of us has to get back to Caroline. Just do what I tell you to do for the first time in your life."

I opened the door slowly. The house was dark in the kitchen we walked into. There were no sounds so I hoped we were alone.

"Let's see if he has some kind of office," I said.

It took us walking through the first floor before we found a locked door. "Go ahead," Sandy said. "Kick the damn thing in. He's going to know we were here anyway."

I did just that, knowing that my kicking the door open like a real movie tough guy would impress Sandy. It actually took five kicks before the door slammed open.

At the noise of the door breaking open, we heard a child-like scream from behind us. We turned and saw the young girl DuSomme had been sleeping with. She was at the bottom of the stairs that led up to the bedrooms.

She was dressed in shorts that were too short. Any shorter and they would have been bikini bottoms. Her blouse was short, ending just below her small breasts, and it was thin enough to expose her child-like breasts to the world. Her hair was colored pink, and it was rumpled from her bed adventures.

"Qui es-tu? Qu'est-ce que tu veux?"

Sandy walked slowly to the girl. She smiled and held out her hand trying to calm the little girl. She spoke in the best French she had, "Please don't be afraid. We won't hurt you."

"Who are you?" the girl repeated in French.

"No one important," Sandy said. "Do you live here? What is your name?"

"I am Teresa," the girl answered. "Are you going to hurt me?"

"No, Teresa," Sandy said. "Do you live here?"

"No, I was just leaving. Alain and I . . . We were . . ."

"I know, I know. If we give you some money, will you be alright? Will you leave and not tell Monsieur DuSomme about us?"

"How much money?" she asked, as if she were asking for seconds on her dinner meal.

Sandy turned to me. "Give her some money. I think she's just a one night stand. She will leave quickly."

I quickly pulled out my money clip and peeled off a hundred Euros. I handed it to Sandy who walked it to the little girl. She held it out to her, and the girl grabbed it and ran from the house, slamming the heavy door closed behind her.

"That poor little girl," Sandy said. "She couldn't be more than fourteen or fifteen."

"Yeah," I said. "But she wasn't a virgin when DuSomme got his hands on her."

Assuming it was too late to worry about anyone else knowing we were there, I walked into what I thought was DuSomme's office and found a light switch on the wall. I flipped it on, and one light in the ceiling above a plain desk cast a bright light through the room. It was a gold chandelier with real crystal drops surrounding the light that was encased inside a paper thin marble globe, thin enough to let the light shine through it.

Immediately my eyes went to a four drawer file cabinet at the left of a big teak wood desk. There was little else in what had to be DuSomme's office. A few pictures of no real value hung on the walls. A clock with a pendulum that swung slowly was on the wall opposite the desk. I laughed when I thought it was there so that DuSomme would know what time it was and when it was time to go kill somebody.

The file cabinet drawers were locked. Sandy found a heavy letter opener in the top drawer of the desk. As she worked to unlock the cabinet I wondered why a world class hired killer would have such a sparsely furnished, common office.

"There's got to be something else here," I said. "If he has anything in his house, it just can't be here if it's important."

Sandy took three minutes, but she was able to pick the lock on the cabinet. We searched through each of the four drawers. There was nothing; household receipts and meaningless communications. Nothing.

We went through the entire house. We ripped through furniture and tore pictures from the walls. We pulled carpets up and emptied drawers. Nothing. There was no use trying to hide what we were doing. DuSomme would know we were there.

After over an hour, we were sitting on a couple of chairs in DuSomme's sitting room, wondering what to do next.

"Is it time to give up, Morgan?" Sandy asked.

"I really don't want to," I said. "I don't want to give up. I came to Paris for a purpose. Bob Sommers talked me into it. I hardly remembered LeRoy Manns; it's been years since I've seen him. But DuSomme has done things . . . To me and to you. I can't walk away from all that. But I have an idea. It means leaving Paris. And I mean tonight. DuSomme will know it was us who broke in to his office and his home. He'll try to find us . . . And kill us. We leave tonight."

TWENTY - The Contract

A month passed by as Sandy and I travelled around Europe. We seldom spent more than two or three days in any one place and never more than one night in any one hotel or Inn. We paid cash for most things so that finding us by credit card use would be impossible or at least difficult.

Peter Jascro sent us boxes of cash by special messenger so there was no trail for DuSomme to follow. In some small town a hundred miles from Paris I bought a five year old Mercedes and left the rental car at the side of the road with a note under the windshield wiper to return the car to the rental company.

Occasionally I would drive out of my way, onto some major highway, and fill up the gas tank using a credit card just to leave a false trail for DuSomme.

As we travelled, Sandy hand wrote translations of the little ledger book we had taken from DuSomme's office safe. If her translations were right . . . Which I trusted were right because Sandy is pretty good at French and Italian and some German . . . DuSomme was either writing in code or gibberish. He wrote about dogs and cats in sentences that had no meaning. She and I together worked on deciphering what he had written.

And while we travelled, Alain DuSomme spent those weeks having his home and jazz club repaired from the damage we had done. Of course, he knew we had done it, and he knew we had his small ledger, a record that would incriminate him . . . If anyone could break the codes he used. But what could he do? We had disappeared . . . Completely.

He had spent almost a month using every resource and contact he had, but he could not find us. Every criminal he had ever done business with in Europe, Asia and Africa had been paid by him to send him information about where we were.

While looking for Sandy and me, he had not gone to his club every night as was his habit. He had been home drinking heavily the night before it happened. He had woken early with a hangover.

Then something happened to stop his search for us and stop his drinking and worry.

DuSomme was on the balcony of his home on an unusually dry and sunny Sunday morning. He was sitting in the sun reading Le Monde, his daily newspaper, and eating a breakfast of coffee and orange juice he had struggled to put together himself in his kitchen. He had let his household staff, an elderly woman who was his cleaning lady, a middle aged lady who was his cook, and the man who parked his cars and maintained them, all go. He gave them each a month's wage and despite their pleas and the women's tears, he couldn't have them around as subjects for the police to question.

After an hour of strong coffee, he had rolls delivered from a local café. They settled his stomach enough for him to think once again of what he could do that day to find us.

His doorbell rang; he ignored it at first because his head still hurt from the whiskey he had the night before. But whoever was at the door rang it twice more. He tossed the newspaper on the tile of the balcony and went to the door, upset at the interruption.

Considering all that had happened in the past weeks, DuSomme had added extra protection to his home by having a steel plate fastened to the inside of the door, covering the glass panel. He could not see out, but he had an intercom system installed at the front door. Without opening the door he pressed the intercom button and asked, "Qu'est-ce?"

"May I speak with you, Mr. DuSomme? I am sorry, I don't speak French."

It was a man's voice, confident English in tone, but with an American accent.

"Who are you?"

"My name is Marc Chalmers. I'm an Attorney . . . From New York . . . I represent a client of yours."

"What client?"

"Please, Mr. DuSomme. It's best we don't talk in public. I'm sure you understand."

DuSomme made a quick decision. Of course, if it was about a client that meant someone who had hired him . . . Or wanted to hire him . . . To kill someone. That was not for the public to hear. On the other hand, too many people would like to see him dead, he thought. He shivered at the thought of me, using the Crew Family money I had access to, hiring someone to kill him.

He said through the intercom, "Wait a moment, Mr. Chalmers. I'm going to get a gun. If you intend anything but talk . . . I will kill you. Do you understand?"

"Certainly, Mr. DuSomme," Chalmers said without any fear or trepidation.

DuSomme walked quickly to his little den which he used to meet with people occasionally, when his office would not be suitable for certain meetings. His den was furnished better than his little office and it put on a better show of wealth and prominence than his office.

Sandy and I had torn the place apart and had found nothing. But DuSomme had a hidden place. He walked to the farthest corner of the room and with the toe of his leather slipper he touched the baseboard at the floor. A section of the baseboard slid toward DuSomme, opening a well-hidden place where he kept a single pistol. It was a Heckler & Koch 9mm VP9SK. It was not a pistol he used when killing people on contract. It was a 'home defense' pistol only; illegal in France, but one he kept at his home anyway. He bent and took the pistol from its hiding place.

From his desk drawer he took a single key and put it in the pocket of his silk bathrobe.

He walked back to his front door, the pistol in his right hand, lowered, pointing at the floor. But he could raise it and shoot quickly if needed. Actually, he had hoped that the mention of a gun would frighten the Attorney . . . If in fact he was an Attorney . . . enough to go away.

DuSomme pressed the intercom button. "Are you still there, Mr. Chalmers?"

"Of course," the Attorney answered. His voice remained calm and businesslike.

"Alright," DuSomme said slowly. "I have a pistol. I am going to open the door. Please be assured I will kill you if you have been dishonest with me.

"I assure you, Mr. DuSomme. I am here on business only . . . Only business and nothing more."

Three sliding bolts plus two keyed dead bolt locks with four inches long bolts, held the heavy door secure. The steel bars covering the outside of the front door added the final word to the security, and DuSomme considered his door breach proof. He slowly slid each sliding bolt open. He took the key from his pocket and opened the dead bolt locks.

His left hand went to the polished brass doorknob, his right hand rose to point the pistol forward, ready to fire. He opened the door cautiously and slowly, using the heavy door as a shield.

The man standing there was smiling. He was tall, and women found him very handsome. He was in his mid-forties and muscular slim. His hair showed the very smallest amount of grey around his temples. His suit was tan wool and custom cut in the American fashion, which told DuSomme the man may have actually come from New York as he said. His pale yellow silk shirt was open at the collar and he did not wear a tie, in deference to the early morning hour.

He carried an expensive, grey leather, elephant hide attaché in his left hand. DuSomme glanced at it and wondered what might be in it. A gun perhaps? Some other tool of murder? If the man were to open it, DuSomme would be ready.

Chalmers was holding a business card in his right hand, holding it out between his index finger and middle finger for DuSomme to take. Both of Chalmers' hands being occupied gave DuSomme some semblance of relief that the man would not try to kill him immediately.

DuSomme took the card. It was not an inexpensive print shop card. It was heavy, glossy and a rich shade of grey. The print was raised, and it held only Chalmers' name with 'Attorney at Law' after it. There was no address or phone number on it.

"May I come in, Mr. DuSomme? I assure you it is most important." Chalmers was smiling, showing gleaming white teeth. He didn't look dangerous, but truly dangerous people seldom looked dangerous.

DuSomme took a step back, still holding the pistol pointed at Chalmers. Chalmers smiled at the defense DuSomme put up. He walked past DuSomme, turned and waited for the door to close.

"I assure you I am not armed, Mr. DuSomme," he said. "You may search me if you wish. And you may look in my attaché."

DuSomme made a motion with the pistol, telling Chalmers to turn to face the wall.

"Place the attaché on the floor, please," he said. "And place your hands on the wall, above your head."

Chalmers did as he was told. DuSomme took notice of Chalmers's hands. The finger nails were manicured, and his hands were soft, not made for killing.

DuSomme patted him down, not missing an inch of the man's body, even the most private parts. Then he opened the attaché and leafed through it. Nothing but papers and a couple of file folders. He closed the case and set it on the floor.

"Alright, Mr. Chalmers, what do you want?"

"May I take my hands from the wall?"

"Yes," DuSomme said as he took three steps backward, away from the Attorney. He kept his pistol leveled at the man.

Chalmers bent to lift his attaché, but stopped and asked, "May I pick up my case?"

DuSomme nodded.

Chalmers asked, "May we go somewhere . . . To talk in comfort and privacy? It is most important, Mr. DuSomme."

DuSomme waived the pistol to his right. Chalmers reached down for the attaché and then walked ahead of DuSomme. He stopped at a door to the sitting room.

"Inside," DuSomme said. Chalmers opened the door and walked into the room. He pointed towards a couch upholstered in red silk with Asian birds stitched across it that sat behind a low Luis XIV table. DuSomme nodded and Chalmers sat.

"There really is no need for the weapon, Mr. DuSomme," Chalmers said. "You know I am not armed. I am not a fighting man . . . Except perhaps when my wife gets angry at me," he laughed. "All I want is conversation about business."

"What business?"

"Won't you please sit, Mr. DuSomme? I mean you no harm. Please believe me."

DuSomme did sit on a gold leafed chair with a blue woven cushioned seat with a white heron stitched into it, across from Chalmers, leaving the table between them. He let the pistol rest on his lap, but his hand was very near it.

"Alright," DuSomme began. "We're sitting. Now what?"

"Mr. DuSomme, my clients hired you to . . . Eliminate shall we say . . . Certain people who would interfere with the discussions between some . . . Business people I guess you could say. I think you know who I am speaking about. That discussion was taking place at the home of one François DeLocke. The location was chosen by the Nation of Iran because of its remoteness. It was assumed to be a safe place and only a few Jews stood in the way. Those Jews were a danger to the people at DeLocke's chateau. The . . . Business deal shall we say . . . Was not completed, and my clients lost a great deal of money. The people . . . The Jews whom I had mentioned . . . You were to . . . Eliminate . . . Are still . . . Alive. My clients paid you five million American dollars as a deposit with a further five million to be paid when your job was done. That job was not done, Mr. DuSomme. The business deal that would have been profitable to my clients was not completed and the Jews remain alive. You did not complete your part of the contract."

"Can I assume that they want their money back?" DuSomme asked. He knew he wasn't going to give whoever hired him five million dollars. If demands were made, he also knew that he would kill this American Attorney as a message to whoever sent him.

DuSomme had no idea who had hired him to kill the old Israeli and whoever was working with him. He had received a package; it was lying on his front porch one morning. Inside the small cardboard box that had been carefully wrapped in brown paper and heavy tape, was a simple one page typed communication telling him who to murder. There was also a large white envelope, 13 by 18 inches that had $5,000,000 dollars in $100 dollar bills, all used and old with serial numbers that were not in order.

DuSomme had used me to case DeLocke's chateau. He had planned to kill the old man Patrice Laurent had brought to me before he could kill the people meeting at the chateau. I, of course, screwed all that up. He had no idea, nor had Chalmers' clients known, that the old man's organization had hired Lorraine Demeaux to kill the people at the chateau. Killing the old Jew would not have stopped Lorraine from killing the people at the chateau.

But all that made no difference to Chalmers's clients. DuSomme had been retained to commit murder. He did not commit the murders. He had not fulfilled the contract.

In answer to DuSomme's question, Chalmers said simply, "Of course."

DuSomme smiled and said, "Well, you can go home and tell your client they can forget about it. I'm not returning a dime. It wasn't my fault the operation fell through. You should have known there were more players in the game."

"I'm afraid I have more than one client, Mr. DuSomme. It was an investment by an entire group of very serious people. You see, they had intended to supply titanium and other materials to the . . . Business people . . . Who were making the deal. And of course there was the plutonium. Materials the United Nations had blocked the sale of to Iran. And that is where the product would have gone. The investment group stood to make a great deal of money. Much more than the five million they gave to you. Therefore they want a return on their investment."

"I see," DuSomme said. "And what is the return?"

"One million dollars American, Mr. DuSomme."

"So they want me to give them six million dollars, is that correct?"

"I will take the cash," Chalmers said. "I assume you do not have six million dollars here at home. You have 24 hours to collect it."

"And what if I tell you and your investors to go to hell?"

Chalmers seemed almost sad when he answered, "Then your life will come to a sudden, very abrupt and very unfortunate end I'm afraid."

"And what if I kill you right now?"

"Then your life will come to a sudden end also. It would be only a few days after my death and you would be dead, make no mistake about that."

DuSomme, a former sniper with the French Army and hired killer for anyone who could pay him, had never before had his life threatened. Chalmers wasn't the type to be a killer, he was merely a messenger. But he seemed to be a serious messenger with a serious message.

He asked as he opened a small gold box and took out a Gauloises, "Just who the hell is this investors group of yours? Investors are people who wear expensive suits and sit behind desks and screw other people out of their money. Who are your clients?"

He lit the cigarette with the gold table lighter that lay next to the cigarette box. His pistol was still in his lap as he stared at Chalmers and blew smoke towards him; Chalmers laughed a short, nervous laugh. He wiped his forehead even through there was no sweat beading there. He straightened himself in the chair. He cleared his throat and then cleared it again. He looked away from DuSomme and in a frightened whisper he said, "Have you ever heard of the Calabresse?"

Of course DuSomme had heard of the Calabresse Crime Family. On occasion people in that family . . . That Mafia family . . . Appeared in the news. DuSomme read the European edition of the New York Times often enough to know of the Calabresse. Yes, he had heard of the Calabresse Family. They ran New York and most of the American Northeast as well as being well entrenched in the West Coast of the States. They were drug dealers, they ran illegal gambling and prostitution, they sold protection, they ran Unions, and they were killers. But they were not in France.

"Yes, I am aware of the Calabresse," DuSomme said. "But New York is an ocean away from here."

"Don't be naive, Mr. DuSomme," Chalmers said. His

voice was that of an adult who wanted to protect a child from unseen harm. "It isn't the 1950s anymore. These aren't people who have big mustaches, wear loud ties, and have shootouts in the street. They are business executives who have offices on Wall Street. And they always make profits from the business they do. And that business is carried out throughout the entire world. Oh, you wouldn't believe the corporations they control. They are dangerous people, still."

"That is impressive, Mr. Chalmers. But the world is a big place. Do you think they can find me if I don't want them to? I am a professional, too, you know."

"In an office, on the 32nd floor of 1 World Trade Center, in a locked safe that even the best . . . Safe Cracker I think they are called . . . Would fail at opening, is a file folder. It is two inches thick. It is your life history, Mr. DuSomme. You cannot hide from these people. I cannot hide from these people, Mr. DuSomme. Believe me I would like to. I have a distinct dislike doing what they bid. But I do it without question or complaint because I like life. And I must protect my family. They pay me well . . . As they have paid you over the years. And yes, this contract that is in dispute is not the first contract you have had with the Calabresse, be assured of that."

Alain DuSomme had seen combat in war. His life was centered on violence. Fear was not a stranger to him, but as with all fear, one must push past it and do what must be done. He was not alone in that. I share that with DuSomme. When fear reveals its face to him and me, we push past the fear, put it behind us, ignore it, and do what we must do. He pushed past the fear to kill; I push past the fear to stop the killings.

He thought, 'There has to be a way out of this.' Yes, he had six million American dollars and much more than that. That was not a problem. But once he handed it over to these people, he would be a fish on a hook to be played by the fishermen in New York. It would show fear, and animals in the jungle can smell fear. There had to be another way. He had to find some way out of this dilemma without paying these people anything.

He asked Chalmers, "In business there is always an option, a second plan, a backup so to speak. What is my backup plan?"

"Alright," Chalmers said. He seemed relieved that DuSomme would ask. He had hoped DuSomme would ask for a way out. He would not have to report back that DuSomme would not return the money and then he would be part of yet another murder.

It meant DuSomme was frightened and would do what the Calabresse wanted. It was a relief to Chalmers. He said, "The business arraignment that was not completed is important to many people. It is being revived. And the people . . . The Jews who you were supposed to stop . . . The people who wanted it stopped are once again going to try to stop the arrangement. You are to do what you should have done in the first place. You are to kill the group of Jews who would interfere."

"And if I do that . . . I will be left alone?"

"All they want of you is six million dollars . . . Or the deaths of the people they want dead. Complete the contract you were hired for and they will be satisfied. But you will not receive the additional five million. That is for defaulting on the original contract."

"Alright," DuSomme said. Chalmers let out a deep breath understanding that he had completed his job. "But I need more information on these people and where the others will meet to complete the . . . Business deal."

The Attorney lifted his attaché to his lap and opened it. He pulled a photograph from it and handed it to DuSomme. It was that of an old man, grey hair and beard. The old man was slightly overweight as so many old men are. It was the old man Patrice Laurent had taken to meet me.

"So who is he?" DuSomme asked.

"He is Hiram Wisekophf. He was once with the Israeli Government . . . In several positions, most of them highly secret. Today he runs a private organization not affiliated with any Government. They kill to be perfectly honest. They believe in the good effect of killing for Israel. Find him, and you find the small group of people he runs. Kill him, and your debt to the Calabresse is paid."

"And where is this business meeting to take place?"

"I don't know that yet," Chalmers admitted.

Alright, DuSomme thought. It would take time, but he could find out. He had contacts everywhere. But something else was bothering him. He asked, "What your clients are selling sounds like bomb making materials. And a very big bomb at that."

"Yes . . . And that bothers me, of course. Believe it or not, I have a conscience, too. But what will be, will be, as they say. There are people . . . Nations . . . Religions out there who hate each other. Nuclear weapons exist, and the vast majority of the peoples and Governments of the world fear these and don't want to see a nuclear war of any size. But there is a great deal of money involved in this, many millions more than the six million we are talking about."

"And you are willing to sit back and watch this happen? If Iran does acquire what is being sold . . . You know what will happen. Israel will be wiped off the face of the world. Millions will die."

"Mr. DuSomme. Perhaps you and I are not that much unalike. I do the work of people who would murder for wealth. You do those murders. Yet, I think perhaps neither you nor I want to see the deaths of millions of innocent people for some silly Religious disagreements. The world . . . I think perhaps you and I would agree on this point . . . The world should be a better place. A place without such religious hatred. But the world is what it is, and history cannot be changed. It would be so much better if we could *learn* from history instead of forgetting it and repeating our mistakes time and again."

Chalmers rose slowly and closed his attaché. His head was hanging low; a sad cloud covered his face. "I must go now," he said, his voice cracking. "You have three weeks to complete the assignment so that the sale may be completed. If you don't complete the assignment in that time, my investors will want an additional million dollars as interest. That will be seven million dollars, Mr. DuSomme."

Chalmers left, leaving DuSomme sitting and staring at the photograph of the old man.

TWENTY-ONE - Justice

In less than a week DuSomme had a lead on Hiram Wisekophf. He had given up on finding Sandy and me. That was good, but if the plan I had didn't work, he would be back after us once again. In the end, a thought I kept to myself and did not share with Sandy, I knew I might have to put a bullet in DuSomme's head. I could not allow him to walk free and someday come after me and my family.

An old man, fitting the description Chalmers had given DuSomme and the photo DuSomme had, had left Berlin on a Lufthansa flight the same day a flight attendant, who slept with DuSomme when he was in Berlin, phoned to tell him. With the old man were four other men. All five had Israeli passports. Their destination was Orly Airport, Paris.

DuSomme clapped his hands together and went to the bar in his home. 'Time for a drink to celebrate,' he told himself. If the old man was foolish enough to come to Paris, DuSomme's home territory, then the old man and his companions would be dead very soon.

DuSomme had purchased a ticket on a departing flight from Orly that he would not take. Having the ticket allowed him to pass through security and be waiting at the gate the old man's flight would arrive at. He sat in a crowd of people awaiting their flight at the gate directly opposite the old man's arrival gate. The old man's flight was late, but that was not unusual. 'Patience,' he told himself.

Finally the jet arrived at the gate. DuSomme watched as Wisekophf and his four companions left the jet in a crowd of other passengers. Orly was crowded, and DuSomme had no trouble following the five out of the gate area and to baggage claim. He stood near the entrance to a ladies restroom as if he were waiting for his wife. He drew no attention.

He watched as they rented a car, a blue Mercedes van, and followed them to the car lot. He took down the license plate number, make, color, and model of the car. He used iPhone's digital camera to photograph the five men and their rental car.

They drove away, but he knew it would be a small problem finding the hotel they were staying at. Once that was done, he would go in at night and kill all four. He would use a knife, he decided. That way there would be no sound. Each would have his throat cut, quickly and quietly. He would then be free.

However, what he assumed would be the small problem of finding the hotel turned out to be a large problem. He spent three full days checking almost every hotel, large and small. His search turned up nothing. They had disappeared in the City he thought was his own.

Maybe, he thought, they were not at a hotel. Maybe they had a place to stay, a safe house perhaps, a home of a friend. But he had the car and the license plate number. He put out the word; 500 Euros to the person who found the car. After a week he had nothing.

But DuSomme had contacts throughout the criminal world of Europe. He put out a contract. One thousand Euros to the person who could tell him where Hiram was. Ten thousand Euros to the person who murdered the old man.

And the sightings started to flood in. Every cheap crook in France, Belgium, Germany and Italy started claiming the contract. But none of these were good leads. At first DuSomme would rush to the place where someone said they had seen Hiram. Place after place, and there was nothing. Then he stopped rushing around.

He demanded photos and proof. The leads suddenly stopped. DuSomme began to worry. The old man seemed to have disappeared completely. What had he left?

More than two weeks of the three given to him by Chalmers were gone, and DuSomme was worried. He had only days before a killer would come for him, as he had done so many times for so many other people. He was distraught, and he began to drink to try to wash away his problem.

Maybe he should run? He had plenty of money. He could disappear. He had passports in a dozen different names from a dozen different Countries. There were places to hide. He could keep on the move; make it hard for someone to find him. He started to think of plans to save himself.

Then at three in the morning as he lay stretched out on the silk covered couch in his sitting room, sleeping away all the brandy he had drunk since noon the day before, his telephone woke him.

He spoke in French automatically, "Oui, qui est-ce?"

A woman spoke. She had an Italian accent but spoke English because she knew DuSomme didn't speak Italian, and she did not speak French. She was a sometime lover of Alain DuSomme and a thief of jewelry. She lived in Rome and preyed on rich American tourists.

"Hello, Alain," she said softly. "Did I wake you?"

He recognized her voice immediately. "Yes, Marlene,

you did wake me. What do you want?"

"I hope you are alone, Alain. You know how jealous I am. You must have sex with only me."

"What do you want, Marlene?" DuSomme asked impatiently.

"Oh, do not be cross with me, Alain. I have news for you."

"What news, Marlene. I want to sleep. If you're pregnant again . . . I am still not the father."

"Do you want to know where this Hiram Wisekophf is?"

DuSomme jumped from beneath the old pale blue sweater that he had used as a cover as he slept on his couch. His bare feet hit the carpeted floor, knocking over the glass of brandy he had laid there the night before, but he ignored that. He was awake.

"Yes . . . Of course . . . Yes . . . Tell me."

"Oh, my love," Marlene said pouting like a child trying to get the last cookie on the plate. "I was told there would be money."

"Yes," DuSomme said. He tried to hold back his anger. He knew Marlene well. She was a money hungry bitch to DuSomme. Once she had even asked for payment for a night of sex. He said as calmly as he could manage, "One thousand Euros, Marlene. You know that. Now tell me."

"But Alain, one thousand is such a small amount of money. Can't you pay more?"

"Alright," he said, exasperated with the woman. "Two thousand then."

There was silence on the line, but DuSomme could hear Marlene's throaty breathing. She was playing a game she loved and a game DuSomme had no time for. He had less than a week to complete the contract.

"Damn it, Marlene!" he growled. "How much, tell me."

"Would five thousand be too much to ask? After all, everyone knows how important this is to you."

"Alright, five thousand. Now tell me where he is."

"And when will I have the money, my love?" she pouted again.

"Marlene, tell me where he is. I will pay you. But I may put a bullet in your head if you keep this up."

"Oh my love," she said. "I do love it when you get rough. But oh well, I must trust you. He is in a small farming village in the Southwest of France. In the foothills of the Alps. It is called Lamarge. He and his friends are in a house just a short distance to the east of the village. There is only one road. You can't miss it. Now, my money?"

DuSomme slammed the phone down. He would deal with Marlene later. He ran to his bedroom and stripped off the clothes he had worn for two days. A quick shower and a shave were next. His head was still spinning from the brandy, but he had to ignore that. He turned on the bedside light and dressed quickly. He would need a weapon, a good one and powerful enough to kill five people quickly.

He retrieved his Jaguar and drove to the warehouse he owned; a place that had been vacant for over three years. He ran inside and used a key to unlock a bookshelf that was on hidden wheels. He slid it aside easily. Behind it was a door that opened into his collection of weapons. Knives, pistols and automatic weapons, as well as explosives were hidden there. He studied them and chose a Berretta 9MM pistol and an HK machine pistol, also 9MM. He took those and extra clips and ammunition. Locking the hiding place behind him, he ran to his Jaguar.

He decided on the black Jaguar because it was the fastest of his cars. He had three but loved the Jaguar best. It took corners easily and could reach 200 km/h when needed.

At half past three in the afternoon he was on the road, carefully not breaking speed limits while inside Paris. Once on the country roads, he pushed the car up to 180 km/h.

It was well past midnight when he saw the first road sign for the village of Lamarge. He had stopped but once, to fill the Jaguar's gas tank and to relieve himself.

He slowed the car as he approached the village and drove carefully the rest of the way. He hadn't eaten since the day before; his stomach told him he had to stop somewhere. He had to be in good condition to take on five people who might well be as dangerous as he was himself.

A roadside trucker's café that was open twenty-four hours a day was ahead, just a few kilometers from the village; he stopped there. Quickly devouring a cold ham and cheese sandwich and a glass of not very good red wine, he was back on the road.

As Marlene had said, there was but one road into and out of the village. DuSomme drove very slowly through the town that was merely a few shops and one tavern. He continued slowly on the road east toward the farm where Marlene said the old man was staying.

'If she lied,' he thought, 'She would die.'

Then he saw the blue Mercedes van the old man and his four companions had rented at the airport. He stopped at the turn of the road, a safe distance from the farm house and studied the surroundings.

It would not be easy. He would be seen approaching the house. There was no cover. He could wait a few hours to make certain everyone inside was asleep, but where could he wait without drawing notice?

As he thought, a man approached the Jaguar and tapped on the closed driver's side window. The man was dark skinned with thick, black, curly hair that hung long over his forehead almost to his eyes. He was tall and not too heavy, but he was burly, tough looking, muscular, and DuSomme had seen him at Orly with Hiram.

The man held a revolver, long barreled and obviously of a heavy caliber. He waived the pistol as he said in English, "Please to remove yourself from the car." His accent was heavily German.

DuSomme opened the car door slowly. His two weapons were in the trunk of his car. He wondered if he could overpower the man. But once standing outside of the Jaguar he realized the man was taller and heavier and younger. He gave up thoughts of fighting with him. He had to save his strength for the old man who was the main reason he was there. He would wait for the opportunity to kill without being killed.

The man pushed DuSomme and turned him towards the farmhouse. With a second push from behind DuSomme started walking. Once he was in the farmhouse there would be at least five men to deal with. He thought the odds were better with just the one man with the revolver. So he swung around quickly, pushing the arm holding the gun away and lashed out with a quick right punch to the man's jaw.

The punch hurt DuSomme's fist more than it hurt the big man. His jaw was broad, his lips thick, his face unshaven for three days. The big man laughed and swung his left arm in a wide arc. DuSomme tried to bend out of the way of the bearlike fist, but it caught him on the side of his head above his ear. It was like a brick hitting him.

DuSomme fell to his knees and hardly felt the second punch to the back of his head.

****

When he awoke he was chained; his arms were twisted uncomfortably down and fastened with handcuffs to the legs of a heavy steel chair. His ankles were handcuffed to the front legs of the chair, spreading his legs apart. A heavy chain was wrapped around his neck and fastened to the tall back of the chair. Any movement resulted in sharp pain. And he was completely naked.

Wherever he was, the room was pitch black and cold. He shivered, and even that slight movement hurt. His eyes slowly became accustomed to the dark, and gradually he was able to make out grey stone walls in front of him. Turning to look to the right or left was not possible without sharp pain at his throat.

When he was a sniper in the French Army he had been trained in resistance when captured. He brought to mind what he had been taught:

- Don't speak as long as possible
- Resist torture until it becomes too much to bare

- Answer questions in circles without revealing too many secrets

- Eat whatever food is given to you no matter what it is

- Drink any fluids given to you

- Do what is necessary to live

- Never give up the thought of escape

Minutes tied to the cold steel turned slowly into hours. He had no idea how much time actually passed. His eyes went left to right without turning his head. There was nothing he could see in the room, other than himself, the grey stone wall in front of him, and the chair he was in.

The cold was frigid against his bare skin. He shivered once again, uncontrollably, but the chains cut into his throat at any slight move. He forced himself not to shiver, regardless of the cold that was cutting through him.

Suddenly the room was flooded with bright light. DuSomme jumped but the pain was too much. He was blinded by the light and closed his eyes against it. A roar of machinery started, coming from behind him; a growling grinding of gears that became louder and louder until the sound became painful. He resisted the urge to turn because he knew the pain it would cause. It went on for what seemed forever. Minutes or hours? Time meant nothing, and it suddenly stopped.

Quiet engulfed DuSomme. The lights went out as suddenly as they had come on, and the room began to warm. Gradually, over an hour the heat became close to unbearable.

Then a screeching wail crashed down around him. It went on for minutes, for an uncounted time. And without warning it stopped. The room cooled, and the lights came on once again, this time to a normal light from a single bulb hanging over DuSomme's head. He raised his eyes to see it.

A door behind DuSomme squeaked open, and the old man, long grey hair and beard as was in his photo walked slowly into the room. He stood in front of DuSomme smoking a pipe and said, "So, you would kill me?"

DuSomme said nothing. He looked down at the cold dirt floor. He couldn't lower his head, but he didn't have to have eye contact with the old man. 'Resist whatever comes,' he thought.

"I understand," Hiram said. "You will not speak, and you will probably not speak if we were to keep this silly light and sound torture going for days. I understand. But I want you to meet a man. He is a friend from Israel who sometimes works with us. He is not Jewish of course, he is an Arab. But his family has lived in Jerusalem for generations, and he is a loyal Israeli even if he is not Jewish."

DuSomme heard soft footsteps on the bare dirt floor. A man walked to Hiram's side. He was short, not more than five feet tall, and heavy weight, shaped like a bowling pin. His face, in shadow from the red and white checked Arabic head scarf he wore, was wrinkled and scarred and bent out of a normal shape. His nose had been flattened and was bent to the right. His skin was dark, and his hair was long and tangled. And he wore a thick, long beard, black and speckled with grey. He wore a cheap black suit and scuffed black leather shoes. He was bent over and looked like some monster maniac from a cheap movie. He carried a canvass bag with him.

Hiram said, "His name he does not want revealed,

Herr DuSomme. But in his work he is called 'The Gardener'.

The little man opened the canvass bag and dumped its contents onto the cold dirt floor. Every tool a gardener would need to maintain a king's garden fell to the floor. Hand-held clippers, branch loppers, several saws, small shovels, and battery powered shears of three sizes, small to large.

"Herr DuSomme," Hiram said softly, almost an apology behind the words. "The Gardener will start with your fingers . . . One digit at a time. When you are without fingers he will snip off your toes and saw off your feet. Your penis will be next. Eventually he will open up your chest, and one by one he will cut and remove your ribs. Mr. Gardener is very, very good at his work. He will keep you alive all that time. The pain will be extraordinary."

"What do you want?" DuSomme asked. Sweat beaded across his forehead; his hair was wet with sweat. His heart was beating too fast, his breath was short. Hiram saw this and smiled.

Hiram answered, "I want to know everything."

"Everything about what?"

"Please, Herr DuSomme. Don't be injudicious. You well know what I want. Who hired you and why? Now, before The Gardener starts his work . . . Tell me."

DuSomme swallowed hard. His vision was blurry and failing. The room was spinning around in his mind. His stomach twisted, and he tasted bile flooding up into his throat.

Death had never bothered him before. He knew that in his life his death was waiting around every corner he turned. A bullet in the head or in the heart; that was acceptable. But a slow and torturous death . . . That was something he knew he could not face. Often he had thought about this. When in the Middle East or in Southeast Asia or on some special mission for France, he had wondered what would happen if he were captured and tortured. Now he was faced with torture and fear overtook him.

His lips were dry, sweat dripped into his eyes. He wanted to wipe his face but his hands were secured tightly. Hiram saw this and smiled. DuSomme spoke, his voice weak and shaking, "I'm not really sure."

"Oh, Herr DuSomme . . . What a shame. Herr Gardener, please begin your work."

"Wait! Wait!" DuSomme cried. The fear of the pain grabbed ahold of him. "I think I know . . . But I'm not sure. I was contacted by an envelope left at my front door. Money was left with instructions on who I was to kill."

"I think you know more, Herr DuSomme. Why don't we start at the beginning? Tell me everything . . . Leave no detail out."

DuSomme tried to swallow through a dry mouth and throat. "May I have some water please?" he asked.

Hiram said simply, "No. You tell me everything now. If you do, you may get water, later."

DuSomme cleared his throat as best he could and began in a raspy voice tinged with fear, "As I said, I found a package at my door. That is an unusual contact, but it was not the first time I was hired that way. Inside were instructions to stop you . . . Kill you actually . . . That was very specific. There were instructions about the meeting at DeLocke's chateau. I was to insure you did not stop it. There was nothing about what the meeting was about, and I really didn't care.

Five million American dollars were in the package.

The instructions said another five million would be deposited to my bank account when I carried out the contract. That was more than I usually am paid for such a kill, but because of the size I knew it was important."

DuSomme paused to lick his cracking lips with his dry tongue. Sweat running from his forehead was in his eyes. He had no way of wiping it away, making it difficult for him to see anything. "Please," he begged. "Please . . . May someone wipe my eyes?"

"No," Hiram said simply. "You will get nothing until I am satisfied you are telling me the truth."

"Alright . . . Alright . . . Please . . . I will . . . I will."

"Go on, Herr DuSomme," Hiram said. He was pacing back and forth in front of his prisoner. The Gardener was standing aside, the tools of his trade lying at his feet. "Was this an easy contract?" Hiram asked. "Did any problems arise?"

DuSomme grunted again, trying to clear his desert-like throat. He tried to laugh, but that hurt his chest. "Problems? That doesn't describe all that happened."

Hiram waited for DuSomme to say something. The prisoner was shaking his head slowly forgetting the pain at his throat. He was thinking of all that had happened since finding the envelope at his door. Finally, he said, "The problems started when one of my musicians became too inquisitive."

"Who was that?" Hiram demanded roughly.

"I want to know what you intend if I tell you everything."

Hiram answered, "If you do not . . . The Gardener will begin his work, and your death will be long and terrible. If you do . . . There is a possibility you may live."

DuSomme tried the handcuffs fastening his wrists to the chair. He moved his legs. He twisted his chest. He would not break free. All he had was the chance . . . Just a chance he knew, nothing more than that . . . To live.

Hiram turned to the Gardener and said, "I think a finger or two. Perhaps that will convince Herr DuSomme to talk to me."

The Gardener bent to the floor and picked up a big clipper, one that might be used on thin tree limbs. He tested its workings, ran his finger across the blades, and looked at DuSomme. He took a step towards him, holding the clippers out, ready to cut.

"NO! NO!" DuSomme shouted. "Please no! I'll tell you."

Hiram put a hand out and the Gardener stopped. Hiram asked again, "Who was it that became too inquisitive?"

"No one important . . . A musician . . . LeRoy Manns." DuSomme was breathing hard, sweat covered his face, and his eyes burned with sweat that he could not clear away.

He went on, "He apparently overheard a conversation. A phone conversation I had with the contact . . . About finding you to kill you and your people. We were talking about DeLocke's chateau. I had planned to wait there for you . . . To kill you and anyone with you before you could kill anyone. He heard too much. He confronted me and told me he would go to the police."

"And so what did you do?"

DuSomme grunted again trying to find some spit in his mouth to swallow into his arid throat. His eyes blinked uncontrollably. He wanted to shake his head but he dared not because of the pain from the chain around his neck.

"I killed him, of course," he said. "I made it look like a hit and run. I had to fulfill the contract."

"That seems understandable," Hiram said softly. "And what happened next?"

DuSomme thought for a moment. His mind was not clear, and his memory was difficult to bring to the front. Fear and pain was changing the previously dangerous killer into a whimpering slave in fear of the torture waiting for him.

He said, "I guess it was some woman . . . Manns' girlfriend, I think. She came to the club and confronted me after Manns was dead."

He paused once again, thinking. Hiram moved very close to him. He put his hands on DuSomme's bare knees causing the tight handcuffs at his ankles to turn and cut into DuSomme's flesh. He demanded roughly, "And you murdered her, too?"

"Of course," DuSomme said as if the question were senseless. His mind was spinning out of control. Terror had overtaken him. I strangled her in her apartment."

Hiram stood away from DuSomme and had started pacing back and forth in front of his prisoner. Suddenly he stopped his pacing. He was standing in front of DuSomme, a foot away, looking down at him. His hands had folded into fists. He said, "And then you came after me?"

"No . . . An American stuck his nose into my business. He was asking questions about Manns . . . The musician."

"And did you kill him, too?"

"No . . . Manns . . . The woman . . . They were nothing . . . Insignificant nothings. Interest in them would fade quickly. The American . . . He and the woman . . . They would draw too many questions. They are powerful, and too many people would want to know how they died. I had to brush them aside . . . I had to keep them out of the way. But I couldn't kill them . . . Even though I wanted to."

DuSomme's eyes went to The Gardener. The little man, a monster in DuSomme's eyes, was standing still, unmoving, looking down at the ground. A horrible automaton who would do horrible things that DuSomme could not allow to happen to him. No, he would talk, he would tell Hiram everything. And then he would kill them all.

"And what of the policewoman?" Hiram asked. "Did you murder her also?"

DuSomme scoffed and said. "Les Flic . . . She was nothing . . . Les Flic."

Hiram turned to someone standing behind DuSomme. He had a questioning look on his old face. A voice, a woman's voice, spoken in a whisper, said, "Les Flic . . . It means . . . It is a dirty comment . . . A slang for . . . It is used by people who hate the police, oui?"

Hiram began pacing again. He didn't stop while he bit the tip off of a long, fat, black cigar and lit it with a wooden match he had taken from his pocket. He blew dark, acrid smoke away from him while he was in deep thought. The little specter with his garden tools at his feet hadn't moved and continued to stare at the cold dirt floor. The woman standing behind DuSomme coughed, clearing her throat. That drew Hiram's attention.

"Alright, Mr. DuSomme," he said, letting cigar smoke drift from his lips as he spoke. "Let us get to the meeting at DeLocke's . . . Little chateau."

"What is there to get to?" DuSomme said trying to laugh, but he was too frightened of his unsure future. "That fils de pute ruined everything."

Hiram looked behind DuSomme. The woman said in

a faint whisper, "Son of a bitch." Hiram nodded.

"I didn't know the Demeaux woman had been hired to kill the people. I wasn't told of her. I would have stopped her . . . I would have killed her so the deal would go through."

"And who was this Lorraine Demeaux?"

"I've only heard of her," DuSomme said. "She has a dozen . . . What is the word? . . . Persons?"

"You mean aliases?" Hiram asked.

"Yes, that is so. I've only heard of her. She is a killer . . . A person who is hired to kill."

"Like you?"

"No one is like me . . ."

"Herr DuSomme," Hiram said. "You are about to die a very slow, agonizing death. Jokes will not lessen that death."

Hiram leaned forward, his hands on DuSomme's tied wrists, the cigar in his right hand. The sudden extreme pain DuSomme felt at his wrists did not stop him from turning his eyes to the cigar. Would he be burned, too?

Hiram whispered, "And now, Herr DuSomme, the meat of the matter as they say. Who hired you?"

"I told you . . . I don't know. I found the envelope at my door."

Hiram smiled. He took the cigar to his mouth, leaving his left hand on DuSomme's wrist, squeezing it as tight as he could. DuSomme did nothing to acknowledge the extreme pain. He glared into Hiram's dark eyes that were hooded in thick, long, grey eyebrows. He wanted to scream, he wanted to plead, but he didn't.

"But you know, don't you, Herr DuSomme. I assure you The Gardener will learn the truth. Please . . . Tell me. I deplore torture."

"Kill me," DuSomme said. "Kill me if you have to. I don't care."

"No, Herr DuSomme," Hiram said. "Your death will be slow if you are not truthful to me."

'So what?' DuSomme thought. What can this old man do with the truth? What can this old man do against the Calabresse? It is a crime family whose fingers stretch across the world. What can he do?

"Alright," he said. Hiram released his wrist and took a step backwards. DuSomme took a deep breath and said, "It was The Calabresse Mafia Family . . . Out of New York."

Hiram was surprised. He looked up at the woman behind DuSomme. She said nothing. He looked down at DuSomme and asked, "Why?"

"They wanted to sell dangerous materials to some Arab group . . . Terrorists I assume . . . Who I guess wanted to build a nuclear weapon. They wanted to sell materials that are banned by the United Nations."

"Are you lying, Herr DuSomme? It was our information that these people were going to destroy Israel's economy."

"I had thought that at first also. But I was told differently."

"And would this weapon be used against Israel?"

"I don't know," DuSomme answered.

"Guess."

"Oui . . . Yes I suppose it would be used, as you say."

Hiram began pacing again. He smoked his fat cigar, the strong, acrid smoke beginning to fill the room. He stopped, bent to whisper something into the ear of The Gardener. The little man nodded in response.

"What else?" he asked DuSomme.

"Nothing. There is nothing else. Please, I did tell you everything."

"So then, you want me to let you go?" Hiram asked, grinning through his beard.

"Please, I told you everything."

"No you didn't, Herr DuSomme. You have a new contract. I know this. You know this. And you lied. Now, shouldn't I let The Gardener work on you? Shouldn't I tell him to take three . . . Maybe four days for you to die? Didn't I make it clear you must be honest with me?"

The fear of great pain and a slow death had overtaken DuSomme completely. He was shaking, not from being naked in the cold of the stone room, but from the nightmare of what The Gardener could do to him. His mind was twisted, not knowing what he should do. But he had to do whatever he could to save himself. After all, he reasoned, what can this old man do against the powerful Calabresse Family?

"Bien . . . Bien . . ." he said, his voice weak, his throat dry. He started to regress into his native French. "Un homme . . . A man . . . He came to see me. He said he was an avocet . . . A lawyer. He wanted me to pay five million dollars to his client for not killing you. I agreed to renouveler le contrat . . . I mean . . . Renew the contract. I would kill you and the debt, it would be erased."

"And who was his client?"

DuSomme laughed a frightened laugh. He looked

down at the floor and whispered, "The Calabresse of course."

"And what is this lawyer's name?"

"Marc . . . Marc Chalmers. That's all I know."

Hiram dropped his cigar to the dirt floor and crushed it with his heavy boot. He turned and looked at the group of people who had been standing in the shadows behind DuSomme.

I walked into the light with Sandy at my side. Mary Huntington from the American Embassy was behind us. Inspector Renard, the Paris policeman brought up the rear.

Hiram asked, "So, did you hear enough? Was I right . . . Did I say the truth?"

I turned to Inspector Renard and asked, "Do you have enough? Can he be prosecuted for LeRoy Manns' murder?"

"I do not think so, Monsieur Crew. This man . . . He made the confession under threat of the torture. The courts . . . They will not allow his confession. There is nothing I can do. There is no evidence."

I had figured that the law . . . The law that all too often interferes with true justice would save DuSomme from the life in prison that he deserved. But I had one last card to play. I walked back, out of the light, to what I had brought with me.

The small laptop computer I had brought with me lay on a small table behind DuSomme. I took both and set the table in front of DuSomme. I opened the laptop. Tapping a few keys brought the computer to life. I stood to the side of the table.

Numbers flashed quickly across the screen, spread sheets opened and were filled before another opened and was filled. When the upload was done I asked DuSomme, "Do you recognize this?"

His eyes widened in shock and disbelief. "These are your bank accounts," I said. "I found them all, Alain. Now, I want you to watch what happens when I touch just one key. You see, I had a program written. I'm not much with a computer but I have my child's nanny . . . Betsy Concanon . . . at home. She's a computer whiz. It was simple enough for her. Now watch."

I brought my index finger over the 'enter' key and paused. I looked at DuSomme. His jaw fell open, and a faint, almost imperceptible "no" rose from his throat. I touched the key and DuSomme watched as his bank accounts were drained, leaving only zeros where many millions of dollars and Euros, and Yen, and denominations from around the world had once existed.

"It's all gone Alain," I said. "The people who have it now will do a great deal of good with all that money. Charities will have fat bank accounts . . . The hungry will have food . . . The sick will have medicine. All the killings and all the sufferings you have inflicted over the years will . . . In the end . . . Do some good."

I looked into Sandy's beautiful eyes. She nodded slightly. I looked at Hiram and nodded.

I closed the laptop computer and looked at DuSomme. He was crying uncontrollably.

My little group from the Embassy and the Paris Police all left the stone cellar together. Sandy and I followed, the laptop tucked under my arm. As I shut the door and we stood in the warm sun, we heard the gunshot. It was a single gunshot. Muffled as it was by the stone walls of the cottage, we knew what it was.

Inspector Renard walked away. Mary Huntington got into her Embassy car and drove away. I took Sandy by her arm and said, "Let's go home."

Part One

The End

Watch for Part Two of this mystery, "And Now Revenge" to be published and released in 2018.